SUMMER REIGN

SEASONS OF TREASON

BOOK THREE

H.L. HINES

Book Cover by Ambient_studios

Illustrations and Formatting by Ravenswood Publishing & Goods

First edition 2023

I'd like to dedicate Summer Reign to everyone who struggles against The House, The Man, The Establishment, whatever you call it. We know we can rise and thrive when we work together. This is our David and Goliath story and it's only together we can create our own ending. The struggle is real, but we won't tire, because we're used to the grind. That is our magic. Let's use that power to improve our world.

TRIGGER WARNINGS

Blood / Bones / Branding / Child death / Cults / Death / Fire / Gore / Infertility / Kidnapping / Murder / Occult / Physical abuse / Poisoning / Profanity / PTSD / Religion / Sexually explicit scenes / Skeletons / Starvation / Torture / Violence /

Preos
Cinbari
Taraq
Cxxus
Devils Spill
Ja Maal
Ocean
Siren Cove

PROLOGUE

3741.02.22

The town was vibrating with energy. Busy feet, dark boots, light-colored sandals, and everything in between scuffled on dirt tracks. Hands big and small, delicate and calloused, clean and greasy, extended in trade. The air was jumbled with different dialects and clashing noise. Ryker watched it all with prideful satisfaction tightening his sharp cheeks.

"Shouldn't we see the Fifth before we begin the hunt?" Kennith, to Ryker's left, asked. Ryker turned and looked up at his friend. His thick, calloused hands twisted as he gripped the reins and shifted in his saddle.

His large friend looked worried. His sturdy mount shifted underneath him, but not in strain. Kennith sat high on his squat beast of burden, which had been bred explicitly for Kennith's people, a *Konan*. It was the only creature that could carry the mammoth of a man. Still under Ryker's stare, Kennith fretted like a schoolgirl caught cheating on a final.

"I'm in no mood for scheming. We'll kill the beast first and then suffer the politicians."

"It's your duty as Third Citizen—"

"Spare me the lecture. I know."

Compared to most, Ryker was a squarely built man with defined features and piercing eyes. He had the bearing of an aristocrat without the tact. In the years before his enlistment, he'd spent time at the academy of Vails. Which meant he had the intelligence of a learned scholar with the arm of a swordsman.

As Ryker's esteem grew, so too did the suspicion of the First Prime, leader of Taraq, who feared any man who held both combat and political acumen in equal regard. Now instead of leading an army, Ryker was the lazy official he'd spent his life looking down on.

The large town of Namndi was under his jurisdiction. These were his people. Well, not all of them. Some were *Preosian* merchants, *Einhart* enlisters, or the wandering vagabonds who called themselves *the Travellers*, and who everyone else called trouble. Still, as long as they were on his land, obeying Tarquin law, they too were covered under his protection, which is why he was eighty spans away from his home — maintaining the citizens' safety.

"If we see him first, he'll throw us a party," Kennith appealed.

Ryker's only response was to grunt, his finger tapping against the reins clenched in his fist.

"Ah yes, free-flowing *kublaas*, townsfolk grateful for our assistance. That sounds awful," Drusti scoffed in exaggeration.

Ryker didn't have to look at his right-hand man to know he'd rolled his merry green eyes and was still shaking his head, but not hard enough to mess up his hair. His roguish friend loved mocking him. *Too much,* Ryker thought.

"Prompt service, too. I think we got here in record time," Kennith added with a hopeful smile. "I think we have time to stop by for a little bit."

"Well, with Lord Wyvier leading the charge, I'm surprised we didn't catch air."

"Oh, please, how could we when we had to stop every couple of hours so you could stretch." Ryker looked over at his blond friend. Already he was fluffing his collar, ever hopeful of festivities.

"What? I didn't want to cramp. Besides, Kennith's pony needed the rest."

"She's not a pony. She's the finest, strongest, and smartest horse in her herd." Kennith's meaty palm slapped the mare's neck with affectionate care.

"Right, she just looks like a dwarf under you," Drusti quipped.

There was something off about this place. If only his friends would quit their antics and pay attention. Since he'd been 'asked' to leave the military, they'd gotten sloppy. All three of them had gotten soft. *The true test will be in finding and defeating the beast of Namndi.*

Ryker shifted forward, straightening in his saddle. He was sure something watched them from afar. And by the friction warming his chest, his instinct told him it was hostile. *Perhaps finding the beast won't be as challenging as I'd expected.*

A commotion of falling pots and pans shocked the trio's horses into a side step and a snorting tangle. Ryker controlled his steed with a firm hand, Kennith cooed to his four-legged companion, and Drusti snapped his riding crop in three successive smacks.

"Parden for the intrusion, m'lard, but you must know. I mean, I have to tell ya." An older woman, bent with age, looked up at them from the corner of her eye. She'd come upon them as they turned towards the commotion and moved as if riddled with pain.

No warrior enjoyed being surprised, and Ryker felt his irritation compound within him like a tight grip against this stomach. His friends may not have been observant at first, but both men were quick to focus. There was something out there, watching and waiting. And maybe this raggedy old woman knew something that could help.

"What is it, woman?" Drusti asked with keen eyes.

The older woman hobbled closer to Ryker, never faltering in her approach until she stood next to his horse. Another uneasy feeling spread through him as she reached for him, one hand on his horse's thick chest, the other near his stirrups. Immediately, Ryker wanted to push her away, but the woman looked frail enough to need the assistance.

"Shadows tremble as a force awakens," she started, looking up into the gray sky, eyes rolling uncontrolled back and forth.

"Destruction rules for those who'd take it
A girl of three worlds moves lost and alone
Travels deep into a land — dark and unknown
Her journey leaves a trail of smoke and blood
from a master whose name is mudd
With the help of my kindreds, dread
will lead her to your heart and bed
But once she's there, she will leave soon after
A wreckage in her wake — a new disaster"

"Damn it, woman, what are you talking about? Stop talking crazy," Ryker scolded from his horse. He lifted his leg to break her contact on his calf, which she clutched tightly. Leather breeches and riding boots doubly protected Ryker from her clawed grip, but he felt her touch long after he broke contact.

"The spirits talk through me to warn you," she mewled, looking up at him despite the curved hump that was her back. A pathetic creature, too pitiful to be cruel to — still, instinct warned Ryker to keep an eye on her.

"The spirits are talking alright, but it's not the dead, only that flask of kublaas that speaks for you," Drusti joked.

"Think what you will, but I'll finish. If you're ready," the beggar woman demanded.

"You might as well let her get this over with," Kennith muttered.

"And you, Lord Ryker Wyvier, will fall on bended knee—"

Lord Ryker snorted and rolled his eyes, but waved his hand at her heated glare, quieting so she could continue.

"Twisted are your fates: intertwined and uncertain
Life or freedom are your only choices
For when she comes — to deny her is to deny yourself
If you turn her away, you'll spell doom for us all
But if you keep her, it will be you who falls"

"Is that it? Are you done?" Ryker asked.

"I think so, whew. Speaking with the spirits is exhausting work." The woman curved her lips into a coy smile. Slowly, her spotted hand reached out, a dirty knapsack extended under her sad eyes. "Honest pay for honest work, m'lard?"

"If you don't pay her now, her sons will steal it from us later," Drusti cautioned. "Though that last part didn't even rhyme."

"It don't all need to! And my kin would never!" she said with wide, shining eyes, hands still outstretched.

"You know, loitering and false prophecy are a crime," Kennith stated.

Instead of answering, the woman straightened out and scurried away, the layers of glorified rags trailing behind her. Ryker watched the woman leave. She straightened herself out, transforming into a small, thin woman in baggy layers and wraps. Gone was her lopsided gait, the hobbled pace smoothed into a sweeping stride. Glancing over her shoulder, Ryker caught her eye as she cursed them.

Travellers — they bring nothing but trouble. Ryker thought with a glare.

"Better watch your valuables. I think we made her mad."

"She's harmless." Kennith shook his head with a grin, and the woman and her 'prophecy' were quickly forgotten.

They were here for a reason. There had been news of another brutal attack on a state merchant cart. They'd lost a lot of goods in that wagon: food, fur, gold, and an experimental medicine to combat a particular rash that had been spreading around the western coast. Their primary mission was to retrieve the cart and get it on the boat to make its way upstream. On top of that, they had to eliminate the threat targeting their supply chain.

An attack on his people wouldn't be tolerated. Warmth spread through Ryker's muscles at the thought of the possible conflict. Combat proved the most exciting distraction, and he didn't get nearly enough of a challenge these days. *Not since I've been forbidden from raising my sword.*

He pressed his lips into a grim smile. After being exiled and promoted, Ryker jumped at the chance to flex his strength. Even if it were to protect a small town from a monster, which was probably a disoriented bear, General Lord Wyvier would take any opportunity to get out of that cage called a castle. Even after nearly a year, he only felt right with a sword strapped to his hip.

"Well, maybe once he finally settles into his position, we can get a real vacation. Then, we can become fat and lazy as properly befitting men in our positions." Kennith leaned back and talked directly to Drusti behind Ryker's back.

"Where have I heard that before, Ken?"

"Enough. Kennith, you stable the horses, get them

fed and pick up supplies. Drusti, you ask around. Let's see what we are dealing with. We'll meet in an hour and hopefully be back by nightfall."

Ryker and Drusti climbed off their mounts and handed the reins over to their steadfast friend. Each man set on their own tasks. The men on Ryker's sides shared a quick grin with each other before parting.

Ryker was used to giving orders, and being in a position of political power that had expanded the scope of his authority hadn't helped matters. Now, instead of directing thousands of soldiers' lives, he had responsibility for nearly a million souls. *Unitas, help them, because I have no clue how I'm going to continue with this charade.*

On the battlefield, he knew what he was doing. There was no time for hesitation or doubt. But when dealing with back-biting politicians and swindling vendors, there was nothing but time in which to falter. Ryker hoped he could accept this challenge with dignity and integrity. He'd never been good at trusting change, especially when strong-armed.

The grasping older woman's strange words left him feeling uneasy; *Lord Ryker Wyvier would fall on bended knee.* Not on his life. If he hadn't knelt for his First Prime, he sure as hell wouldn't bow down for a woman. Not in this life.

CHAPTER ONE

Lana
3742.05.28

A single bruised, swollen eye opened at a child's soft, scared sobs. *Bastards. What kind of monster throws a child in a dungeon?*

"Hello?" Lana called out.

Her raw throat produced a raspy whisper — a tickle formed through the pain of her bruised neck, throwing her into a coughing fit. Had the child spoken, she wouldn't have heard it over her own wheezing.

Holding her breath, Lana tried to use every sense she had to locate the child, possibly the only other inhabitant in this vile dungeon. She just hoped his cell fared better than hers. The warm draft of the balmy Eastern Islands was the only thing moving the smell of blood, mold, and waste.

"I'm Lana. What's your name?" She tried to project her voice while keeping it soft, not to scare the child, but her broken canine tooth made her words whistle.

For the first day, Lana had thought the undead warrior had smashed all resistance out of her. Had she really thought she could find her brother on her own? What had she been thinking, to leave the protection Ryker provided?

By the second day, Lana had decided whoever locked her up had forgotten about her. What strength she had waned, and so did her fighting spirit. But she still thought herself a fool. Lana the Unlikely, her friends had called her. *Yes, the Unlikely. Unlikely to survive.*

"Rue." His little voice quivered, sounding muffled. He was to her left, which seemed closer to the door. If only she could see! If only she could connect to the *metis*, the energy that maintained all life, then she could... *What, burn everything?* She sighed heavily, spurring another coughing fit. Metis was tricky and dangerous in the most ideal circumstances, and this was far from ideal.

"I'm scared," the boy whispered.

Lana imagined big eyes welling with tears and shaking with cold and fear. The image reminded her of what had urged her to leave the protection Ryker had provided in Taraq — her brother, Charlie. Chased by the same group of zealots and greedy bounty hunters that had formed a mob and chased her into these cursed lands.

"It's okay, Rue. I am, too. I was really scared when I first woke up here. No amount of shouting or crying brought me any answers. I was feeling lonely until meeting you. So, even though we can't see each other, neither of us is alone. Tell me more about yourself. Are you from around here?"

Her throat burned, and Lana swallowed hard multiple times. She couldn't keep talking. The pain was starting to compound. The undead puppet that had caught and beaten her had damaged her throat when he'd strangled her unconscious.

She remembered how Lord Ryker had all but called her crazy for her decision to leave.

"How long do you really think you will last?" Ryker slammed his fist on the table. Plates jumped and clanked, Lana's tea spilt on the pressed cream table runner. He'd startled her and her heart fluttered rapidly.

"As long as it takes, I hope." Lana tried to keep her face blank. Let him try to figure her out. She couldn't stand the thought of him knowing how his emotional reaction affected her. Or how she wished it meant more than it did.

"There are too many after you. There's no way for you to remain undetected. Why are you doing this? Now is not the time for romantic notions." In one step he stood in front of her, his hands behind his back.

Lana felt her body jerk at the word 'romantic', until

her reasoning finally caught up with her embarrassment. "It's not fanciful to think I can help my brother." Lana didn't give him the satisfaction of looking up at him. In fact, she didn't spare him a glance, instead she just sipped her tea.

"That's not what this is about, and you know it."

In the end, Ryker had let her go and helped her in all the ways he could, but now she wished he hadn't. Really, what had she been thinking? That she could avoid the monstrous creatures roaming the wild, the bounty hunters forever haunting her shadow, or King Paul's army of Shining Knights? Did anyone believe that Lana could find and save her brother within a week when teams of professionals had tried and failed? Ryker should have called her stupid, because that's precisely what she was.

But Lana needed Rue to feel comfortable with her and trust her. It might be the one thing that kept him alive long enough for her to set them free. For them both, the boy had to have faith. She may have failed herself, but she vowed here and now not to fail him. Not like she'd failed her brother.

What a fool she was; she still believed she could survive. There was a way. There had to be. Lana, daughter of Harding and Anabell Colton, the last of the rebels, king killers, and freedom fighters for the people, would not die forgotten in a destroyed dungeon among piles of shit and decay.

"Rue?" Lana called, her voice cracking.

"I was just exploring, and I know I'm not supposed to be in the castle, but everything is so cool! But then the ceiling caved in, and I couldn't get out! I don't want to be here anymore."

Lana thought she heard him scuffle around. Maybe he was pacing.

"I'm sorry. I'm sure your mother is looking very hard to find you. You'll be out of here soon and you'll feel better once you leave this place."

She heard a moan and the soft pants of pained breaths as he moved around his cell. Lana pressed her forehead against her hands, trying to block out the feel of the slimy wooden bars.

Eventually, Lana found the strength to walk around the small, uneven room, looking for weaknesses again. Lana looked for any give in her prison, from the rain-damaged ceiling and rusty nails in the door, to the rotting wood. Lana's injuries didn't hurt any less, but she was learning how to shift her weight to alleviate the brunt of the pain.

"Lana?"

"Yes, Rue?"

"I'm so cold, and I hurt really bad." His voice pitched, and it brought a swell of regret to the surface. Lana hated that she couldn't spare him his pain.

"What hurts?"

"My 'tomach."

"Have you eaten anything funny recently?" she asked, as she inspected the last wooden bar in her door.

The cement that had been holding it in place now had the consistency of clay. Gripping the wood, Lana twisted, and the cement crumbled into a sandy paste, slowly churning up more as she turned. Excitement spiked through her, and she twisted faster.

"I ain't ate nothing in days."

Pausing mid-turn, Lana pressed her bare forehead against the flaky bars, trying to see down the dim hall. The only movement was the rats in the shadows. The scratch of their claws against the rough-cut rock was an almost constant sound. Outside, waves crashed against a rocky shore, a continuous splash and spray that had become part of the quiet.

"Listen, Rue." Lana struggled to find a deep breath. "Eventually, I'll get us out of here, and you'll be free." She worked on hollowing out the space around the bar. It had disintegrated a little, but remained stubbornly in place. Still, she turned, yanking it forward and back, sweeping around the sides of the hole.

If the cement wouldn't break, the wood eventually would. Would it be in time?

Lana had been down here almost two days herself. And no one had come down since she'd been awake. The little boy would quickly weaken without any nourishment. He had to have fallen when she passed out. *He couldn't have been down here before her, right?* Either way, Lana knew she would have to work fast. She felt the effects of malnutrition herself, and she didn't have to be a healer to know a child would fare worse.

Lana dug her dirty nails through her pockets, looking for anything useful. She had a few trail rations, but they were dwindling, as was her strength. Lana's bloody, possibly broken finger snagged on something hard and sharp. When she pulled it up, the protection charm the

Viridate tribe had given her dangled — *fat lot of good it had done.*

"I'm scared. It's so dark." His little voice broke into a soprano. She heard muffled steps, a soft slap, and then a soft fleshy slide against the rock wall.

Shoving the charm back in her pocket, Lana gripped the bar, throwing all her weight at the weakest point of the door. Jerking back, her shoulder jolted with sharp and deep pain, and she wondered if she had just dislocated her arm. The door's integrity held far better than her battered and bruised form. Frustration and pain blurred her vision, and a scream tingled her throat, heavy in her chest.

"Arrg!" The echo of the shout silenced the child for a moment as it ricocheted down the narrow cell-filled hall. Now that she wasn't pressed with emotions and could think about it, this was an advanced imprisonment system for as old as this castle was. Did that leave room for escape?

"Tell me, Rue, when you fell down, what direction was the front of the castle?"

"I don't know." His voice was tight, like he was expecting her to yell at him.

"Do you see a door, or have you seen anyone?"

"I don't know. I don't know. I… I'm scared."

"It's okay, Rue. I was trying to determine where the exit was. Do you know where we are?"

Any information would be helpful; she just had to keep her and Rue's minds off the situation.

If she could keep him talking — Lana paused, her breathing becoming irregular. She needed him to say something, because she was now the one terrified. Being closed in and confined had never seemed severe compared to her other fears. However, when she looked into the darkness, it seemed to span into the end of her life.

"Why, you don't know?" He sounded surprised. "This is Castle Krunos. Home of the Deathless Master."

The Deathless Master — his words rang true. She'd felt it all along. Power pressed against her, literally smothering her access to the elemental metis around her. Lana was once again smacked with another layer of terror. Oh, Light Bearer, what had she gotten herself into?

CHAPTER TWO

Ryker

3742.07.14 Castle Wynthros, Taraq.

3742.04.16
Addressed to the Third Citizen of Taraq, protector of the lands between the Lalow Swamp and the Nostu River, Lord Ryker Wyvier of Wynthros.

Father,
The further we travel into this land, the

more it takes my breath away. I'd never admit it to anyone else, but it's indescribably beautiful. Waterfalls that stretch past the clouds, flowers the size of a grown man and with a fragrance that fills the senses so thick you can taste the smell. When the wind blows from the north, picking up speed through the gorges, pollen and humongous umbrella seeds ride the currents, pelting everything with velvet puffs.

Though there are dangers just as magnificent as the beauty, it seems like the most beautiful are the most deadly. Those man-sized flowers that attract all with their scent are meat eaters, the tacky leaves are a potent numbing agent, and their bicep-thick prehensile vines spread so invitingly that once disturbed, they can wrap a man up in their deadly embrace.

We picked up a Preosian ecologist, Kartrellos Sritharans, at the port of Rost. She seems to be very excited by this land's many marvels. It has become taxing, the amount of time the woman spends on botanical pursuits. I've never seen an adult giddy to sort through patches of weeds and dirt.

While she proves useful, I must concede, the woman's careless enthusiasm lost its charm after the first death. Though she did save my life by creating what she called immunoglobulin serinum after an unfortunate incident with another particularly aggressive venom. Still, her clumsiness is as much of a hazard as the landscape. But, alas, I can't just drop her off and leave her to her own devices. It would be a terrible death sentence.

We've come across a few beasts. None so far have been as challenging as the gormadon we faced. I'm trying not to be disappointed. After we passed through the Ulta Superior, the temperature abruptly changed. It was almost too much for Kartrellos; her damned delicate Preosian immunities left her with a terrible sickness. Though she refused to stop, she slows us down.

What's worse, I believe she knows more than she says. I'll keep my eye on her. I'm hoping to gain more to my name than a map expansion and a few pelts.

I've sent within this letter a sample of the flower, and the elixir mentioned earlier.

I'm sure the benefits of its potency need not be explained. The girl seems confident that it will benefit those affected by a disease sweeping across her country. If Asa Ve is interested, then I'd be honored to donate it to their labs.

Please ask Grandmos Kinzi to say a proper blessing to Unitas. Meanwhile, lasting peace to the people. Blessings and victory, Father.

D. V.

Ryker read his son's letter one more time. An unsettling feeling nagged at him. Though Tarquin parents prided themselves on healthy child-rearing, they adopted a more hands-off approach as the child neared adulthood. Ryker had always thought it essential for a child to grow up comfortable, relying on themselves. Daiviad was learning the hard way, by trudging through dirty mistakes.

Now he wished he could warn his son to stay away, to venture deeper into the unknown and make a name for himself as the explorer he was. Setting the letter down, Ryker jotted a letter to ask a friend to check into this Preosian addition. The aggressive scratching of his writing utensil against the thick-grained page rang out into the quiet room.

After completing the letter, Ryker turned back to the special missive that had been taunting him. Reading it over again, he shook his head and crumpled the page, throwing it into the fire. A dozen or so crumpled rejects littered the area surrounding the fireplace. The quiet mocked him for being a fool, thrice over.

As of late, the castle halls hummed with an empty ring. Cold stone and baited dread beat in the hearts of the staff. There was no survivor of Lord Wyvier's displeasure. A hair-trigger temper and sharp orders replaced the fair and firm directions of before. When heavy steps stormed in the hall, the servants scurried away.

Three short knocks, and Ivok, Ryker's personal man, opened the door. Normally he wouldn't be so bold. It must be important.

"What is it?" Ryker's husky voice demanded.

"The letter from the First Prime has—"

"Hurry up!"

Striding through the room with four long, controlled steps, Ivok scrambled to the desk in the center of the back wall. Ryker covered the letter he'd been hovering over with a stack of books. As his man approached, he shoved a pile of failed correspondence off onto the floor towards the large fireplace barely lit with a small fire.

With long arms and a flick of the wrist, the letter landed in front of Lord Wyvier. In the time it took Ryker to reach for the letter, Ivok had nearly shut the door behind him. It was a soft click that boomed through the silence, where even the fire was mute. Once more alone with his swirling thoughts, his frustration mounted like the thick rolling frills of a starched Einhart necktie. Anxiety and desperation rolled into one another, choking him of breath.

The worst kind of tension was the buildup that led to nothing. For weeks, Ryker had been expecting word. Twenty-two letters sent to friends and allies, and only three replies.

The light leather roll was tied in the royal knot, the only seal and signature needed when carried by the royal courier. Disappointment clouded his face as he held the small letter. Disembarking orders were usually large, needing to contain all the commander's orders and decrees. However, this document was nearly as delicate as a lady's handkerchief; it did not bode well.

Shoring up the little patience he had, Ryker released the knotted lock, pressed the letter open, and revealed the hard scrawling of burnt characters; short, choppy, and most unlike First Prime Zuul.

3742.6.08

By order of Zuul, First Prime of Tarag, champion of the citizens, peacemaker of Preos, defender of damsels and the Pillars of Unitas, protector of the five eternal laws and the chalice of Lamazie; to his ever-loyal Lord Ryker Wyvier, the Third Citizen, civic servant for the Tarquin people of the Wynthros regions of 18-28.

It is my great displeasure to inform you that by our people's standards, and with their best interests in the forefront of my consciousness, I've decided that combating the supposed Einhart mobile infantry is inadvisable at this time.

I have reached out to King Paul to see if he would be willing to compromise his efforts against Miss Colton. If she is to be your wife, then any attack made against her either on or off the soil of Taraq would be subject to the umbrella clause. However, until the good news breaks, she is still an Einhart fugitive and subject to their laws. That goes for all Einhart deserters, until they formally pledge allegiance to the land. Until then, they are visitors with a home elsewhere.

As for now, Miss Colton is still miss-ing, and as your friend, I think it best if you held off on further pursuits that may lead to unnecessary embarrassments. As per

Setting the letter down carefully, grave doubt compounded on his chest. Guilt tethered him to his chair. Ryker was caught in a wave of indecision, and the hesitation highlighted an unknown fear. It had been a long time since he had needed guidance, and he didn't relish asking for help now, but it seemed there was no other alternative.

A historical tapestry was being crafted by hands yet

unseen. More was at work in the building of countries and the destruction of lives than usual. It was a cold shiver on a warm day that woke his soul in warning of war games at play. As a commander, Ryker had been around war too often to have forgotten so quickly the taste of manipulation.

The time for waiting was over. News had come, and with it, more questions and frustrations fed his discontent. Inaction was no longer an option. It was time to bring Lana home.

CHAPTER THREE

Terra

3742.07.15

Terra's head spun, and it wasn't from being one hundred and fifty spans in the air. The Preosian contraption she and the general rode in lifted them none too easily. The device taking her to her jail was a small metal box attached to a few cords, with a mechanical pulley system that creaked as it clicked them up the mountain.

Amidst gray skies and thick clouds, Terra had no idea how the contraption worked, but she knew she couldn't continue worrying about the forceful wind knocking the lift off its track. No, Terra had to focus her attention on the small herd of hardened hunters she was about to encounter.

The box jolted to a stop, and Terra's stomach lurched with it. Lord Wyvier pushed the gate open. The hinges squeaked, and Terra watched the weathered wood and rusty frame move and act as a handrail to the narrow bridge leading her into a stone room. The narrow footing was all that kept her from falling off the side of the mountain.

"We can end this now if you just tell me what I want to know." He wanted her to tell him she was a bounty hunter, what clan she worked for, which pack she hailed from. When she told Lord Wyvier the truth, he hadn't believed her, so she didn't know if she wanted to bother now.

"I told you, I'm not working for anyone."

"Okay, if that's how you want to play it." The Tarquin general rolled his eyes and pushed her through. For a brief moment, Terra sprung forward with uncontrolled momentum, hovering so high she couldn't see the individual people below; just tiny ants moving under patches of clouds.

The walkway led into a closed-off stone courtroom, unlit and unused for decades.

The only way out is down.

"Why are you doing this? I've broken no laws."

"Unregulated hunting and littering."

"I've done no such thing."

"You've been found guilty of both counts."

"By whose authority?"

"Mine. Your sentence is two nights in the tower."

The way he looked her over, his upper lip raised with a sad shake of his head, told her exactly how he thought she'd fare.

"This is bullshit."

"Perhaps, but it's your own fault. All this could have been easily avoided." He still wanted her to admit to something much worse — hunting his woman.

When Terra merely glared with a raised chin, the man shook his head once more and walked over to the built-in shelf. It may have once stored legal reference, but now it stored a short stack of everything a prisoner would need. He pulled out a thick bundle, tucking a utensil inside a wooden bowl, and folding a wool blanket around them.

He tossed it to her, the inside rattling as it hit her chest.

"Here," he chuffed abruptly. His meaty fist stretched between them. Slowly, hesitantly, Terra extended her open hand under his. Then, his hand opened, and a thumb-sized whistle dropped into her palm.

"Three short bursts and I'll get you out. Three short bursts will tell me you're ready to talk. Good luck."

His hand now rested on the lever inside the wall. When he pulled it down, the wall split, and two massive stone slabs spread open. The room inside was dimly lit, with a central fire illuminating the walls of her new cage.

"If you want my advice, find the biggest guy and either take him down, or make him heel."

"I can take care of myself."

"Yeah, I've heard that before." He shut the door, leaving only his self-deprecating chuckle.

After taking a staggered breath, Terra faced the dark room. The quiet sounds of the contraption chugged behind her. Inside was silent, except for the whipping wind. Movement echoed from each edge of the round hall.

Large forms numbering nearly a dozen watched her silently from the shadows. Her sweaty palms flexed against the rough fabric. It took a great effort, but Terra lowered the blanket — her shield — letting it drop to her side.

Lord Wyvier probably thought she'd use the whistle before he got to the bottom of the mountain. Hell, at the moment, she was considering it. Ego, bravado, and maybe a little bit of greed kept her from using the whistle concealed in her fist.

Two nights — he would only keep her here for two nights. The rest of them were convicted hunters, but Lord Wyvier could only keep her for petty charges like littering. *I can do this.*

After, while they were stuck up here, Terra would be out and back to business. Apparently going rogue did have its advantages. Striding forward with a confidence she didn't feel, Terra headed towards the fire. *I can't afford to look weak.*

A fifteen-length fire pit took up most of the central chamber. Around it, a narrow ledge of smoothed mountain wrapped the nearly perfect circle. Leaning casually with her back to the flame was the only thing she could think to do.

The vast nothingness inside the deep well shocked her. More Preosian contraptions? There was nothing that she could see that would feed the fire as steadily as a large flame like this would need.

She had no idea the alliance between the two countries had gotten so warm. Still, the proof was undeniable. The fire's flames reached higher than she could throw a stone in the air.

To the right, a cold draft bellowed, and sunlight streamed through an opening. Not even thirty paces away from her was the gaping hole of mountain. It looked like a kind of chiseled-away patio.

The ledge had no railing, but still a few men laid on the edge, perched to overlook the death fall the mountain provided. *No way in hell.* Slowly the shadows moved once more, circling.

There was a deeper cubby carved into the wall, one where barely any light reached. Her skin pulled towards the darkness. The weight of their eyes pulled the hairs all over her body to attention. Too many, everywhere.

Why don't they step out of the shadows? Circling the well of fire, Terra skirted the dark room. The sensation followed her movement. For a second, every inch of her flashed with tingles, reaching for something she couldn't yet understand.

With her back towards the pit, Terra's newly adjusted

eyes scanned the area. Three men stood out as especially dangerous. The tall, hulking man in the deepest shadows of the dark room; she could barely find the line of his form, but she could feel a primal awareness with every ounce of the *wyld* spirit inside of her. The wyld connection warned her of danger all around.

The two hunters circling her moved slow and with confidence. One was slim and tightly wound, with vicious intention pulling at his lips, while the other towered over his partner. His large, shiny head and stocky frame densely packed with muscles moved with shorter strides to accommodate his shorter friend. With a slow and steady turn, Terra faced the pair.

The larger man had to be nearly seven lengths tall. *Great, a Konan.* Born in the highlands of the Wynthros Mountains, the Konan people were first reported as giants; highly aggressive and very territorial.

Terra had heard her father mention only one Konan bounty hunter — a man who went by the name Crusher, for his tendency to crush the bones of troublesome captures. Though Taraq had a reputation for breeding big, bulky men and women, the highlands put them all to shame.

The other man stalking nearer was too nondescript to recognize. Most likely an Einhart who traveled abroad.

"I don't have anything for you."

"Don't sell yourself so short." The smaller man grinned.

Terra frowned in response, not liking his tone or the greedy sweep of his eyes.

"Are you the hunter they call Crusher?" Terra turned

her attention back to the giant. The other man probably outweighed her by at least a hundred pounds, but the Konan had to be at least twice his size.

Hopefully if I can get Crusher to back off, the other will follow his lead. Like Lord Wyvier said, make the biggest guy heel. But how did Lord Wyvier even get this guy up here? Especially without breaking the lift?

Terra stepped forward towards the Konan. With a stiff spine and jaw, Terra made sure to keep her knees ready. There was a fine line between looking firm and being stiff.

"You've heard of me?" Even his voice was big. Loud and low. The man, Crusher, spoke volumes above a shout.

Terra flinched. She couldn't hold her reaction. The only saving grace was that men all around the room jerked and startled with her.

"Of course, who hasn't heard tales of your victories?" Terra tried to imagine what Josef would say. She knew no one better at talking than him.

It seemed to have worked. The big guy stopped and smiled at her, his mouth stretching to reveal a crooked-toothed smile.

The brief moment of charm lasted only long enough for her to notice the other man. The one with the greasy stare hadn't stopped. He was making his way closer.

Acting on the instinct screaming in her head, Terra jumped back, closer to the man. Her leap landed her within his reach. Terra slammed her elbow upward.

While she intended to strike his nose, her jab came up short, catching him in the throat. *Whoops.* Without stopping, Terra spun. She needed to keep moving to stay out of range of his angry flail.

Scanning the small room to see if anyone else wanted to try something, she ended with a long-held stare at the smaller man.

"You come at me again and I'll rip out your eyeballs."

She didn't know where the threat came from, only that it was his stare that unnerved her the most. So that's what she would target first. Growing up in the migratory pack, she knew well what it was like to be surrounded by those bigger, badder, and better than herself.

But it was his eyes she hated most. They had an angry, reckless tilt to them, that looked at her as if she were prey. No, that she couldn't tolerate.

The smaller man stepped forward, undaunted by her promise. If Terra needed to, she'd rip out his eyes and eat them in front of him. If that's what it took to keep the rest at bay. Her life depended on showing the others she was not one to be messed with.

Crusher reached forward, his long arm filling the space between him and his friend without moving a step closer. His large, dusty palm set heavy on his friend's shoulder, holding him back.

Terra smiled and nodded.

That's right. Fear me! I might be a crazy bitch willing to do some crazy shit. You don't know me. You don't want to. The internal speech stopped abruptly when both men's eyes looked not at her, but behind her. *Oh shit!*

Terra been so focused on the two men, she'd forgotten about the presence she'd felt in the shadows.

CHAPTER FOUR

Lana

L ana was just about there. She could crawl into the next chamber if she could make it to the balcony that overlooked the jutting rocks and grinding ocean current. Hopefully, once inside, she could find a weapon. Then, Lana could make her way back down into the dungeon and free the boy, Rue.

Why would anyone put a child in a prison? I don't

know what they have in store for us, but I know we won't be around long enough to find out. I need to focus on escape. First this dungeon, then this castle. Then the real test will begin.

After a while Lana found her escape. Not through her dungeon cell door, but through the hole in the wall separating the cells. On the other side, Lana crawled beneath the debris, past what may have been an abandoned rat's nest, to get to another destroyed wall she could climb over. Of course, that led to several dead ends, and back into the rat tunnel she went.

From there she had to dig her way through a collapsed partition, which led to another wrecked wall. Now she stood overlooking an endless expanse of ocean, with a small peninsula off to the right, just as dilapidated as this building. Whatever had happened to Castle Krunos, it hadn't fared well.

Lana wasn't stalling per se. She was debating how long the rails would last before they broke off. And they would break — they were flaking chunks of rust as Lana watched. But, if she could sprint, she could use them to propel herself into the blast hole and into the next room.

If not, she would tumble to her death, breaking her body on the jagged rocks and debris below. On the other hand, who knew what waited on the other side of the wall? Its breach was part of the main building, but inside was hidden from view.

The ocean air formed a brine on the back of her tongue. Heavy saltwater spray had corroded the very foundation of the estate. The only thing that seemed to be keeping the outer wall together were layers of muck, grime, and a penetrating root system. Ivory roots punched through the stone walls, weaving through cannon holes and pockets of deterioration.

Closing her eyes, Lana prayed. She could only take two steps back; anything more than that, and she would fall under the building, again, to her death. It wasn't much to build momentum, but Lana was determined. What made it difficult was the angle between the hole in the wall and the missing ground behind her. She would have to throw herself to the left at the last moment.

If she made the ledge, and if it didn't crumble beneath her, she might be able to jump up. Then she could dive into the two-length-wide hole four lengths up the wall, which may lead her nowhere. *Well, I never thought escape would be easy.*

Now was as good of a time as any, she supposed. If she didn't figure something out fast, she would be left foraging for rats and saltwater mold. Taking a deep breath for strength, then another for fortitude, Lana sprinted the two steps and, as she breached the opening, tried pushing off the crumbled wall.

Crystalline spores cut her hand, but the effort propelled her forward. Lana bounded through the air, long legs stretched, tired arms ready to grasp at anything. It was as if Lana hung suspended in time, with nothing but the wild currents underneath her. But when her foot did land on the compromised metal, she only had enough time to shift her other leg ahead before the bolt keeping the railing up started to rattle and shake.

It nearly threw Lana off balance. Waving her arms, trying to flap herself forward as her hips dipped back, she punched forward in a desperate attempt to keep her footing. *I'm not going to make it!*

The depressing thought rang in her head longer than she figured the railing would last. She was on borrowed time already. Every move sank the rail lower and lower as the hole holding it upright split and chipped away.

Her hands, stained with old and new blood, wrapped around a thick root system. Her fingertips pressed hard into the shredding fibers. With eternal slowness, she crawled until the roots turned to stems that wrapped around a rusted piece of rail.

As Lana found her balance, the railing she'd been holding onto snapped in her hand. There was no slow break; no creaking to foreshadow the drop. When Lana fell, the air billowed underneath her. With two, then three swimming kicks and a string of slapping palms, she frantically attempted to find purchase.

Lana's descent stopped abruptly, wrenching her already damaged shoulder when her hand wrapped around the thick root system once more. A surface-level numbness spread across her fingers.

The metal she'd been climbing on only moments ago crumbled in on itself, disintegrating in her hand. The collapsing barrier bounced down the once well-formed stone wall and down the rocky mountain cliff. Lana watched it fall. Nothing but the heart-shaped flowers with waxy leaves remained, ripped and tangled within the iron bars.

It was good, Lana told herself. She was lucky. Lucky to just be alive.

It was fortuitous that she'd jumped in time. But if her

entire hand went numb before she made it to the opening, her luck would run out. She tried creating momentum as she dangled over a hundred paces in the air.

Twisting, kicking, wiggling, her body rolled like a caterpillar. Eventually, she started to swing with her ankles locked around the ivory roots. With every swing, she moved closer to her destination. It also sent fine debris of dirt and stone loose, pelting her steadily.

Lana blinked away the flakes as she eyed the thick support that stuck out from under the stacked stone. She could have made it already. If she could just let go.

Heights never ranked on her list of fears. Dangling up here changed her opinion. *Remember Rue*, she thought. This escape wasn't for her alone. Lana had to make a move; she tested Fate too much.

The opening wasn't the dead-end that she feared. Lana crawled into what looked like an antique parlor room. The floor seemed solid; at least, it didn't shift when she stomped her foot.

What was once fine furniture was either tattered or moldy. A full-sized, undamaged cannonball rested where it had landed long ago. An imperfect sphere hammered through stone walls was nested in the floor, lifting the wood around it.

Still, the smell of this room was a significant improvement from the rat hotel she'd been crawling through. Listening carefully, she tried to discern anything man-made. There were no shuffling feet or clanging of cleaning. There was no smell other than fresh salty air and dusty funk. The only noise she could name was the howling of the wind through the destroyed walls.

Lana walked, inspecting the room. There were fine knickknacks, either broken or layered with soot and dust. And the pictures, once wiped down, showed mostly stuffy men in an assortment of stately posturing. The only thing that Lana thought would make a fine weapon — or at least a web destroyer — was a tall candlestick. It reached the length of her arm, and it felt comfortable in her hand. Not as comfortable as her short sword would have been, but beggars couldn't be choosers.

Lana tried to make an effort of creeping, but as she walked, she realized the layers of dirt softened her steps and left a trail. Besides, she reasoned with herself, anyone around would have heard the crashing. If they hadn't come running, her escape probably wasn't a priority.

She could only imagine what her unknown captors would prioritize in this mess. Not that it mattered. Rue was her priority now. Then later — freedom. Freedom from this dingy building, this cursed land, and the dreadful forest. Then freedom from Ryker and his lies. But first, she had to leave the parlor.

The rooms that she passed were like the first — way past dusty. Decades of dust and humidity had layered the surfaces with a kind of murky goop. There were about a dozen walls that had caved in, making the castle look like a long-forgotten battlefield.

As drafty as most big buildings are, the room Lana walked through was just plain windy. The air current lifted the dark stray hairs that escaped the remainder of her hairpins, brushing her neck and cheeks, heavy with filth. When she ventured into another room, this one a bedroom, Lana took the opportunity to use a sheet and some rainwater to clean her face as best she could.

The image in the mirror was shocking. Not that Lana had expected to wake up gorgeous. Not after getting beaten nearly to death, kidnapped, and thrown in a cell for days. And that was before rolling around in rubbish and rat refuse.

Still, her cheek was so swollen it had split, and the tooth she lost in the fight left her gums inflamed. Both eyes were blackened, and if her face wasn't smeared with blood, it was covered with dirt. She didn't have the time to try to mess with the dark clump that was her hair; it was most likely affixed with blood, grease, and dungeon goop.

Lifting her neck, Lana inspected the bruise. It was healing, but it must have been pretty bad initially. She was surprised the giant hadn't snapped her neck when he was thrashing her against the ground. He had plenty of chances to kill her, now that she thought about it. He could have just crushed her skull when she fell unconscious.

Instead, he had hauled her up and tried taking her who knows where. Well, she survived the giant only to be bested by her traveling companion. Story of her life. If it's not the unknown devil that surprises you, it's the friend that betrays you.

Shaking herself off as best as she could, Lana tried to shake the feeling back into her skin. Lana picked up her candlestick and carried on, unable to bear her reflection anymore.

Down the hall, she found a small kitchen. After rummaging she was able to snag a few jars of what looked like pickled fish. While she didn't imagine it would be delicious, she hoped that it was edible. Cracking the seal, Lana squeezed and popped the top. The smell hit her immediately. A combination of the worst smells in any kitchen: fish and vinegar. But at least it didn't look spoiled.

Without hesitation, and in a manner befitting someone who had starved for two days, Lana dipped her fingers into the liquid and pulled out the slimy flesh. It hovered over her open mouth, the juices dripping on her tongue and chin. It was pungent, but not rancid.

She'd already swallowed a significant chunk whole to save her the taste when she realized there was a thin strip of frail bones left in the fish. Slowing down, Lana picked off the inedible bits and swallowed the flaky meat a handful at a time. It was all she could smell for a while.

Rummaging through the cabinets, the drawers, the bare pantry, and the drop-down seasoning rack, Lana found a knapsack. Two jars of the fish and what looked like jam or fruit spread were rolled in towels to keep them from clanking. It wasn't a lot, but Rue had to be weak with fatigue by now. Lana only hoped she could get to him in time.

What she didn't understand was if no one was here, if the castle was abandoned, who had put her in the cell? If the Deathless Master had been dead or asleep, who commanded the deathless puppets? And why go through all the trouble to leave her there to starve and rot?

Long corridors were void of anything delicate or valuable. Heavy and ornate pedestals stood empty, while others laid tipped on their side and cracked. What would have once been richly colored walls were sun-bleached and bare.

Lana's footsteps, hesitant as they were, occasionally crunched over broken glass or destroyed floorboards. Each step still echoed in her ears. Hauntingly quiet as this place was, her every step felt like a bomb blast. Looking up to the tall ceilings, Lana had to ignore the scurrying that went on overhead. The ceiling corners were so densely packed with cobwebs it looked more like a community of wasp nests.

She couldn't think about what lived above her head. She didn't want to imagine what could be slinking down to drop into the nest of her hair. With practiced determination, Lana focused her attention on the destruction before she started swatting the air above her.

Every kind of devastation Lana could have imagined had befallen this place. Wind, water, war, and what looked like a fair bit of looting had laid the undoubtedly once proud castle low. Lana could only imagine the courage it would take to sneak into this place. Some things weren't worth the loot, especially with it being the home of the last Deathless Master.

What kind of desperation dared bait Fate? Was it fear or a lack of imagination that led them to pilfer the halls and the rooms of this ghostly manor? Walking through the dead and empty spaces brought forth a surge of dark ideas. The memories of a warning, too long-buried to remember, filled her with irrational dread.

A string of terrifying and horrible deaths that followed an eternity of un-life. Who would be stupid enough to tempt that? Like her thought had summoned the beast, the screaming started.

CHAPTER FIVE

Ryker

3742.07.16 Castle Wynthros, Taraq.

"So, what are you going to do?" Kennith asked with a choppy huff. His thick arms raised just in time to shield against the boot aiming for his face. The sun was blazing overhead without a cloud in the sky, but that was only part of the reason Kennith dripped sweat.

"The only thing I *can* do," Ryker said, before

attacking with a quick combination strike. He used fists, elbows, and a swift chop to his friend's collar bone. "Prepare for the worst." Ryker shook his head and stepped away from his friend, instead facing The Peak, a prison carved from the tallest mountain. He noticed a group gathered around the edge and it gave him pause before he assumed a sparring position once more.

"The legislature is already starting to coalesce. They're just waiting for you to overstep," his long-time friend cautioned once more.

The stocky giant braced himself as Ryker pulled back. The half-spin kick and cross-body combo bounced Kennith back a step, but he recovered quickly. Kennith and Lord Ryker had been sparring for decades now. He knew how to brace for his commander's attacks both on and off the battlefield.

"I'm sure the rumors of my judicious cruelty have spread through every loose tongue in the district." Ryker gritted his teeth, not in irritation but exhaustion. The sparring grounds were no place for a conversation, but Kennith enjoyed keeping him out of breath. With his attacks absorbed, Ryker continued his aggressive charge. "It doesn't matter what they think," Ryker added, emphasizing his point with a jab that had the full force of his pivot. "I made a promise to her that I would keep the bounty hunters off her trail for as long as I could."

Who "she" was didn't need to be addressed; Lana, the young foreigner who'd sailed into his life and thrown his world upside down. The damn girl that had been on his mind non-stop since she'd left. When she'd ended their association, she'd severed his role as protector and told him in no uncertain terms how much of a cad he was.

The fact of the matter was he had been, and still was, a bastard. Ryker had let his pride and his assumptions of the girl and her family ruin the one thing that made his exile exciting. Now he was scrambling to fix his mistake before Lana was gone for good.

"Some would say," Kennith started hesitantly, "that by promoting the rumor of her presence here, you've done just that."

The blistering look Ryker targeted Kennith with had him raising his hands in surrender. Ryker took the opportunity to strike low. That one, his old friend didn't block.

"I never said I said it. Only that it was being said." Kennith raised his hands, an easy grin on his big face.

"As long as I'm the Third Citizen, I will use the full weight of my authority. Besides, as the Third Citizen, any person, foreign or domestic, that breaks the law is subject to my rule. I am the ultimate voice of law and order, am I not?"

"You are the ruler of Wynthros, the leader to the people, and the protector of the land," Kennith said with a cautious lift to his voice. "I just don't think anyone in the position has ever taken its role quite so literally."

Again, Ryker attacked with an explosive assault. Even though his muscles burned, his arms were shaking, and his legs felt knock-kneed, he persisted. The sweaty lord didn't stop until his friend and target was completely on the defensive. This was their fourth round of practice. He'd only been training for two hours, but if this had been a siege, he and Kennith would've both been dead.

"Or so vigorously," Kennith added in an exasperated gasp. The grass underfoot was still crunchy from winter, but it was the loose rocks that were the real danger.

"I need this." The training cut his body back into shape and prepared him for the bounty hunters that continued to flood into his land. It also helped him work off the constant agitation that shadowed him.

Never had he been so unprepared. He'd been spending his time managing bickering farmers and checking merchants' coffers; his sword arm had gone soft. He was ashamed of himself — many things of late shamed him. Breaking off from Kennith, Ryker grabbed for the cup attached to the water pot built into the stone perimeter, shaking some sweat from his brow like a shaggy dog caught in the rain.

"What's there to say? I'm honor-bound and determined to fulfill my duty."

He wouldn't fail again. Lana could be lost or hurt. His people, the unit he had selected to guard and guide her, had failed. And now Lana was out there, alone once more; the one thing she feared most.

He had failed Lana. She was his armful of sparks and fire, the gentle voice in what was a hard, brutal existence. It had taken losing Lana for Ryker to realize that she'd made a place for herself in his life. That was his burden to bear. If Lana hadn't left without a backwards glance, he never would have realized how asinine his assumptions of her setting up a marriage trap had been.

I thought she was trying to trap me, so I did every-

thing in my power to deny her. And in pushing her away, I've only denied myself.

"It's a shame more officeholders didn't share your passion." Kennith gasped from the previous blows. "But not too long ago, it was considered toeing the line when you went on your hunts. Remember the flack you received for slaying the daimon of Namndi?"

"I have a vague recollection," Ryker lied.

The people and Bogar the Fifth had nearly prostrated themselves before Ryker after he and his men hauled in the mutated beast that had been terrorizing the area. However, once news had spread to the First Prime, an informal censure was issued on Ryker for depriving professional hunters of a good wage.

"Well, speaking of vague recollections, have you given any thought to what that crone said?"

"You'd better not let Hagitha hear you call her that, or you'll be eating nothing but cold oats for breakfast, lunch, and supper."

"What?" Kennith looked over each shoulder twice, shaking his head. "No, not Hagitha! The crone we met in Namndi."

"Who? Oh, the old bat that tried swindling us?"

"Yeah, do you remember what she said?"

"No, of course not," he lied. "Because it doesn't matter. That stuff never comes true. You're better off putting your money and your faith in your armorer. At least they'll actually save your life."

"Well, from what I remember, she turned out to be fairly accurate. She predicted Lana."

"Fate controls nothing. The woman was a fraud, not

a soothsayer. We are the masters of our future," Ryker said, shifting.

"I'm just saying—"

"I know what you're saying, so spare me." Ryker's twisted eyebrows lifted for a moment, and he made a note to check out the soothsayer. It might be desperation, but he was willing to try anything. Ryker stretched his shoulder, twisting his spine to avoid Kennith's sympathetic eyes. *I did both of us a disservice with how I treated her,* Ryker admitted, if only to himself.

"You're going to make things right."

Ryker swished his sun-warmed drink around his mouth and spat it to his left. He stared off to the north while his pulse thudded in his neck. It was the direction Lana had headed a few weeks ago. For a long moment, he could almost imagine connecting with her again.

In those brief flashes, she seemed to consume his senses. He didn't know whether the connection they shared was real or a figment of his wayward imagination, but the feelings swept over him like tingling ice, every sense heightened until they burned out. A few seconds later, Ryker shook his head. It was hard to pull out of the memories, but there were too many dangers to linger.

"We don't know that," Ryker added, still looking off into the landscape. Between the two of them, they had plenty of enemies. Lady Lana had been right to hesitate at making a formal alliance with him. However, he could feel a change inside her. If nothing else, he knew she needed him now more than ever. And if he answered that call, they would need each other and would have to call in every debt and ally they had, because what would come after them would swallow the world.

"Have you heard anything?" Kennith asked quietly, even though no one was around.

"Just more reports of outsiders invading our land."

"The First Prime has refuted those claims."

"Yes, he has." Ryker looked to the horizon at the angry swell of sickly clouds. The birds were gone, and only the sharp howl of the wind tunneling through the mountains remained. A storm was coming, and there was still a lot left to prepare.

If the rumors of Tarquin's borders being breached were true, then there was a bigger problem than Lana being in danger. And if it was true, then Ryker was training for more than protecting his woman. He was preparing for war.

CHAPTER SIX

Terra

Turning on her heel, Terra ran into a chest with the density of a brick wall. Tilting her head up, she stumbled back. *What the hell?*

The man had been standing behind her so closely she was surprised she hadn't felt his body heat until now. He was a mean-looking fighter, not nearly as tall as Crusher, but close, with broad shoulders and stern eyes.

Terra couldn't see the color of his eyes — his glare hadn't left the pair behind her. It wasn't until they left, walking towards the opening, that he tilted his head to look down at her. And that's when she noticed the long white scar running down his cheek, barely concealed under the wild edges of his short beard.

His sunlit, honey eyes roamed over the curves of her face, tracing her cheeks and lips all the way down to the swoop of her throat. His eyes, which were already caught in the throes of the wyld, flared when their gazes met. When a wyld glow swirled, lighting his eyes up from the inside, something shifted inside of her.

Locked in his stare, Terra frowned. After Josef, she'd told herself her focus had to remain on the job at hand. So why was her heart's fluttering choking her in silence? Why did the wyld spirit inside of her want to test the man in front of her?

"If you're looking to try me—"

"You'll pluck out my eyes, too?" His voice was dark, like a deep-throated whisper. As heavy as it sat on her senses, she didn't pick up any signs of aggression or hostility.

"I might, if I have to."

"I don't think it will come to that, do you?"

No. "I haven't decided yet."

Slowly, as if not to startle her, he leaned forward, keeping his hands at his sides. His body bent until his eyes were almost parallel to hers. Frozen in place, Terra's gaze dropped to his lips. His short beard framed the sharp twin peaks of his upper lip as it came closer to her own.

Parting her lips, Terra stilled. Then, he sniffed. Four slight flares of the nostrils of his patrician nose. Short sniffs, like a wolf tracking his prey.

Tensing, Terra flexed her hands, barely resisting the urge to shove him back. Fear kept her from an attack. It would make her look even weaker if she shoved and he didn't budge. Jerking her eyes to his warm honey gaze, similar to her own, her hand curled into a fist around the whistle.

He pulled back slightly, his eyes sparkling in amusement. Then, she did punch him. The hit landed with surprising force on his chin.

The sharp *thump* of her bony hand meeting his equally hard jaw ricocheted around the stone walls of their prison, ringing in her ears. *I can't believe I just did that.*

"Rude," she said instead. Turning away towards the fire pit, she got only one step before the man's hot hand wrapped like a vice around her arm.

Instead of giving in to her panic, Terra forced herself to look him up and down. If she learned anything in her previous hunts, it was how to mask her emotions.

"Because you're a she-wolf, I'm going to let that slide. But if you hit me again, I'll hit back."

"Get your hands off me." Terra felt her wyld spirit rise, ready. Ready to do what, she wasn't sure.

Taking his time, he released her, but his eyes never left hers and she still felt caught by him. Part of her felt fear and hesitation. He was a large man who absorbed her punch like a splash of water. There was another part of her that felt sparks of excitement, which always spelled trouble.

That other part of her — the reckless, devious, prideful side of her — wanted to climb up on the edge of the fire pit and launch herself at him. She was fairly sure that when she had her legs wrapped around him it wouldn't be a fair fight. The same spirit that urged an attack wanted to play conqueror.

He called her she-wolf, a term hardly used by their people anymore. It meant wild woman — a female who could just as easily choose seduction or violence. The term was an insult, but it didn't feel degrading when it came from him.

"Do it," he challenged when she said nothing, caught in her indecision.

"Do what?"

"Whatever it is that has you biting your lip."

If only we didn't have an audience, I just might. She tried to appease her ego by reminding herself she had to play her time here smart. *I'm not here to find a man.*

"Why did you do that?" Terra asked instead.

"What? Save you?"

"One," Terra chuckled, "you didn't save me. I saved myself and you just unnecessarily backed me up. And two, I didn't need your help." She turned up her nose, ignoring the smell of evergreens and lemon that stirred every time she shifted around him.

"You can lie to yourself, but you can't lie to me," he said with a smirk.

"It's not a lie."

"What are you doing here?"

"I'm a murderer. Real crazy shit." *Don't mess with me!*

"You can't lie to me." His eyes slid up her chest and neck until once again he stared into her. There was something familiar in his eyes, but she couldn't figure out what.

Images flashed in her mind — his naked body underneath her, his hand sliding up her back and down her bare hips as his teeth sank into her shoulder. A ripple of lust bubbled up from her stomach and she jerked her body upright abruptly, clenching the feeling back down.

My imagination needs to cool down. There will be none of that.

"I want to know why. Out of everyone here, why did you help me?" Terra demanded, as the hand on her hip clenched into a fist.

"You know why."

"Because we're both wyld?"

"Sure."

Terra had to shift to her other foot, pressing it into the ground to avoid it tapping. He was so damn tight-lipped, it was infuriating! His stare didn't waver; he just silently waited.

"Well, fine then. Forget it," Terra huffed, shaking her head. She turned, preparing to leave.

"Stop." His deep command brought her up short. "Come back here."

"Bite me." Terra flipped him off over her shoulder and forced herself to keep walking away.

"If you insist."

He wrapped his arms around her chest to keep her

flailing under control. He pulled her back, spun her around, and lifted her so that she sat on the ledge of the fire pit. In a quick, controlled motion, his wide hand fisted her hair, holding her in place.

Squirming, Terra pushed, but her arms shook under the strength of his pull. He brought his lips down to her chest. Terra felt his nose lift the fabric of her shirt, trailing slowly past her collarbone.

She threaded her fingers through his hair, considering resorting to hair pulling and scratching. But as Terra struggled, she caught the intensity in his eyes and it locked her into place. She felt a whip of desire lash through her as his canine caught the swell of her breast. He grinned at her, dragging his lips slowly back up her neck.

Stuttered breath echoed in her ears. Something inside of her shivered, stirring to life. His cheek scratched her chin, and Terra shifted — not to pull away, but to lock eyes with him once more. Their breath mingled just moments before making contact. Terra's head raced, thinking of everything but their audience.

For a moment, The Peak was theirs alone. Belatedly, Terra came to her senses. She felt eyes on them and, in an uncharacteristic flush of modesty, she balked. She was no longer trying to strong arm him. Instead, she slapped at him, trying to wedge her hand between them.

"Woah, bad," Terra scolded.

"You're welcome."

"Excuse me?" Terra snapped, adjusting her clothes. She looked around the area, her face on fire.

"That should protect you from the rest. As long as you don't do anything too stupid."

That was all for show? Oh hell no! "How dare you!"

"No need to thank me."

Glaring, Terra shook her head and scooted away. When she was outside his reach Terra hopped down and sat on the other side of the fire from where he stood. There was never a time when she wasn't acutely aware of eyes on her, but when she finally looked over her shoulder, he was gone.

Back in the shadows again. The thought of him watching her from the darkness sent shivers down her back. *Three days, two nights. I can do it.* Terra nodded to herself, gripping the whistle for dear life.

CHAPTER SEVEN

Lana

Lana wondered if the layouts of these buildings were intentionally confusing. She had to go up to go right, then had to take stairs down to follow the hall, only to discover that the gallery led to the servant's wing and a dead end. Perhaps if she turned around and went back the way she came, the stairs to the dungeon were behind a closed door?

Sighing, Lana turned, hating that she was back to walking towards the unnatural howling. She heard the pain and rage. Lana wanted to believe that it was just a wounded animal, a creature caught in the chaos of the castle's destruction. But fear had taken seed. The haunting sound chilled her blood.

Gripping the cloth sack and candlestick tight in each fist, Lana crept forward. Though she'd yet to encounter resistance, she continued to feel as if an attack was always around the next turn. Perhaps the next door, or was that the sound of someone who'd snuck up behind her? As open as the destroyed roof was, the halls had a heavy, confining feel. Fear pressed into her.

But it was hard to maintain fear. Coincidentally, it was easy to get bored, and Lana's confused sense of direction was becoming a problem. If only the cries would stop for a moment. Then she could think.

She felt like she was getting close. Lana knew there was a dungeon underneath her, and she knew it faced north and had an ocean on the west. Lana didn't know exactly where she was, but she knew it wasn't smart to stay long.

By her count, she was already at least ten days behind schedule. And if she'd been transported, Lana had no way of knowing how far away she was from Exxus. *Well, I may miss the meeting with Drusti, but that just means I have longer to search for Charlie.*

She would get there. It was merely a matter of when. And her brother, Charlie, would have to forgive her after all she went through to find him. *Besides*, Lana thought as she looked down at the pocket that held her compass. *I come bearing gifts.*

Wait. The wailing had stopped. Closing her eyes, Lana breathed a sigh of relief. The bated breath that she'd been holding felt cleansing as it expelled. *Thank you.*

The time going through each room seemed to move faster. Lana felt guided by intuition. Lana knew it; she just needed to be able to think clearly. Her confidence in herself was renewed. After all, she'd survived so far.

Swirling white, gray, and blush lines ran smooth streaks across a long marbled floor. The long, flat expanse met with massive black columns, each branded with detail to pay tribute to the god of old. It rivaled the ancient temples, almost mockingly. The person who built this had a big ego.

What she could gather from the bits that were left was that this had once been a powerful house. This ball-room alone showed that to be true — thick marble, multiple ton columns that led the eye to the ceiling's artwork. An epic rendering of a fable lost to time.

She was near to the middle of the dance floor, her neck craned to look up at the ceiling. She was trying to follow along to the story above her head. If Lana was reading the images correctly, the young hero's lover was dead at her feet, killed by a betrayer.

Fresh air filled her lungs as she ran into another hole in the ceiling, just as the young hero was about to confront the killer. *Figures.* Lana flicked a disdainful look upwards, tripping over some trash.

Catching herself hard on her palms, her injured wrist

caved under the weight. Lana spilled further down and came eye to eye with a mutilated body. Her natural reaction was to gasp and scramble away. When she inhaled, she took in so much death and decay it soured her throat like poisonous gas. Expelling a closed-mouthed scream, Lana franticly tried to get her knees under her.

Her shin hit the body's femur, and it snapped and crunched under her. Rolling her eyes away from the sound, trying not to gag, her eyes met once more with the open eyes of the corpse. When she stood, the eyes followed her movement.

Gasping again sent Lana into a coughing fit, but she was already turning to run towards the two pairs of double doors. Something slimy grabbed her leg, and against her bare flesh, it held her. Lana screamed in terror, though her bruised throat cracked with the sound. Afraid she was about to be swallowed up by the undead nightmare, Lana kicked.

It pulled her down, trying to drag her deeper into its clutches. Lana raised her arm, and her ornate candlestick smashed through its skull. Its gilded curves splattered with coagulated blood, shaking in her hand like gelatin.

I have to get out of here. The feeling of beetles crawling beneath the body's waxy skin wasn't a figment of her imagination. The puppet was still attempting to grapple her, and it spewed beetles from its ribcage as it shifted. They flew out of its mouth in a jet of ink, taking to the air like oil-saturated flutterbys.

Rolling, Lana kicked, closing her eyes to focus, but there was no time to find the metis to connect with. Lana lifted the candlestick again and beat the creature until it released its grip on her. Standing abruptly, Lana stumbled backward, away from the carnage and into a wall.

Turning her head slowly, Lana looked into empty, milky globes. The body of an old man, dressed as a meager shining light priest with the outdated, traditional bald, tattooed head, his throat slit. He stood like a shade of myth and legend, and when she shifted, he followed.

Lana's breath caught in her lungs, and her sweat felt like plaster against her skin. The air in her mouth was hot and stagnant, and tasted sour on her tongue. Looking between the two animated corpses, Lana couldn't decide which was worse — rotting flesh, or the morbid disguise.

She didn't want to see any more, but she couldn't tear her eyes away from the gray face of the priest, colored only by the blood that dried against his skin. Not even the clanking of bones on marble could distract her. That undead creature was too grotesque to stomach.

"Don't mind her. She forgot she was dead." A dark-haired man slowly walked across the room. With sparkling eyes, he looked more like a ballroom rogue than a demon summoner.

Lana paused a long moment, then turned to the only other lucid being in the room. Dipping her head in respect seemed the only appropriate action. Even covered in scars and surrounded by ghouls, the man still had the bearing of a nobleman.

A smile brightened his face, which was shielded by an antiquated bevor-like device wrapping around his neck and curving over his delicate jaw. It may have been actual armor or just an intimidating statement piece. But when he turned his head, the skin parted, exposing for a brief second the pinkish inner workings of his neck.

"A polite warrior. Well, I never would have guessed." His voice was hoarse as he looked over her.

The metal device surrounding his head curved just over the crown, protecting his skull, while the long, intricately carved ancient symbols etched into the sides dropped low, protecting his throat from an attack. The whole piece of armor looked to weigh a bundle since, from the looks of it, the metal was thick, and most likely metis reinforced — resilient.

"Who are you?" Lana asked, trying to hide her growing nausea. It was one question Lana pulled from the dozen spinning around her head.

Though he was tall, his long legs wobbled as he hobbled towards her. His tight smile and heavy eyes warned her of deception. But he moved around her despite the tax it put on the delicate threads of skin holding him together. Unease shifted in her breast, and his smile made her stomach curl. Caution pulled her back in warning.

"My name is Dimitri, but don't worry, soon your fears will be silent. Just come to me and accept my grace." His hand, graceful and tapered, lifted towards her, palm open, fingers laid waiting.

Lana didn't know what his 'grace' was, but she knew she didn't want it. Reflexively, Lana blocked the slow arms of the priest as he reached for her. His pallid hands gripped her shoulder with surprising strength. Lana couldn't stretch herself far enough to avoid the slow-moving palm.

"I don't think so." Lana shook her head, trying to find an escape.

As Dimitri reached for her, Lana saw red cracks against his skin. It looked as though bloody thread stitched the flesh together. A scream shredded the inside of her throat, but she didn't care. It felt purifying to release the fear boiling in her heart.

Lana tried to lift her leg to kick Dimitri away, but he managed to avoid it. All she felt was cold as two hard fingers pressed against her forehead, stroking down her cheek and around to the base of her skull.

Then, it was all heat. Energy stretched between them, actually sparking the air. Or maybe that was her flesh that was burning.

The wretched man tore apart her insides with a single, delicate touch. It felt like he was heating her organs, burning her from the inside out. Lana shrieked and cried as Dimitri laughed.

The pain made her twist and turn out of reflex. Anything to dislodge the touch that devastated so thoroughly. Though she intended to move, her body refused. Like a statue, Lana was frozen — immobile.

Before her eyes, the thin threads that held Dimitri together grew and strengthened. She watched with horrifying awareness as he healed before her eyes. *He's taking from me to heal himself. He's going to suck me dry and kill me.*

His touch lasted what seemed like hours, and she thought she would disintegrate into an ashy pile. Until finally, her finger jerked; just once, but she knew control was coming back to her body. Lana rolled her gaze towards the man. His blue eyes were pinched in a secretive smile, pulling his lips into a long, thin line.

Invigorating herself with determination and control, Lana leaned back, breaking Dimitri's contact with her head. With two precise movements she disengaged his touch by biting his inner wrist. There had been nothing holding her in place except for the vortex of power transferring between them. Her legs were shaking, though she couldn't tell whether it was from exhaustion, the effect of whatever damage he'd inflicted on her, or just a final burst of energy before she succumbed to death.

Whatever fueled her, Lana ran. And if she fell a quarter-mile away, like a deer after it's been shot, she was happy to die as far away from there as she could get.

She didn't need to see the priest to know he pursued. Marbled floors and ornate walls passed in a blur. With Lana's battered and beaten body, half-starved and sleep-deprived, she didn't know if she was moving fast or if her vision was failing. All she knew was that she wouldn't be sparing even a second to turn and check the chaos behind her.

She'd never been this far into the castle, even after all the dead ends and wrong turns she'd made earlier. It reminded Lana of the split-second decision she'd had to make long ago on her journey to Ryker. That decision had cost the life of Bobette.

Now Lana had a similar choice: keep to the destroyed parts of the building, staying within the reaches of the light, or venture down the darker and more structurally sound halls. Lana sent up a prayer — a

desperate plea where she begged for guidance and life —
then set off into the dark.

Slowly, the light faded as she jogged deeper into the
hall. It took a bit for her eyes to adjust, and she was left
groping the dirty walls. Lana had to still the nagging
voice in her head telling her she needed to rush.

No headlong charge into the unknown. She'd done
that already. It hadn't turned out well. But now she knew
why her friend Josef had feared this place and the Deathless Master that ruled here. At the time, she'd thought
her friend absurd, but time had made a fool out of her.

She used the moments in the dark to move noise-
lessly. Lana's ears strained to hear anything that may
serve as a warning for another attack. She calmed her
breathing with the metis exercises she'd struggled to
learn before. Now each breath whistled, either from her
broken nose or the missing canine. The shrill sound was
a beacon of her location.

As she passed several closed doors she thought of
the priest's clumsy grab, and Dimitri's rigid movement.
Hopefully that meant she had an advantage. Her body
was tight and painful; the beating she'd taken had indeed
dislocated her shoulder, which accounted for the blessed
numbness in her hand and wrist.

She had to leave this place. Perhaps she would be
able to come back for Rue and save him in time. But, if
what she'd just encountered was what had thrown them
in the dungeon, then maybe he was better off dead
sooner rather than later. Lana's stomach rebelled, heaving. The loud whistle of her heavy breathing pierced the
air.

Scrambling, Lana reached for one of the doors that lined the walls. The handle fell apart in her hands, and the door moved with a heart-stopping squeak. Crouching down, Lana looked back the way she'd come. There wasn't any movement, not even a shadow.

Cracking the door open just enough to get through, Lana nearly wept at the sight of the bedroom. Small and neat, everything tucked into its place. Bright light streamed in through the intact window on the far wall. It was there, in what may have been the only untouched room, that Lana threw up pickled fish and blood.

Then, just as she had feared, the energy that had sustained her escape was wiped out. Lana had enough momentum to stumble to the dusty bed. Crawling on the rotted blanket, Lana folded her hands and tried to keep the image of her family in her mind. The tear that rolled down her cheek was the last thing she felt.

CHAPTER EIGHT

Ryker

3742.07.17 The city of Wynthros, Taraq.

"**N**ext!" Ryker shouted towards the open doors. Lazy slaps of slow, fat raindrops hitting the dry rock did nothing to soften Lord Wyvier's bellow. There was nothing that could distract from the irritation in his command.

People fled the streets, darting in front of the open chamber doors just long enough to peek inside before racing away. Ryker watched impatiently as the people outside looked over their shoulders with suspended dread; some towards the open doors of the public chamber and the angry voice inside, and others towards the queasy green sky threatening overhead.

Still, there were a few who hesitated to enter the open threshold of the council chamber, reluctant to face the real storm inside. Many preferred the impending deluge to the fury of Lord Ryker.

"I said, *next!*" Ryker shouted. One man pushed aside fear and with great reluctance entered the chamber. The amber lights, kept as low as possible, cast monstrous shadows across the walls. Lord Ryker sat half over the arm of his chair, his stare direct as the tall younger man approached. It took a moment too long for Lord Ryker to pull back from his thoughts to recognize the man. When he did, he was merely rewarded with a nod.

"What does the town's second-best blacksmith need from me now?"

"I ask for news—"

Thunder broke in a deafening crack that echoed within the chamber. Whatever Brayden said was lost in the noise. Not that Ryker needed to hear what the man said to know why he'd come.

"I have none," Ryker said with irritated authority. His tone was clipped, and though he barely raised his voice, the chords rang with tension.

"What do you know of their last rendezvous?"

"I know they didn't make it through the night before a mob formed in the town. Those that lasted through the night were to be strung up by morning."

"And what of—?"

"Drustrudian is en route at my behest, and that's all you need know."

"And what of Lady Lana? Have you heard nothing of her as well?"

"You should worry less about things you cannot have, blacksmith." Ryker ground his teeth. *First, he plays my friend, wrapping Drustrudian up in knots, and now he's after Lana too? I don't think so.*

A soft creaking of tired wood on tight hinges ended the conversation as a group entered, uninvited. Ryker had never been happy to see the High Council of the Citizens, but tonight he welcomed them with a deep nod.

Ryker turned back to Brayden. "You may leave now." It wasn't a question.

There wasn't a thread of pretense in Ryker's voice. Begrudgingly, Brayden nodded in respect and left gracefully. He hadn't gotten any answers, but at least he hadn't been sent to The Peak for the night.

CHAPTER NINE

Ryker

Ryker tried to keep his foot from tapping while the bleating old goat finished his speech on jurisdictional boundaries and occupational duties. It was the same address he'd used in every introduction since being elected. It must've worked. After thirty years, even the public could recite it.

Ryker just didn't have the patience to wait the three more minutes until the conclusion. Clasping the elder — Lourum — by his narrow shoulders, Ryker silenced the man with a small shake. He felt a nudging temptation to thrash Lourum around and watch his long neck whip around like a ragdoll.

The frustration inside of him that had been building for weeks nagged him to lash out. Ryker pushed the desire down, clenching his fists in the official's cloak, as his colleague gaped at him. Finally, the old councilman sensed the threat before him. Ryker's control was finite, and he struggled for calm.

Releasing his grip slowly, Ryker rolled his eyes and turned away. Lourum had brought two underlings, as per usual, who benefited from his counsel and support. Ryker looked them over as they stepped back, almost as one.

He didn't recognize them. They must've been new. And what a first impression he'd made. *Well, sometimes the rumors are true. It's good for them to know now; better to be disillusioned early.*

"Why have you come, Elder Marqit?" Ryker asked.

"I've come at the behest of many of my — our — people. There have been... a few complaints. It appears you've become quite an ass."

Ryker felt the first crack of a smile in almost two seasons. His lips struggled to spread into the familiar position. It was uncomfortable for both men. Shaking his head, Ryker sat down on the bench, ceding to the old man's wisdom. Direct confrontation. He agreed; it was about time to get intentionally aggressive.

"Maybe you're right, Lourum. Should I resign my commission as the Third Citizen under the law of bias?"

"Nobody wants that."

"Except for me."

A crack of lightning rippled in the crevices of the mountain. Deep, throaty echoes of thunder purred like a libidinous harem on the night of a full moon. The faint screech of a child in fear pierced the storm's song, a somber reminder of just who Ryker served.

"What are you saying?"

"I'm a better general than Third Citizen," Ryker acknowledged.

"The people know they are protected under you, and we flourish for it."

"My focus is split, and we both know how dangerous that is."

"This is highly irregular. You can't claim bias on yourself."

"Why not? I'm the best to know."

"It must be demanded by the citizens. No one's ready to throw you to the wolves, yet."

Thrown to the wolves — a literal expression deeper in the country. A trial taken from the laws of nature. The only acceptable final solution for a people so out of touch with modern advancements and moral liberation.

When excised leaders fell out of favor in Taraq — after their rank was revoked and their civic brand was cut off — the accused faced those who they had wronged. Sometimes the matter was settled in court. But it was common practice to resolve the matter with combat.

"Not yet," Ryker added. "But what happens when war breaks out among an unprepared people? Who gets thrown to the wolves then?"

Ryker turned the conversation towards the actual problem. The First Prime's insistence on heeding the opposite of everything taught by both the academy and life. The territory of Taraq was hard-earned, and now they were asked — no, ordered — to sit on their heels as another nibbled away at their border.

"You ask me questions that no one can answer, "Lourum said.

"What are we if we stand by and do nothing?"

"By the word of the First, the attacks on our borders are misinformation and rumors."

"Are we men, or are we sheep? Both of us have lived through territorial skirmishes. Do you really believe our borders are safe?"

Boom. The conversation ended abruptly when lightning struck and cast a looming shadow over the two men. A lone figure stood proud against the storm, striding towards them. They shook the rain off themselves, obscuring their identity.

"Announce yourself," Ryker ordered, and turned to put the old man and his acolytes behind him.

A flurry of rain poured in from outside until the intruder closed the towering doors, one at a time. When they were finished, the figure turned, lowered their hood and bowing. Genie, niece to General Orla and number one on Ryker's shit list, stood in front of them, blinking the rain from her eyes.

"How dare you interrupt us." If Ryker were a wolf, his maw would have snapped.

"This is too important. I have word from Orla."

Genie's hair was waterlogged and sticking to her

flushed cheeks. Her skin was a few shades darker than the last time he'd seen her. Her body, too, was toned with muscle. What had she been up to since Lana left?

"What is it, child?" Elder Marqit stepped closer, his warm eyes wide, head turned to the side with his good ear towards the commotion.

Genie stepped into the group's circle, staring at the underlings who crowded too closely.

"You have word of Lana?" Ryker's eyes brightened as his hands clenched.

"I'll only speak of it with you."

Elder Marqit drew himself to his full withered height. The apprentices under his care noticed the affront and took to his sides immediately. The two soft-faced young men floundered wordlessly, lips rounded as they fretted in confusion, fussing over the elder.

Ryker turned to his old friend and extended his arm towards the door, dismissing the first local leader to accept Ryker after his banishment. The man looked at Ryker with open-mouthed surprise. A curt nod changed his expression from charming bewilderment to vexation, as the powerful lord walked them to the door.

The news board, with a single light masked by thick layers of rain and hail, stood as a lonely vigil in the storm. Ryker almost felt bad for sending the frail man out in the foul weather. A strong enough gust could tip his fragile form over.

If Lourum had been alone, Ryker could have petitioned for him to stay. After all, with age came wisdom, and he wasn't known as an elder for naught. Still, there were many matters a local civic servant need not know, like how truly desperate Ryker had become for any news of Lana.

The two acolytes Elder Marqit had taken under his wing had yet to be tested, and for that reason alone, they could not be trusted. Hell, Orla had triumphed through the fires and still, she failed him. *If it wasn't for her fuck-up, Lana would be back by now.*

But the girl had come bearing news. Important news, if her urgency was to be believed. One thing Orla would always be counted on for was her commitment to self-service. A smart woman with a determined mind and a hidden agenda was dangerous, to be sure.

He'd only wished he'd seen it sooner. Unlike others, Orla understood the strategy of political games. He would have to scrutinize everything Genie said.

The sigh Ryker tried to swallow came out as a long exhalation. With a fierceness borne from desperation, Ryker turned towards the young woman. She had been Lana's best friend while she'd been living with Ryker. Once upon a time, he'd thought warmly of the girls' friendship; now he couldn't help but see her as the same failure Orla had proven to be.

He'd thought the general was dead. Ryker had already provided the service for her empty pyre, honoring her for dying in battle and for protecting Lana. Now he knew that Orla lived. Now he had to wonder and worry about Lana's survival.

Looking to the western mountain range, towards the direction Lana had set off, Ryker prayed it wasn't too late. He took a deep breath to prepare himself for what was about to come. Then, he sent up another silent prayer for strength and patience.

Finally, word had arrived.

CHAPTER TEN

Terra

Terra had always had a hard time standing still. When her body was at rest, she always felt a pervasive soreness. Perhaps the cause wasn't the lack of movement, but rather the complete lack of action — time spent doing nothing became torturous to her.

Propped up against the fire pit, Terra kept a tired eye

out for trouble. Her mind was stubbornly reluctant to stay alert and vigilant. Her tired eyes watched the tall stone walls pulsate, slowly closing in on her.

It was easy when there was a rush of emotions to rely on. Now, however, the absence of anything at all lured her into a doze. "Oh no, girlie. You don't want to do that. Not here."

Snapping upright, Terra reached for the empty spot where her prized blade once resided. Before her crouched an old man. His threadbare tunic did nothing to hide his concave chest. Gray hair, curly and unruly, spread across his entire body like a fuzzy rug.

"You're a bounty hunter?" Terra asks skeptically.

"Nah, just a nuisance. You?"

Terra debated her answer before shrugging. "I got picked up for littering."

"Littering, eh? That Lord Wyvier sure is getting peculiar. Too big for his boots, if you ask me."

Terra looked the older man over. Undoubtedly, he once was as big as any of the men here. Age, however, had zapped the majority of his bulk, and the trials of time had beat him into the hunched form he now had.

He was probably the closest prisoner to her size, which meant he would be the safest bet for a companion.

"I'm Terra." She didn't know why she lowered her voice. Her eyes flickered to the darkest shadows, and she felt a blush heat her face. *It's just the fire.*

"Haggerdy." His tone was gruff, but he extended his hand out respectfully.

Terra gripped softer than she normally would, careful not to bruise his frail skin. He, however, gripped as hard as he could and shook her arm violently with a wily grin. Terra pulled her hand back, feeling the throb in her wrist. She turned back to the man, her eyes looking him over a little more carefully now.

"You don't have to worry about much here. This place ain't bad. Fresh water from the well, food comes in every day from the bucket. And if you can fall asleep on the hard stone and sleep without getting killed at night, you'll find it's not too bad here. But you look like a creative gal — I'm sure you'll figure something out."

"I'm not scared. The men here are bounty hunters, there's no money in cold-blooded murder."

"Murder ain't the only thing you have to worry about, kid. Besides, most become hunters because they prefer existing outside the law, living by their own set of rules. And here, there is no rule of law, just survival. Being trapped has a way of making men crazy."

"You sound like you agree with Lord Wyvier."

"No, he's an ass. But I do understand his logic," Haggerdy clarified.

"Logic?" Terra scoffed.

"When a man has the power and ability to protect his family, he does it, no matter what. Because there's nothing in the world more crippling than not having the power to help, and having to watch your family be torn apart before your eyes."

Damn. What the hell happened to him?

"I don't agree, but I do understand. If I had his authority, I would have done the same."

"So, what do I need to know? Because understanding Lord Wyvier's motivation doesn't get me out of here."

"Well you already met the two big players."

"Right, Crusher."

"Meh, Crusher's a slab of meat, mostly harmless as long as you keep him from getting too upset. But, his new best friend, Sentillies, now, he's a mean one. Spiteful. He won't forget what you did earlier. I hope you know how to sleep with one eye open."

Before she could suggest a partnership, he rose from his knees, both joints and an ankle cracking as he stood.

"Hey, if you ever find yourself with a little extra food, I'm always happy to help a friend," Haggerdy said.

"Do you mind watching my back as I sleep?"

"Oh, well, I don't sleep much myself you know, and so when I do sleep I'm out like a light. I'd be no help. And besides, I'm not going to get in between you and Sentillies. You should try Allister, he seemed partial to you."

Allister, you say. That must be the man who came up behind me. Allister. So that was his name. Terra looked into the shadows, feeling an electric pull that didn't dissipate after she turned away.

Nope. It's only two nights, I don't have to sleep.

CHAPTER ELEVEN

Lana

The time was now. With her heart beating like a war drum, Lana moved. She pressed herself against the chipped walls, heedless of the cuts on her back and arms. She had woken in the same room she'd passed out in, with a special guest patrolling her door.

If she slowed her breath, she could hear shuffling

feet. It was close; less than a dozen paces heading towards the west wing. Pacing back and forth, the puppet that guarded Lana's room continued its patrol. The mottled corpse walked with leaded steps. The vines that must have been growing near his body remained within him after he'd been reanimated, and now dragged behind him like a limp tail.

It made him easy to locate. If she could sneak past the guard there, she would be able to outrun and outmaneuver the creepy bastard. Then, she'd be able to roam free, find a way out, get to the dungeon, and rescue Rue.

That was if he was still down there, alive. Lana had no idea how long she'd been unconscious, but she'd promised the boy, and she wasn't going to give up on him. Lana would keep her word.

First things first, she had to sneak away. She had no idea how these puppets sensed their surroundings. They were dead — could they see and hear? She didn't know, but the very little lore she had picked up centered around how vile the creatures were. There were stories across the world that told of great evil that contaminated life. They were the reason knowledge of metis was destroyed, and the metisians able to manipulate the energy were so thoroughly eradicated.

When the mottled gray puppet shuffled to the left, turning the corner, Lana made her move. It would take sixteen seconds for the shambling form to make his turn. From her previous attempts, she knew there was a corridor to the right. *I have to go faster! Time is ticking, and I still haven't cleared the hall.*

The shuffling steps of the puppet were getting louder.

Lana slid through the entrance just as the creature rounded the corner. She pressed herself into the crumbling wall, behind a toppled pillar. It was the first time she'd been able to get a close look at the patrolman. His movements were sluggish, with one leg unable to bend and the other dragging behind him like a club. The puppet seemed to be whole, with clothes and not the deteriorating rags she expected. Only a few mounds of bright orange fungi sprouted from his head and neck, looking like overgrown acne.

Once the sounds of her patrolman's steps faded, Lana sighed in relief. At the moment, there was no one around, but she couldn't stop herself from walking on the balls of her feet. Any squeak from the stairs stopped her heart. The briefest movement stopped her in her tracks.

She continued down the hall, the deteriorated carpet squishing underfoot, until finally she found a set of stairs leading down.

Yes, finally. This has to be it. Rue might still be down there, and even though the musky smell suffocated her, Lana continued. If there was a chance there was a little boy down here dying, she owed it to him to attempt a rescue.

It was sheer luck that she was able to find the entrance that led to the underground prison, and it had only taken her wandering around for a half hour. Now she and Rue could leave this place. His mother was probably scared stiff. *And then I can go back to searching for my brother.* There was a nagging voice that reminded her she did have another option. *I could go back to Ryker, a defeated woman. Accept his marriage proposal and go back to dealing with his vindictive mistresses.*

I'd rather be dead. As soon as the thought entered her head she felt an uncomfortable shift in her gut. Lana was lucky to be alive. Did she dare tempt Fate?

Slowly, Lana made her way to the bottom, watching the light stream in from the giant hole in the ceiling. Rats the size of her foot scampered over the destruction. Huddled in the corner of the first cell, shadows stretched on his protruding spine, curled a small form, crying. Lana could barely hear him over the squeaking rats and crashing waves.

"It's okay, child. I've come back for you, just as I said. Come on, let's go."

Rue's scrawny form froze, then leaped to the far corner of his cell, pressing in the shadows. The poor thing. He was confused and terrified. Lana had to get him out fast, before someone spotted them and she wound up behind these bars again.

Searching through the wreckage, Lana yanked a loose bar off a broken door. It had weight to it and was longer than her arm. Wedging the bar in the small space between the door and wall, Lana pushed and wiggled until it was secured. Then she pulled, putting all her effort into prying the door free. It took multiple tries with her tired and bruised body straining against the force. When it popped open, it moved only a small distance, but it was enough.

"Come on, Rue, hurry!" Lana grunted.

"Lana. Is that you?"

"Of course. Hurry before we're found."

Looking over her shoulder towards the upstairs door, Lana prayed.

"I didn't think you'd come back. I thought they killed you."

As weak as he had to be, he ran into her, wrapping his arms around her waist with a surprising amount of strength. With hands shaking from fatigue, Lana held his matted head. When she pulled away, greasy tufts separated, sticking to her palm. The boy's tears stopped, but he still clung tight.

"I'm hungry," he said.

"I know, Rue. We'll get you something to eat as soon as we get out of here. Are you ready?"

"What if they're waiting for us?"

"Then you'll stay behind me, and if you get a chance to run, you take it. Understand?"

He nodded, but his hands remained clutched around her. Reaching behind her, she unwound his arms, noting the unhealthy feel of his skin. Pulling away from his outstretched arms, Lana stepped back out of his reach and squatted down to look at him. She wanted him to see that she was here, to see the concern in her eyes.

But instead of the green eyes she'd imagined — a mirror of her brother's — she came face to face with vacant pits. Two black voids that stared unfilled. Lana couldn't stop her gasp. She fell back and skittered like a crab until her back pressed into the rubble.

Lana raised her hand to her mouth, but pulled back after the clump of hair scratched her jaw. She gaped silently at the boy. His mouth was smeared with blood and chunks of fur. His cheek was split open, exposing small, rusty pearls - two uneven rows of teeth.

This time Lana couldn't control the retching that swelled in her throat. She scrambled up and inched away from the boy who was no longer a boy. His arms stretched towards her, seeking. Black fingers, thin and stained, wiggled, searching. Lana watched as his grotesque mouth puckered and trembled.

"What's wrong, Lana? What's the matter?"

Lana could feel her pulse pounding at her temple. Which was odd, since she was pretty sure her heart had sunk to the vicinity of her knees. *Oh, Rue. The poor child.*

He didn't even know he was dead. Though his eye sockets were raw and exposed, the meat beneath his expression shone clearly in the dim light. Confusion, hurt, pain, and fear. *The poor boy.* Tears tightened her throat as she fought them back.

"Nothing, it was just a rat."

A muscle in her jaw started to tick as her tongue swelled into the roof of her mouth. The background noise fell away, and her ears felt the pressure of her emotions. The boy was long dead, and still, he suffered. A solemn thought stole her breath. *What if I'm dead too? Stuck here and just pretending to be alive. Confused and eternally damned.*

"I'm here, Rue. Feel my hand?"

"Yes."

The flesh of his palm was waxy, beaded with sea salt and muck. She wouldn't leave him here to suffer alone.

The only thing she could do for him now was to help him find peace.

Lana swallowed past the bile in her throat, caused not by the wretched sight of the boy, but from the horrible thing she was about to do. Yet again, she would kill using her metis. Another mark against her soul, but this one she would bear proudly. This time there was no doubt holding her back. Still, it would be another nightmare in her head.

When Rue came to her, Lana opened her arms to accept him. Again, he wrapped his arms around her, nuzzling her belly. She searched within Rue for the dark thread that bound him to his un-life. Finding the foreign energy was easy. Releasing its control over his body was something else altogether.

It was different from last time. When your life is on the line in the heat of battle, making a connection is as easy as breathing. Now, when she had thin arms wrapped around her waist in trust, Lana faltered. A spark fizzled, then failed as soon as she reached for it.

Nothing. *Impossible!* Again, she couldn't access her metis in this infernal place. Its depravity smothered her.

"F-follow me, Rue. We're…we're getting out of here."

Maybe once they were out of the dungeon, she could give him peace. What would come after that was still a blur of uncertainty, but Lana owed him this kindness. He deserved better than this torment. The tears that she'd been fighting off spilled, but at least Rue would remain unaware. It was a small blessing.

Grabbing his hand, Lana led him up the stairs.

"My tummy hurts," Rue cried.

"Shh…" Lana reached back and rubbed his bony shoulder as she helped guide him. "I know, little one, I'll make you feel better. But first, we have to be quiet so we don't get caught," Lana whispered.

Guilt hit her doubly for her deception. Tears streamed down her cheeks, and she swallowed around the pain of containment. The only thing she knew to do was cradle his diminutive hand in hers.

They were nearly there. Lana could only hope that once she cleared these walls, her power would return. If not, then she might be just as damned as Rue. It wasn't something she wanted to dwell on. She knew what she risked when she left Ryker's protection.

Well, becoming an undead puppet hadn't been a consideration. Not what she expected, but she'd run into the lost forest knowing the rumors. It was her fault for thinking them only exaggerations, mere Einhart propaganda. She'd been wrong. Dead wrong.

What would she do if her metis still didn't work? Lana didn't have any other ideas. When they reached the stairs, Lana was met with another slack face. It was the puppet that had been guarding the hall. It didn't make a move to stop them, so Lana maneuvered Rue in front of her, shepherding him away. The puppet stalked behind them, his eyes staring at their backs. Lana felt the attention, and how Rue kept shifting and turning; he, too, felt its disturbing presence.

Lana wished, as she had many times before, that she knew what to do. What powers did these creatures possess? How could Rue speak and act like an average child, but the watchman behind them couldn't look her in the eyes? Fear and anxiety of the unknown assaulted her. Together they filled her head with all of the horrible possibilities she had yet to contemplate. She had to get out of here.

Up until now, her entire focus had been on freeing the boy. Rue had reminded her so much of her brother, Charlie. He'd left for the academy at about this age. He could have ended up looking like the boy cradled in her skirts, pocketed and filled with maggots. Oh, how she hated the power within her! All the twisted and vile ways it shaped Thrae.

Lana felt his presence before she saw him. Heavy, like sulfur on the roof of her mouth; power, or the vacuum of it, drew her focus. The knowledge came intuitively, perceived with an incorporeal sensory organ. Lana sank in its presence, falling deeper into the dark. Rue's hand squeezed hers, and now it was her turn to cling to him. It took a moment, but Lana found her focus once more.

Opening the eyes she'd closed in fear, Lana squinted at the corpse in front of her. Unlike last time, it didn't attack. There it stood an arm span away, a rotten flesh statue, staring her down with alert eyes. Lana pushed the boy behind her, stretching her hand out, keeping him away. But the puppet that watched them did nothing. Lana skirted around him and rushed Rue's stiff and sluggish body forward.

"It's okay. I think I saw a way out, just a little bit more."

Grabbing his hand, Lana led him down two halls.

The slow-moving puppet was trailing behind. Lana tried not to watch over her shoulder. There were still too many uncertainties ahead. The exit was to the east, out a side garden, long overgrown. At least, she thought it was an exit.

Two double doors shining with sunlight was one of the most welcoming sights she'd seen in months. The air outside the building was lighter than the heavy oppression that came from inside. Everything was brighter than her eyes could stand, but she refused to shield her gaze and return to the shadows. The smell of citrus filled the air, a clean breath of victory quickly spoiled by a pair of dead villagers.

Lana studied the face of the first woman, who was carrying piles of laundry and linen. Overtop the piles of clothes and cleaning powder, the woman had a familiar pointed jawline, with the same little cleft on her chin. Silently, Lana wondered if it was Rue's mother who had just passed them.

She, too, was dead. Unlike her son, there was no outward tell of her cause of death. The two passed each other silently, without a glimmer of recognition. Lana had imagined that the woman would lay eyes on the child and there would be a spark of recognition.

The pair continued their progress, unaware. Lana strayed behind, looking after them. She didn't have time to gawk; the puppet was still following them. At first, Lana thought the guard would try to round her up, but the puppet maintained a stone's throw distance, ever watchful and patient.

Crouching down in front of Rue, Lana tried once

more to access her metis. She wanted to shut him down and give him peace. Again, when she made the connection her own power evaporated. Lana was left clutching the young boy's shoulders. Fear turned to panic, and panic to rage.

It was time to consider the worst-case scenario. Lana was dead. She was as dead as the corpse child in front of her.

Did it happen when that man sent fire through her soul? Perhaps the giant killed her, or she'd died in the dungeon? Had she been dead this whole time? Was she now being controlled by the Deathless Master?

No. Lana fought against her despair, refusing to believe it. She was alive. Lana might look like death, but her bruises were healing, and that had to mean something. The problem was this place, not her metis. At least, that's what she prayed.

Lana told herself to push it away, focus on Rue. If she couldn't give him peace, what would she do? The last undead had been impervious to weapons. If she couldn't save herself, at least she would find a way to save him.

CHAPTER TWELVE

Ryker

"What news do you have?" Ryker demanded.

The young blonde raised her chin. "First, I need—"

"The only thing you need is to tell me what you know of Lana."

"I can only do that if I have your assurance—"

"And quickly. The people who disappoint me end up at The Peak."

"Please, Lord Wyvier. I do not mean to anger you. I want to help. And I will help… after I have your promise that you won't throw me in jail for the news I bring."

That doesn't bode well, Ryker thought. The young girl had grown up since the last time he'd seen her giggling with Lana. There was a hard tilt to her chin: determination.

"You have my word. Now start talking."

"Two days ago, I received a letter from Orla—"

"Let me see it."

Genie hesitated. "She ordered me to destroy it after reading."

Convenient.

"Why didn't she send it to me directly?"

"I, well, I think she wanted to ensure that her story had an unbiased narrator."

"She should have faced me herself."

"I think we both know why she couldn't do that. But she wants me to let you know how sorry she is about Lana. And that it wasn't an accident. Orla's party was ambushed."

"That's ridiculous. Orla wants me to believe that one of my people has betrayed me?"

"Not just anyone. Lord Wyvier. General Orla. She was given orders by her supreme commander to eliminate a potential cause of war. She was asked to sacrifice one for the many. Believe me, it was a decision she has come to regret greatly."

Not as much as she is going to. There was a subtle tremble in Ryker's chest. It felt like a snow flurry, but in his ears sounded like a war drum. The news was far worse than he had expected. The reach of this deception, the scope of its effects, sent his mind racing. *Show nothing,* instinct warned him.

"Were you involved in this plot, Genievet?"

"No! I promise. Lana became a worthy friend, and it happened organically. I wish that no harm has befallen her because of this."

"I think it's a bit too late for that."

Ryker turned away from the girl with heavy steps, but the large room was still too small. Was this why there was no news? Was he being silenced?

"Please. There's more," Genie said, tentatively.

Holy Unitas. Wasn't this enough? Did the Great Equalizer not find his burdens sufficient? Unitas, the Divine Collective, never doled out a trial one could not overcome, Ryker reminded himself.

"Our First Prime ordered Orla to leave Lana at the town of Carthy. There, her people were supposed to be waiting to transport her back to her country."

Translation: take her out of sight and kill her.

"But before they made it to Carthy, word had somehow gotten out about Lana and her bounty. They were ambushed, and Lana fled into the Lost Forest. Orla ordered a guard with her, for protection, but neither of them came back."

"What else?"

"After mercenaries killed some of Orla's party, General Orla went to Set. She wanted to give the news to the First Prime in person. Before she could schedule a meeting, she discovered First Prime Zuul in a meeting with Einhart lower nobles. Orla said that the Einhart nobles were giving orders to First Prime Zuul, that he was…" Genie struggled with her emotions. "Supplicant to them."

"That's ridiculous. Easily one of the most unbelievable stories I've heard. Tell Orla she's going to have to do better than that. You should leave now."

"I will, but there's more. Do you still want me to leave?"

"Finish."

"They spoke of a small band of Shining Knights cleaning up the border towns. You see, the rumors are true! And what's worse, our First Prime not only knows, but holds back his protection!"

"I want proof."

"So did she. Orla went to the village named Chortle. A small coastal settlement, not even big enough to be considered a town. There, she found the people who had survived the battle. The people swore it was the Shining Knights. They picked seemingly at random the people they wanted. They were fearless."

"Tarquins wouldn't surrender any of their people."

"No. We don't. General Orla found a small pile of shining armor, remnants of the slain."

"I want *proof*."

"How's this?" Behind Genie, slung over her shoulder, was a misshapen bag. What she pulled out of the bag eliminated all doubt and brought forth a wave of shame: a mirrored helmet and visor — a Shining Knights signature.

Genie handed the headgear to Ryker, and when he held it in his hands he was surprised at how light it was.

The edges were caked with dried blood. When he turned it over in his hands, something fell to the floor.

Genie was quick to kneel and pick it up. Her outstretched hand held a dried fireburst, the bushy, coastal counterpart to the climbing vine, firebell, common deeper inland.

It was proof. Explicit confirmation that Shining Knights had breached their border. Whether the First Prime was aware of it, he couldn't say for sure. But at this point, he wouldn't be surprised if it was all true.

Looking the young girl over, Ryker understood why Orla would order her to destroy the letter. This information was dangerous. If the First Prime was weak, if he allowed their people to be subjected to the Einhart elite army's brutality, things were much worse than his lover going missing. Something had gone terribly wrong.

Now the question remained: what was he going to do about it?

"Get word to Orla that she is to find how deep this goes."

Ryker herded her out into the rain. He felt a perverse degree of satisfaction at shutting the door in her face — her hopeful innocence melting under his cold dismissal. Orla might have a good reason for her betrayal, but she had still betrayed him.

She was smart not to come around, and that just made her more of a threat.

CHAPTER THIRTEEN

Terra

The night brought a terrible storm. Most of the rain and hail pelted the outside of the mountain, but occasionally a few small pellets of ice tumbled nearby. Terra wrapped the blanket around herself tightly, shifting it once more. She had tried sleeping next to the fire pit, but the ledge was too narrow, and there was nothing inside the pit to stop her fall. Besides, her nerves wouldn't let her relax.

So here she was, resting with her back to the fire. She figured it would be warmer next to the fire than anywhere else, but even Crusher and his friend, Sentillies, had ventured into the depths of the dark room. Standing up, she stomped some feeling back into her feet and exhaled on her hands, reaching to bring them towards the flames.

If only I weren't so exhausted, I could nap on the edge. Again, she leaned forward and peered into the deep well. If she fell, she would freefall thousands of spans without anything to grab hold of. *Maybe not.*

Terra took to pacing around the fire to keep herself warm. She was restless, but lacked the energy to pick up her speed. From one lap to the next, the wyld man, Allister, stood before her, blocking her path. Lightning flashed behind him, casting a shadow on his face, but she could still see the irritation in his brow.

"It's time to come in now."

Who the hell does he think he is? "I'm good."

"You can lie to yourself, but you can't lie to me."

That's going to get obnoxious fast.

"Is that the only thing you know how to say?" Terra snapped.

Again, he said nothing. *Infuriating man! Well, I'm not going to let some guy tell me what to do.*

"Just return to your cave, or I'll make you."

His brow lifted, unimpressed by her threat. "I'm not accustomed to having to repeat myself. It's time to come in now."

"Neat story. Goodbye."

Thunder shook the walls and rattled her heart in her chest. Terra spun quickly with a glimmer of light-headedness and restarted her trek counterclockwise around the ring. Allister stayed where he was, watching her while she stubbornly ignored him. Soon she would come upon him again.

Do I go around him? I could stop and turn around and do a half circle. No, that would make me look foolish. I'm not scared of him. What can he do?

It was the truth; she didn't fear him. The wyld spirit was too strong in both of them. When it came down to it, wyldons protected each other. Nature or instinct would urge them to get close and work together — that was half the problem.

There was something inside of her that wanted the companionship — maybe even needed it. That scared her worse than anything he could do. That needy part of Terra wanted him to grab her. There was something in the silent set of his jaw, the promise in his eyes.

What kind of reputation would I get from that? Nothing good. Besides, what if word got back to my dad? Gross. Terra watched him. She slowed as she neared until she stood in front of him. He was so damn tall it boiled her blood having to look up at him. Now that she thought of it, almost everything about him was infuriating.

"There are vents for warmth, and I'll keep you safe. Don't think twice about what that old fool told you," he said slowly, obviously trying and failing to keep the irritation out of his voice.

"Yeah? What's the cost? Because I'm not going to share my food or anything else with you. I'm good."

"I don't need anything from you, Terra."

"Do I know you, Allister?"

"No, but if you keep using that tone, you will."

Like a magnet, Terra's eyes shot back to his. A dark promise glimmered, a preview of things to come if she didn't follow him into the cave.

"What the hell does that mean?"

"What is your aversion to being warm?" Allister asked instead.

"What's your aversion to listening? I told you, I'm good." Terra tilted her head to the side, raising her voice. Still, the noise of the downpour outside drowned her out.

There was something almost invigorating about walking away from him. The energy of the storm reflected the turmoil inside of her. Terra waited with bated breath each time she circled near for him to grab her. His eyes told her he wanted to, the same way she did, but he restrained himself. His control was probably the sexiest thing she'd seen in a long time. *And I want to see how far I can push it. What's wrong with me?*

"Go away," she said in her snarkiest tone.

She shoved at him, digging in to gain purchase. Nothing. Another flash of lightning lit the chamber, and an eruption of thunder followed.

"Get inside." His voice was as deep and foreboding as the gale. The discharge of electricity, or maybe something else, sizzled across her skin. Everything inside of her clenched, and her already uncomfortably hard nipples stiffened. Though her heart was racing, she still tilted her chin in defiance.

"What don't you understand? You're the kind of controlling asshole I left my pack to get away from," she huffed.

"Careful, you're injured. Getting winded up here is easy, especially when you're all worked up."

Maybe that's what's got me so breathless. It's not him, it's the thin air. "I'm fine. I don't feel any different." Terra rested a hand on the fire pit ledge, breathing deeply through her nose.

"It's how they keep us under control."

"I said I'm fine."

But she wasn't. *Where's the whistle?* Terra immediately wanted to slap around frantically, searching for the tiny instrument in the near pitch-black night.

Another bout of lightning flared, and she searched the ground desperately. Allister was a long-forgotten threat, one that she could only face knowing she had the whistle as backup. *Would Lord Wyvier even hear the whistle in this storm? Oh fuck, no, probably not. I'm on my own. I'm really on my own. What was I thinking?*

"Calm down."

"Fuck you. I don't—" Terra gasped. *Need any help from you,* she finished silently. The air was a little too thin for her to catch her breath.

"Yes, I know." He knelt in front of her.

"You don't know me. I'm—"

"Yes, you're a dangerous she-wolf. But that doesn't mean you don't need someone at your back now and then."

"I don't trust you." She glared with gritted teeth. Terra clenched her jaw so tight that pain shot up the back of her skull, making her head spin even more. Anything to hide her panic.

"You don't have to trust me completely, or forever. Just trust me tonight."

Terra meant to shake her head, but her vision blurred into a panoramic streak of white and black. *Damn it, no. I must stay alert.*

"No harm will come to you while we're here."

"Your oath?"

"Yes, you have my oath to bind. No harm will come to you. Not from me, not from anyone."

From outside the cave, an unfortunately familiar face grinned. "If you don't want him, you can always share a bed with me." The condescending chortle of Sentillies immediately set her nerves on end. Cringing, Terra pulled back, glaring at the intruding man.

Allister must have had the same thing in mind, because when he turned he turned quick and with his fists ready. Terra didn't know if it was the thin air, but she'd never seen a man move so fast he blurred. The space between him and Sentillies was cut short in seconds.

Allister didn't say a word. The only communication shared between the men was of a more primitive language — fists. Grunts and the thud of heavy fists pounding into flesh drew a crowd.

From inside the cave, Crusher's massive form stepped closer. His form towered over the rest, and Terra started to get nervous. *Could Allister handle both men?*

Should I step in? That thought was immediately shot down. *No, I want to see what he can do.* There was something thrilling about seeing two men fight. Especially when it was about her. Not that it mattered who won; she wouldn't be Sentillies' prize.

The fight was over too soon. Allister stood before her, bloodied and breathing heavily. His body glistened with sweat and rain, the flashing lightning illuminating the red welts across his form. He held his hand out to her, a silent rage of the wyld he had inside still stamped in his eyes.

Slowly, Terra took his hand. The discipline in him invigorated her senses more than any storm could. He jerked her forward into his body, and this time she didn't resist. When he lifted her into his arms Terra felt his strength and restraint tighten his muscles, and she nearly purred.

She waited for her instincts to pull her back to her senses, but they never did. The freezing wind whipped through her hair, but their closeness warmed her body. Allister leaned down and didn't hesitate to claim her lips.

The kiss was hard and fast. It was just as brutal as she expected; possessive and free in a way she'd learned only wyldons could understand. When they stepped into the cavern another layer of humid heat settled on top of her exposed skin.

So, he hadn't been lying about the vents. There's that, at least.

He laid her down on a stone slab covered in folded blankets. The layers dipped in the center, still warm from the heat of his body. Allister sat next to her on the edge of his bed.

Terra felt him move, but he didn't lie down. Instead, she imagined him scrubbing his jaw, working the residual tension and aggression from his body. She wondered if he was irritated at her. Would he blame her for the fight?

In a moment of weakness Terra reached out, grabbing his shoulder and tugging. Two quick pulls, just enough to clue him in to what she wanted. He had promised her she would be safe with him tonight, from Sentillies and himself.

Where she came from, your oath was your life. And tonight, with another of her kind so close, she didn't want to lose the opportunity for something she'd missed for so long — skin to skin contact.

Terra had already spiraled into self-doubt in the time it took for him to move. *Is he angry at me?* It only took him a few seconds, but Allister laid prone next to her. At first, his hand settled lightly on her hip, sending tingles of awareness like a trail as he went.

Terra shifted in a subtle flex she hoped he felt. She loved knowing his promise forced his control, and tempting him made it all the sweeter. How utterly delectable it felt to have a man grasping for control.

He pulled her into his body, his significantly larger form curled around hers like a wall of heat. It might be the thin air, but she felt protected; it felt right. And for the first time since she had ventured out alone, Terra slept deeply.

CHAPTER FOURTEEN

Terra

The sunlight barely lit the cave. Only the faint rosy glow of sunset bounced off the smooth stone walls of the inner chamber. Terra had a vague awareness of movement deeper in the central room. She and Allister shared a smaller chamber; nothing fancy, just a hole and a bundle of blankets to lay on. It was nothing like the last cave she stayed in, but it gave them a small amount of privacy. Outside, the sounds of some of the others settling in for bed barely registered.

Smiling, Terra stretched, pushing her hips back into the warm body behind her. A heavy hand dropped on to her waist. Allister's palm moved against the flare of her hip, his thumb grazing back and forth under the hem of her tunic.

She knew she should pull away; there were too many people who could get the wrong idea. But he felt good at her back. Besides, this was her last night, what was the harm. *I could think of it like a wild weekend, a quick vacation on a prison mountain.*

Heat radiated off of him. The muscles that lined his body were rigid, yet yielding. The hand that lazily stroked her skin or the heavy arm resting on her side didn't feel suffocating or claustrophobic. *Yeah, I could let him touch me all day and call it a vacation.*

As Terra turned into him, he pulled his hand away from her hip. Once she settled, it was the first thing she reached for. She wanted him and his heat back. Terra rolled her body, weaving her leg in between his. She smiled sweetly up at him as her hand snaked around his body, grabbing his muscular ass and pulling him in. *See how you like it.*

With the pressure between them increasing, she felt his pleasure pressing into her stomach. Again, she looked up at him, watching the fluctuating control flit across his face. The hand on her hip grabbed her bottom and squeezed, flexing like he was savoring how she filled his large palm.

Burying her face in his chest, Terra hid her smile. His hand tapped under her chin, but when she didn't take his lead and lift her head, the hand wrapped around her neck and forced her to. Swallowing hard around the firm grip, Terra watched him with wide, excited eyes.

"You're starting something we can't finish." His voice was raspy and deep, but his eyes were focused and intense. It was a combination that sent shivers up and down her spine.

"You're right," Terra agreed with a sigh. "I'll behave."

His only response was a groan, his grip stopping her abruptly when she started to scoot forward.

"Not yet."

A thumb slipped under her waistband, grazing over-sensitive skin. Terra's heart pounded. She warmed at every place he touched. Her skin pulled as if reaching for his touch. Slowly, as if he were teasing them both, the hand on her throat lifted to her chin, bringing their lips close enough to graze.

Excitement coursed through her and she rolled her shoulders, practically throwing her breast into his hand. He eagerly accepted the gift, rubbing and rolling the plump mound with one hand while the other swept back and forth, so close to where she couldn't allow it. She should push his hands away, but she had to fight the urge not to wiggle and thrust towards him.

Deep, even breaths didn't do a damn thing but bring in more of his delicious scent. It claimed her from the inside out.

"Allister."

"Don't make a sound, or the others will hear," he whispered into her ear.

A shiver tightened her scalp and tingled its way down her spine. He hadn't moved since he spoke, but it took Terra a moment to realize it. He was waiting for a response from her. Terra's hips jerked, and she closed her eyes, trying to calm down.

Eventually, Terra opened her eyes and nodded. His hand squeezed tightly at her breast, then pulled away. A small mutter of protest escaped her, and he glared down at her.

Bowing her head, Terra buried her face in the crook of his neck, masking any more noise she may make. One hand slid inside her trousers, pressing into her mound and sliding lower, while the other fisted her hair. He held her in place, her face buried into the hot skin of his neck.

Instinct or desire demanded she taste his skin. Terra kissed and licked up to his ear, where she turned to needy bites. Her hand followed his example, tracing down his tight stomach, slowly savoring him. When her hand cupped him he flexed under her touch, and she knew he was just as affected by her as she was by him.

Together they stroked each other with only quiet, heavy breaths to hint at what was happening. Terra's grip tightened on him as she neared the ecstasy of his touch. When she came, she pulled back, and his mouth covered hers. He tasted like blood. As soon as his tongue teased hers, she unraveled again.

Before she calmed, his hand wrapped around her wrist, pulling her touch away.

"When I come for you, I'll be inside you. I haven't

decided where that might be yet, but I know it won't be here." He whispered his dark promise into her ear, finishing with a hard bite on her earlobe before sitting up.

Euphoria filled her, and she flipped on her back to sigh in relief. Terra brought her arm over her head and laughed, shaking her head as she watched him walk away.

CHAPTER FIFTEEN

Terra

It was their second night together; their last day. Things had been as close to peaceful as one could expect in jail. No one had bothered her since Allister left Sentillies a broken heap in the storm. There was a part of her — the foolish, irrational part — that didn't want to leave. *I could lay like this forever.*

Allister's body pressed hard against hers. The hands that held her hips squeezed a shade harder than pleasure, but not quite pain. It was like he held himself back by holding her down. Terra wanted him to melt against her. The only way for her to feel the calm in the middle of this storm of sentiment was for there to be no space between them.

There had to be a moment in the dark chamber where the others knew; the sounds they were making were far from discreet. Yet, Terra didn't care. There was something thrilling about having others around. Allister would hold her, stroke her, and make others scream in pain if they dared get too close. It was the wyld way.

The primal part of her wanted them to try. She wanted them to hurt. She wanted to see Allister bruised and bloodied for her again. Power — that's what this moment felt like. It tasted like buttered berries warmed by the sun. In his arms, her body sang.

They didn't have long. This was the end of Terra's last night, and after seeing how thoroughly he throttled Sentillies, she wanted to give him something. He promised protection, accepting her when she gave nothing in return. Now it was time for Terra to pay him back.

Terra wiggled, sliding down his chest underneath the long line of his tense body, dragging her nose and lips along his bare skin. His muscles contracted, his fingers snaking through her hair. For a moment, Terra thought he would stop her. Instead he pushed, rolling his hips, his rigid member bobbing between them.

Terra's grin was for herself alone as she wrapped her arms around his hips and thanked him. Just as her tongue made its first swirl, the grinding sound of the lift chugged in the distance.

"It's Lord Wyvier, and he's come alone," an unknown hunter called out.

Pulling back, Terra grabbed Allister on either side of his muscular hips and pushed. *That's my cue.* Slipping her legs over the bed, Terra shook out her hair and shrugged at him over her shoulder. In the time it took her to give him a half-assed grin, his anger had doubled.

Too bad you can't do anything about it until you get dressed. Terra stepped to the entrance of the sleeping chamber. From a distance she watched as some men formed groups, while others took to the shadows.

A jolt shot through her. When she first arrived, tactics like this had frozen her insides. Now she felt foolish. They took to the shadows not to cause fear, but to escape it.

"Why do you look so smug? Do you really think you can tease me like that and get away with it?" Allister tilted his head, leaning against the wall next to her.

"In fact, I do."

"When we get out of here and I've got you all to myself, I'm going to spend days teasing you the same way you tortured me."

When his hot, naked body settled behind her, Terra shivered. *Why did I think he'd shy away from being naked in public?* The answer was easy: she'd been spending too much time around outsiders.

His arm wrapped around her stomach, his thumb sliding underneath her pants, grazing the delicate skin of her lower belly. The touch was soft, but without hesitation. Allister gripped her as if he already possessed her body.

The same touch had thrilled her in his bed, covered by his body and shielded by blankets. Now out in the open, it just pissed her off. Jerking her elbow back without restraint, she struck true. His arm pulled back, tucking under his ribcage as he bent over.

"She-wolf," he coughed.

"Not in public. You never should have forgotten. Now put some clothes on, the Winter Lord is coming." Without looking away from the impenetrable door, Terra stepped closer. The lift groaned until it came to a clanking stop. The rest of the men stayed back, but she knew something they didn't. She was about to be free.

Terra sighed, flicking her eyes back to the dark chamber that held so much frustration and promise. She would leave this place and continue her hunt. While everyone was locked up here, she would have the lead.

So, Terra decided then, she would have no regrets. She wouldn't waste time looking backwards. Sitting next to old man Haggerdy, Terra grinned at him.

"I wonder if he's letting us go?"

"Us? No. Me? Yeah, I'm out of here," Terra said.

But as the Winter Lord stepped forward, her eyes locked with Allister. His eyes were a kaleidoscope of emotions — rage, betrayal, lust, and the promise of something more, something she didn't have a name for. She knew this wouldn't be the last time she saw Allister, and when they did meet again there would be hell to pay.

Lord Wyvier cleared his throat, bringing her attention back to him, where it needed to be. Terra walked towards him, undaunted. It was time to finally face her future. Her destiny awaited; she just knew it.

CHAPTER SIXTEEN

Ryker

3742.07.18

Guilt hung over Ryker's heart. *I shouldn't have left that girl at The Peak. What if they hurt her?* He stood between the lift and stairs that led to the jailhouse. Ryker chose the lift.

It groaned up the thirty flights, chugging along on its choppy journey up the mountain. The jailhouse and courtroom stood at the highest peak on the edge of the city. It stood as a brutal reminder of the danger in tempting Tarquin authority.

The mechanical rise, barely used and rarely maintained by Preosian mechanics, took ten minutes to grind its way to the top. Steps no bigger than a lady's hand were all that marked the path. Ryker figured it reckless to maneuver them this early in the season. Those stairs, used to intimidate criminals about to stand trial, were too slick for the strength of the wind today. But after the fourth lurch and screeching start, Ryker regretted his decision.

Regret kept company with desperate determination. Lord Ryker Wyvier of Wynthros had made a mistake; or, at least, rushed to judgment regarding the female prisoner. It may have taken him a couple of days to think it over, but he was here to make it right.

Aside from making a mess and trying to trap him, the girl had done nothing wrong. Each man in this prison was dangerous; they posed a threat not only to Lana, but to his people. But this girl was no threat to anyone.

When the lift finally stopped, Ryker secured the lift box to the deck railing. It was a structure sound enough to hold four men comfortably, and was the one security measure the jailhouse had against a breach. To make sure he could get down the way he came, he pulled the chain, testing the hold.

The courtroom was directly attached to the deck. The judiciaries mainly used it for sentencing to keep themselves separated from a prisoner's influence. Its indestructible columns were carved in long lines, creating a scalloped edge in the foundation blocks.

An ancient race, long ago, wrote words of justice, freedom, community, unity, and peace along the base of the pillars. When Ryker had first been expelled to this city, he'd had them rubbed so he could translate the old tongue. The words were powerful, but they were only words.

This place was what the criminals feared — towering above everyone, cold and hungry, exposed to the elements and time. There were no cages; nothing that inhibited movement. But without a doubt, they were trapped. Isolated on top of the tallest mountain, high above the city, with only the clouds to entertain them. Though he supposed there were enough people packed into the cave that entertainment wouldn't be an issue. Another pang of worry shot through him.

The bounty hunters would be looking for a way out, and they were welcome to try to escape anytime. The only way to do so safely was to use the lift or to secure the bridge, which, like the lift, could only be lowered on the opposite side.

He'd noticed that a small group had banded together and were watching for any newcomers. Like they had when Ryker had brought the girl, the others had crowded around the bridge, waiting for it to be drawn. Ryker had two men stationed at the bridge after that day. Those he'd imprisoned were waiting for an opportunity, and growing more impatient each day.

The hollow courtroom was cold and sparse. It was a place that hadn't been used since almost two months before the surge of bounty hunters. Now the jailhouse was practically full, and the judiciaries were crying foul.

Soon, if he weren't careful, it would be him climbing these steps.

Let them all choke on their whispered words. Ryker knew better than most what awaited his people should he slack in his duties. That was why he was finding it so hard to leave.

Lana was running out of time; he could feel it. In each brief flash of awareness that bridged the distance between them, he felt a darkness closing in and her desperation rising. And what was worse, even though she reached for him, Lana was also the one to shut him out. Whatever was happening to her, wherever she was, she was trying to shield him. *How ridiculous.*

Ryker unlocked the door and threw it open. Most of the inmates were outside, lingering in the sun. They sat on the half-rails, sprawled on the stone slabs theorized to have once been a sacrificial altar, and leaned against the pillars. When Ryker stepped inside, only the young woman and a town regular sat in the inner chambers.

The two of them sat huddled around the center fire, heads together. When the rusty hinges squawking in protest didn't grab their attention, Ryker cleared his throat. The girl stood and stepped forward. She had obviously had a hard time up here and was ready to leave.

"No more hard-working bounty hunters to falsely accuse and wrongly imprison?" The older man's crooked smile beamed up at him condescendingly. If he were a lesser man he'd find the bum's stare galling.

"Mr. Haggerdy, you're not a bounty hunter, you're a beggar. And you were caught stealing."

"Lies."

"I found you running down an alley with nothing but widow Miribet's wedding tapestry wrapped around you."

"I told you, I had to borrow that... for personal reasons."

"Look here, girl," Ryker ordered, ignoring the town crackpot.

Slowly, she did as he asked, her chin tucked while her eyes scanned him over.

"I'll ask you again. What is your name?"

"My name is Terra Hallowbit of the Wrenshaw pack. But you already knew that, didn't you?"

Of course. Ryker had received her complete history, short and uninspired as it was, earlier today. He knew of her people and their terrible choice of allies. Even that unfortunate bit with her elder brother.

"But you're not sanctioned by the Wrenshaw pack, are you?"

"No, but technically I don't need to be sanctioned to attempt a bounty."

"This isn't Einhart. Private citizens can't bring in bounties."

"Which is why you're unable to charge me as a bounty hunter, right?"

"Technically you're correct, but as I'm the highest ranking official for almost eight hundred thousand spans, I don't know who could stop me," he said blankly. "You will leave my land and abandon your bounty on Lady Lana Colton," Ryker demanded, letting the command be felt.

"And why would I do that?"

"Because I'm hiring you for another job. If you agree, I'll release you," he said. "Do we have a deal?"

The girl's eyes trailed back to the group hanging outside in the small strip that led to the drawbridge. The men sat, stood, or leaned together, intent on their conversation. *That doesn't bode well.*

"We have a deal." Terra stuck out her hand, and he accepted it in a tight single shake.

"I'll make a deal with you too!" Haggerdy smiled with bright, hopeful eyes.

Ryker turned to the dirty old man. Haggerdy was a drunk and a layabout. He had no family and no place to go, yet he still sulked around the city taking handouts — and if Ryker's suspicions were true, swindling old widows.

"You have nothing I want. Maybe next time you run through an alley drunk, you'll make sure you have your clothes on," Ryker said with finality. Before he closed the door he watched as Terra shot a quick, almost contrite look into the den. *She shouldn't feel bad about leaving Haggerdy, the man's a good-for-nothing fool.* With a frown, Ryker set the lock, ready to put this place behind him for good.

CHAPTER SEVENTEEN

Ryker

Terra followed him into the courtroom where her few belongings were laid out on an ornate table. Ryker didn't watch her rummage through her supplies, checking to see if anything was tampered with. Instead, he secured, locked, and checked the second door to the ancient barbican jail.

All of her things had been looked through. Aside from an absurd collection of Lana's bounty sheets, he'd found nothing overtly suspicious. Ryker had searched through everything personally to find out who she was. Nothing had been misplaced or broken, but he gave her time to check it over anyway.

Ryker tossed a small bag of coins on the table next to her things.

"What's this?"

"That's a down payment; another condition of your release. You work for me now, exclusively. You will search for Lady Lana's brother, Charles Colton, and you will inform me when you find anything. Should you prove useful, you'll receive a second payment and something worth even more — I'll name you myself," Ryker vowed. "Here, take this." Lord Wyvier slapped the packet against her chest in a careless flick.

"What is it?" Terra asked, her eyes glaring over at him, suspicious.

"It's a file on Lady Lana. It has her and her family's known allies, past and present, throughout Einhart and Preos."

"For an outcast and an exile, she has a lot of contacts."

"She's a woman of many worlds." His face pinched for a brief moment, and his eyes were lost in a memory. But just as quickly as it started, Lord Wyvier was back and giving orders. "There's a map that I've marked to show her route and where she was headed. Any destination with a mark has a person of interest in the area. You can refer back to the list."

"I see that you've coded your notes."

"I'm thorough." Ryker glared, crossing his arms in

front of his thick chest. "I've also had an artist make an accurate sketch of her."

It was a stark contrast to the sharp and severe image the Shining Knights provided in their bounties. Instead of the pointed nose, cold, pinched eyes, and the bitter press of her lips, this picture had been sketched with tenderness. Lady Lana's features were soft, gently swooping, elegant. Her eyes were lit with curiosity, and her mouth discreetly pulled with good humor.

"She has a kind face." Terra traced the edge of the paper. "Do you create such a complete dossier on all of your women?"

"Just the ones who run," Ryker quipped.

"I don't see how this is going to help me find Charles."

"He was sent off quite young. Not much is known about him. I'm hoping Lana's known contacts could be useful in uncovering him. He's likely changed his identity; hopefully a Preosian contact will be more useful."

"Is there anything else?"

"Yes, here is a token of my service. Use it only in an emergency, and only in the lower half of Taraq. No one is to know you're working for me, so keep that closely guarded. Do you understand?"

"I understand. This will be plenty to get me started." Terra nodded and stepped back.

"If you come across any word of Lana, send a falcon immediately. My address is in the file. Do not approach her. Just follow her and keep me apprised."

He knew the Einhart crown was offering nearly double his amount. What he offered was a nice down payment for a lineup of steady income. Ryker only hoped it was enough.

"All right, I'll do it."

"How do you plan to start?" Ryker asked as he unchained the lift and started their journey back down the side of the mountain.

"I'll start at the last place she's been seen and follow the trail. With all this information I can begin right away," Terra offered.

The young woman kept her eyes squarely on the folder. Ryker realized the shiny hesitation in her eyes was fear. She clutched her belongings with one hand, while the other wrapped around the railing. Her voice was tight, and she had rolled into herself, eyes closed. Ryker felt the urge to rattle the lift a little just to watch her shit her pants, but he didn't have that much faith in the Preosian contraption.

When the lift hit the bottom, and Terra had her feet on soil, she took her first breath without restraint. It was a complete breath that revitalized her fully. Her color was quickly starting to return.

"How did you gauge the competition?" Ryker asked.

"They were looking for a quick hunt and are growing angry with being held. It's only a matter of time before they escape."

"Escape is impossible. The Peak doesn't release her guests except in death."

"Don't underestimate them, they grow more determined by the day."

"Focus yourself on finding my—" Ryker paused. "Focus on finding Charles."

"Don't worry, Lord Wyvier. I'll keep an eye out for her, too," Terra promised. "You know, there's a Formless group of Travellers, the Viridate tribe, I think that they have an association with your woman. They have a connection to the spirit world that I can't even begin to explain. They might be able to help you find her."

"I don't need help from a bunch of thieving vagabonds. Just do the job."

While everyone else was focused on finding Lana, Terra would be finding what Lana had left him for — her brother. Hopefully, Terra would be able to cut Lana off, maybe find her by finding Charlie.

The others had nothing to prove. Undoubtedly, these bounty hunters had more experience and a higher trophy count. They thought Lana would be a steal — low effort, high reward. Then they stumbled into his trap. But not this one, no, she'd made him come to her.

Shaking his head, Ryker rolled his tight shoulders. As green as she was, he saw a hunger in Terra's eyes. Terra Hallowbit of the Wrenshaw pack had been vicious enough to survive The Peak, but only time would tell if she had what it took to succeed.

CHAPTER EIGHTEEN

Lana

This was torture. Lana could feel the stress sucking away her strength and determination, but she wouldn't quit. Not when they had finally made it.

"Are we out yet?" Rue asked.

Lana felt him turn to the left and look over his shoulder. She couldn't bring herself to look at him in the sunlight. She was a coward. The fear of seeing his decay soured her already twisted stomach.

"Yes, we're in a garden courtyard."

"Why can't I see?"

Because you're dead, and the rats have eaten away at your eyes.

"You just need to give yourself time to adjust," Lana soothed.

"We're close to my house. Do you see a small dirt lane towards the bay?" Rue pulled at her hand, dragging her in his excitement.

Everything was so overgrown it was impossible to differentiate any path other than what was most likely an animal trail. Looking back towards the entrance, Lana figured that there would have been a path between the broken water fountain and what remained of three large statues. Though the sculptures were smashed into anonymity, they were undoubtedly meant to be the garden's focal point.

Rue didn't give her time to answer. Instead, he led her through the weeds. It took a few minutes, but Lana finally saw the town.

Some of the buildings were toppled entirely, while others were punched by the same cannons that had laid the castle low. The rocky terrain was reclaimed by nature, making the path all the more dangerous. Vines and tall grass — plus a phalangeal moss network — spread on the northern edge, making the rocks, boulders, and any remnants of the town's buildings slippery.

Rue pulled Lana along with such confidence that Lana doubted his blindness. If she hadn't seen the fleshy inside of his eye sockets herself, she would have thought it was a theater mask. The way he climbed, scrambled, and pulled himself up, then reached a hand back to help her, expanded her heart. He would have grown up to be a fine man. Again, the tears swelled. With a determined sniff, she pushed them down.

"Rue? Are you able to see now?"

"Not really, not yet. I think the dungeon must have done something to my eyes."

"How do you know where you're taking me?"

"I just do. Maybe because I know this place, so I don't need to see as much. Come on, we're getting close!"

Rue doggedly dragged her to one of the few buildings left intact. It was the only home still standing in its block. It was a slim, single story with a peaked roof. It had stable but worn outer walls — a single stalk in a harvested field. The building to its left was cut in half; its guts laid bare. To the right, there was only a single pillar surrounded by rubble and covered by vines. This town had surrendered everything for its master. What was left fell to time.

Lana's survey of the town brought her attention back to the ever-persistent hound. Still, it followed. The puppet's stiff and uncoordinated steps were set at a steady, determined pace. His apathetic stare always fixed in their direction.

Rue marched forward, unaware of the demon nipping at their heels. His youthful enthusiasm so prominent that Lana could almost imagine him running between the rows of knee-high border shrub, laughter lighting the air.

He walked into the building without hesitation, oblivious to the door that wheezed like an old man sitting in a low chair. The home's sandy walls were crumbling, revealing the metal reinforcing the structure. It was a raw wound exposing the bone underneath.

The image of Rue alive and well was imprinted in the tan landscape as he hopped inside. When Lana followed his halting progress, she half expected the home to have a hearth fire crackling.

"This is it. Isn't it beautiful?"

There were many ways to describe the interior — beautiful wouldn't have been at the top of her list. Furniture was thrown about the small flat. A thick layer of dust coated everything, even the cobwebs. Shelves had been ripped from the walls, and it looked like the planks had long been busted from underneath the home. The only thing left untouched was a small bed, tucked into the corner, a deteriorated quilt laid limp but folded with an intentional and loving hand.

Perhaps bandits or grazers had come through, looting what remained. Standing in the middle of the room, Rue stretched his arms wide, glad to be home. Lana eyed the small bed, the sick feeling in her stomach doubling. *This would do.*

"My mom should be home shortly. When she is, she'll make us something to eat. She's the best. She'll be so happy I'm home," Rue said.

"Yes, I'm sure she will. You'll have to apologize for

scaring her like that." Guilt hit her hard in the throat, causing a tremble in her voice.

"I will."

"It's been a really long day. How about while we wait for her, we take a little nap. Doesn't that sound good?" Tears pooled in her eyes again, but this time she didn't try to swallow them down.

"But I'm not tired."

"I am. Will you lay with me?"

"All right, I suppose. But just until you fall asleep."

"Deal."

Lana wasn't sure the bed would hold, but like the rest of the building, it had been built to last. Rue crawled into his bed, cradled on her lap, and Lana stroked his molting hair, discreetly wiping clumps of brain matter away. She didn't know when she started rocking, but by the time she realized he'd already curled tighter into her.

"Tell me about all your favorite things," Lana asked.

"Well, my most favorite thing is exploring. I love sneaking into the castle and looking at all the cool old relics. My mom says I'm not supposed to take anything, or Lord Dimitri will get angry and punish us. So, I just go in and explore."

That must have been how he wound up in the dungeon. He fell through and was trapped in that cage. All alone, until Lana.

"But I liked helping my pa. He built this house for me and ma. He built it with his own two hands. He let me help make the shelves and build a ladder to my fort. Wanna see my fort?" Rue smiled, already starting to get up.

"Later, Rue." Lana pushed gently on his shoulders. "Show me later. Just keep talking."

Lana stroked his falling hair and rocked with her eyes closed. They had been followed and it was only a matter of time before she was found, but she couldn't rush this. He had started listing all his favorite foods when Lana found the spark of life inside him once more. This time, instead of trying to ignite or smother it, she studied the thread.

When she reached for it, something different happened. Like a fraying cord, it opened up. It was light and hot; it burned her eyes even though they were closed. The intensity scorched a path through her, but she did not flinch. Even when she felt another presence nearby. *Stay calm. You can't mess this up.*

Lana reached for the tiny sun inside of Rue, acting on instinct alone. It quivered in her control, then melted. Instead of fighting the deathless for control, Lana relinquished the struggle; she opened herself and let her own spirit follow the thread. Like water on a red hot skillet, the power inside Rue dissolved.

Energy rushed through her, and she held the boy as the light dimmed inside of him, words of love and longing still on his lips. A seizing quake ran through her, and this time she welcomed the tears, Rue's lifeless corpse held tight in her rocking embrace. She wasn't ready to let go.

Lana didn't know how long she stayed there. Even with the threat of capture ever-present in the back of her head, she held fast. With gentle reverence, Lana carefully lifted Rue's calcified body from her lap. Laying him back down in his bed, she wrapped him in the quilt his mother had no doubt painstakingly stitched together. All she had left to give him was the comfort of a makeshift death shroud.

Well, there was one more thing. Looking around for anything she could use to set the place on fire, Lana came face to face with disturbingly familiar blue eyes. The puppet master that had tried to drain her dry now stood in the doorway with another vigilant guard.

If the choice was between dying in a blaze or being a puppet, Lana knew her preference. Even as she heard the tired door open, Lana frantically searched for anything she could use to burn this home down. She refused to look over to the now filled bed. Lana tossed every dry piece of wood she could find into the center of the building.

Looking the youthful man in the eye, Lana held out a hand, a pitiful barricade as she tried to focus on igniting the tinder. *I can do this*. It wouldn't take much. The wood was ready to end her existence along with the rest of this forsaken town.

But when she reached for her power, though she felt revitalized, nothing came. Not even a spark. Shaking her head, Lana tried again, trying to keep the desperation away. The deathless one stepped inside, watching her quietly. Lana pushed her hand forward, a silent attempt to hold him back, and air shot out of her hand.

The force wasn't enough to push him back, but he did stop.

"What do you want?" Lana demanded.

"You surprise me, again. What is your name?" He

tilted his head to the side, the red lines circling his neck stretched taut, and he winced before straightening himself.

"What do you want?" Lana remained firm.

"How do you feel?"

"Why do you care?" Lana refused his questions. She was just trying to stall him, to buy herself some time to find the fire inside of her. Now that he was in the building, maybe she could take him down with her.

"Why do you?" he parried.

He wasn't the same man as before. This time he held lucidity in tight control. It didn't matter. He controlled the dead; what use did he have to keep her alive? Lana was going to have to end this.

There was only a brief pause at the thought of Ryker. She could almost imagine connecting with him, enough that he could read her dizzying emotions, and she felt the warmth of his flashing silver eyes. It was enough to steady her.

He would be able to do it. For his life and the lives of all the others, Ryker would have the strength to end it. And so would she.

"Why did you do that? Why did you show the child such kindness?" The man pulled Lana back in to the conversation.

"What a silly thing to ask. A better question would be why anyone would raise a child to begin with."

Accusation salted her tongue. She wished she had better control; there would be nothing more satisfying than hurling a fireball at his pristine face. Lana would watch as it melted and fell away, along with the rest of this tired home.

"It was an accident. My loose power draws many. It was never my intent to force him awake. That's why he was different from the rest; he didn't have my soul brand. I had no control of him, so he could control himself. I would never intentionally make a child suffer. I'm not the monster you assume."

"I don't see how."

"I can help you," he soothed.

"Again, I don't see how."

"You have so much power and very little skill. Whomever your mentor is, they should be ashamed of themselves."

"I have no mentor."

"Then your academy. Let me guess, you're from The Golden Harvest. They always were overly ambitious."

"I don't know what you're talking about. Such things are forbidden. Stay back!" Lana shouted her demand, hoping to emphasize it with another force push, but again, nothing. *Damn it! Is it me, him, or this place that's blocking my metis?*

"What is your name, girl?"

"Don't worry about it." Soon it would be irrelevant.

"If you want to leave, then go. But there's no need to burn down this home."

"I'm keeping Rue safe from your evil manipulations."

"You are definitely trying." The man's tone was pure, condescending pity. "I can't bring him back, I promise.

You can come out now," Dimitri coaxed, stepping back out of the house.

"No."

Lana shook her head. It was a trick. But when she looked back at Rue, she hesitated. Confusion paralyzed her. Indecision crippled her, while guilt stole her breath. She didn't know what was right and true, but she knew she had to make a decision. Her metis wasn't coming, and she couldn't maintain a standoff with a Deathless Master.

I just had it! It's got to be him. He's doing something to my metis.

Lana felt the hairs on her arm stand and knew Dimitri, the Deathless Master was doing something. Fractured breath ripped through her throat and Lana hiccupped on it. Wiping the trail of tears dripping from her chin, she turned her face away. She felt compelled to hide her disappointment and shame. *Did I make a mistake? Have I failed Rue?*

"See? Nothing."

Lana stepped out of the house, unable to bear the sight anymore. Her head was starting to pound, and she was losing hope. Dimitri, with not even a hair out of place, kept his distance.

"See. I'm not a monster," he said.

A tremor rippled down her consciousness. Not even a year ago, she made the same declaration. Perhaps they weren't as different as she'd like to imagine.

"I can teach you how to use your grace."

"It isn't grace. It's a curse."

"If you truly believe that, then it's no wonder your

access is limited. At your age you should be training others. I don't know what happened while I was… asleep, but whatever you think you know is wrong. Let me prove it."

"How?"

"I'll show you how to access your grace."

"How can I trust you, after you ate me earlier?"

"Don't be vulgar, I ate from you," he scolded. "Either way, you shouldn't trust me, only a fool would trust someone they just met. All I'm asking for is a chance."

"Why didn't you kill me?"

"Because you're the one who woke me and I owe you a debt of gratitude. Besides, I like to wake with council. Fear not, I have no plans to kill you yet. You need me, as I need you."

Chills ran down Lana's back. She felt his power down to her toes. Though she didn't know how she'd done it, she remembered the creeping worry that she kept pushing aside. Was she responsible for waking the Deathless Master?

"What do I do?"

CHAPTER NINETEEN

Ryker

Lord Wyvier's northernmost estate, Munstriale, city of Nostrus, Taraq.

"So, they've brought in the cavalry." Ryker hid his grimace by shutting the door to the office.

Ravetta turned, the long line of her cutting through the room. Her crimson waves, nearly the same color of the rich curtains behind her, rolled like fire and silk down her neck and shoulders, stopping halfway down her back. The noonday sun was behind her, and, as usual, there wasn't a strand out of place. She was elegant and classic, everything meticulously decided. But what didn't show was her brutal streak and her penchant for quick insults and long vendettas.

"Well, I don't know about that. I'm just passing through." She lifted her bare shoulder in a casual shrug.

"Did you bring Stella?" Ryker asked with a hopeful spark.

"Had I known we would be heading this way, I would have."

"How is she?"

"Stella's coming into her own. You know how children are. You nurse them, watch them grow in your arms. One day you're coaxing their first steps, and the next, they're trying to start an uprising to overthrow 'barbaric rituals of academia.' It warms a mother's heart." Ravetta looked up and to the right, staring off into the colorful ambition she saw in their daughter's future.

Ravetta was in for a rude awakening when she learned that Stella's current passion was cultivating medicinal flora — chimeric horticulture, if he remembered correctly from the letter he received from their daughter last week.

"Well, as much as I would have loved to see her, it's for the best. She doesn't need to know of such things," he said ruefully.

"You say that as if she doesn't already. How cute. You know, she accused me of being a spy the other day."

"Aren't you?"

"Aren't we all agents for kin and country?" Ravetta countered, with an old, familiar phrase.

Ryker's brow raised, but he said nothing of it.

"Are you here to spy on me?" he asked instead.

"Why would you think that?"

"I've heard things are changing. Ravetta, tell me the truth. Tell me what you know."

"Me? I'm just a *betnoir*, a *che-tro*, a common whore."

"You are many things, but common is never one of them."

"Our relationship might have lasted longer had you employed more of your flattery." She angled towards him, looking up at him with mischievous eyes and a tempting mouth.

It might have lasted longer, but it would have been more of the same.

"And what will flattery get me now?" Ryker stood straight, catching the lingering scent of feminine soap. Ravetta was all legs and gentle curving lines; classically seductive. He knew she would be soft, and would sink into his arms like a sultry swan.

But it would be nothing compared to Lana's charged touch.

"What is it about this foreigner?"

Caught off guard, Ryker ducked his head. Then he looked over at his old friend and lover with a bashful grin. The soft look lasted only a fraction of a second, but her eyes lit in amusement. Ravetta saw more in that moment than he'd been able to admit in a month.

"You're not jealous, are you?" he asked instead with a curling grin as he passed by the small drink cart.

"Why do men always assume that? Never mind. Yes, my life ended with you. I can't stand the thought of you with anyone else. I want you back. I need you here. Now. Take me." Ravetta sat on the edge of the desk and splayed her hands on either side, arching her back. Her faux impassioned pucker cracked with a peeking eye.

"Really, Ravetta. There's no need for dramatics. Men just know these things."

"Don't confuse wishful thinking for knowledge. You'll set yourself up for disappointment."

"Are you insinuating that I'm not knowledgeable?"

"When it comes to martial matters, I know of no one better."

"But…?"

"But with women, especially their hearts, you're pretty oblivious."

"We were at war with the Chargers. I didn't have time to pick flowers for you."

"Oh no, Ryker. Flowers were never what I wanted from you. But I'm not talking about me, or us for that matter. Lana is an Einhart, born and bred; practically royalty if the rumors are true." She stepped forward. "She's going to have expectations. It will require a certain gentleness," she said emphatically.

"I know that," he said with a scoff. "I just need help finding her. I'm not worried about what to do when I get her."

"Careful, Ryker. Men have hunted and killed wild

beasts since the dawn of time, but women have been hunting and taming men for just as long."

"Are you saying she's tamed me? I'm not an animal. I've been general to thousands, and the chief and protector to millions."

"Of course." Ravetta rolled her eyes. "Just trying to help."

"If you want to help, tell me what you know." The time for waiting for information passively, whether from Terra or the countless missives he'd sent, was over.

"I know First Prime Zuul does not want you two together. He fears a family between you two is the first step in an Einhart invasion. If we accept Miss Colton by rights, we'll have to accept all metisians, or worse yet, all of Einhart. He's worried about national instability."

"That's fear-mongering. Worse-case arguments are suitable for a commoner or standard elder, not our First Prime."

"He's worried about the future of Taraq. That is a concern suited for the First Citizen and every Tarquin." There was a glimmer of defensiveness in her eyes that Ryker found out of place.

Normally, Ravetta didn't get emotionally invested in matters of state. For her, intercepting and manipulating letters and reports was enough. Changing the tides of war and peace with whispered words and carefully placed brush strokes was what she did best. While his position was weighted with heavy responsibility, his duties paled in comparison to her work.

But, for almost as long as he'd known her, protecting their daughter had been her primary goal. Now, something had changed. There was a new edge to her emerald eyes.

Ryker took a hard look at his ex. Now that he'd started seeing it, there was no room for doubt: Ravetta was different. Could her loyalty still be trusted? It seemed Fate had decided to throw him another surprise. Was there anyone beyond reproach?

"Lana's life is in jeopardy. I feel it. Trivial concerns should not be the excuse that fails to bring her home."

"Home, Ryker? You really do love her."

"Don't be ridiculous."

"You are her home. Or at least, you want to be. If that's not love, then perhaps you need to reevaluate."

"And when did you become an expert on love?"

"What, you think a whore can't understand matters of the heart?"

"I'd never—" Ryker had learned long ago not to follow her into arguments. "Are you all right?"

"Of course," she said quickly, bristling.

"Well, if the person you love makes you feel cheap and common, then perhaps it's you that needs to reevaluate."

The quip was enough to bring out the familiar flash in her green eyes. It was a grim reminder of the past and of the countless truths better left unsaid.

"You know what, Ryker Portellum?" He cut her off.

"Did you think that by calling me by my old name, you would shame me?" *To what end?*

"You're right, what was I thinking? I should have known. You can't shame the shameless."

She wanted to say more. Ravetta always got that

pinched expression when she was about to lay into him. Instead, she turned and walked to the metallic drink cart quietly, as if debating her words. She made them both a drink and handed him a glass.

"Let's start over. Ryker, darling. I heard your latest enthrallment is wanted by the Shining Knights, a mad king, and a horde of bounty hunters. How did you two meet?"

"She asked for my protection after she told me to get lost."

"Well, I like her already."

"She's a good person. There are no power plays or manipulations with her. She's strong, but fragile. She makes me feel like I don't need to protect all of Taraq — shielding her is enough."

"Well, with enemies like hers," she muttered, "why did you let her go?"

"The decision wasn't mine. Lana wanted to leave, damn near strong-armed me. I wasn't going to stop her." Ryker took a long pull of the amber liquid.

"And so, like the fool you are, you hid and sulked."

"What do you women expect? What do you want from us?"

"To explain it would deprive you of your journey towards understanding." She muttered another one of her favorite lines. He'd always hated that one. He figured it was pretty much a roundabout way of saying she didn't have an actual answer.

"You sure that's it?"

"What does that mean?" Ravetta turned in a snap,

her perfectly sleek hair tousling with her abrupt movement.

"Only that you seem to be going through something, and maybe it's affecting your judgment."

Ryker remembered Stella mentioning some things being unusual the last time she'd returned home from the academy. *It's a shame I didn't bring that letter with me.*

"Unbelievable Ryker, I travel near the Din Draug Forest for you, and you want to question my motives?"

"I didn't mean it like that, Rav." Ryker reached out and placed a hand on her delicate shoulder. They were close enough that he noticed the faint smell of murdosh flower, fresh and sweet, unlike the dark, rich flavor that Ravetta usually scented herself with.

"Lord Wyvier, there's a man out here—" Genievet walked into the room and halted abruptly, mid-sentence and mid-step. The girl looked between Ryker and Ravetta, and he could see the her head spin. Though Genie voiced none of her accusations, the mulish bunch of her lips and forehead said it all.

"What is it, Genievet?" he asked, lowering his hand and feeling foolishly guilty.

"There's a man here to see you. He says it's urgent." Genie's voice lowered as she glared ahead.

"I'll be out in a moment." Ryker nodded, turning back to his ex until the sound of nothingness irritated his awareness. "You may leave now, Genievet."

"Yes, m'lord," she said, as she begrudgingly made her exit.

"I should get going too." Ravetta stepped away,

smoothing out her unwrinkled skirt. "I have an important meeting I need to prepare for."

"Did you come all this way to tell me nothing?"

"Of course not, darling. I left a letter on your desk. It would be best if you read it before you see your guest. Then burn it."

Espionage and subterfuge were Ravetta's tools of the trade. She was a master at deception and had a cut-throat proclivity that most warriors dreamed of. Ryker had always thought it was one of her most endearing qualities.

Not that he could judge. Lately, between his temper and his heavy-handed law, he hadn't made many friends. And the allies he thought he had in court and on the battlefield were dropping contact with him left and right. His career was a sinking ship, and his associates were bailing out while they still could.

But that did bring some core questions to the surface. Why had Ravetta shown up here, and now? Who was she working for? And how did he and Lana fit into their plan?

CHAPTER TWENTY

Lana

There are inherent risks in everything one does. Even the most fervent actuary couldn't take into account the vast probabilities of devia-tion. All bets, even the kind ones, would have called for Lana to be dead by now.

Whether it was strong will or good — some would say dumb — luck, Lana had survived every challenge directed at her. She had no doubt that things would end poorly for her eventually.

Since her travels, she had been afforded plenty of time to consider her death. She figured her demise would begin with licking flames, or maybe a cold knife from behind. Confined to a rotting castle had never made the list. After all, King Paul was a man of action; he didn't have the patience to sit idle and let justice sort itself out.

Lana forced a smile at the Deathless Master next to her. He'd held out his arm, again playing the gentleman, and Lana accepted it, keeping her touch as light as she could. He led her back into his crumbling estate, effortlessly looking past the piles of filth and rubble.

He'd asked her to give him a chance. A chance to prove that he wasn't the monster that history had painted him out to be. *Only time will tell where the truth lies.*

He led her to the room where they first met, where he had tried sucking the very life out of her. The painted ceiling was the only thing that remained the same. All of the debris had been cleared, and the corpse Lana had smashed had been removed, revealing the chipped tiled floor, swept but not polished. A large table sat in the middle of the dance floor.

One of the servants, a tall, gangly man with a beak of a nose, pulled back a thick wooden chair to the right of the head of the table. Lana tried not to shiver at the crawling dark energy that seeped from the puppet. Before her laid a great feast, but all she could think about was the walking corpse.

The curtains that draped over the huge windows were pulled shut, and the entire room was lit by hundreds of candles. Crystal placed meticulously on white and dark streaked wood decorated the beautiful room. Rainbows of color danced across all the walls. Lana had never seen anything so beautiful in her life.

"You wanted a council, my lord. What would you like to speak of? I'm well versed on many topics."

Never in her life, never in her wildest dreams or most fevered nightmares, would she have imagined sitting across the table from the most notorious metisian in the world, a Deathless Master, at that. All the surviving historical texts tell of one brutal, unstoppable master — a man, a fiend, a spawn from the Devil's Split, a great evil come to steal life and spirit. Now it looked like she was about to break bread with him.

"Well, let us talk of art."

"I find Quain's *The Beginning*, the interpretation of the beginning of time, to be quaint but dull. His colors are purposely muted, yet his use of wax tones down the already staid colors, making what could have been a beautiful contrast into a murky blundering."

"So, I take it you are a fan of Nexis? I must agree, *The Beginning* is dull. But I think it expresses the bleakness of the era he was trying to emphasize; the decaying afterbirth which was what he felt life sprang from."

She intentionally spoke of the few true classics she knew. From what little remained, she figured he'd been 'asleep' for nearly two hundred years. Who knew how old he truly was.

"Nexis uses bright colors, which I enjoy, but I don't think he should be considered a counterpart to Quain, who usually has wonderful, but always dull and dreary paintings." Lana shook her head and pressed her hands into her lap, her knuckles quickly turning white. *Keep it going, keep talking. Act normal.* "Ah, Nexis passed away too young to have the steady handed mastery I think he would have grown in to. Though, what he lacked in skill he could have made up for in raw talent one day, had he lived long enough. No, I prefer Netty Vulm who is both whimsical and witty. Her mixture of bold colors and intricate detail leaves me breathless."

"He died young? That is troubling. I was always very fond of him. I don't know this Netty Vulm, and I grow tired of this conversation." Dimitri's tone turned sharp, and Lana knew she'd messed up.

Leaning back, she crossed her legs with her ankle on her knee, a pose that she had seen many men assume. She'd always thought it was a confident and powerful pose. She couldn't hold it for long; it made her feel too exposed. His eyebrow lifted as she fidgeted, but he said nothing of it.

"How did you learn of the metis?" he asked bluntly, snapping his fingers in the air. One of his puppets, another fungus-filled corpse, stepped forward before the snap had finished ringing in her ears. He had paper thin, shelf-like layers stacked down his neck and back, attached to his bark-like skin. He dripped with goop and spread fine wood dust from his shoes as he walked.

It may have been common practice to see and speak of such things when and where he came from, but to her it was still very taboo. Speaking of such things was as good as a death sentence. Even among close friends, such things were not spoken of lightly, and never at the dinner table.

"If you'll excuse me," Lana patted her mouth with a napkin, trying to swallow the saliva that pooled on her tongue. "I'm still trying to get comfortable talking about such things. Where I come from, even talking of metis would get you killed."

"Why? Metis is all around us. It is in everything. It's life, death, and all the elements in between, including the soul. Are you uncomfortable talking about love and war? Are there bans on mentioning the weather? We are surrounded by metis always. Cutting yourself off from that would be like refusing to breathe."

"Knowledge of metis, or anything metisian-related, is treated with the utmost suspicion. The dark works of metis are responsible for killing thousands of people." Lana tried to explain, though in truth she never understood it well herself.

"More than that, I'm sure. And without the knowledge of metis, I'm assuming people still die. Millions of people find ways to kill themselves every day. Do you close the roads and shut down living to preserve life?"

"Metis is dangerous. Surely you can admit that."

"Of course. So is trusting someone in your relationships. I mean, look at me. I was one of the most powerful metisians the world had ever seen, but it wasn't my manipulations that killed me. It was my family. My point is, the very act of living is dangerous. The trick of it all is control. You can't control the world around you, you can only trust yourself to handle what life throws your way. You must take all the gifts and advantages given to you and make the most out of your life, and you can only do that with control and self-determination. So, how did you first learn control?"

Lana paused, choosing her words carefully. She turned her head to help keep her eyes from wandering back to Lord Ballroom or his ever-present puppet. The undead man wasn't physically imposing, but was still bone-deep intimidating. Instead of looking at the puppets, Lana's studied the faded red curtains, dancing in the wind.

"I learned it while I was traveling."

"And what are you searching for?" he asked probingly.

"Safety." Lana shook her head. "Freedom," she corrected.

She leaned forward, looking into the Deathless Master's eyes. They were a dark shade of blue. What she saw in his eyes didn't comfort her. In them was madness; a raw, fanatical concentration. What was worse, Lana saw herself reflected in the zealous globes.

"What you did earlier, I felt it all the way down to my bones." Dimitri leaned forward, his eyes tracking her fidgeting with a frown. "Your connection to the metis is remarkable. Your loose power alone woke me and a handful of my guards. So, do I believe that you're new? Yes, anyone with experience protects their line of power. Anyone with a semblance of experience would know how to control themselves."

"I didn't know; it was the last thing I wanted to do. Is that why you attacked us? Because of my power?"

"I thought my enemies had sent you to finish me off."

Then that meant Marcus's death now weighed on her conscience. He'd saved her, protected her from the mob looking to collect the bounty on her head, and she'd led him into the Deathless Master's trap. It also meant that any who fell at his hands would also stain her soul. She'd unknowingly unleashed a monster.

"What do you plan on doing with me?"

"Why, Lana…If I tell you, will you run from me? Will the truth send you scurrying away? Do you fear me?"

"No, I do not. You may be Quain, but I am Nexis. I don't need a light touch when I can use the heavy hand of the metis to destroy you."

"If you can, then why haven't you?" This was one of the first hints of genuine amusement to lift his thin, pale lips.

"Not every situation needs to be solved with violence," Lana bluffed.

"Wise words. But not all problems can be solved by conversation."

"You said you only wanted council. Why, then, did you invite me?"

"We've already discussed this, I wanted you."

"Why? For what?"

"Come here and I'll show you."

Instinctively Lana recoiled, but he came prepared. Two puppets held her down in her chair as another pushed the chair towards Dimitri. The ear-piercing scrapes rang in her head, but fear eclipsed the noise.

"No, please don't do this again."

"Don't worry, this will be the last time," he promised lightly.

The Deathless Master reached forward and threaded his fingers with hers, slowly digging in. She tried to avoid his touch by pressing her palm into the chair's armrest, but his determined strength won out. He pulled from her, drawing her life's energy out of her though the small connection they shared.

Lana tipped her head back and shouted. Pair ripped through her, starting at her head and surging down through her arm. Worse than the pain was the numbness, the cold emptiness that left her hollow and drained.

"See? That wasn't so bad. I just need you until I get my full strength back."

He'd been awake for less than a week and he'd already raised, both intentionally and accidentally, nearly two dozen puppets. What would he be able to do at full power? Lana was afraid to know, and much too tired to ask.

"Besides, what is a Master without an apprentice? What is a teacher without a pupil? There can be no knowledge or power without a price."

"Why waste your time having to train me when I could become a true danger to you?" she asked through gritted teeth.

With her energy still fueling his healing process, the patchwork scars lightened before her eyes. Some of the light pink scars faded discreetly into his skin. Even the purplish wound at his neck looked thinner, smoother, and less angry.

"Don't be ridiculous, Lana. You could never be a threat to me. I can't be killed. But with you I will smash my enemies and retake my lands."

Lana slowly sat back in her chair. Dimitri's conviction would have been hard to fake; the anger in his face impossible to replicate. She was rubbing her temple when the butler came back, carefully holding a tray with sparkling, delicate glass saucers and cups.

"When will this be over?"

"Only you can answer that. Come now, you must eat, drink, and rest. You start your training in the morning."

A small teapot was positioned on the tray between Lana and Dimitri, the handle angled towards her. A plate with a half dozen tea cakes sat behind the tea. A tall, thin crystal glass of juice sat to Lana's right. She tried to find comfort in the thankfully mundane task of pouring both of them a cup of tea, pretending she wasn't surrounded by corpses, sitting across from the most hated man in history, discussing death and political revolution.

CHAPTER TWENTY-ONE

Ryker

3742.07.20 Somewhere deep in the Avoscion Forest.

"**Y**ou move against the First Citizen's recommendation and orders, you might as well consider yourself gutter-bound." Kennith's lecture swam in his head, even though he was nearly half a day behind him. It was his final comment as they parted ways. His friend didn't have to remind Ryker of what was at stake.

It didn't matter, Lana needed his protection. So, he donned his sword, breaking the covenant between him and First Prime Zuul. Until there was a formal relinquishing of power, he was still the Third Citizen. And until a document came and formally abdicated his position, Ryker acted as a public servant. He thought it best for all involved.

The path he traveled was quiet. Some might find loneliness in isolation, but not Ryker. The steady trot of his horse carried him through the Avoscion Forest once more. This section of forest had been thinned to maintain roadways. Even though the winter season had laid up the construction efforts the road remained clear as he passed through. The fallen leaves, wet and decomposing, looked like rubies on the ground, a sea of sparkling red as the light streaked through.

Word had come from his inside source that there might be a way to track Lana. He had to find and convince the Viridate Traveller tribe that he meant Lana no harm. His history with Travellers wasn't one of trust and friendship. Alas, he had more wyld connections. Wyld families had taken homes across Taraq's unclaimed territory, and with them they brought their strong, familial bonds and an animal-like ferocity against transgressors. Now he rode to the scourge, in need. Desperate need.

He yearned for Lana. A need pulsed inside him that clouded clear thought. Though he would be happy with word, he wanted most for that intimate connection they shared. He wanted it so badly he could almost see her violet eyes flash through the fog of his mind. The image vanished as quickly as it had appeared.

He couldn't help but wonder how much of the information blackout was politically motivated. Was there just not any information to spread? Why hadn't she reached out to him? He had to find out.

But he would miss this place. Though it was a gilded prison, Ryker had started to find a peaceful purpose in this land. It was distinctly different from his other estates, where the bustle and innovation were constant bombardments on his attention.

Few things silenced the warrior spirit, but just as the elders had promised, "the country air" did. Mountains opened up to land, land to rivers, and always in the distance, tall, stalwart mountains dotted the landscape. Yes, he would miss this place.

Now he was set on a task like no other. He'd served as a judge, chief guard, and mayor all in one for nearly the last decade. Now, instead of mending relations between neighbors, he was going to have to build a relationship with people who Ryker had not even a few years ago deemed vagabonds and swindlers.

As the Third Citizen, he'd made a habit of restricting their access and holding them accountable for their scams. Ryker had been proud of that. His people approved of it, and often mentioned their appreciation for the more equitable trade deals. Now he wondered how it would affect Lana.

Would they hold back their help to spite him? Here he was, in command of nearly a million lives, struggling to deal with a group no more extensive than the average family unit. How Lana had even come across these people and survived seemed remarkable to him.

By all accounts, they were dangerous cutthroats. Usually docile, until their opinion changed. Then they lived by no rules save their own. It would be nice to walk into the tribe and demand answers, but these were not a people used to obeying orders. They were so isolated he had no idea about the intricacies of their hierarchy, or whether they even had a government.

Now that the stream of bounty hunters had slowed to a drip, Ryker divorced himself from his people. He figured he could start the separation now, so when the First Prime denounced him, the people weren't surprised. It wasn't like he was abandoning them; he was just fulfilling personal obligations. But then why did he feel so guilty?

Ryker was a man caught between duty and freedom. He'd made a promise to Lana as the Third Citizen, not as Ryker, her lover. Most critics wouldn't see it that way, but they weren't there. Besides, 'What I would have done' was a nonsensical statement. If they were going to do it, they would be Third Citizen, not a loaf, gossiping in front of the general goods store.

Ryker and his horse snorted at the same time, and it pulled a smile from him. Ryker had left his war horse back at Wynthros. The poor old creature he'd driven into countless battles was soft from the stables and wouldn't have done well on a journey like this.

Instead, he'd selected Chet, the young chestnut stud. He was an emphatic horse whose expressions and character had grown on him. Byron, the stableboy, had all but sworn his life on the horse, and that kind of insistence was hard to deny.

When he found Lana, when she was back in his arms and sparking at his touch, he would make up for his mistakes. She would know that she was free, and he would become an extension of her. Never again would she feel she had to run from him. When he found her, she would never again be on her own.

All he had to do was discover the nomads' current location, track them down, convince them to help him find her, and then put himself in her path. Easier said than done. He'd gotten word before he left that a tribe was spotted north of Vearilly, a small town with historic sulfur springs said to cure everything short of death.

He hoped it was the tribe he needed. Ryker didn't have the patience or the spare luck to be chasing faulty leads. Lana had been missing for too long now. He didn't have the time to waste.

Though he was still two days out from Vearilly, he intended to make it to the springs by midday if Chet's stamina and hock survived the hills and shifting slopes. If the steed proved reliable, there was a basket of treats in it for him. If not, he would have to trade the horse in at the nearest market. And horse trading was not something you wanted to do mid-mission. Ryker was guaranteed to lose money. Not to mention, he really hated bartering.

As Ryker traveled, he enjoyed the nature springing to life, an innocent excitement that had nothing to do with war and death. The long pause in distractions set his mind to wonder where his future would lead him.

In the past, when he had been a warrior, he'd expected to die in battle. But through all the wars and injuries, he'd survived. From there, it had been a natural progression to take office.

Who better to confront conflict than someone hardened by fire? Who better to decide when to tempt war than a warrior who knew the horrors of battle? As his success grew and his influence expanded, he figured that if he were going to die before his time, it would be defending his people.

But now, Ryker was once again encountering a shifting future.

All things considered, the roads were safer. And his people were happier, healthier, and more prosperous. Perhaps, for all his efforts, he'd done well in the time he'd had. If he was excised as the Third Citizen or thrown to the wolves, Ryker knew he'd done right by his people.

So what if he bent a couple of laws to hold back the loose-cannon bounty hunters? It wasn't indefinite, just until he had Lana back — definitely before he stepped down. And as for the others — once they hurt a Tarquin, they were protected by no laws superior to Ryker's will.

He may have done well defending and maintaining the law, but these roads were in bad shape. He could probably send people in the summer to fill the ruts and potholes. Maybe even angle it better for run-off. Snorting, he tried to shake off the thought.

Soon, the First Prime would hear of his departure. No doubt Zuul had spies everywhere. Come summer, he could have an entirely different life. The idea amused him. It was exciting not knowing what the future held. Still, even though the title would be gone, hopefully he would have time to wrap up his community affairs before relinquishing the job. He might as well determine the best way to patch the roads, as well as which roads to prioritize and who to make accountable for the work, especially across districts.

It was after a particularly brutal hole that Ryker heard an unusual noise. At first, he thought his axle had snapped. But there was no dragging. He pulled on the reins and stopped the horse. Swinging off the bench, Ryker stood before the wagon. The wooden cart was low and without a top. He could clearly see his wheels were even and undamaged.

A tingle rose the hair on the back of his sword hand. Though he was never graced with an active power, Ryker liked to think of this extra sense as a metis aware-ness. Long ago, Ryker had developed an ability to sense when something suspicious was going on. It had come in handy when waging wars, calming villagers, and assessing the fiery foreigner he'd let slip through his fingers.

Quietly, Ryker pulled out his dagger. The leather sheath, oiled over time and with care, released the blade without a whisper. He made a show of patting his horse, kicking the wheels, and knocking on the cart walls, but his focus was on the small bundle hidden within a stack of blankets. Between two barrels and a small fortune in furs, medicine, and swords made by the best blacksmiths in Taraq, the pile of blankets shifted.

"Okay, you found me." The girl from earlier, Orla's

kin, appeared. Her hair was threaded with straw and her face was flushed a dark red.

"What is this about? Why are you here?" he demanded, though the answer was obvious.

Genievet, had begged Ryker to allow her to accompany him on his quest to find and save Lana. But she reminded Ryker of the turmoil Lana had suffered in their time together. Stubbornness on both sides had cut the time they had together short, with bitter regrets. No matter how many times the girl asked, finding and cornering him inside and outside of his estate, he refused. Orla's kith could not be trusted.

"Lord Wyvier, please listen. Just hear me out, okay?" Genie climbed out of the other side of the cart, giving them both plenty of space.

"Don't make me ask twice," Ryker warned.

"I know I can help. Lana is my friend. Please, don't let your anger at General Orla keep me from helping you. I can take care of your horse, make meals, run errands. I can fight."

Genievet struggled to keep her hands at her sides. They kept rising, but before they could finish the begging clutch, she lowered them. What she couldn't control was her pleading tone.

But Ryker would not be swayed by pretty words or promises of comfort. Genievet's connection to Orla had been confirmed by his sources. The only question that remained was whether his general had betrayed him intentionally, or if it was her ruthless ambition that had betrayed them all.

"What makes you think I want or need your help? Are you a warrior?"

"You know I'm not, but I have received training."

"Oh, you're in training! How many years?" Ryker grinned in faux enthusiasm.

"Well…one season."

Well, I'm sure those defensive rolls they teach to first-season recruits will come in handy.

"Impressive," he said, deadpan. "Can you track?"

"No."

"Hunt?" Ryker continued, taking pleasure in how her form shrank away.

"No."

"What's the most dangerous beast you've pursued?"

"Only you, Lord Wyvier," she answered bowing her head.

Ryker glared at the cheeky and unexpected response. "How can I trust you not to be Orla's spy?"

"My lord Wyvier, you don't know me, but when you stormed the infernal castle of Krunos, I asked about you every visit into the city. You are an inspiration; your tale had motivated me long before you became Third Citizen. When you were hurt in the hunt against the wild sabic, I prayed for you every day and harvested some of the medicinal herbs used in your recovery. I believe in you, but more importantly, I believe in Lana. She and I might have only known each other for a short time, but I consider her to be part of my family. And as possibly the only surviving member of her family, it is my right to lead this rescue mission."

Ryker didn't need her to finish the train of thought

on tradition. Because Lana was not his wife, he wasn't considered entitled. Instead, he was only her shield and protector. That made him honor-bound to see to Lana's return to safety — or to serve justice, should she come to harm.

Ryker had only Genievet's word that she and Lana had, in their short time together, somehow 'bonded.' Under normal circumstances, word was enough. But her associations were in doubt, and that cast a long shadow. Could he trust her not to be Orla's eyes and ears?

"I'm not asking to lead this. I know Lana would do better with you. All I want is to help bring her home," Genievet pleaded.

By law, she had the right. But if he was going to travel with the runt, the air would be clear between them. The heavy sigh was born from not only acceptance, but an unwanted truth. Genievet may have thought he'd yielded, felled by her convincing speech and moved by her passion, but the truth was a bit darker.

"What is your connection to Orla?"

"She and my mother were good friends, and she has added her sword to shield me. She was supposed to introduce me at Asa Ve this summer. She's my *kataem*," she finished. A kataem was a non-blood-related adult who took an active role in guiding a child. It was a powerful bond.

"Fine, you may join. But you're walking. This journey will be difficult enough for the horse without you adding a burden."

"Thank you! Thank you, Lord Wyvier. I won't disappoint you."

"Just remain quiet until I call for you."

It was cruel to make her walk the trip, but her brother had suggested this horse, so she should know its limitations. Her walking would slow them down, but losing the horse now would be worse. He'd been played, and he'd lost this round. If Orla was behind this madness he would have to keep one eye open, always.

If Ryker had made Lana his wife like her father had intended when she'd stood in the council chambers before him, then Lana would have been protected by Tarquin law and custom. But no, Ryker liked his independence. The casual dalliance suited him, or so he'd thought. It hadn't taken Lana being gone long before he'd realized he missed the grace she brought to the vast estate. But by then it was too late.

Ryker had messed up, and now he was doing what he could to make it right. Damn the consequences, and to hell with anyone who stood in his way, be it metisian travelers, wyld bounty hunters, or an army. Nothing would deter him. It was no longer a taxing duty, but a task of the heart.

Ryker needed to keep his eyes open for the right opportunity. Eventually, the right time and place would reveal itself; he just had to be ready to make his move. One of the most valuable lessons war had taught him was not to play the immediate game, but to look further ahead and plan a path that ended the game. And that, he could do.

CHAPTER TWENTY-TWO

Ryker

"Help! Please, help! Is anyone there?" The plea for help echoed, distorted by the trees.

"Did you hear that?" Ryker asked Genie, scanning the area.

"Hear what?" Genie asked.

Ryker stopped the horse once more, jumping from the cart, his worried eyes scanning the area. The call for help sounded close, as if the woman was running towards them. Ryker didn't see how the girl could have missed it.

"This is exactly what I was talking about. Things were going well on my own. Now, look!" Ryker returned to where he last saw Genie and the horse, but they were gone — the girl, the horse, the cart, and the road, all gone. Now Ryker stood in a foggy clearing, with nothing but small gray boulders peeking up through the thick mist.

"Help!" A tingle of awareness warned Ryker. There was something unusually familiar about that distorted voice.

This time the cry was close, within a stone's throw of his location. But now he knew: Lana.

"Where are you, Lana?" Ryker bellowed.

"I don't know. He's coming. He's going to find me! Help!"

His long legs ate up the distance, but still, he saw nothing. Turning, Ryker scanned the area. His heart pounded in his ears like a war drum. To be so close and not be able to find her was gut-wrenching. Lana was practically within reach. Maybe if he found her and could hold on tight enough, he could pull her out of this misty netherworld. The chance he could pull her out of this nightmarish realm that had her trapped drew Ryker deeper. Deeper and deeper into the fog, with only her screams as a guide.

Fear — no, terror — trembled her shouts, and the desperation inside Ryker's chest compounded. I will find her. "Lana! Stay where you are. I'll find you."

Searching the fog, Ryker swiped at the low-hanging

clouds, hoping they would reveal tracks he could follow. Anything that could lead him to her.

Then he saw it. Dark movement heading away from him. Running as fast as his legs could carry him, Ryker sprinted towards the looming shadow. There was a vague notion, just a prickling awareness, that something wasn't right, but the pressure of possibilities weighed on him too heavily to hear it.

Lana's long shriek of tormented pain broke just as Ryker reached for the figure he chased. Grabbing a fistful of the cloak, Ryker pulled Lana back and into his arms. Immediately he knew it didn't feel right. Too heavy, too tall, and too hard. Ryker let go of the form, but not in time to miss the sharp swipe of polished steel.

Fire ran like liquid across his chest, settling deep into the bone. It felt like he'd been cut in half. But there she was, behind the cloaked form, curled into a ball. Even with tears streaming down her cheeks, eyes tight with horror, she was still the most beautiful sight he'd ever seen. Lana was alive — in danger, but alive. Fight, survive, protect. Those things Ryker understood to his core, so that's what he did.

With sheer force of will, Ryker swallowed his pain and charged. He grabbed the attacker Lana feared so greatly and threw them away from her. The form fell prone, and their cloak slid back, showing a bone mask for a face.

He didn't need to know who or what was behind the mask. Ryker needed only to eliminate the threat.

His fists smashed the soft spots he knew had to exist; Ryker wailed on the stomach, throat, and kidneys. He stopped only to slap the flashing metal away, and when Lana scrambled forward, grabbing the attacker's hands, helping to pin him down, Ryker spared a second to nod in appreciation.

He stopped when the figure lay limp. Ryker's lungs burned hotter than the cut on his chest. Next to him, Lana shook. Blood splattered her face and neck, but he pulled her into his arms without reservation. He knew he squeezed her too hard, but she held him just as tightly.

Lana pulled back, looking up at him with sparks lighting up her violet eyes. Her mouth moved, but no sound came out. He gripped her, even as she tried to pull back. If there was a chance he could bring her back, he would try with all his strength.

Lana shook her head, her hand resting on his shoulder. The smile she gave him was weak and trembling, but it made his heart soar. She's not too far gone if she can smile. *Ryker rested his hand over hers and brought their heads together.*

He had her. Ryker had found her. Finally.

"Lord Wyvier, are you okay?"

When he opened his eyes, Lana was gone and he was back on the road. Genie stood next to his horse, holding the reins. Jerking, Ryker twisted, looking around for any remnants of Lana. *Was it all just a dream?* He rubbed his pounding temples, his chest screaming in opposition.

"Your chest, you're bleeding. It came from nowhere," Genie whispered.

Ryker pulled the neckline of his shirt down so abruptly he startled the horse next to him. The creature swung its head to look its rider over. Leaning forward, Ryker patted the mount, muttering his apologies.

"What was that?" Genievet asked.

"Nothing. Let's go. Keep up."

Underneath his shirt, a long cut bled from nearly shoulder to shoulder. The skin above his navel to below his neck felt tight and enflamed. But Ryker felt the connection to Lana down to his bones. The pain of the wound was nothing compared to that.

CHAPTER TWENTY-THREE

Lana

The sound of bone skidding on broken stone vibrated in the air next to Lana's ear. The chalky bone figure stumbled but charged forward, held together by metis and thick vines. Its loose-hinged jaw flapped as it ran; Lana recognized a battle cry.

The skeleton continued forward, running into and

toppling over the quarter wall Lana had ducked behind. Reaching forward, Lana pushed her hand towards the humanoid frame with all of her focus. The blast knocked the vine-entangled target back into its bramble patch grave. A plume of bone fragments, dust, and mold ballooned into the air, pelting her.

Raising her hands to protect her head from the dust exposed Lana's unprotected chest. It was an opportunity that Dimitri struck at ruthlessly. In these lessons of war and battle, Dimitri spared no pain.

The attack snapped a rib. Lana felt the force of the hit and the internal snap high in her stomach. She stared, fixated on the foreign object protruding from her chest. There was no pain, but a shocked cough popped a bubble of blood caught in her throat. It sprayed from her mouth, warming her chin and neck.

"And, dead." Lana finally looked up. Behind the skeleton wielding the sword was Dimitri. His high armored collar concealed his pout, but the boredom was unmistakable. And that was how she died for the fourth time — eyes locked with the cheery-eyed devil.

Thunder shook the earth under her body. Falling to her knees, she was unable to keep her balance. When she tried to stand, she fell to her knees once more as lightning rained down around her. The ground underneath her was shifting, rolling.

A terrible drum filled the sky instead of thunder, punctured only by cracks of lightning. Fear pressed in at her from all sides. This isn't right! *No matter where she went, pain and paralyzing fear followed.*

No matter which direction chose, she was rewarded with another strike. Whipcord pain lanced through her chest. What would happen if she just laid here? What could she do to make it stop hurting her?

The horrific storm surrounded her with no shelter in sight. The ground continued to shift under her feet, and she knew, even though she hadn't seen, monsters were waiting for her to stop moving. So, Lana climbed to her feet again and shifted to find a pattern to the rearranging landscape. A beat that her battered body could keep up with. Now was the time. Lana surged to her feet and—

"Wake up, Lana." a little voice called abruptly, right in her face. Charlie, thank the Light.

"Little brother, what are you doing up so early?"

Lana groggily opened her eyes, but the pull was too strong. Her eyes drifted down again. A cocoon of warmth surrounded her. Though she didn't want to drift back to her nightmare, she lacked the strength to climb out of bed.

"Don't you want to find me? Why did you stop looking for me? Don't you love me no more? I'm not dead yet. Are you?"

The words slowly sank in. But when they did, Lana's eyes shot open, and she darted out of bed. Slowly, Lana turned on her heel towards Charlie, her shoulders tense, but he dashed past her and outside. Too fast to grab and always a little out of reach.

"Lana, wake up."

Slowly, her eyes opened. Lana saw nothing but darkness. *Am I blind?* Shaking her head and waving her hands in front of her face only increased the panic bubbling beneath the surface. After a few seconds, however, there was some difference; the light was growing. Slowly, she was able to make out the shape of her hand.

"Come, Lana, we're not canceling the rest of practice because you got knocked out again," Dimitri mocked.

"You didn't knock me out, you killed me!"

"Stop being so dramatic. I nearly killed you. And I'm doing you a favor, not everyone has the benefit of a Deathless Master being able to revive and accelerate your healing and skill. A little gratitude would be nice."

"What happens if you accidentally kill me?"

"Don't worry, my dear. It wouldn't be an accident." A cold shiver shook her shoulders, but she climbed to her feet.

Twisting, Lana rolled her shoulder. The long line of her spine cracked deeply. It felt good, like she could breathe freely again. Lana tested out the rest of her body. She wanted to keep track of her aches; they were what let her know she was still alive.

"Excellent, Lana. Again."

Did he care that she was progressing, or was she just a means to an end for him? Did he heal her because he didn't want her to die, or because he wasn't through with her yet? *And at what point will I become too much of a burden to waste energy on?*

As much as she was learning about her metis, she still had a *long* way to go. She could only access her metis for a second at a time, making her attacks more like a scatter blast of fire and forced air. Each burst grew more and more exhausting. *After hearing Dimitri's stories of legendary metisians, I'm nowhere near where he wants me to be.*

"What would happen to me?" Lana probed. She couldn't take another beating, not so soon.

"If you died?"

"Yes."

"Don't worry about it, you'd never find true death around me. Now, again."

"But I mean, what would happen to my metis?"

Dimitri sighed heavily. "It would leave your body and join the *metitonne*, like with everyone else." Lana knew she had to be careful. Even gently probing the Deathless Master for information could cause his irritation to spike hard and fast, which was usually followed by a ruthless attack.

"So, you can't control my metis through my corpse. I would be powerless?" Lana asked slowly.

She knew she risked his anger, but she needed to know. The thought of him using her lifeless corpse to bring forth destruction on an unsuspecting world was quickly becoming the first and last thing she thought about before going to sleep. *Whenever I can get some sleep.*

"Of course. If I could control a metisian's power after they were dead, there would be no need for me to suffer though this torturous training program. Life rarely allows for such blatant advantages. Now, you're never going to succeed until you get the basics, so, again."

With a wave of his hand, Dimitri beckoned his puppets forward.

At least I don't have to worry about that. If someone like Dimitri could control metisians after death, there would be nothing powerful enough to stop him.

Again. Again. Again. Lana shook her head to clear it of the repeat. Again. She didn't know how many agains she had left in her.

"Don't you want to find me?" Charlie's childish voice called to her. Yes, she did want to find him. Lana only hoped that she survived Dimitri's training long enough to try.

CHAPTER TWENTY-FOUR

Lana

Four, thirty-seven, eleven hundred and eighty-two — the numbers that separated her and freedom. The four times Lana had tried escaping. Thirty-seven steps until she was outside the castle walls. Approximately eleven hundred and eighty-two seconds was the longest she'd been free. All attempts to escape had ended with Lana swarmed by puppets and deposited back in her room. Then the next thing she knew, she was half-drained, and another undead puppet was added to patrol the halls.

If she didn't make it out this time, she would never be able to make it out of the building without being spotted. Eventually, she would outlive her usefulness. It was then that she would die at the hands of Dimitri and his swarm — she had no doubt.

There were just too many of them; she'd never be able to fight them all. She needed to find freedom, and soon. Dimitri's lessons weren't going well, and his impatience was growing.

If I don't improve or escape, he'll kill me and use my corpse as a stool, Lana thought as her head spun.

Already weak from Dimitri's feedings and his 'training,' Lana struggled to focus. If it wasn't bad enough, the puppets shuffling and shambling as they paced the halls all night kept her from sleeping. And knowing she was dining with corpses in the room made it difficult to eat.

Where would she go, and what would she do when she found a way out of this cursed land? Those were questions for later. Right now, Lana was leaving. Peeking through the cracked door, she watched the puppets meander.

Their commands were simple: patrol the hall, watch and follow Lana, then signal for the others. When the puppet wearing a blue sash around his waist turned, Lana slammed open the door he was about to pass with a light flick of her wrist. Mr. Blue Sash and his shambling partner followed the sound.

Lana crept down the hall, knees bent, balancing on the balls of her feet. She snuck past the undead servants inspecting the noise. She wished she could lock up the creatures in one room and burn them all.

Dimitri had used the puppets to guard her, contain her, beat her both in training and in surprise attacks, as well as to handle all the household maintenance. They were everywhere. He trusted his puppets, and Lana supposed he loved them in his own way. But if she never saw another moving corpse, it would be too soon.

She darted past the door when they turned their backs to her. Disabling her guards wasn't an option; there were always more. And locking them up or blocking their path hadn't worked. They seemed to have some telepathic link to Dimitri.

Fifteen seconds. At the top of the stairs, pressed into a chalky pillar, Lana waited for the next batch of undead patrolling the ballroom. *Hurry up!* The blue sash puppet and his partner were likely to return any second.

Thirteen, twelve, eleven — time's running out! Lana debated turning around and going back to her room. It was better to try again discreetly than to get caught for the fifth time. But then, the puppets' steps on the smooth marble floors faded.

Instead of racing down the steps, which had gotten her caught the second time, Lana slid down the banister, using the currents she created to give her speed. Lana would need all the speed she could get. The ballroom floors were one of her biggest obstacles; any noise in that room rang out in the open space. It was an alarm that brought all nearby puppets down upon her.

This time she had a better plan; if she could launch herself high enough from the banister, she would be able to slide into the balcony. If she could make it to the balcony, she'd be able to climb down the vines that over-whelmed the exterior. From the ballrooms' balcony doors, the forest was within sight. Excitement surged through her.

I can't believe I've made it this far! Lana shoved the tender emotion down, knowing well the price of getting her hopes up. But she was so close, she could taste the salty-aired freedom.

All Lana had to do was exit the castle without being seen. Scale down the three stories, survive, and then run along the jagged coastline until she made it to the wooded area. *I can do it,* she told herself.

Exit through the front and side doors had proven impossible. There were just too many puppets moving about inside and outside of the decrepit estate. It was a lesson Lana had learned on her second and third attempt. Puppets designated for household tasks would drop what they were doing to pursue her. Lana figured it had some-thing to do with the way Dimitri commanded them.

Her mentor was always so tightlipped about himself and his abilities. Lana had learned practically nothing about the Deathless Master, but she had learned plenty about herself.

In her time with Dimitri, her powers had flexed. She rarely had a rebound when she channeled now. Even though she still had the terrible migraines, the motor function lag was nearly a thing of the past. She still struggled to control fire, but manipulating air had become significantly more accessible, even within Dimitri's stifling border.

So when Lana pulled the air around her, pumping her arms to catch speed, she sailed through the air face first. With her legs tucked underneath her, Lana shot through the open doorway and into the balcony. Twelve paces traveled in seconds with nothing but the quiet sound of a wayward gust of wind.

Manipulating air was easy. Stopping the forward momentum was a more difficult and unexpected challenge. The speed she needed to get through the ballroom was her enemy on the balcony. Pinwheeling her arms to keep her balance, Lana desperately pushed against the current she rode on. It barely slowed her down, and wouldn't be enough to stop her fall.

No, no, no, no! Scrambling, Lana frantically pushed against the stone slab she was about to land on. The final burst of air was just enough to soften her landing as she tumbled uncontrollably.

Eventually, Lana caught the stone railing. She had only the flash of a second to pray that it didn't tip over, like all the other dilapidated structures within this dying building. It held without even a cracking groan, and she pressed her forehead into the aged stone slab in gratitude.

Lana wrapped her arms around the ornate pillar; bruised face pressed up against the edge, dirt and muck greasing her cheek. She registered the filth on her skin for half a second, but she'd had worse. What her mind couldn't ignore was her feet dangling so high above the ground.

Lana pulled herself to the side, one railing at a time, until she pressed herself into the green wall. From there, she was finally able to get her feet perched against the rough stone wall, nestled into a tangle of massive vines.

Since she'd had a near-miss each of the last few times she had climbed, Lana's reservations about free climbing had grown. In her childhood, Lana had pushed herself to keep up with her best friend, Henry. Together they would play dangerous games like climbing trees, startling nesting srikers, and barrel rolling down the steep hills of Calanthea. If only Henry could see her now, nearly forty paces above ground, with only her tiptoes holding her weight. Lana smiled at the thought.

Her heart may be skittish at the sight, but there was nothing that could stop her now. One step at a time, one controlled jump to the next precarious ledge, and down she went. The accomplishment she felt as her feet hit the soft sand was barely outweighed by her relief.

Now all I have to do is get back to the Lost Forest and fight my way past Dimitri's barrier.

Her prideful relief was short-lived. When she turned, she faced Dimitri. He sat on one of his puppets, leaning against an ancient tree in the shade, casually sipping from a glass. The image would be forever stamped in her mind, like one of the classic paintings hanging on the walls: *Deathless Master's Beach Day.*

Lana shrank back. *So much for fifth time's the charm.*

"Lana, so delighted you could join me. And what a remarkable performance. There may be hope for you yet."

"Lord Dimitri, how unusual to find you here."

"Lana, darling, we really must address your habit of wandering eventually. You're going to get hurt."

"Is that so?" Lana asked, inching away from the incoming flanking unit of puppets. With a stone wall at her back, her front blocked by Dimitri, her left a cliffside, and her right closing in, Lana had few options and little time to figure out a solution.

"Come, come. Is it so bad here?"

"Being surrounded by your undead minions isn't exactly how I imagined my tutorship."

"Are you not learning about our history and growing your skills? Does my library not answer any question that you ask?"

"Yes, I suppose."

"I just saw you flying out of the window. Could you have done that a week ago?"

"No, I suppose not," she admitted.

"I don't think so either." He paused, assessing her. "You know, I'm not doing this to be cruel. It takes time to bridge the gap between your powers and your mind's control. What we're doing is a shortcut; hard and painful, but effective."

How could Lana put into words the fear she had of him? His mere presence tempted the monster in her. Hell, he encouraged it! It was his very nature and at the core of his abilities to consume both power and life. It wasn't a question of who she would be at the end of their training, but what she would become.

"Am I a prisoner here?" she asked.

"I'll tell you what, Lady Lana." Dimitri stood so he could smile down his nose at her defeated form. "When you're strong enough to leave without deception, you can go. Until then, you're obviously not ready. Now, meet me in the training field. It's time we shift tactics."

Dimitri turned sharply and didn't give her a backward glance. But Lana looked after the Deathless Master. The man had a dancer's body, a nobleman's stride, and a cutthroat sense of humor — literally.

Closing her eyes, Lana stalled. By the pressure in her head and on her heart, it seemed the depth of her disappointment was swallowing her whole. She thought she was so close. And now she would suffer the consequences.

Her life and death were always in the hands of her Deathless mentor.

Lana didn't know what he meant by 'shifting tactics,' but what were the chances it would make her life better? *One thing is for sure,* Lana thought as Dimitri's posse started to close in on her, shepherding their wayward sheep. *I'm about to find out.*

CHAPTER TWENTY-FIVE

Lana

Later that night, as Lana was preparing for bed, a soft knock on her door stopped her abruptly. Setting her nightgown down, Lana crept towards the door, heart pounding. *Was it Dimitri? Would puppets knock?*

She'd been recovering from training, nursing her wounds and pounding head, and didn't think she had the strength to deal with the Deathless Master so soon. Lana's head spun while she reached for the door handle, all the while trying to see a future that didn't involve corpses. Standing before her as she opened the door was a real, living and breathing woman.

She was short and slender, looking especially indistinct dressed in all black wraps. The women stared at each other, both startled. After her shock settled, Lana smiled and started, "Hello, my name is—"

"Lana, yes, you are Master Dimitri's pupil. How very fortunate you are."

Well, that's one way to describe it.

"Who are you? How did you get here?" Lana asked.

"My name is Wyn, and I felt the call."

"What does that mean?"

"Lord Dimitri requests your presence before you get ready for bed."

Lana nodded trying to smother her frown as she followed the woman.

The hallways were almost completely dark by now, with no candles to light them. The other woman did not keep to the shadows but still kept quiet, her steps soft, but not hesitant. Lana thought the girl sounded too young for such darkness.

Lana tried to picture the sharp curve of Ryker's cheek to distract her; his supple lips pressed in a firm, straight line, his strong jaw, and even stronger shoulders. He had soft skin over hard muscle and a touch that burned. Even his expression when he looked at her — a mixture of aggressive passion and resolute control — was what she thought about when she wanted to *feel*. No amount of hushed intimidation could provoke the fight or flight reaction that Ryker's look could inspire.

When Lana arrived at the door she took a steadying breath. The woman who was still elusively eclipsed in the shadows knocked, then stepped back further into the dark corner. *Who is this woman?*

A tall, lanky servant, more skeleton than man, opened the door and stepped aside for her. As Lana entered, the fireplace roared to life, going from dim to blazing in an instant. The room was decorated in red velvet and cream satin; it would have once been beautiful, but was now worn and tattered like the majority of this blasted castle.

"You may leave us."

Silently the tall servant ducked out, the heavy door closing without a sound. Dimitri had his back to Lana, looking out the window. He stood before her in a silky version of his earlier outfit, swapping his fitted jacket for a sleek robe. He'd also traded his gadgets for the full nightcap in his hand.

Turning slowly, he walked towards Lana. The fire sank down, dimly lighting the room once again, but it was enough for her to briefly see the pinkish lines running across his throat.

"You called for me, Lord Dimitri?" Lana said, when silence continued to lapse.

"Here, have a drink." Dimitri leaned over his liquor cabinet and poured her a tall glass. He handed it to her even as she shook her head. Her hand gripped the fine crystal as she stared at more of those pink lines encircling his wrist. Under his watchful stare she brought the amber liquid up to her lips, nearly grimacing at the potent smell.

Taking a cautious step around the brooding man in front of her, she walked towards the window he was just gazing out of. The weather was dreary, the air heavy and warm, rain just waiting to start pouring down. The window was slightly ajar, the sweet smell of sun-warmed grass slowly clearing the musky smell that persisted inside.

"I realize this has been hard for you, so I found you some company. Some living company."

"How?"

"Apparently, I have a cult. The Order of the Undying — terrible name, I might have to tweak that, but who would have guessed not everything about me has been erased."

That thought didn't sit well with Lana. Two women stepped forward, Wyn and another larger woman. Neither of them looked at Lana or Dimitri directly. Instead, they kept their gaze steadily at their feet.

The other woman was a head taller than Lana, with a wide set of shoulders and a masculine stride. She reminded her of Orla, the warrior woman who had risked her life to get Lana to safety. The stronger-looking woman took up the rear, and made a point of ignoring both Lana and the shadowed woman.

"Are you ready for your next lesson?" Dimitri asked, taking a long pull of his drink.

"It's nearly midnight," Lana groaned. She followed his lead and brought the glass to her lips. She didn't actually drink, but she made sure to make a show of pretending.

"Do you think the bounty hunters will only attack during the day?" Dimitri asked over his shoulder. Lana knew very well that they didn't, and with tight shoulders, followed him out of the room.

Wyn and the other woman stood on either side of her. That was when she saw the true purpose of the women's presence — they were just a living pair of watch dogs.

They didn't walk for long before they were inside a dueling arena. Dimitri pulled a helmet on as Wyn readied an arm band decorated with more ancient symbols. She strapped it on next to Dimitri's other metal device, stacking both on his left wrist.

Lana had to shake her head at the complicated contraptions. Dimitri took to the far side of the court, flipping down a visor as Lana took her place at the other end of the court. Shifting and shaking out her hands, Lana tried to get herself ready.

Before she had a chance to ask the question that was bubbling in her head, a red-hot bolt of energy flew towards her from Dimitri's hand. Gasping, Lana dove to the ground, barely missing the shot. The sound of energy fizzling on the stone wall echoed abnormally loudly inside Lana's head.

Three more shots. One struck Lana hard in the thigh. A shout ripped out of her as she was flung to the ground. This time Lana rolled with the momentum. Popping up to her feet, she leaned heavily on the gate, keeping weight off her injured leg. Her dress had been seared, showcasing the open wound.

Damn that wrist contraption. All he had to do to throw a fire ball was squeeze a pump in his fist; the Preosian device does the rest.

"Fire back, Lana," Dimitri yelled as he shot two more red balls at her. "You can't force push your way out of this fight. Use your fire."

"That's easy for you to say."

"Try. Face me and focus."

Lana hopped to her feet. "Stop! Stop! I can't do this. I'm not ready."

There was no reply, only more red shots fired at her. One hit just below her knees, and the other rolled off her shoulder to hit the back wall. The force of the hit knocked her back, and she forced herself to put momentum into the roll until her feet were underneath her once more.

Three more shots and Lana jumped up, holding out her hand. Again, nothing happened.

"Get with it, Lana. Defend yourself! Attack me! Do something!"

"I can't! Nothing is coming. It's too soon!"

Four more shots: two hit the wall on either side of her, one just above her head, the last one hitting her directly in the chest. Lana was thrown into the wall, her head slamming hard against the stone. She gasped once as the light started to dim.

She fought to open her eyes. Dimitri was standing over her, a worried look fading as she looked up at him. He grabbed her under the arm and lifted her to her feet, shaking his head all the while. Lana looked down at herself; her dress was ripped, but the skin underneath was pink and freshly healed.

"Concentrate Lana, even when you're in pain and being shot at. Calm your center, connect with the metis. Feel that energy build in your center, breathe through it. Remember, your every anxious breath feeds it, you grow more powerful. It's all energy, you just have to tap in to it and control it."

Lana closed her eyes and tried to concentrate. She searched inside herself for the metis. Lana took a deep breath, remaining still even when she knew Dimitri had fired another shot. She stood her ground.

At first, nothing happened except for his blast continuing to hurtle right at her. Slowly, she felt the budding of power tingle down her arm. Lana grinned and lifted her hand. The shot that was aimed at her face fizzled into nothingness. She drained the energy from every volley he sent forth, just as every blast she fired was blocked by some invisible shield.

"Try and get it through my guard, Lana," he pushed.

Again, she tried to put more and more energy into her shot, only to have it fizzle uselessly. She tried to move, combing his shields for a weak spot, only to waste time and energy. Finally, she let her hand fall to her side as her headache blurred her vision. She shook her head to clear her vision, which only made tiny rainbow dots fall in front of her eyes. Slowly, she leaned against the back wall.

"When you're in battle you can't just call it quits when you get bored, Lana." Dimitri's voice was overly loud and angry as he walked towards her.

Lana smiled as her hand shot up one last time, a shot hitting him hard in the stomach. Dimitri bent over wheezing. She felt guilty for a breath, until she remembered the beating she took just moments ago. When he finally stood, instead of the anger she was expecting, a look of satisfaction lit up his face. It left Lana feeling more than slightly suspicious.

"Finally, Lana you learned the lesson. It only took hours of being hit." Dimitri grinned, almost looking proud.

"And what lesson was that?"

"Hold nothing back. If you're fighting your enemy, there is no such thing as a low blow. When you're fighting your enemy, anything goes." Standing in front of her once again, he held out his hand and helped her lean forward. "I guess we can take a break."

"Do you get a headache—"

"Yes. Whatever it is inside of us that lets us control the metis, it's like a muscle — the more you work it, the stronger it is. Eventually, your headaches will lessen. Anytime you push yourself too far, they will be there to let you know."

"So, you've built up a tolerance?"

"It took me a very long time to build it as much as I have. Still, I need this to help monitor how much metis I'm using, and it alerts me when I get too close to an overload."

Dimitri held out his wrist and Lana leaned forward to get a closer look at the gadget. Thick leather straps secured twin metal bars that bent up the front of his forearm like a cage. The curved metal protected two tiny glass vials of fluctuating blue matter. Small gears worked inside a slim glass box affixed to the inside of his wrist. Now that she saw it close up and had a chance to see how it all worked, she couldn't deny that she was intrigued.

"How long do you think?" she asked.

"Until?"

"Until I'm ready."

"We make our move soon, whether you're ready or not."

"Why? You'd think—"

"He will be on the move from the palace estates to the sacred lands where he, as King, must make pilgrimage every three years. He's nearly there now. We'll attack on his way back."

"But perhaps King Paul's pilgrimage will straighten him out."

The moon slid from behind a cloud. Lana looked up at Dimitri. His eyes caught the rays, lightening from a dark blue to an electric sapphire. He was the first to start laughing; Lana smiled, then started to giggle as well.

Dimitri snorted in a most ungentlemanly manner, shook his head, and walked off to dab his face with a towel and order his two cultists about. Meanwhile, Lana leaned against the wall, sipping her water and thinking very hard about murder. On the battlefield she understood self-defense, but to be the aggressor seemed reprehensible.

"I don't know if I can commit cold-blooded murder," Lana confessed.

"How do you feel about your parents being killed? Not a pleasant thought, right?"

Dimitri spoke so easily of her family's death that Lana almost didn't see it for what it was: a manipulation. Lana stared out the window across from her into the considerably abundant untouched forest that surrounded them; she wondered if anyone on the outside thought of her. Who was left to care if she never returned?

Lana tilted her head back and stared up at the stained, faded, and battle torn ceiling, trying to swallow any emotion that the destroyed building brought forth. She lived in a home all too similar to what the estate once was, and she couldn't help but wonder what had happened to it. In these walls she could see the past as clearly as the present.

Clean, sparkling walls, tall and proud, would stand as a testimony to the authority and glorious life of the lord of this seaside paradise. Gleaming stained glass windows arranged in a beautiful mosaic of serene, upturned faces, so that the placid villagers could hold their heads high in pride.

She could only imagine the bustling village that surrounded the castle. It would have been a place where adults worked, and children playfully ran from their nannies. A smattering of stately homes, arranged aesthetically down the well-manicured roads that led out of the city, would have paled in comparison to the floating castle overhead. The people would have felt safe, even excited for the future, and they would have been determined to make the village better for their children.

But this town, this castle, and these people were

gone forever. They were long dead. Had anyone cared about them when they were being wiped off the face of Thrae?

"Everyone has a choice, Lana." Dimitri spoke when it became clear that Lana wouldn't.

"Then shouldn't our choice perhaps be considered for a little bit longer than a couple of weeks?"

"How long? How long would you like to ponder? I've had plenty of time to consider my options." Dimitri swept his arms out in a grand gesture, his jerky movements reflecting the irritation in his eyes.

Lana supposed he had already spent his time debating the merits of murder. He had reached his conclusion and would now waste no more time in following through. She knew she had to tread carefully — he would not allow her to deviate from his path.

CHAPTER TWENTY-SIX

Ryker

Chaos. Ryker had walked into chaos. Without a doubt, he'd found a traveling tribe. Now to find out if it was the one he was looking for: the people that could help.

He looked back at the cart where Genievet lay curled under the blankets, dark circles under her closed eyes. She'd passed out two days in, though she'd walked and kept up with Ryker's brutal pace without complaint.

In a sandy clearing next to a quiet lake, children ran

around with glee. Colorful caravans spread wide in a large protection circle. Some of the carts had a stretched cloth covering to shade from the unrelenting sun.

Ryker walked beside Chet, nearly running into a man who raced from the water as if he'd spotted a snake. The strange man had a basket of wet clothes in his arms that reached his forehead. He paid Ryker no attention other than to mutter under his breath.

Others, however, weren't so oblivious. Most stopped mid-conversation to stare at him. Children huddled together in fear, looking for their guardians. With a shout, three men rounded the corner: two held weapons, the third stood behind them. He was a substantial form, a warrior cloaked in mourning.

"I'm looking for the Viridate tribe." Ryker lifted his hands as a show of peace, trying to keep everyone within sight.

"And what do you want with them?" the sharp-eyed man asked from the back.

"A mutual friend is in need."

"Well, why didn't you start with that?"

"So this is the Viridate tribe?"

"Yes. I'm Elias, the leader here. And you are?"

"Ryker. Lord Ryker Wyvier of Wynthros."

"An honor and a surprise. And our mutual friend?"

"I thought all Formless tribes had a soothsayer. Shouldn't you know?" Ryker tried to ease his glare. Even though he was here, Ryker still had his reservations about these people. After all, he didn't need Kennith, Elder Lourum, or anyone else to tell him what a long shot this was.

"I'm afraid we are a tribe in mourning. Our soothsayer has transitioned and taken our leader, her husband, with her. I've taken my place as leader, but no one has or can replace Petra."

A gentle wind curled around the men, bringing the smell of fragrant wildflowers and the sweet peel of sun-warmed berries with it. Elias tipped his head back and seemed to glory in the perfumed air. A bittersweet smile tugged at the younger man's mouth.

"I'm sorry for your loss." If they had no soothsayer, how would they find Lana? He truly hoped this trip wasn't for naught. *Maybe I should leave, they have nothing for me here.*

"Come, Lord Wyvier, the spirits welcome you. What can we do for the Third Citizen of Taraq?" Elias looked at Ryker, then nodded to a long-faced man with similar features and gave him a wordless command, gesturing towards a weary Genie and a hungry Chet. Elias beckoned Ryker towards a blue home with a green mossy roof.

Outside the open door were three chairs and a small table. Elias took the chair on the left and offered Ryker the chair on the right. Each piece seemed well-used and tenderly taken care of.

"A year or so ago, I was gifted with a message from your ancestors. The beggar — I mean, oracle spoke of a woman who would come into my life." Ryker sat down heavily in the chair, centering himself towards the man.

"Yes, she would come into your life to leave soon after." Elias nodded with a sagacity he was too young to have.

"You know of the prophecy?"

"I'm familiar with it. Get Vedoma," Elias ordered. A herd of children went running. "I also know Lana. She came to us, asking for help."

"I heard you have a way of tracking someone. I need this done, now."

"Unfortunately, m' lard, that is beyond our power."

"Because you lack a soothsayer?"

"Formless is limitless potential, but some things are just beyond our control."

"And what of the tracking devices you plant?"

"I'm sorry, what?" Elias looked genuinely perplexed. Perhaps he wasn't the one Ryker should be talking to. Either that, or he was an exceptional liar.

"A year ago, your tribe helped her. Help her now."

"I don't know what you're talking about."

"The hell ya don't." A woman rounded the bend, wavy blond burnt caramel hair wrapped in a silk scarf, hanging loosely around her shoulders. With her hand on her hip, the look she gave Elias would have boiled water.

When she turned her ethereal stare on Ryker, all he could do was watch her amber eyes shift in contemplation. Her plump lips set in a mulish glare as she inspected him, but Ryker had no clue what she needed to see.

"Vedoma," Elias glared.

"We took her in for da night. What do ya want of her?"

"She's gone missing, I'm trying to find her," Ryker explained.

"Ya da one she was goin' ta meet?" The lit *yeezba* between her lips bounced as she spoke around it.

"Yes."

The woman, Vedoma, switched her stance, her layered skirt rolling in the wind as she looked him over again. Finally, she nodded. It wasn't to Ryker. It wasn't directed at Elias either, but Elias replied with a sigh of acceptance anyway.

"I'm no Petra, but I'll scry for her."

"So, you can?" Ryker emphasized.

"I can try. We may 'ave given her somtin to protect herself while she was here."

"The pin?" Ryker had noticed Lana had always worn the silly thing. It didn't look like something her family would have given her. He wished he would have asked about it.

"Yes, a protection charm, a gift to help her practice and warn her when danger was near, or her metis was too high." Elias looked around the tribe, as if looking for a reason to escape the conversation.

"So, how do you track her?"

"We don't track, we connect."

Vedoma was already carrying a map, a chain, and three coin-sized smooth stones. She set the first two down on the table as she took a long pull from her yeezba roll-up. Then she unceremoniously dragged a chair between them and sat down.

"What Vadoma means is that she's going to try to tap in to the energy of the mark. When she does that, she'll be able to pinpoint her location on the map."

"The brand." Ryker hadn't had a lot of experience

with Formless metisians in his travels, mainly just running them off. But he'd heard they were singular in their ability to pool metis. As individuals, they were dangerous, but combined the effect was devastating. Surely Lana wouldn't have allowed them access to her in such a way.

"Lana came to us on the edge of ruin. We did what we could to bind her metis into something controllable. If we hadn't, it was unlikely she would have completed her journey," Elias offered.

"I'll do a reading, but dis will cost you," Vedoma said.

"What exactly do you want in return?"

"Oh," Elias turned his head to the side, away from him. His eyes sparkled, coming close to enthusiasm. Not a good sign in a negotiation.

Ryker came prepared to pay for the information. It would be worth it, especially if Ryker could track Lana himself. Elias' grin told him he knew damn well the cards he held, and he was willing to take a gamble to make the most of it.

"I'm sure we can work something out. After all, we want Lana returned safely," Elias nodded with a solemn sincerity that Ryker didn't trust.

The unease that had been his silent riding partner grew inside of him, and he wondered what he would have to lose to get Lana back. He didn't know if he was angry at himself for letting her go, or angry at her for pushing him away. Damn that woman. Her pride would cost him once again.

"Come." Vedoma smiled. "I'll channel 'er using our connection. It shouldn't take long."

Vedoma shifted on her stool, eyes closed, scarf and hair lifting in the wind. With her hands flat on her thighs, she started to rock, her full lips muttering prayers or a chant in an ancient language. In her hand she spun the stones round in circles, their sharp clanking and grinding turned into a smooth vibration. Soon the woman fell into a trance.

Meanwhile, Ryker sat straight and stiff, a hand at his knee and the other at his hip, near his dagger. He might have been asking for their help, but he was no fool. These people, this tribe, were treacherous; he couldn't forget his previous dealings with them because they played nice now. Ryker knew how quickly people's attitudes could change.

"There's a problem," Vedoma hesitated, pressing the stones silent in her palm.

"What?" Elias asked before Ryker could.

"I can't find her." Vedoma's voice was soft, the meaning clear.

No, impossible.

"Try again," Ryker ordered.

"M'lord." The seer was about to argue, but Ryker would throttle her if she denied him.

"Try again, Ve," Elias urged.

Looking to the right at Elias' tight brows, Ryker saw the man's agitation. Whether it was for Lana's safety or the small fortune of treasure they would miss should they give him bad news, Ryker was unsure. Still, whatever the cause, he pushed his seer to continue, which was good enough for now.

Bowing her head, she shrank, falling deeper into herself as she searched for his woman. After ten minutes she lifted her head, again in failure. Vedoma didn't need to say a word, her sad eyes spoke volumes.

"Perhaps, my lord, if you have something personal of hers. I can connect directly to her."

Damn! Out of all the things he'd brought, not one of them belonged to her. Frantically, Ryker ran through his inventory, hoping that there may be something that could be used.

"I have something." Genie pulled her fist from her cloak pocket and stretched her hand out, long before closing in on the small table. A delicate chain with a lone pearl dangled from her fingers. The girl set the bracelet down next to the seer, and it pooled in a spiral.

"Lana's mother gave it to her on her fifteenth year. She gave it to me, to keep safe should she not return. It was her dream to refill the bracelet with pearls, which she had to sell on her journeys. Is this good?"

"It has her past and future. It's perfect. I should warn you, if I can't find her, it's because she's dead."

A howl ripped through his head, and he barely bit back his denial. Lana couldn't be dead — she'd just visited him not even three days ago. He refused to believe he'd made that up.

Ryker almost called her to stop. The breath was in his lungs, the word suspended on his tongue. His hand lifted under the table, ready to stop this madness. But

Genievet's earnest look as she clutched her hands to her heart stilled him. The truth wasn't for him alone.

He tried to relax his thick fist, marbled with scars that traveled up his arms. They were the tribulations of his life, both failure and fortune. Ryker stared into the mapping of his scars. To pass the time, he tried to remember which scars came from which battles. By the time Ryker had made it to his wrist, he felt eyes on him.

Genievet startled when confronted with his direct stare. Her sky blue eyes widened and watered. Within seconds she was looking down, around, anywhere but near his head. He didn't know what Lana saw in her; enough, apparently, to give her an heirloom for safe keeping.

"I feel 'er, she's trapped. No, she's in danger — with dead all around. Fighting for 'er life she is, with smoke closing in. Soon it will be too thick to breathe. Some-where—" She paused, her head drooping a little to the side. Vedoma's hand hovered over the map, but her eyes remained closed. Her lips formed and shaped wild words, but nothing over a hissing whisper could be heard.

Ryker felt torn in two directions. He was glad she lived, but felt damned in the knowledge that she suffered. Genievet mirrored the turmoil within him.

If there was any question of the girls being bonded, Ryker had his answer. Genievet was kin to Lana. And because of that, they shared motivation. He would work beside her to reach their mutual end goal: saving Lana. But that didn't mean he would stop watching her. Far from it.

"Salty air, a giant shroud covers the land three-fold," Vedoma whispered.

"Anything more specific?" Ryker asked, deadpan.

"She's in a place touched by the shadow of the Lost Forest, but the night reveals a glowing sea."

"Before going any further, let's discuss solutions and payment," Elias inserted.

And there it was. The negotiations have begun.

"I'll give you fifteen furs, a crate of medicine, and a dozen of the finest crafted swords."

Elias would counter with the addition of an obscene amount of coin; Ryker would strike it down, and then the volley would begin.

"I accept your kindness." Elias surprised him with an easy acquiescence. "I ask for one other small thing."

Here it was. Ryker was guessing it would be somewhere between 150 silver and two gold bricks.

"I want your written consent and an immediate enactment of law that the Andoran people are allowed to own land, and to freely traverse and trade on Tarquin soil."

What? Ryker smothered his groan. *Where did that come from?* Never in his lifetime had any of the tribes settled down, so who were they helping?

"Who the hell are the Andorans?" Genievet asked. Ryker agreed with that sentiment wholly. The conviction in Elias's face fell flat, deflated by the question.

"That's the ancient name of our people, all metisian Travellers and tribes."

"I can't speak for all of Tarquin, but I have the ability to open my borders to those Andorans who wish to try for citizenship. Though I cannot, nor will I, guarantee anyone's acceptance," Ryker argued.

"What must the Andorans do to prove they are worthy of citizenship?"

"What every other deserter and alien must: accept our culture and be accepted into an established house."

"You won't ask us to change our customs?"

"As long as you follow the laws, conforming to the Tarquin standard, no."

"That's acceptable. And as agreed, Lana is here." Elias' tapered finger pointed to Parlopian Bay. "Is that specific enough?"

"She's in *Elukranos*?" Genie murmured.

"Deep in the lands of Elukranos. It's a place even we never venture; it moves and shifts endlessly. It's a very dangerous place, even without the monsters that hunt there." Elias nodded at her, looking her over. "But you must hurry. Send for Josef," Elias ordered over his shoulder.

"Monsters?" Genie asked.

"Who's Josef?" Ryker demanded.

"That's the boy Lana met when she was here. She called him a friend," Genievet explained.

Ryker pressed his lips together, irritated at how much the girl knew about Lana. They spoke of things personal and private. Things Lana had never mentioned to him. Was he so much of an asshole that Lana hadn't felt comfortable talking to him? The answer was a resounding yes.

"Josef will help guide you." Elias nodded to the younger man who walked up to the table.

"But I have to—," Josef protested.

"I can't be responsible for another kid. I need someone trained and experienced."

"Josef's no boy. He's traveled across Taraq, has had multiple encounters with the Shining Knights, and defeated the enforcer of the Ironmaw pack. He's the most experienced man I have.

"Besides, it's for Lana." Elias looked both men in the eye, which stopped their grumbling short. "This map will help you find her. You'll need it to navigate the Lost Forest." Vedoma pressed the map and a hollow coin in Josef's hand.

"Can we go back to the monsters?" Genievet questioned, her voice quivering with fear.

"Yes, there's plenty of them. The lost that die there are reborn twisted. It's a tricky forest. Careful where you bed. Hallucinatory fungus grows there thick; it's beautiful but dangerous. A plague doctor's mask should protect you," Elias advised with a low tone of caution.

"Lana waits, and she needs you; her spirit is becoming tainted. If she isn't saved in time, all our futures are lost," Elias added. He stared Josef down. Though the boy had a strong jaw set in defiance, in the end he nodded.

Ryker smothered his scoff at their dramatics. Still, he agreed that he needed to get to her quickly. The vision world she shared with him confirmed her dire situation. Even the tribe was worried for her.

"There's one more thing I need you to do," Ryker added, turning back to Elias.

"And what's that?"

"You have the authority to bind a couple in marriage, yes?"

"Our people, of course."

"And that brand makes Lana one of yours, right?"

"Lana will forever be a woman of many worlds."

"Well, I need you to marry us."

"I'll be happy to when you bring her back."

"No. Now," Ryker demanded.

"I can't do that."

Ryker dropped the bag of silver on the table between them. "I have one hundred and fifty reasons you can."

"But what if she don' want ya?" Vedoma protested.

Irrelevant. "There's only one way I can truly ensure her protection, and that's as Lady Lana Wyvier."

"No. Elias. Dis ain't right. Don' do it," Vedoma protested.

"Lord Wyvier, I don't think this is how Lana would—" Genie began.

"Enough," Ryker hissed, silencing everyone.

He didn't need more objections. He knew well how Lana would feel when she found out. She was the kind of woman who probably dreamt of her wedding her whole life. No, she wouldn't appreciate this at all. *But if it helps me get to her in time, I can make it up to her.*

"Alright," Elias nodded slowly, his eyes searching in the distance. "But you'll have to grant everyone in this tribe immediate citizenship under your name, since it carries so much weight."

A greasy feeling slid down his spine. "Deal." Out of the corner of his eye, he saw the boy, Josef, shake his head and walk off.

"Leaf by leaf and breath by breath may you grow stronger together. I, Bogdan Elias Silviu of the Virdiate tribe bless this couple in matrimony. Lana Colton, I now pronounce you Lady Lana Wyvier. And by your traditions, as I understand them, Lord Ryker Wyvier, I now pronounce you Lord Ryker Colton Wyvier. Together as one, and what not. Eh, you'll have to figure out the naming on your own." Elias ended it in a rush, obviously flustered by the unusual request. "How's that?"

Ryker responded with a nod. "It's good enough."

"I don't envy you, Wyvier. There will be hell to pay when you tell her."

"If I find her alive, I'll gladly accept it. Now tell me, Elias, how many people are in your tribe?"

"Forty-six. Why?"

"So, I have forty-six witnesses that will be willing to claim they were there for the wedding?"

"Yes, m'lard, forty-six new citizens to establish an alibi," Elias reminded.

The subtle insinuation was unnecessary; Ryker knew well what stakes were on the line. If anyone were to find out what he'd done, they were all doomed. Though he knew the marriage was hardly legally binding, something inside him settled.

They were connected. If worse came to worse, he could call on kin to fight for her. It wasn't a lot, but it was enough. In fact, it might be all he had to give.

"Take their cart," Elias spoke softly to Josef.

"But it's yours," the young man argued.

"No. It's yours. It was always meant for you. It's what they would have wanted."

The two men embraced, and Ryker once more noticed the resemblance. Side by side he realized they were brothers; the twin looks of fear clearly reflected in their eyes. Ryker didn't have time or the charity to wonder what it was that Josef left behind. He could only look forward — he was now once step closer to Lana.

"Come. If we're going to travel, we'll do so comfortably." Josef glared at Ryker as he opened the back of a brightly colored caravan cart.

With a fresh horse saddled next to Chet, Ryker, Genie, and Josef were on the road heading to the haunted hills of the Lost Forest. Towards Elukranos, the most haunted land in history. There they would travel into a land where unnatural creatures lurked in the shadows, and tortured souls lured the weary astray.

The things I do for this woman.

All on the word of a couple of vagabonds, and with only the trainee of a betrayer at his back. The things a man braved for fortune were nothing compared to the torments he'd endure for the heart. *Lana better be happy to see me.*

CHAPTER TWENTY-SEVEN

Ryker

3742.07.30

I t takes time and patience to travel long distances; Ryker knew this well from the endless military campaigns he'd organized. Even though they weren't expending much energy sitting in the back of Josef's caravan cart, a soldier's vigilance could never slip.

"Snap out of it! You're still on watch."

He nudged a dozing Genie with his foot. The pressure wasn't hard, but she snapped alert, scanning the landscape out of the window. When she finally cleared the sleep from her sight, she looked at him like he'd hit her.

"You didn't have to snap at her like that," Josef said, glaring over his shoulder.

Ryker swallowed down his irritation. *They are not my kids, they are not my men, and they are not under my control. Not even Genie, even though she did promise to make herself useful and not be a burden.* Nodding his head, he took a deep, calming breath. Then another.

"No, it's okay, Josef. He's right. I shouldn't have fallen asleep. This is important."

"Danger lay around any and every corner," Ryker reminded. "It could be a pothole that breaks a wheel, a downed tree hiding an ambush, or something as basic as traveling through the wrong creature's territory." He had seen it all and had no time to waste on any of it.

"Listen, both of you. I know you're young and inexperienced, but you should know these things." *Already.*

"We've been traveling nearly non-stop for a week now."

"Yes, exactly," Ryker agreed.

"I don't follow." Genie shook her head, but her eyes never left the window.

It takes a good leader to bring the best out of their people, but I don't have the patience for this. I can't worry about Lana if I'm worrying about them.

"It's about time something happened. Our journey has been too easy and smooth," Ryker warned.

"That's probably because you're not the one who has to ride with you," Josef grumbled. That did get Genie's attention. Her head whipped to the front, where Josef steered the horses. Her eyes were wide with disbelief, but she said nothing.

"Do you have something else you want to share, Josef?" Ryker asked.

"Yeah." Josef pulled on the reins and abruptly steered them off the road. They were halfway up the Nostrus river, but were nearly seventy spans away from the Borsmar swamplands. It was too close to the ruthless cutthroat camps that made the swamp their home to stop.

"What the hell?" Ryker faced him with a thunderous glare. "Put us back on the road and drive," he ordered.

"You have no idea what I left behind in order to help you on this farce of a mission."

"What are you talking about?"

"We've all sacrificed something to help you get Lana to safety. But this isn't just about you, and you might be someone important where you come from, but not here. Now is as good a time as any to stop. The horses and I need a break," Josef said flatly.

"Do you know what kind of men live near these parts?"

"Yes, bad people travel from all around the world to find sanctuary in the swamps. I get it, but we're not in the swamps. We'll be fine. Besides, it's my cart and my abilities that you need to find Lana. So, you guys can leave if you want, but I don't see how far you'll get without me." Josef shrugged and jumped from his seat.

Ryker had half a mind to snatch the reins and leave

that brat behind. *He better not make a habit of this.* Ryker climbed down, ready to make the most of their downtime. While he knew very well how beneficial breaks were, he'd have preferred to choose the spot with a little more care and a little less attitude.

"Genie, head west no more than thirty lengths and look for food. We have no idea how long we'll be in the Lost Forest, we might as well bump up our rations. This land is abundant with wild fbardi and gooseberries, see if you can find some.

"And Josef, well, you just do whatever you want." Ryker felt his glower pull his lips into a snarl, but he didn't care. *Kids, they think they know everything.*

"Actually, I was thinking this would be a good time to check the map again," Josef snapped.

"Good. Make yourself useful," Ryker called over his shoulder, noting the young man had already set out crystals in a circle around him and the map.

A few moments later, before Ryker had a chance to walk off his irritation, Josef called him back.

"What is it? What did you find?"

"I don't know. I found Lana, but she feels different — darker. She's drawing in too much metis. She's lighting up like a torch. I've never seen anything like it."

"What does that mean?"

"It means she's outside the Lost Forest barrier. It means something's tainting Lana, and the more she uses her metis the deeper the stain. It means we don't have much time. We have to get to her before she goes dark." Josef rubbed his arms and shivered even though it was too humid to be chilly.

"What do you mean by going dark?" Ryker thundered.

"I mean…" Josef hesitated before turning to him. "It means that soon she'll be consumed by metis. There's only so much energy a body can take before the metis takes over. If we don't get to Lana soon, there won't be enough of her to save. She has to get out of the Lost Forest. We're not going to get to her in time."

"Genie! We have to get moving. Find Genie, our little break is over."

Ryker's head swirled with thoughts of Lana. The last time he saw her, in his dreams, she'd been beat to shit and terrified. If these dreams did connect him to Lana, maybe he needed to find a way to get through to her.

Like his worry had summoned her existence, Lana blinked into being before him. Unlike before when Lana had come to him in a dream or in flashes of awareness, now he saw her standing before him, watching him watch her.

Ryker knew immediately that this was no ordinary flight of fancy. He wasn't daydreaming; Lana's form was too true-to-life, the emotion dancing behind her eyes too vivid to be imagined.

Lana watched him watching her as she approached. A curious expression spread across her pallid face, one that matched her unusual, antiquated black dress. When she stopped within arm's reach of him, once more his world fell away. Now there was only Lana and the thick mist rolling out from around her.

The look she gave him was the only warning he needed to know she was not doing well.

"No, this is my daydream. You don't get to look at me like that."

"I don't think this is a normal dream, Lana." Ryker wrenched his neck to survey the area. It was an empty space filled with mist and a soft, lavender light.

"Well, at least it's not a nightmare," Lana murmured. "Why can't I move?"

"I'm in control of this fantasy," she grinned, stepping around him, her hand trailing down the length of his back. "I've always loved how wide your shoulders are."

"Let me go, Lana."

"I don't think I want to, Ryker."

"Then come before me," Ryker demanded.

Too easily, Lana ignored him. Instead, she looked up at him with hooded eyes and a mischievous smile as she skirted around him once more.

"You know, I've been thinking about you," Lana chuckled. Her hand slid up his arm and rested on his shoulder. She gently pressed down, and Ryker sank to his knees as if he'd been kicked. "The real you," she whispered in his ear, finally stepping in front of him.

"I am the real me."

"No. You only think you are."

"What have you been thinking?" Ryker said instead. Grunting with strain, he tried to lift one leg to rise, but it took every ounce of willpower he had to elevate his foot an inch. Each movement felt like fighting against a body of sand. Slowly, she reached forward and closed the gap between them.

"I've missed this," she sighed, resting her hand on his chest. "And as much as I want to hate you, I can't help but to think of you. And I hate that even more!"

"Why?" Ryker asked, searching her face. Her brows were pinched and her eyes tightened, disgust clear for him to see.

"Because of the way you treated me. Because of your continued denial. And in spite of that, you're still another thing I want and can't have. When will I learn?" Lana lifted his chin with another gentle touch. Abruptly the touch became a hard crack against his cheek. "You have no idea how long I've wanted to do that," Lana laughed, her head tipped back in childish joy.

To Ryker, her laugh seemed a bit maniacal, confirming what Josef had said not three minutes ago. "You have me. Tell me where you are and I'll prove it to you."

Ryker struggled under her tight control. He strained against the force tilting his head back. With gritted teeth, Ryker pulled Lana to her knees in front of him. He might not be able to stand, but he would have her look in his eyes. *Maybe if she could just see it's really me.*

"We always want what we can't have, especially when it's bad for us."

"Those days are in the past. I've missed you, Vahejara."

"Ryker, I..." Lana hesitated.

"What?"

"I realized that I continue to pull you into my dream world because I need the distraction I know you can provide. And also, because I need to face some things I've been avoiding."

"And what's that?"

"Well, first, that I loved you. As stupid as it is. My time in Wynthros was the wildest and most exciting of my life. Completely maddening and awful as well, but I fell for you."

"Good. And the second?"

"That time for you—the real you, meant nothing."

"That's not true," Ryker denied with a hard shake of his head.

"You're just a figment of my dream trying to protect me from a truth I need to come to terms with. I am alone — except for him."

There was a lot to unpack in that statement, and Ryker didn't know where to start. "You're not alone. You have to trust me on that. I don't think this is a dream. In fact, I think you may have pulled me out of—"

"Enough!" Lana sat tall, commanding him with finality. "I need to say this and I don't know how much time I have so shut up so I can get this out. Maybe then I'll stop dreaming about you."

I hope not. Ryker stared into her eyes and fell silent, as was her will.

"I'm never going to be an uncomplicated ally. And as much as it hurts me to realize, I can't ask you to change, and I'll never lower my standards in a partner. I will not be one of many. I'll find someone who wants me and only me, or I'll die alone. Either way, I live by my rules. I'm no longer a damsel, I will take care of myself."

"You know why I think you dream of me?" A look flashed across her face, but Ryker didn't recognize it. She'd once told him she struggled to read him, but tonight, like this, it was she who was indecipherable.

He drew his arms around her, and instantly she relaxed. That was all he needed to know. The weight around him lifted.

Ryker forgot their tumultuous past and the way she was currently controlling him like a puppeteer. Lana needed him, and with every fiber of his control, he opened himself up to let go. Eventually, the struggle fell away. His hand slid up her spine while the other traced lower.

"I think you dream of me because to you, I represent protection and strength. You bring me to you when you need it most. Because in your hour of suffering, you know who you need, even if you can't admit it in the waking world. You may not be a damsel, but no one can survive alone."

"Maybe you're right. But I'm not alone."

"Because he's there with you. Who is 'he,' Lana? Why have you been using so much metis? Is it one of the King's men?"

"You know it's not." Lana flicked a befuddled look up at him, as she stood and turned away. Once more, a force kept him immobile, and just like that, she slid out of his arms.

"Because I'm a part of your imagination and so I would know everything that you know," Ryker said slowly, trying to keep up. "But I don't know. I don't know

who you're with or what you're doing, so doesn't that prove anything?"

"No. Your ignorance proves nothing." *Lana puzzled over him for a moment.*

She's going to wake up. I need to get through to her, but, how?

"But if I'm a part of your subconscious, maybe this is a question you need to be asking yourself."

Lana reflected on that for a second, then answered. "I'm taking back control of my life. Eventually, they will come, and we must be ready."

"Who's 'we'?"

"Why are you so curious?"

"Is 'we' you and I?"

"No, I'm training with a master. He is very knowledgeable, but also very demanding."

"What does he want?"

"He wants to use me to take back what was once lost. He's teaching me a great many things."

"Is he good to you?" Ryker asked, quietly. He looked over at her, needing to hear something positive.

"I think, he's... trying to be."

Jealousy ripped through Ryker, but he held it in tight control. Was he the one that hurt her last week? *I'll kill him. No, calm. I don't know if this training is good for her, but I know she's always feared the power inside of her. If this 'master' is helping her find confidence and control, then I must be grateful. So why do I still want to rip out his throat?

A bloodthirsty nagging inside him kept wondering about this mysterious trainer. Who was this metisian master that had taken Lana under his wing? Did he care for her, or was she just a tool, a weapon to be used at his side?

It was the same fear Lana had of Ryker the first time they met, and now he understood her reservations. What I had assumed was Einhart arrogance was really her fear of being used and taken advantage of. What else might I have missed?

Ryker stared down at her. She'd always felt small underneath him, but now with her hesitant touch and shadowed eyes she felt downright diminutive. So damn breakable it made his heart crack.

"Lana, I've been searching for you. Tell me where you are, let me bring you home." He made his demand like he always did, without thought or hesitation that someone, especially she, would disobey.

"Home? I have no plans of making Wynthros my home. I had no plans of returning," Lana scoffed.

What? "You agreed to marriage. You would have stood me up?"

"The real Ryker didn't want a marriage, he made that very clear. His proposal was purely to mitigate the damage my presence might stir. Just as my acceptance was to placate him into letting me leave so that I could find my brother. I have no plans on becoming Lady Wynthros."

I'd like to see her say that to my face. *A nagging self-recrimination jingled in his head.* Now might not be the best time to tell her about the arrangement I made with the Viridate tribe.

"Don't look at me that way," Lana said, glaring.

"It's almost like you don't realize you're a figment of my imagination. You don't get to ask such questions or give orders here. And I don't have much time. Let's not waste it talking."

With a boldness that should have surprised him, she grabbed him by the back of his head, threading her fingers through his hair, and pulled him in. His hands cupped her neck, and as much as Ryker struggled against her force, he felt her pressed into him. All he could do was clutch her in a punishing embrace.

In this dream world he had no choice, but she couldn't control him completely. Lana might have initiated the kiss, but Ryker quickly took control. His strong hands gripped and squeezed, drawing her in and lifting her to meet his demanding mouth.

As soon as he fell along into her fantasy, the layers of resistance fell away. A soft moan escaped her as his tongue and lips trailed his possession across her jaw and down her neck. Her hand lifted to his chest, a delicate pressure over his heart, while the other squeezed his shoulder, a gentle encouragement.

"Tell me how to get to you, Lana." At her pause, his touch grew lighter. Ryker's lips trailed tender kisses across her neck. His strong fingers cupped her chin and lovingly tipped her head back.

"You can't take me from death." Her answer stopped his heart, and as soon as she pulled back, she slipped through his fingers. He remained paralyzed once more. Lana glided out of his arms, sliding around him, her hand gently tracing down his cheek. She turned his head to whisper in his ear. "So don't even try."

And just like that she was gone. She'd vanished like smoke in a gust of wind. Her sad chuckle was the only thing left between both worlds; the chime of a bell caught in the howling wind. Or maybe that was his shout of denial that broke through the air; a desperate bark that sent Josef and Genie back a step.

"What was that?" Josef asked slowly, as he and Genie shared a look.

"He does that sometimes. It's like he just zones out," Genie said.

"Back up," Ryker growled. They stepped back, both watching him wearily. It took him a second to come back to his reality.

Still on his knees, Ryker fell forward until his hands fisted the rich soil. Digging into the dirt, he punched the newly upturned soil. *So close. I was so close.* Tears heated his eyes but he squeezed them tightly shut to deny them their purchase. His hair was a dark veil concealing his bittersweet thoughts.

"What happens?" Josef asked after a beat.

"She pulls me into this dream world."

"Lana can pull you while you're awake?"

"Yes. Whenever she needs."

Pain built quickly on Ryker's shoulder. He ripped his shirt over his head, and with dirty hands he traced the spot on his shoulder where Lana's hand had pressed not even ten seconds ago. A new brand formed inside the hand-shaped blister — a circle was starting to form. Ryker watched it with dawning understanding — a crescent moon pierced through the middle by what looked like an arrow.

"What is it?" Genie asked.

"It's an *Owein*, the mark of a mate and protector." Josef's hushed voice mirrored the shock within Ryker.

"But the marriage wasn't real." Genie frowned, sitting cross-legged on the ground as she stared at the brand on his chest.

"It looks like Fate decided otherwise. And that mark might be the only thing that can help pull Lana back from the brink." *It might be able to do a lot more than that.* Ryker stood and headed back to the cart, contemplating the future without realizing his finger still traced his new mark.

"It won't be that easy," Josef hollered after him.

"Why not?"

"Because I felt something else when I connected to her. Something far worse for Lana."

"What?"

"I felt the deathless energy."

Ryker's heart stopped cold. It took a moment for his head to settle before his mind could process his jumbled thoughts. Slowly, Ryker turned back to Josef, his eyes swimming with fear and sadness. Josef looked as if he thought all was lost. *No, never.*

"What does that mean Josef? She's not dead, your seer would have felt that."

"No, Ryker. She's not dead, not yet. It's worse. I feel them, the deathless. They're close to her. The Deathless Master has risen once more."

CHAPTER TWENTY-EIGHT

Lana

"It's remarkable the things you can learn about people by reading their energy." Dimitri stared with relaxed eyes at the space around Lana. He stood near the fourth bookshelf, hanging on to the ladder.

While she'd been lounging on a chaise, reading a book on dream manipulations, he'd been studying her *myit*, her personal energy field. He had been slowly circling her, examining her from different sides, and now heights.

Lana paid him no attention. Slowly she flipped to the next page, careful to remain focused on the words and aware of Dimitri's movements. *Focus. Look for anything that could explain my dream world.*

"Any metisian can be trained to see it, and everyone has their own field. Even puppets, to a certain extent, will take on traces of their master," Dimitri droned, climbing down.

"So, tell me, have you performed any intricate ceremonies involving a high priest and the well of Elumira? Joined any secret cults, or syphoned the life out of anyone?" He scrutinized her for a minute before shaking his head, pacing in front of her. Dimitri walked the length of her chaise, back and forth.

"Have you ever 'accidentally' eaten boisin berries," he started, "hallucinated for a week," he rested both hands on the arm of the chaise and leaned forward, "and awoke to find yourself at the altar of the dark master?" He stared her down, seriously gauging her reaction.

"Dimitri!" Lana snapped the book closed. Her finger held her place, and she gripped the book firmly. Sitting forward into Dimitri's space, she swung her legs down and back into her boots.

"I've never done that either, I was just checking," he amended promptly, with playfully batting eyes. She pulled on her boots and they both shared wicked grin. Lana chuckled and tried to not to imagine Dimitri waking up half-naked and delirious, curled around some bloody, gruesome altar.

"Well, one time…" Lana hesitated, debating whether she wanted to bring it up.

"What?"

"Well, when I was on my journey into Taraq, I came across a tribe of Travellers. They helped me."

"Tell me everything."

For the next ten minutes, Lana did. She explained to him how generous they were. How they invited her into their circle, how the Bogdan's wife, Petra, took her in and made her feel welcome. She explained the dance and how Bogdan Silviu narrated the ceremony for her, telling her how the Formless metisians, Andorans, rose to power and fell with equal vigor.

But when it came to the latter part of the night, Lana stalled.

"What's wrong?"

"I don't know, it's all blurry."

"What do you mean blurry? Your memory?"

"Yes."

"Did they drug you?"

"There were drugs involved."

"I'm impressed, Lana." Lana thought Dimitri's impressed smile odd, but kept it to herself. "Tell me what you remember."

"I remember Josef leading me back from the woods. It was night time by then. I was offered a rolled yeezba, there was some more dancing, then I was in the center of a circle. They were all chanting, then I felt a burn." Lana gently stroked the brand she gained that night.

"Show me."

"I can't, it's covered." Lana rolled her eyes, slowly covering the ties that held her top in place.

Dimitri stood in front of her, his hand reaching for her shoulder. Flinching back, Lana raised her hands only to have Dimitri respond with a disapproving eye roll. With both hands he pushed her neck and pulled open the neckline of her shirt. Startled, Lana slapped at him.

"I can't believe you let them brand you." Dimitri shook his head and looked away. He gave her some privacy as she opened her neckline; his heavy sigh emphasized his disappointment.

"They said it was necessary for me to use their portal. It doesn't mean anything. I'm already slated for death, what's one more allied brand?"

"You don't need a brand to travel through a portal. Anyone can do it."

"What? But they said—"

"Are you ready to show me the mark?" Dimitri inquired sternly.

"Yes." Lana pulled her head to the side, her knee bouncing as apprehension filled her.

"That's not an allied brand, Lana. That's much worse."

"What is it?"

"That's a sypherian mark — a binding sigil. It's a one-way metis transfer. It's no wonder your access is so spotty. Whoever did this gave themselves primary access to your metis."

"What are you talking about?"

"Honey, they stuck a straw in you and have been

drinking you dry all along. You were a metis taphouse, long before you met me."

Fragmented thoughts swirled and churned in her head like a typhoon. It was difficult differentiating between what she remembered happening and what her mind filled in. Between what really happened, and the story she told herself.

"I feel sick."

"Look at the brand," Dimitri urged, handing her a small mirror. "Do you see how this line connects to this spiral?"

"Yes," Lana nodded.

"It's unidirectional, which means you're giving them your metis without being able to access theirs. They stopped you from accessing your metis. It's theft. It's treachery. It's ingenious."

"So how can I use any metis at all, then?"

"Well, metis is in a constant state of regeneration. Yours especially, since loose metis almost seems drawn to you. You're probably only accessing the surface level before it gets syphoned away. It's no wonder your access has been so irregular, and why my feedings are always so hard on you."

"So that's what they did?"

"I'll have to tweak it, but I'll need to do some research first." Dimitri spun on his heel and strutted towards the bookshelves. "We're going to have to do something quick, because I can't have you at my side in battle with your arms tied behind your back."

"What?" *Do I really want to get rid of the seal?* Lana

looked after Dimitri, who had started buzzing around the area.

"I've got an idea, Lana. Finally, things are starting to progress. But we don't have much time."

With a wicked grin over his shoulder, he climbed back up the ladder like a man possessed. As he searched, a curious bounce aided his climb. Whether the lightness in him was due to the thought of freeing Lana's metis, having a stronger ally, or just having something fun to do, the small grin never left his face.

CHAPTER TWENTY-NINE

Lana

"You're going to do what?" Lana scooched back, her fingers dipping into the cool rainwater that collected in the old fountain in Dimitri's *second* ballroom. Dimitri stood in front of the destroyed southern wall. A pile of rubble was all that kept anyone from plunging off the cliff.

"I'm going to cut off a patch of your shoulder, heal you, and then I'll burn the correct sigil into the brand."

In the back corner, movement caught her attention. The room was cut in half by a golden haze, obscuring whatever shifted behind the rays of sunlight. The room's ample lighting was part of the reason Dimitri had wanted this surgery — procedure, ritual, spell, w*hatever this was* — done here.

"Wait a second," Lana raised a finger to Wyn and Gertie, who broke through the barrier of light and had already begun to start closing in on her. Wyn winced in the direct light and skirted the edge of the shadow, per usual. "Explain it to me," she demanded. It was enough to keep them from closing in, but all it would take was a look from their Dark Master.

"You feel this line?" His fingers traveled up the curving line of the sigil connecting the swirling sides. His balmy finger pad dragged along her scarred flesh. Lana nodded, and watched him study the brand. "I'm going to cut here," he tapped under her collar bone, "to here. I'll cut this little line, heal you. Then with a red-hot iron I'll redraw the lines here and here that will create balance within the sharing of metis."

"Why not just cut the whole thing out? Why not sever contact?"

"Because you'll have access to all of their metis now, too. Lana, darling, you might just become the most powerful Formless metisian alive. And you know what that would make you?"

"What?"

"A Queen, darling!" Dimitri's grin widened and he

twirled with his hands in the air. He stopped suddenly, tipping his head back and rumbling a devious chuckle. *Had this been his intention all along?*

"I don't know about this." Lana shook her head and leaned away from him.

"This is going to work," Dimitri nodded, "but I need you to promise to be in this with me, a hundred percent. There can be no hesitation," he added.

"Of course. I know you can heal me, but what I'm concerned with—"

"Because I feel you holding back, Lana," Dimitri continued, brushing her off without a look.

Oh boy.

"This is no small thing; you are going to come into a lot of power. Luckily, I'll be there with you. Besides, you should be separated from direct contact with their collective. That should keep you from getting overwhelmed," Dimitri continued.

"But this kind of power is only suitable for a Queen. You've got a gift that you've made your own, and it packs a punch, but something keeps you shackled to this mousy facade. You're too timid to make a scene or cause a ripple.

"From everything I've heard, this generation could use a good shake-up. So, before we do this, I need your oath that you will become the Queen I need you to be."

"What?" Lana blinked at him.

"A new persona. There's truly only one way to gain a title, and that's by taking it." 'Kill a king to be a king' justified a large part of Einhart history. "You'll never be able to make a difference if you don't change this image." He poked her shoulder, hard enough to push her back. "But even after you have total access to your metis, you still have much work to do."

"What else would you have me do?" Lana tilted her head to the side, giving him a look.

"You need to let go of the image you have of yourself. You are no longer the boring village farm girl. You are as you have been: a remarkably strong, intelligent woman of noble and notable birth."

He grabbed her hand and turned her to face the fountain. The mechanics of it no longer worked, but it was filled with rainwater from the damaged roof. War and nature had conquered this stronghold, but Dimitri refused to leave the grounds.

"Until you see yourself as someone who is a remarkably powerful force, you will constantly be fighting it. So, picture yourself."

"I am who I am, I don't want to change that." Lana struggled against his grip. Though he was marginally taller than her, his delicate build would give under her strength, especially as weak as he still was. His grip wasn't hard or painful, just demanding as he nudged her forward with passion.

"Quain once said, 'The only mask people care to see is the one you present.'" When he pulled her towards her reflection in the fountain, he lifted her hair. "You have an opportunity to reinvent yourself to present to the world the person you want to be. Not this obedient shell you cling to."

"Well…" Change the mask she presented to the world, re-invent the person she was to become. What were traits that she admired in others? Bold vision and quiet assertion. "What did you have in mind?"

"We need to change your look. Maybe when you look like someone who does what needs to be done, takes what they want, and doesn't stop to apologize, you'll realize that it was you all along."

"Is this another lesson?"

"Yes." He cocked his head to the side, rolling his hip. His intentionally unkempt hair wobbled. "What do you look like when you lose all fear? What does your smile feel like when you're in control? How would a woman like that react to someone targeting her and her family? Or to someone who stole her power?"

Lana's smile grew and darkened, until the end of his speech. "They didn't steal my power. It was a trade. At the time I was thankful for help. You can't understand how scared I was of it. How impossible it felt to control." Lana looked at her hands. She'd grown up fearing them. The energy felt unstable, always bubbling to the surface, easy to summon but impossible to control. And it still was, even with the seal on her metis. "Maybe I don't want it back."

"You didn't know then what you know now. We have trained your body and mind for this moment. So, don't be ridiculous. You were meant for this power. Fate sent you to me, to raise me so that I could make you a Queen." Dimitri drew himself into a rigid line, his lowered face now solemn, looking especially humbled by his new role.

"What's so important about that? I'd be a queen of nothing! The most powerful Formless metisian — so what? No one aside from the Travellers practice; I'd be the ruler of a nomadic tribe that I'm not even a real member of." Lana rolled her eyes and shook her head. *He's not going to get it, and he sure as hell won't accept it. I'm not the hero he's hoping for.*

CHAPTER THIRTY

Lana

"I've seen moligned mortals of little to no talent and of average blood achieve awesome feats. Between the two of us, we can handle a single man, even if he is a King. If you want change, you need a war, and do you know what's a sure way to lose a war? Not having an army.

"Who's going to follow Lady Lana into battle? No

one, except for maybe me. But what happens when the mysterious Elle, Queen of the Formless, Mistress of the Lost Forest commands her denizens to gather?"

"We don't have denizens — never mind. Don't act like this isn't just one small move in your grand scheme. It's still murder, Dimitri."

"It is. It's also clean, and eliminates mistakes." Impatience furrowed Dimitri's brow as he started to pace. They had been arguing in circles for hours, and it didn't seem to be going anywhere.

"Well, I'm sorry, but I just don't think a haircut and a new wardrobe will change my mind and cure me of my morality."

"I'm just suggesting you be the change you want to see! Ugh!" Dimitri slapped his thigh and turned away abruptly.

That struck Lana *hard*.

She had always turned to others to find answers. Ryker would shield her. Her brother would fight for the family name. The rebellion would eventually gain ground and safeguard the people. It was always someone else. When would she turn to herself to take responsibility?

"It's not about the wardrobe." Dimitri softened, approaching her slowly and grabbing her hands. "It's about feeling confident and powerful for yourself, so that you can *be* everything you need to be. But, to be fair, it never hurts to come dressed in a little black leather," he winked.

"Alright. Let's do it." Lana's smile wobbled.

"Removing the brand?"

"Yes," Lana reassured.

"And then?"

"Leather it is. Studded perhaps?"

"Now you're thinking," he said, chuckling.

As he pushed her onto her back, Lana pulled the strings of her shirt loose, exposing the Viridate brand. Dimitri nodded discreetly to Wyn and Gertie. Quickly, they moved to either side of Lana. Wynn took the spot on her left, angling one arm to act as a brace while the other extended for Lana to grip.

It's just a small piece of my shoulder, I'll be fine. Soon, I'll be better than fine. Soon, I'll be the next Formless Queen.

Gertie sat at Lana's feet and unwrapped a roll of fabric, revealing a thick, knotty root.

"What is that?" Lana asked. In Einhart she knew some herbalist secrets, but this far north there was hardly any foliage she recognized, and she'd never seen such a bright white root.

"It's from an epoch tree, it will help with the pain. Set it between her teeth," Dimitri ordered Gertie. "Now, before I cut — and I mean right before I cut — bite down. It's going to be bitter, but don't spit it out."

"Can't you just knock her out, Master?" Wyn asked.

"What did I tell you about talking to me?"

"I must never do it. I am a lowly worm, and lowly worms don't get the privilege of talking to you," Wyn repeated blankly.

"Exactly. I don't want to have this conversation with you again." Dimitri's voice was eerily calm.

Frowning, Lana spat out the root and sat up. "Why don't you just knock me out?"

"Because you're going to need to be awake to control the metis that might surge through you. Besides, pain builds character." Dimitri winked as he grabbed the root and shoved it in her mouth once more. "Hold tight and scream if you must, but whatever you do, remain still. Do you want to take one last look, Lana? Because after this, you'll be a Queen."

Lana took a deep breath and laid back down. It took four calming breaths around the root before she gave Dimitri a curt nod and turned her head towards the ceiling. Dimitri nodded to the women. Gertie pressed Lana's knees into the stone while Wyn flexed her fingers.

The poor girl looks as nervous as I feel. Surely it can't hurt worse than dying. But, what if I go through all this and it doesn't work? What if it does, and I can't control it?

"Now, Lana. Bite!"

Lana's teeth clenched around the hard exterior of the root. Almost immediately, the fibrous skin broke, and a bitter milky sap squirted the back of her throat. Lana nearly gagged as the liquid dripped from the roof of her mouth.

Well, that's not too bad. As soon as Lana finished her thought, two things happened: another gush of sap coated her tongue, and Dimitri made his first cut. The pain was sharp and instantaneous, and all Lana could do was hold her breath, squeeze Wyn's hand, and try to swallow the thick, bitter syrup.

"Don't let her move!"

Gertie applied more pressure to Lana's legs, but she barely felt it. Turning towards Dimitri, Lana watched him as he used a small, thin dagger to carve her up. He worked on the small area between her collar bone and breast. He held the dagger with a look of concentration tightening his eyes and lips.

"You've done this before, right?" Lana drawled around the root. *I probably should have asked that before he started.*

"This specifically? No. But I saw it done once, and I once had to cut out a fungal infection that one of my people picked up overseas. The man's skin had started to toughen like bark. This is slightly similar to that. I just have to get under it."

I never regretted asking something so much. Dimitri took his time, deepening his cuts as needed. Four incisions, and Lana felt them all through the milky haze. *This isn't so bad. It just feels like he's pinching me.*

Then, Dimitri pulled back. He let loose a long breath and repositioned the dagger. "Are you ready, Lana?" Dimitri didn't wait for her to respond. He leaned forward, bending over her once more, and with a quick swipe he held the neatly torn and bloody flesh over his head.

Oh! I felt that. Lana gasped and twisted, shoving Gertie back a step. With her mouth gaping like a fish, Lana could finally draw in air past the sting.

"Let me see," Lana gasped.

Dimitri dropped the scrap in her free hand. While she stared, bewildered at the single branded line that had imprisoned her so completely, Dimitri started weaving her skin back together.

Lana screamed and twisted, trying to shove him away. "Why does that hurt so bad?" Gertie pressed harder on Lana's legs until her bones ground against the stone beneath.

"Complete regeneration is more taxing than mending and repairing. I'll need to use your metis as well," Dimitri explained as he grabbed onto her arm. Like all the other times he had fed off her energy, Lana felt as if each cell in her body were being squeezed. Lana's scream cracked and ended in a high-pitched wail.

"Just a little more, Lana."

"What's taking so long?" Lana spat out the root and looked over at him in confusion. *A little more? They've been holding me down for at least an hour. I thought this was supposed to be quick and easy!*

Lana thrashed, and with each twist she felt the newly formed and still tender skin pulling. The discomfort of that was nothing compared to Dimitri's syphon. *No more. Please, finish this!*

"Your brand was deeper than we'd thought. I had to cut further than I'd expected. You're doing fine. Count down from ten with me. Ten. Nine."

"Eight. Seven."

Somewhere in the count, the weight on Lana's legs lifted. Lana tried to keep calm, but the best she could do was to keep her tears from falling as she stared up into the bright blue sky. *The clouds are so pretty and fluffy today.*

"Three," Dimitri reminded her.

"Two. One." Lana exhaled a staggered breath.

Inhaling once more, Lana turned back to Dimitri just in time to see him lower the red-hot iron towards her. Jerking away, Lana screamed when the sounds of her sizzling skin hissed in her ear. It took her a long handful of seconds before she realized the pain was bearable. Compared to the syphon, the prolonged searing brand was nothing. Sighing, Lana looked into the watery reflection of the fountain. Their movements rippled the rainwater, and Lana tried to get lost in those tiny waves.

"Stay with me, Lana. You're going to feel it soon. Girls, step back," Dimitri ordered. Wyn squeezed Lana's hand in two quick pumps before stepping behind Dimitri.

"I don't feel any different," Lana said.

Her voice sounded strange in her ears. *How long will that sap last?* She sat up, and looked around. Dimitri and the two women blurred into the checkered floor and ruined walls of the smaller ballroom.

Lana lifted her hand towards her wound and stroked the smooth skin. The flap of old skin, a rectangle of flesh, sat next to her, but there was no seam on her chest to show it. Only the newly raised blister, seared above her heart.

Sighing, Lana turned back to the fountain, inspecting the new mark. She bowed her head, pulling at her hair in hopelessness. *It's failed.*

The clear water rippled just as she was about to splash away her reflection. Her stomach dropped like a suspended weight. When it fell, as if shattering a glass barrier, Lana immediately felt the flood.

A hurricane washed through her. The frenzy rushed down her legs and tore up her chest, rising like fire. Bending over the edge of the fountain, Lana threw up the pearlescent sap and chunks of epoch root. The whitish liquid slowly spread towards Dimitri, who side stepped it with a curled lip of disgust.

"You're still in control over there?" he asked, stepping closer hesitantly.

Lana could only nod and clutch her stomach. An unusual gurgling churned in her midsection. *Am I going to throw up again?*

"Don't fight it, Lana. Let it surge through you," Dimitri encouraged.

"I can't. It's too much."

He crept closer until he sat next to her on the fountain edge. With a tentative touch, Dimitri tapped the back of her hand like he expected her to be on fire. He jerked back as a spark jumped between them.

"It's not. It's yours. You can handle it."

Shaking her head, Lana bent forward, groaning in pain. She felt like she'd eaten enough for an army, and all the food had stretched the lining inside of her. All it would take was a deep breath or the wrong move and she would burst.

Dimitri inched ever so slowly closer. Lana watched as he tried to cloak his uncertainty and fear with confident determination. Again he reached out, this time grabbing her hand and holding tightly. He held her hand almost as if he expected an explosion to tear them apart.

"Let it go. I'm here with you. I can syphon what you

can't contain." His words were sure, but his tightly closed eyes and stiff shoulders told a different story.

With a deep breath that sent a sharp pain down her ribs, Lana let go. Through the connecting channel, metis rushed through her. What she thought had been a swell, once released, became a surge. Like a waterfall during flood season, energy filled her. This time, it didn't hurt.

This new rush of metis filled an aching void. For as long as she'd had access to the energy inside of her, before she'd been locked away from it, she'd feared it and starved it. For what felt like the first time in her entire life, Lana took a full breath.

CHAPTER THIRTY-ONE

Lana

The next morning, Lana entered the training grounds. A score of deathless puppets turned towards her, unsheathing their weapons. Dimitri was silent as he stared her down, and Lana followed suit, turning to face him, ready for his puppets to charge. For a long moment they stared at each other in silence, his battle-ready puppets as still as statues, waiting.

"Are you ready?"

Wyn and Gertie knelt on either side of Dimitri. Both sported fresh bruises and smears of blood. When Lana stepped forward, Gertie looked up, her eyes hardening before she dropped her gaze back down to the red smears surrounding her knees.

"Yes. I'm not leaving until I get what I came for."

"And what's that?"

"Freedom. I know how to leave now, but until I can better control the metis inside of me, I'll be just as trapped out there. I have Mad King Paul and his army of zealots to face, not to mention a horde of bounty hunters that want my head. I'm as close to understanding my power as I'll ever be. I know now that I need to be here. And I can't leave until I can protect myself, or I'll never be free."

"I'm proud of you," Dimitri said with a smirk. "Most people never see past their instinctual fear."

"Well, no one is going to save me but me. I have to accept that."

"No one but me," Dimitri insisted.

"Yes, no one but you," Lana repeated expressionlessly.

"Not even your lover?"

"Who says I have a lover?" Lana asked, pulling back. Panic flashed within her. *Did he know of Ryker? Could he know about the dreams?*

"Your face. It takes on a tender look whenever you

think of him." Dimitri tilted his head to the side and looked at her with a raised brow.

"I have no lover."

"Because he betrayed you." Dimitri didn't ask. Though they'd rarely spoken of her life before waking him, and never of Ryker, the Deathless Master seemed to understand.

"Yes."

"Come, Lana. Let us talk and get acquainted, shall we?" he smiled.

Lana hesitated as Dimitri waved her forward. He held out his arm, ever the gentleman, and Lana accepted it with a newfound comfort. The Deathless Master led her to a banquet already laid upon the table in the next room.

"I should have done this earlier," Dimitri grimaced, shamefaced.

"It's beautiful. But, how? How did you get all of this?"

Dimitri only cast her a mysterious smile as he led her down the long, opulent table. Red curtains were pulled shut over the huge windows, and the entire room was lit by hundreds of candles. Light reflected off the crystal bowls, casting rainbows of color dancing across the walls, and the table, freshly polished, was now decorated with a delicate tablecloth. What was once a ruined room was now almost back to its former glory.

She'd never seen anything so hauntingly beautiful in her life. *How did he accomplish all of this?*

"I realized last night that I've worked so hard to piece myself back together because I was so afraid to show any weakness that I cut out the part that made me human. Music, art, fine dining." He wiggled his eyebrows and, in a grand motion, swept his hand over the table with a radiant smile.

"I avoided everything, even conversations about things other than metis." Dimitri sighed with sheepish eyes. "You know, I used to love going to events. I would drag either my wife or my lover to balls, operas, races, exhibits, oh!" Dimitri clapped, his eyes lighting up in a rare display of excitement. "Lana, you should have seen it. The extravagance! Women's dress trains so long they needed an entire fleet of girls to help them move. And the men, Lana." He laid a hand on his heart, then began to fan himself with a wry grin. "The men were so sharp and dapper, the absolute height of masculine magnificence."

Slowly turning to take it all in, Lana smiled up at an amused Dimitri. This time, the smile wasn't fake or forced. There was something different about him today. Her smile grew as he nodded his head and led her to her seat. With a bow, he welcomed her to dine with him.

Lana faltered. The truth was, at times he was downright cruel and terrifying. This Dimitri was almost an entirely different person. She was struck with a sudden urge to know who and what he truly was. Was he the erratic, apathetic, energy sucking Deathless Master, or was he the gentle ballroom lord?

"Can you tell me what happened to this place?"

Dimitri winced and automatically shook his head. "No, I don't want to ruin the mood."

"Please. I can't be surrounded by all this destruction

and not know." What Lana really needed to know was he the erratic, apathetic, energy sucking, Deathless Master, or was he the gentle ballroom lord?

With a flick of his wrist, Dimitri dismissed Wyn and Gertie. He sat in silence while the women scurried out of the room. For a long moment after the doors shut behind them, Dimitri sat staring through a section of the wall felled by weather and overcome by the thick vines clutching the castle.

"I was betrayed by my wife and my lover. The more powerful I became, the more they feared. The more they feared, the more they conspired, until everything I did was a grand plot against them." Dimitri's eyes shifted. Lana didn't think he saw the table setting, but rather the tangled web of his past.

"When my son started to show signs of my power, they killed him. And then they held me down and cut out my heart. Which didn't kill me," Dimitri laughed, staring into a pile of apples. He quirked a brow, and a bitter smile darkened his features. "I admit, I probably could have handled that better. But I had two choices: attempt to save my son, or get revenge."

There was a darkness in Dimitri's blue eyes. Lana saw the same storm rage in him that raged in her. Lana had thought she chose to save her brother, but looking at where she was and who she sat next to, knowing the direction this was all headed — now she had to wonder if this is what she had truly wanted all along.

Lana waited on bated breath. "What… what did you choose?" she asked, though she wasn't sure she wanted to know.

"My son, obviously. I'm not an actual monster. But I had to take him down to my altar here at Castle Elekuranos. This is where they cornered me."

"Did you save him?" she whispered, her voice hoarse.

"No, Heloise and Kinsin injected him with some kind of alchemist concoction. His body repelled my metis." Dimitri lifted his hand in the air in front of his face, as if, after hundreds of years, he still couldn't understand his failure.

"I am forever separated from him, in life and in death." His stark features were shocked as he stared into a tormented memory. He snapped out of it abruptly, taking one, then two more sips of wine.

"Three fleets. Eighteen ships in all. There were so many they were stacked four deep in our sea. Oh! And two legions of ground troops that blocked the exits. I almost forgot about those." Dimitri started laughing, his hand tousling his hair as he crossed his legs, leaning towards her.

"I'm sorry, Dimitri." Lana gently touched his arm as it rested on the edge of his knee.

"I've never told anyone this. I never had a chance to tell my side of the story."

He shook his head, and his lips thinned as he pressed them tightly together. Tears shone in his eyes, but he smiled past the swell. Lana watched the display and her heart dreaded what she knew was about to come.

"They sent two fleets to lay siege on the east end and worked their bombardments westward towards the castle. I think they wanted to cause panic and herd the villagers into one place.

"And as their cannonballs tore holes into the mountain holding up my home, they destroyed the delicate balance that kept it afloat. The more they tore into the mountain underneath, the lower my castle sank. Since they couldn't get to me, they brought me to them.

"As parts of the mountain fell, it destroyed the town below, killing innocent people. But they didn't care; they cheered. A riot of applause as each devastating chunk broke loose, destroying the people below."

How awful. Lana shifted, crossing her legs. She leaned closer in rapt attention. Dimitri remained unmoved, frozen in his memory.

"I remembered thinking once the cheering stopped that it was over, but then they continued to hammer us with more cannons, until damn near everything had been laid flat. Everything but me. Since they couldn't get to me, they made sure to leave me with nothing.

"They advanced on me. Their leader was my wife's new lover, and with him was the greatest betrayer of them all — my best friend and lifelong lover. They challenged me while my wife stole my son from me, again!"

Dimitri slapped his hand against the table. It was only then that she realized he'd been casually twirling a knife in his hand as he spoke. He noticed it too, and set the utensil down gently.

"When I faced my nemesis, my hate grew, my control swelled, and all the destruction they caused became fuel to me. I had never touched the dead before. I was a gentleman, a healer, a scholar, a sage; but in that moment, I felt all this death around me and I knew. I knew I could tap in to that, too. That it was its own kind of power. It had its own taste." Dimitri gazed into the distance, slowly swirling the wine in his glass.

Lana realized belatedly that she'd been holding her fork in midair for far too long. She didn't want to fidget, but the silence was intense between them. The heavy emotions he had stirred whirled around them like the wine he spun in his glass.

"And so, when they chained me down and cut me to pieces—" Dimitri broke off, breathing deeply through his nose. Lana watched his brows furrow as he glared, lost in the memory he desperately tried to control. She wanted to reach out and hold his hand, but they were clenched in fists.

"The fools buried me alive. Oh, I'm sure they thought I was dead. What they didn't know was that while they were cutting off my limbs, I was drawing in the death around me.

"You see, the harder their army worked at killing my people, the stronger I became. Sure, my consciousness was in and out, but something inside me kept drawing it in, until it stopped. Something kept me alive, even when all I wanted to do was die.

"At first, being buried was a blessing. They were gone, and the pain wasn't, I don't know, active? But then the throbbing began, and the weight of the dirt they had buried me under felt like a compounding injury.

"The dirt surrounded me and packed into my wounds, stinging worse than the knife they cut me with. And then, I was left there, suffocating and suffering endlessly. Alone with my rage and able to do nothing but feel the agony and plan my revenge."

Dimitri took another sip of his wine, finally looking at her. His bright stare pierced her, rendering her immobile. The pain in his blue eyes tore at her.

Just yesterday, she'd feared him. Before that, she'd hated him. Now she felt the anguish of his despair as vividly as if it were her own. Whatever revulsion she'd had for him fell away, and while she still feared his abilities, and now the direction of his motivation, at least now, she understood.

"In a time that accepted all metisians, even the deathless, I was known not for my dark arts, but for my love of the arts. I was one of the greatest philanthropists of my time. And now, all anyone remembers of me is… Well, nothing good." Dimitri flicked his eyes towards the spot where the cultists once knelt, a dark streak of disappointment shadowing his expression.

Are his admirers not living up to his expectations? "I'm sorry, Dimitri," Lana started hesitantly. "I shouldn't have acted so irrational. I knew nothing about you, so I let fear and a long history of misinformation color my opinion of you."

"I'm sure it isn't all fictitious. It's not your fault. I woke terribly angry and afraid, afraid of everything. History might have forgotten my true character, but that doesn't mean that I have to. But now, I'm afraid that I don't know who I am anymore."

"Some things you have to discover for yourself." *Like what you really want from me.*

"Agreed. I understand how it would be hard for you to be by yourself. I sometimes forget; I have dozens of people to entertain myself with. You, however, have only me, and I'm not always the best of company."

"You're doing pretty good now." Lana smiled hesitantly. *If only you were always so calm and open. Maybe then I wouldn't be second guessing your motivations.*

"So, what's your sad tale? Tell me of your tragic past. I just bared my soul, so don't disappoint," he warned without any subtlety.

Lana sat for a minute. *Why does he want to know? Does he actually care to know about me, or is this all just another lesson? Another trick.* Besides, how could she follow that?

"It's a tired tale of a metisian under the thumb of Einhart thought-police. On the run, cut off from everyone." It was only then that Lana winced at her use of 'cut off.' "I've had a bounty on my head for almost as long as I can remember."

"Einharts," Dimitri spat.

"I fled to Taraq. My father held a personal debt to the Third Citizen, Lord Wyvier. I was supposed to call it in and find relative safety outside of the Mad King's reach.

I thought I could get lost in the badlands. Surely, the Shining Knights wouldn't follow me into hostile territory."

"And so you fell in love with Lord Wyvier."

"No!" Lana immediately regretted her telling outburst. "We had an understanding, or so I thought."

"Did his rages scare you away? Did his punishments scar your body and mind?"

"What? No!"

"So, he broke your heart by taking other lovers?"

Pain bit into Lana's palm. The fork she had in her white-knuckled grip dug a painful streak into her now reddened skin. Lana flushed with mortification.

"Tarquins are notoriously anti-monogamous. I knew a Tarquin general who had fifteen wives. Now that was a party." Dimitri chuckled, making light over a wound that still cut her self-confidence beyond repair. *He didn't want me. I must accept that and stop pulling that fictitious Ryker into my dreams.*

"He mentioned something about that," Lana muttered, shaking her head. "But that wasn't why I left. I went so that I could find my brother; he's the heir to my parents' legacy. The few remaining Preosian contacts Charlie and I shared sent word to Ryker that Charlie was in trouble. He was about to jeopardize everything. But Ryker kept those letters, and news of my parents, from me."

"Probably to keep you from doing something foolish, like leaving his protection," Dimitri nodded. Lana countered his reasonable and accurate assessment with a glare.

"I don't care, he made a promise to keep me informed. I struggled and fought under the thumbs of others making decisions for me. I thought he understood. But he chose to keep me in the dark, leashed to his side."

"Oh, you poor thing. He leashed you?"

"No! Of course not."

"Oh, well, you should be careful with that term then. Leashing is considered to be an acceptable way of training your wife or breaking in your war prize — at least, it used to be. The Tarquin general I spoke of did that with his thirteenth wife. He refused to let her stray more than six lengths from him. He kept her collared like a pet. Now that I think about it, I'm pretty sure she killed him."

Lana shook her head, trying to get that image out of her head. "I just meant, I felt shackled." Lana waited for Dimitri to challenge the term. He did so with an exaggerated frown.

"Chained, bound, tied down." Dimitri shook his head at all of them. *Holy Light, how many of their 'training' methods involved bondage!*

"Never mind!" Lana flung her hands in the air and continued, ignoring the particular feeling nagging her. "I knew that if I could talk to Charlie, I could help him remember what this was all for. I just had to get to Cypt."

"Oh, Cypt, what a fantastic city. Home of the greatest mechanical marvels of the world. A city of ingenuity and freedom. Have you ever been there?"

"Once, after my family was exiled." Lana sighed, tapping her finger on her thigh under the table. "My mother's parents had a summer home in Cypt. We stayed there for a couple of days in hiding."

"Your family must be well connected to have such Preosian contacts."

"My mother was Preosian, but her family cut her off the second she married my father. They never knew we stayed there. They probably would have called the Shining Knights on us, had they known."

Lana hated her Preosian blood; she hated her connection to such an apathetic people. It had taken being surrounded by giant barbarians before she realized she had never really felt attraction to the men of Einhart, either. Compared to Ryker and the Tarquins she knew, they just seemed so frail. *Maybe I have a type: emotionally distant, sharp-tongued, wide-shouldered warriors.*

"Yes, we can be a bit snobby. But to be fair, I bet we're still the number one place to vacation."

"Actually, no. Preos has become extremely xenophobic, they've kept to themselves and rarely open their borders to tourists." *Which is why we decided to enter Preos where their border control was the weakest. Even Preosians fear this haunted land.*

"I'm sure we have our reasons."

"My parents always said Preos was nothing without their technology. That they were so afraid other countries would figure out Preosian mechanics because they were worried they would have to share intellectual property, and then might have to negotiate repair fees and lending agreements that would put Preos at a disadvantage. That they were isolating themselves so they could better control the strength of their economy."

"Your parents were very smart indeed."

"Not smart enough to outrun capture."

"They were killed?"

"They were publicly executed last year. I bet the crowd laughed and jeered for them to die. And after who knows how long they spent in the hands of King Paul."

"King Paul — of what lineage does he hail?"

"King Paul Kinson of House Enillia."

Dimitri stopped as if frozen. Slowly, he looked at Lana, studying her for any sign of deception.

"Of Enil and Illia?"

"Yes."

The drink in his hand whipped across the room, smashing against the wall. Gasping, Lana turned to him and tried not to stare. His teeth were gritted, but Lana was more focused on his puppets jerking in place.

Standing abruptly, Dimitri tilted his chin in the air and dismissed her with a flick of his wrist. Reeling like she'd been slapped, Lana stood. She left, knowing better than to argue. *See, I am learning.*

CHAPTER THIRTY-TWO

Lana

A scream woke her. Pounding and moaning echoed, and seemed to come from everywhere, all over the estate. That ghostly wailing warned her not to move, but Lana heard the pain in the cries and slid out of bed against her instincts. Maybe if she hummed loud enough, it would be enough to drown out the sound.

The puppets guarding her were slamming their heads against the walls. Wyn skidded down the hall into Lana's room and slammed the door behind her. The smaller woman looked up at Lana frantically, with wide, watery eyes.

"You can't go out there, my lady. The animated have gone mad!"

"Stay here and lock the door behind me. Don't come out until I come back."

"But—"

"Now!" Lana hissed, pulling her robe tighter to her throat.

Lana followed the sound, slowly growing accustomed to the thrashing puppets. The closer she got to the sound, the more violent the puppets' self-harm became, until their coagulated blood splattered the walls and splinters of their bones crunched underfoot.

"Dimitri?" Lana whispered. In the center of the main ballroom, in a single beam of moonlight, Dimitri lay curled tightly on his side, crying and shaking. The pile of blankets around him twisted in his hands.

"Dimitri? Are you okay? What's going on?"

"Go away!"

"Dimitri, it's okay. You're okay."

"I said go away." He turned to her, striking out his hand in her direction.

Lana didn't know what he expected to happen. All the nearby puppets were in shredded piles on the floor. Slowly she stepped forward, coming to the edge of his pillowed fortress.

"You can talk to me."

"I can't!" He wailed as he turned. Dimitri shook his head violently before pulling his face into a pile of blankets, muffling the noise of his screech.

"Yes, you can," Lana reached for his shoulders, grabbing him firmly until he turned in a snap. His eyes were sharp, and fat tears ran down his beautifully angled cheeks. Lana recoiled, but didn't break her grip. "You can, because you need to. You need to talk to somebody, and you need me just as I need you, remember?"

Silence.

It stretched between them, dark and burdened. It filled the space between the squishy sounds of residual energy coursing through the corpse puddles. It was the sound of Dimitri's puppets clinging to their suffering master, struggling towards action, though there was nothing left of their bodies to move. And still, more silence. Lana waited. She wanted to show him she wouldn't run away, but she also didn't want to push him.

"They cut me up, and they laughed," Dimitri whispered as he looked up at her, their eyes connecting in the soft moonlight. Lana swallowed hard, confronted with his raw and naked pain. Slowly, she sank to her knees, sliding on the blankets against the marble floor.

"They cut me to pieces, and they laughed about it! Heloise and Kinsin — my wife and my best friend. They laughed." Dimitri's voice shook, watery with the mucus that filled his nose.

"I'm sorry, I should never have asked earlier. I should never have brought it up." Lana pressed her eyes closed. Tears welled. She squeezed her hands into fists;

her nails biting into her palms helped push the pity back. *Get control of yourself!*

Dimitri continued rocking and sobbing into the blankets as if he hadn't heard her. He probably hadn't. He was too thoroughly consumed by the memories he'd held on to, too filled with pain and sadness.

"They laughed like it was nothing!" Again, Dimitri looked up at her. This time when she raised her hand towards his shoulder, he leaned in. It was only a slight shift, but Lana immediately closed the distance.

"They laughed like it was fun, like they were enjoying themselves. What did I do? What did I ever do to deserve that?"

Heavy tears ran down his cheeks and chin. He rocked, holding her to him, shaking in grief. Lana held him gently, stroking over the scars on his back, feeling the raised lines she now knew were the still-healing flesh where he'd been cut apart.

Confronted with such visceral evidence of cruelty, Lana pressed her cheek to the top of his head. Together they cried, and he held on to Lana for dear life. His pain and confusion tore at her heart. A new anger built inside her, dark and filled with grief, not unlike his.

"I'm so sorry you had to go through that. No one should ever."

"I hate them for that. I had hoped they burned and suffered when they died. But they didn't. They ruled and started a family together after they took mine. And I hate them for that even more."

"I can't imagine," Lana pulled back.

"And now his kin are ruling Einhart still. I want Paul

to feel the pain and torment that I've felt. I want his family to be ripped away, and I want that treacherous bitch's bloodline to end. I swear to you, Lana, I don't care what I must do. I will see this through. I will make Enil pay for what he's done, even if it's been two hundred years. Even if it takes two thousand years, it will never be too late."

Lana rested a cheek on the top of his head. She hugged him tight and sighed. She understood his fury, and prayed he never found out that she, too, was of house Enillia.

CHAPTER THIRTY-THREE

Ryker

"Stand up. No, sit down. Kiss me."

Ryker stood, then sat, jerking from one position to another against his will. His body shifted at her command. Already, Ryker was reaching forward to bring her closer for a kiss.

A look of frustration contorted her face before she turned away. Ryker sighed, trying to relax his muscles like Josef had suggested. I am in control of myself.

"Why won't this work?" Grabbing her hair by the

fistful, Lana's screech filled the void of the empty dream plane.

"It won't work, Vahejara, because as much as you want to be in control, you need what only I can give you."

"Oh yeah? And what's that?"

"Release. Let go of your grip on me. It's okay." Slowly, he felt the invisible vice clamping his body loosen. It started at his shoulders, and he used his now free hands to beckon Lana back to him. She complied begrudgingly.

By the time he could use his legs, he stood before her without the heavy press of her command. Still, his movements were leaded, as if she were unable or unwilling to let go completely.

"You know you are protected when you're with me, in my arms, or in my home."

Lana turned and snorted. Then she looked up at him with a blush.

He continued, ignoring her outburst. *"You like how I make you feel, Lana. You want the release you found with me, don't you?"*

His stare penetrated her, catching every squirm and following every shift. His calloused hand lifted, cupping her cheek. He lifted her eyes to his.

"Don't you?"

"Yes." Her voice was a hoarse whisper.

"Then let go — let me go. There are some things you just can't force, and passion is one of them. Let go, so I can touch you where and how I want to, how you want me to. Don't think anymore. Just let go, and feel."

"I... I'm scared. You both keep telling me to let go, but I don't think either of you will like it when I do."

"When you are with me, you don't have to be scared. Do you remember what I promised you the last time we saw each other?" When she nodded her head, he asked, "what did I say?"

"You said that if I can handle your control, then you could control your handling."

"That's right, Vahejara. You could never scare me away. I won't let you down again. Let go, Lana. Let go so I can give us what we both need."

Like a cool breeze hitting his body, the last vestiges of her pressure released, and he wasted no time fulfilling his oath. His hands ached for all the soft curves of her body, and he couldn't help but to grab and squeeze as he held her. Her bright eyes hadn't left his. They swam with questions and a fear that he would gladly spend a lifetime putting to rest.

"Do you remember when I caught you in the greenhouse?" Was that his voice that rumbled with a dangerous depth? Just like that, a seven-length bench, thick and sturdy, materialized behind her. "Good, Lana. Very good."

Her arms circled his neck, and the hesitant but hungry expression in her eyes nearly brought out another growl of pleasure. Sweeping her into his arms, he lifted her into a kiss. At first, he tried for a gentle graze, more restraint than hesitation. But now that the long, delicate line of her pressed against him, he didn't want to let go.

Lana's light touch wouldn't be enough this time. He

needed more. Dropping her the short distance to the bench, Ryker had the satisfaction of watching her expression transition from uncertainty to shock to anger, until she let out an exasperated chuckle. He didn't allow enough time for her irritation to settle; instead, he caught her by the thighs and pulled.

Ryker stepped between her legs, and he felt her shiver. Pressing against her lower back, he held her in place, keeping her still for his kiss. He had her. Then, her long legs lifted up the sides of his hips and wrapped around him, closing the distance between them, and he was left wondering who had whom.

His hands began palming her thighs, drawing her skirt up until it was balled in her lap. Hot skin greeted every desperate touch. She burned for him, and he for her. Ryker's fingers were drawn to her supple skin like moths to a flame. Each teasing touch slid away just before reaching her yearning desire.

Her desperation tightened her grip around him. It was the kind of grip he wanted — the pressure they both needed to find release. Even though Ryker controlled the tension between their bodies, it was still a disorienting dance on the knife's edge. He knew better than most how easily this manipulation could cut both ways.

"Ryker, please. I don't know how much more I can take."

"You'll take it all. You'll take everything I give you."

Lana's eyes widened in a snap. He knew she understood exactly what he meant. Her eyes traced the bands of muscle running down the length of his body. Biting his hand, she flashed a grin up at him, and the world narrowed down to her delicate mouth.

Whatever she saw, whatever expression his face held, she worried her lip for only a few heartbeats. Then slowly, Lana released her legs. His hands wasted no time dragging up her smooth inner thigh.

Grabbing his shoulders with a shuttered breath, Lana closed her eyes, seeming to savor the moment. She responded to every lingering touch with leg muscles that clenched, rolling her stomach into a spine-curling movement meant to direct his hand where she wanted him to go. But Ryker knew it was just as much about drawing out the expectation as it was giving her what she craved.

While still grazing and exploring her exposed body, Ryker couldn't help himself from feeding on her pouting lips. When she moaned at the contact, his will fractured.

"Take off your clothes, Lana. All of them. Now."

By the time he pulled in a breath, her dress was gone. As were his clothes.

"Lana, I said—" he grumbled.

"I know what you said. If you get to see me, I get to see you, too."

"Lana."

"My dream, my rules."

Her gaze swept past his broad shoulders and down his body, and his muscles tightened as if stroked. There was no shame or modesty in him. He'd spent most of his adulthood in the military, half-naked.

He watched her bite her lip again, wicked indecision battling on her face. It was his turn to clench, hoping for the touch he craved. Finally, Lana reached out, her soft hand sliding over him like silk on fire, and his hips bucked under her stroke.

Instead of tightening her grip and pulling him closer to her, her wrist rolled, and with firm pressure she trailed up his narrowed hips, running her fingers over his abdomen. So, she wanted to do a little teasing of her own. His hands lifted to her hair, and he fisted the strands, pulling her up until her breasts pressed against his chest. Ryker's hungry mouth devoured her. She opened herself up to his plunging tongue, and together they dueled for dominance.

His knee planted next to her and his arm wrapped around her, overwhelming her with his larger form. With determination, he pressed them skin to hot skin, and Lana needed little encouragement to wrap her legs around him again.

Rolling her hips, she instinctively slid her slickness against his pulsating shaft. His kneading hands gripped her by her plump bottom, lifting and lowering to keep the pressure heavy between them without penetration.

"Ryker, please." She whimpered against his neck as he bit a trail down her throat and shoulder.

Grabbing himself, he pulled back only enough to line up to her entrance. He glistened, weeping for her. After so much time apart, he struggled not to sink home impatiently. Once they came together and her heat surrounded him, he was whole.

Sighing, overcome by a particular feeling, Ryker held on to Lana's hips, keeping her rolling and bucking under control. It had been too long; there was too much *desire and heat, and he thought he might explode from another one of her breathless twitches.*

Soft, eager hands stroked down his sides as her back arched. With that one slight movement, his eyes rolled back. Ryker had wanted to give her time to adjust and acclimate to his size, but when her nails dug into his back and her hips twitched, he could wait no more.

Five pounding thrusts hammered her into the bench, and her nails only dug in harder. Her enthusiastic mewling urged Ryker on. With one hand wrapped around her shoulder and the other gripping her hip, he took her.

No gentle slides or soft strokes; nothing slow and easy. Ryker claimed her like a man possessed. He slammed into her like a man too long away from his woman, expressing all the fear, the anger, the struggles, and the trials that had built up and accumulated inside him. He worked out his frustrations on her equally desperate and willing body.

Neither had any idea what the other endured in their absence; they only knew they could let it go in each other's arms — so they did. Together they reached for fulfillment, a reprieve from loneliness, and the peace that came after the rush. Wrapped in his arms, she accepted his strength, thundering into her depths. And he, with her squirming, moaning, and panting against him, fell into the dark heat, letting her singe away his burdens, reborn.

Her legs gripped him, locking him in place until her rolling hips stalled and her thrashing head tipped back quietly with an open mouth gasp. She flushed with a raw, naked beauty as she peaked, and her clenching pleasure was all it took for Ryker to finish with her. Together they found release, rolling and grinding to keep the raw desire wrapped up between them.

Then, when it was over, a wave of emotion crushed Lana. He saw it fill her eyes and bend her body. She tried to turn away, but Ryker refused to let her go. She pressed her lips into a thin line, and her eyes sparked like she had a brief thought to strike him. He half expected her to make good on her impulse, but instead she leaned into his chest and hid.

He pulled Lana into him and wrapped his arms around her. What more could he do?

"It's okay." Lana managed a smile.

But it wasn't okay, and they both knew it. Resting her head on his shoulder, Lana let the tears that had weeks, if not months, to build stream down his shoulder.

"I don't know why I'm crying. Only that this feels real, and I feel alive for the first time in what seems like years. Why is it the only time we make love, it's on the eve of tragedy?"

The last time they'd come together it was the night before she rode out. After she decided she didn't want to wait around forever for him to make up his mind. Once she knew there was a good possibility that she might not survive.

"Because you're a fearless woman who refuses to — how did you put it — settle your standards." Ryker quirked a brow and shook his head.

His cheek rested on her head, and he held her as her tears fell. He didn't have an answer to her pain or fear. Not that she would listen to him anyway.

"If I don't survive this, I'm glad you were here tonight."

"You will survive your training and any other trouble that crosses your path."

"Don't. You don't know. You don't know the things I've done or the things I'll do."

"Then tell me. I might be a difficult asshole to get along with, but I'm never going to judge you. Besides, I might be able to help."

"No. The less you know the better."

"Are you doubting my ethereal existence?" Lana looked away sharply, and he had his answer. "I know who you are, Lana. You're a survivor. Strong, curious, and adaptable. You will continue to survive until we can be together again. I'll bring you home."

"No! Don't! You can't." Lana sank her nails into his arms.

"I will."

"Please, Ryker, you mustn't look for me."

"It's too late, Lana. I'm already on my way to the Lost Forest. We'll be there in less than a fortnight."

"Then you've doomed yourself to a fate worse than hell. If you come here, I won't be able to save you. I'm not even sure I would try. If you are real, please, do not come into the Lost Forest," Lana begged. "I don't need you charging in with a rescue."

Ryker held the hand that pleaded with him. "Will you respect my wishes?" she asked. Unable to answer, Ryker forced himself awake.

CHAPTER THIRTY-FOUR

Lana

"Why must we do this?" Lana sighed, with a hand on her hip.

She leaned against the megalithic stone structure and watched a puppet shove Dimitri's cultists to their knees. They'd waded into ankle-deep water at low tide to get to the massive rock Lana now leaned on. Dimitri had been insistent on two things: one, a sacrifice must be made tonight, and two, the sacrifice must be performed here, in the water.

"Because we need to be as powerful as we can be before we make our move. Besides, I need to know you can do what needs to be done. It's one thing to snuff out the life of a corpse and another to take a life. Decide now, who lives and who dies?"

Lana looked between the two pleading women, torn. Their tangled fingers and begging didn't ask her to spare them, but to *choose* them. Both wanted to be their Lord's sacrifice.

"If you don't pick, I'll just kill them both."

If Lana thought the decision would be hard, she'd overestimated herself again. "Gertie," Lana chose smoothly.

What surprised Lana was both women's reactions. Wyn looked at her with a wicked glare, unusual for the typically mild-mannered woman. Gertie grinned, her thick squared chin lifted triumphantly, finally taking her first real look at Dimitri.

"Well, that was less hassle than I expected."

"I like Wyn. Sorry." Lana shrugged to the still glowering woman.

"Alright, Gertie. You know what to do."

The older woman dropped to her knees at the base of the stone, ducking under the water and patting the ground. Meanwhile, Dimitri sent Wyn and his puppet back towards the castle with a flick of his wrist. The puppet passed a knapsack to his master before marching back to shore. Dimitri was very particular about his pets getting exposed to the elements.

Wyn, on the other hand, hesitated. The younger woman looked between Gertie and the puppet for a long moment. When she finally turned away, she had tears in her eyes and Dimitri glaring a hole in the back of her head.

Best not to keep your Deathless Master waiting.

"What's so special about this place anyway?"

"This used to be my altar. During the bombing the entire west wing collapsed. This is all that's left."

That's when she saw it. Small whimsical musical notes ran around the stone. What she'd thought was smoothness caused by the crashing waves was actually smoothed grooves that would fit a body.

"There's not much of anything left."

"That will all change once we finish our mission."

Gertie popped up, eyes red and swollen from the sea water, with a manacle in hand. It was the first time Lana had seen Gertie smile. She looked at Dimitri as if she had just provided him with the finest prize east of the Respit Ocean. *Does she not realize we're going to kill her?*

"Good, now find the other one," he ordered. Immediately, the woman swallowed another big breath and sank back underneath the waves. Lana watched her body float on the surface while she scoured the altar's perimeter. The sharp sting of the salty sea spray burned Lana's eyes and dried out her nose.

Gertie's head broke the water's surface on the other side of the stone altar. Though Lana couldn't see the woman, she heard her exaggerated gasp before she crashed into the break once more. The woman's kicking feet splashed seawater in both Lana and Dimitri's faces.

"You're torturing this poor girl."

Lana tipped her head back to avoid the briny splatter. The sun's bright rays warmed her cheeks and put her at ease despite what they were about to do. It felt like the first time she'd had the sun on her face in months. *They both wanted to die. There's nothing to feel guilty about. They knew what they were getting into. In fact, they asked for this life.*

"She's glad to do it."

"It doesn't make sense. That water has to burn her eyes."

"Oh, I'm sure it does. But she knows the pain won't last forever. Why do you think they came to me?"

"I always tried not to think about it." Lana remembered Wyn once mentioning hearing *the call*. But she had never explained what that meant.

"They're both terminally ill. This life was cut short for them, so they wanted to ensure their next life was eternal."

"Just when I thought people's stupidity couldn't reach further depths."

Dimitri whipped a glare at her just as Gertie popped up again, this time coughing and spitting up water. With another lungful of air, she sank back down. Lana gave him a pointed look, and eventually Dimitri shrugged in acceptance.

With the depressing castle behind her, Lana could almost look into the horizon and imagine she had a regular life. She tried to imagine what it would be like to live a parochial existence, maybe as a fisherman's wife living quietly inland. *Work, worship, family, not necessarily in that order. It would be beautiful and fulfilling in its own way — the perfect life filled with love and peace.*

But a normal life had never been in the cards for Lana. She'd known that ever since she was a child. And that was before she'd become the apprentice to the world's most notorious Deathless Master.

"Got it!" Gertie gasped. In her fist was another manacle; the cuff's long chain was threaded with seaweed and plankton.

"Perfect."

"It was buried, but I didn't want you—" Gertie squinted her watery eyes against the sun.

"No. No. You still don't get to talk to me." Dimitri nodded to the first manacle she'd found. "You know what to do. Show me you are worthy."

Gertie bowed her head with her arms extended and crawled to reach for the other iron shackle. The older woman stumbled on one of the slick rocks and bobbed under the surface. A sudden heat flushed Lana's cheeks as she looked away from the struggling woman. *If I can't watch her fumble in the water, how will I stomach her death?*

"Why are you so mean to them?"

"I'm not mean. I'm testing them." Dimitri stood abruptly straight; he eyed her up and down, his weight on one leg.

"You don't let them talk to you; you won't even let them look at you," Lana countered.

"I don't want to know them. They came to me to die." Gertie interrupted as she popped her head up, sputtering then splashing. Dimitri sighed, ignoring her. "So that their lives and deaths serve a purpose and have meaning."

The woman quieted down, pressing her back into what was left of the groove, both hands gripping the rust-covered cuffs.

"Everything I do, I do for a reason. Especially this." Dimitri pushed the knapsack into Lana's chest. He maintained eye contact for a few steps as he approached Gertie. The woman took a deep breath, facing the sloshing waves with a stalwart stare.

"Today, you are going to serve a purpose. My purpose. You will transcend into something bigger than yourself. Today you will become eternally connected to me. Are you ready?"

"Yes. I'm ready to be immortal."

"Then take your final breath. You may now look at me," Dimitri ceded.

Gertie's eyes swam with tears as her gaze slowly climbed up his body. She looked at him, and her eyes slowly grew wide. In a flash, Dimitri gripped Gertie by the throat.

She could have let go — the manacles didn't actually bind her. Instead she tilted her chin back and opened herself to him. Dimitri didn't squeeze; he didn't have to. Lana watched as a blue-white light poured out of her and rolled like lapping waves up his arm until they settled in, seeping into his pores.

Is this what it looked like when he took from me? It

was so painful, like he was trying to squeeze my bones dry. How can she look so joyous?

"Do you want to join in?" Dimitri asked. His breathless sigh and fluttering eyes told Lana all she needed to know. The power that he drained from her was euphoric. A part of her wanted to try. She wanted to taste the power that made his sickly pallor turn into a healthy flush.

"Um, no. I'd better not."

The Deathless Master didn't ask Lana again; he only stepped closer to Gertie and leaned forward. His nose dragged across her wet face, tracing the curve of the woman's cheek. *Is he going to kiss her? Should I turn away?*

"I serve you in death," Gertie gasped against Dimitri's lips. There was nothing passionate about their kiss. In fact, the Deathless Master's lips never touched the woman's, but he consumed her nonetheless.

Lana wobbled on the sharp rocks. Staying steady in the low tide had been manageable, but now the waves crashed into her legs higher and higher as the tide came in. Each wave dragged a little stronger, making her fight harder while he finished his meal.

"The tide's about to take over, Dimitri. Bring her into your service now. We must go."

"Bring her into my service? Why would I do that?"

"Isn't that what you planned on doing?"

"Of course not!" Dimitri laughed, sidestepping Gertie's floating body.

"You lied to her!"

"I told her that her death would serve me. It has. Where's the lie?"

"You know what she thought," Lana scolded.

"Her assumption isn't my concern." Dimitri lifted his shoulder in a casual shrug.

"Why did you kill her?"

"For the energy, of course."

"Well, what do you plan on doing with her then?" Lana asked with an incredulous shake of her head.

"Something even better. Her death will serve a greater purpose. Hand me my bell," Dimitri ordered, extending his arm towards her.

"Excuse me?"

"The bell and the horn in the bag." Dimitri snapped his fingers at her. Lana reached inside the bag at a snail's pace. *I'll swim back to shore, I don't care. Snapping your fingers at me like that. Humph.*

"Kriton!" Dimitri shouted out into the sea. He pulled out a bell and whipped the handle back and forth a dozen or so times before stopping. "I know you hear me. I'm back, old friend, and I give you a gift. Bless us on our journey. I will take back what was mine, and soon the bay will be filled again."

"What's a Kriton?" Lana asked.

"He's my oldest friend, a Parlopean whale I rescued as a child."

"A whale?"

"Don't scoff; he's among the most intelligent and compassionate creatures I've ever met. To see him has always brought me good fortune," Dimitri muttered as he scanned the waters, looking for his friend.

Then, he pulled out a simple but well-crafted horn and started an irritating twiddle of high-pitched notes. Lana shook her head in exhaustion and waded back to the castle. *He doesn't believe in religion, but he has faith in a fish. We're in trouble.*

CHAPTER THIRTY-FIVE

Lana

The ruby and gold dress Lana wore clung to her curves; its long, ruffle train belied the predator in silk. Lana looked around the room, concealed by the delicately carved bone mask Dimitri had insisted they each wear, as she watched for any signs of the King.

Reports from Dimitri's cultist contacts said the Mad

King was scheduled to make an appearance at this masquerade to console the noblemen. No doubt by making promises he couldn't keep. Not that it mattered — after tonight, one of them would be dead. And then, it would finally be over.

I didn't travel through another one of those damnable portals just to walk around a ballroom with a crowd of overdressed cowards. Who would have guessed Dimitri had a working portal, maybe the last remaining intact portal in Thrae, in his backyard. *The entire time I was looking to escape, dreaming of freedom, it was just a brief walk along the shore. He sure knows how to keep a secret.*

"This is a bust, he's not going to show," Dimitri pouted sourly.

"Keep to the plan," she muttered under her breath. He turned to her with a fake placating smile as he patted her hand. The thin, gold inlay of his mask caught the light. Even with his mask, Lana could see his impatience grow the longer he remained away from his infernal castle. It was the only place he felt safe. But Lana knew there was no such thing as safety, only varying shades of undisturbed.

She placed her hand on top of his, smiling up at him coyly. If they were to play a besotted couple, he was going to have to stop watching every man with a fine form. Lana patted his hand and gave him a pointed, blank smile. He chuckled.

"This is too much. I can't handle this. We have to go," he muttered, through gritted teeth.

"Not yet. Just wait."

"I don't have much more 'wait' in me."

"I've noticed you don't get out much. Since I've been with you, you've left your castle...never," she joked, nodding benignly to a younger woman walking towards them. The young woman's hair was set in soft curls, expertly layered to frame her cheeks, complete with a pretty little lavender bow. Her date looked down at her adoringly. His hair was salted at the temples and his stride was strong and experienced as he guided his companion past.

"It's hard to get out when you have children in the street who know more than your pupil."

"Well, not everyone has had centuries to accrue knowledge." Lana smiled up at him in pretend adoration.

In truth, even after reconnecting her access to her metis, she still struggled with her inability to fully utilize her spirit. She'd spent so many years denying herself and ignoring the swell, she was worried it may have permanently handicapped her. It was like trying to use an arm after it had completely atrophied.

The graceful swirl of people who all seemed to look down their noses at her only highlighted her insecurities. It felt like a lifetime ago that she had to worry about people noticing her unusual features. She was too tall and too bulky for this elite crowd. Lana had almost forgotten the scorn of her early years.

Dimitri had focused on cultivating her control, and Ryker had made her feel perfectly beautiful, and all other opinions had faded. But now, the fear and unease resurfaced. Lana wanted to reach within and touch the metis building inside of her chest next to her anxiety, almost as if she needed to remind herself of her power. But she didn't dare. Anyone sensitive would feel the swell and alert the guards. It wasn't worth it; not for a brief relief from these pretentious fakers.

Lana wondered how many of them had called her father friend as they helped to dismantle his influence. Would anyone recognize her, even with her mask? She'd been told she was the spitting image of her mother, if not a bit stockier.

"High Priest to your right." Dimitri called attention to the older man in formal attire gracelessly snoozing against a pillar. Dimitri pulled her closer to him to avoid another couple as she looked over the priest. *He has just as many stray hairs on his head as he does on his chin.* Dimitri nodded to the other man and continued leading Lana around the room.

It was an Einhart custom to have multiple lines walking clockwise and counter-clockwise in a loose pattern around the dance floor. The older generation said it was to aid digestion, but Lana knew it was just another way to see and be seen. It also served as a prelude to the dancing, where people who wanted to participate in the more active aspects of the ball would be able to reserve partners throughout the night.

Lana shook her head and bowed to a gentleman to her right. She dipped low enough that the man's focus would be on her décolletage and not her anxiously shifting partner.

"If worse comes to worse, I'll run a distraction and you hit him."

"Just wait," Lana cautioned. His obsessive determination to destroy the King and all who helped him would get them both killed. She figured that living for centuries would have taught him some patience.

"It's almost midnight." He scanned the crowd, his finger tapping against the back of her hand. The gilded pillars reflected the swirling, colorful dresses dancing about. Silkscreen wall art stitched with meticulous detail stretched across almost thirty lengths of the wall. People were strolling by in a leisurely, connected way that allowed for brief conversation.

The couple in front of them — a gentleman and his date, dressed in the yellow and gray color block standard of Preosian formal attire — nestled close, talking quietly to an older gentleman in a stiff suit jacket.

"Oh look, that's Captain Armaar," the woman walking behind Lana loudly whispered to her partner.

"Who's that?"

"Him, right there, in the green tunic. He's a retired death squad member. I heard he's personally responsible for the deaths of over a hundred metisians."

Lana looked the man over. He laughed and smiled amicably, but it never reached his eyes. His spotty hand lifted to cover his cough with his handkerchief, and Lana saw his hand tremble.

"I don't know how you can tell who anyone is with these damnable masks on."

"He's been wearing the same outfit for the last thirty years. Oh! And look who he's talking to!" The woman's enthusiasm lifted her voice.

"Shush, woman! They'll hear you."

Too late. Though the trio never turned, all three of

them stiffened at once. The look passed between them was a casual warning; whatever they spoke about, they didn't want to risk anyone overhearing.

"It's Mr. Birial, the headmaster of Demiskus Academy, I wonder how they know each other."

"If we hit the priest now it will cripple the whole," Dimitri muttered, unaware of the drama unfolding around them.

Sighing, Lana turned back to the old man. He had his mask pulled down to block out the light as he gracelessly snored just inside the ballroom. The High Priest looked as old as Dimitri and twice as senile.

Dimitri was growing impatient. He had been ever since he started mentoring Lana nearly seven weeks ago, but now it was as if the threads of control were starting to split apart. His revenge was all that was keeping him together.

"If we attack half-cocked we lose all advantage," Lana whispered. "We wait."

"No. We go for it."

"Then your—" Lana was cut off by a commotion from the entrance to the ballroom.

"Announcing your most beloved leader of Einhart, the great King Paul Enillia."

The King stepped through the double doors, accompanied by a young woman. The couple stood proud in cream and pastels. The King's date was dressed in layers of cream silk topped with floral-embroidered taffeta. A dreamy smile was fixed on her face as she draped over his arm.

He was taller and stronger than Lana had imagined.

The King, the only one without a mask, looked young for his age. He had a clean-shaven face, a masculine jaw, and an easy smile. His blue eyes shone crystal clear as he scanned the crowd.

Lana panicked, afraid now that the moment was upon them. He descended into the crowd, which parted before him. He passed Lana with a curious look. When their eyes connected Lana swore she saw recognition in them.

Impossible. There's no way he could recognize me through my mask. Right?

She half expected him to call for the guards and have them dragged out of the building. Instead, he dipped his head in a generous bow. His companion's dreamy smile never wavered. A glittering, multicolored gemstone stood stark against the clustering of smaller settings on her pale fingers.

"She's so high she doesn't even know where she is," Dimitri muttered.

Lana's eye was drawn to that delicate, limp hand, cradled firmly in the King's manicured grip. "That's probably why they drugged her up." The King was a known womanizer — only the tales of his madness and murders spread faster than those of his sexual exploits. It was a running joke among the press and was considered an acceptable pastime. *Better than murderous rages, I suppose.*

"Do we attack now?" Lana asked.

"No. Now that he's here, we wait for his guard to relax. Maybe we'll be lucky and be able to get in close."

The King made his way through the corkscrew rows

towards the art screens that were the room's focal point. To celebrate their honored guest, their gracious hosts had a three-sided painting on display one of Quain's better known pieces of an Enillian noble making the first pilgrimage that King Paul was currently on.

Lana and Dimitri had seen it three times already. Each time they circled the works of art, four seats remained empty. Now she knew why. They were reserved for the King and his favored guest.

"Excuse me." An average looking man cleared his throat behind her. Lana turned, Dimitri angling with her so they both faced the royal courier.

"Yes?"

Drawing up every ounce of willpower she had, she focused on containing her building spirit. It felt like she breathed with half a lung, but she felt the extra sense close. Lana had gotten so used to accessing that part of herself that when it was gone, the room quieted, dimmed, lost a certain richness.

"I asked around, and no one seemed to remember your name," the attendant inquired with a raised brow.

"Oh, how dreadful. I must not be leaving much of an impression."

"I assure you, that is not the case. You've certainly made quite the impression on our King. He's asked for your attendance."

"How lovely," Dimitri said with a chuckle.

"I'm so sorry, sir, but not you."

"Ah, yes. How fortunate for me," Lana lied. "I believe it's time for you to mingle." Lana nodded to Dimitri and took the man's waiting arm.

A flash of comprehension struck his face when he looked back at her, but almost immediately it was gone. He led her like a lamb to slaughter. How many countless girls before her had followed him just as she did, walking docilely to their early grave? *But I am no lamb, and there will be no more slaughtering for you, dear King,* Lana vowed silently.

"I still need your name, to announce you."

"Ah, of course." Lana's mind raced, quickly reviewing the fake backstory that Dimitri had crafted for them. "You may introduce me as Lady Elle, Mistress of the Lost Forest."

His eyes flicked to hers twice, looking her over thoroughly. With a single raised brow, he stood to attention before the King.

"My Liege, Lady Elle, Mistress of the Lost Forest."

"Thank you, Torrin. You may leave." With a final bow, Torrin dismissed himself seamlessly. "The Lost Forest, how about that?"

"Does that surprise you, my lord?"

"It does, but I love a good surprise. So, tell me, are you a good surprise?"

"As much to you as you are to me, I'm sure." Lana smiled sweetly and looked up at him, meeting his suspicious stare directly.

"Oh dear. Well, if you aren't just magnificent." King Paul circled Lana. He was only marginally taller than her, but with his shoulder pads and tassels he commanded space. When he stopped his inspection he stood in front of her, blue eye to blue eye.

"You flatter me, my King."

When Lana stared into those rich orbs, it was difficult to believe he was responsible for thousands of
deaths, and even more abductions. He didn't look like
the deranged King everyone claimed him to be. *No, he
looks like a second son, destined to reign only in cata-
strophe.* Which is exactly how he won the throne.

"The Lost Forest — what stories must you have to
tell."

"I love stories!" The King's companion jerked
forward abruptly.

"As do I," Lana agreed belatedly.

"Please," the King ordered, "allow me to introduce
you to my partner for the evening — Lady Theresta of
the Ba'hirvian Plains."

"Lady Theresta, it's a pleasure to make your
acquaintance."

"Oh, hmm…" the beautiful young woman trailed off
and pulled her hands to her chest, a faraway look filling
her empty stare. *Okay.*

"Don't mind her, she's not very talkative today. Sit."

Hesitantly, Lana sat across from the King and adja-
cent to his date. *Just relax. Is my smile tight? Should I
smile brighter?* Lady Theresta now had a generous smile
for everyone who passed through her fixed stare. The
promenade continued, though the King's guards kept
everyone at a distance.

"There's something familiar about you," The King
said, inspecting Lana with a shrewd smile.

"Excuse me?" Lana's tongue went dry, and she used her
glass to conceal her mouth. Lana's heart pounded. Here she

was sitting across from a King with sweat beading down her spine. A dark instinct pushed her to strike now, before she lost her opening. *Just wait. It's one thing to kill the King. It is another entirely to get away with it. I have to be patient.*

"I must say, you're absolutely magnetic. I never imagined being attracted to your power."

"I beg your pardon?" Lana froze. *I'd heard about the King's exploits, but has he no shame?*

"What? Do I surprise you?" King Paul leaned back, kicking an ankle over his knee. His light hair shone like spun silver and gold in the light, and his glittering eyes never left her. She had only his persistent inspection and the almost amused smirk to gauge him.

"You could say that."

"Good. So, why are you here?" he asked, leaning forward. He rested an elbow on his knee and regarded her with his complete attention.

"I came to see you." She smiled coyly. Her eyes kept catching on Theresta's hand, brushing thoughtlessly back and forth on the chair's velvet arm.

"And what do you want of your King?"

"Perhaps I want nothing from you."

He gave her a raised brow and a laugh. "Alright, perhaps it is just I who wants something from you."

Here it comes. "And what's that, my King?"

"A dance."

The King held out his hand, his gaze so focused on her Lana was transfixed in his stare. She didn't need to look around; she knew the guards surrounded her, waiting for anything remotely suspicious. Lana lifted her hand and gently rested it in his. Locked in his stare she waited again, preparing for the worst.

His grip was tight as he led her away from the chairs and the painting. As soon as they touched it had felt like water rushing up and down her arm. She knew immediately that this was a mistake. The Traveller charm vibrated its alarm inside her wallet.

"Tell me, Lady Elle, how long have you been a practicing metisian?"

She felt him push his myit into hers. It was a spiritual invasion that revolted her. The heavy swarm of his energy field pressed against her, but she refused to shy away. Without flinching, Lana did what she did best — she swallowed the energy. If he wanted to play, she was all in.

"You surprise me again, my King."

There was no way to deny the power that flowed between them like a battery. There was an eerie exchange of energy, and the understanding behind that truth was too much for her to contemplate. *How could he be a metisian?*

"And you surprise me as well. To think how long I've been searching for you. And here you are, an uninvited and unknown party crasher. Finally, I've found someone who might actually be able to take it all."

There was a directness, a greediness, in his stare that made her core cold. He wanted her for something far more damaging than sex. The King held her in a tight, unrelenting grip.

"I don't know what you're talking about, my King." Lana tried to discreetly pull out of his grasp, but his hands gripped her like a vise, pulling her along in their dance with long, sweeping steps.

With a menacing grin, he leaned in to whisper in her ear. "I think you might be the one." Before she could react, King Paul spun her, then tugged her into him with a snap. He pulled her into his chest against typical dance protocol.

"The one for what?" Lana asked, trying to get her feet underneath her to counter the imbalance his position created. He held her so close, so tight, there was no space to move to the steps. Instead, he practically dragged her, spinning her around the room like a doll.

Lana could only hope that Dimitri had been doing his part while she played distraction. If things were going to plan, Dimitri and his followers were sowing the seeds of chaos. All Lana had to do was sit pretty and wait. *I certainly have the King's attention, but what am I going to do with it?* That was something that she and Dimitri had never discussed.

"You're the one I've been waiting for. You might just be the one that can save our country. I only hope I can salvage your wit, too. I can see your mother's influence. It'd be a shame to ruin you when I break you in."

Lana jerked, startled by his admittance. *So he did recognize me. But how?*

"Like you did her?" Lana nodded towards Lady Theresta.

His fingers ground into the bones of her wrist, but he never missed a step. Lana snarled up at him as he pushed and pulled her in the dance, still stuck in his clutches. He gazed down at her with eyes that didn't truly see her; he saw only the dream he imagined her to be.

"Yes. You're going to serve your King and your country well."

I bet he says that to all the girls. A shout behind them jerked the King's attention. Then a chorus of ladies screamed as the first man dropped dead. *Finally. That's my cue.* The first guard scrambled to come to his King's side.

"No, my King." Lana gritted her teeth against his painful grip. "I think not."

Lana threw her weight down and rolled with her momentum, just like Genie taught her before she left Ryker's estate. Instead of King Paul's grip detaching in the spill and Lana tumbling to her feet as planned, the King fell with her and they both became tangled in the excess fabric of Lana's dress.

Paul grasped wildly at Lana's arms as Lana crawled away from his assault. Another bloodcurdling scream reverberated through the ballroom. Dimitri's inside man, a flat-browed clergyman, flailed into the crowd with his poisoned needle.

Several guards tackled him, bringing him to his knees. On his last dying breath, he shouted his family name, calling Dimitri his Eternal King. Then another choked cough and a hard drop. Another scream, alerting another death.

The statuesque soldier moved towards the King, his red cape flapping behind him. His heavy boots stomped noisily on the marble floor as he rushed in a sure-footed march through the sweeping crowd. He had intelligence in his eyes, though his crescent face didn't spare anyone a look, let alone a pardon.

Even the extravagantly dressed men and women bore the full brunt of the mans curt dismissal. For the kings head of guard treated them all the same. If they stood between him and his king they were a problem.

"Yes, you'll do well."

King Paul's heavy form blanketed her, pinning her arms over her head. His mouth slammed down on hers as she struggled underneath him. An unfamiliar drop hit her stomach, like a plug being pulled.

Visions flashed in her eyes, too many, too fast, too jumbled to recognize. They pooled into her mind, filling her head with screams of fear and pain until the scent of charred wood and burnt hair filled her nose. Lana jerked, too caught up in the throes of a vision to decide whether the screams were real or in her head. The only thing that felt tangible was the King's body pressed down on hers, his knee jammed between her legs, pinching the skin on her thigh.

It was that pain, that discomfort that was all hers, that helped pull her out. When he pulled back, her eyes began to clear. She could only cringe at the way he smirked down at her, like he'd seen her at her most compromised and couldn't wait to use it against her. Those ice chip eyes swept over her face and upper body. Lana's wrists ached in his crushing grip as she fought with all her strength to keep him off of her.

"Who would have thought Fate would be so cruel as to bind us together. But now that I know you exist, I won't let you get away," he whispered in her ear. "You and I can change the world."

"Oh, I plan on it. Now, get off of me!" Lana twisted and used her mind's eye to push him off of her. The King rolled, pushed back into his companion's legs nearly ten lengths away.

A guard dragged Lana to her feet, his metal-strapped arm locking around her throat. He swung to the left, yanking her with him. Lana wiggled her fingers inside the straps of the armor, slowly gaining leverage.

"Don't kill her!" The King shouted, struggling to his feet.

It felt as if time stood still. Even as more knights and guards rushed towards her, Lana couldn't move. *Alright, you want to keep me close? Then feel my burn.* Rage-fueled heat melted her gloves. Molten silk dripped down her fingers, burning itself out before it hit the floor. Lana raised her hands and grabbed the guard's arm.

His barking shout abruptly cut off as he jerked away, his arm a mutilated peg at his side. His long face paled as he grasped his mangled arm. "Come on, my King. Why don't you try to take me now?" She crooked her finger at him as she snarled.

An incendiary blast shot from her outstretched hand just as another guard caught her wrist, jerking her arm away from the King. It was the only thing that saved the wicked monarch from his just reward. Sparks sizzled and smoke bloomed as the shot set a nearby tapestry afire. And that's when the real chaos started.

CHAPTER THIRTY-SIX

Lana

People were screaming. They ran like rats, desperate to escape Lana's heated blasts. Each shot spread like claws ripping through the frantic crowd. A manic fervor arced within her like electricity, and as her eyes connected with Paul's, Lana knew the King felt it too.

In the background Dimitri was shouting her name

over the scrambling nobles massing against the doors and beating at the walls, lost to hysteria. But Lana couldn't tear her attention from the King's drugged date. Her delicate hands were wrapped around the leg of a table.

It had taken the world slowing down for Lana to realize what had been bothering her about Lady Theresta. The King's companion was wearing her mother's heritage ring. The ring her mother, Anabell, had given to Charlie before he went off to Demaskus. Which meant, the King had found her brother — Charlie was dead, or worse.

Lana tipped her head back and wailed. It wasn't a warrior's bellow, but the grief-laden scream of a woman who had just lost the last of her family. It was the shout of a woman with nothing left to lose.

The room tipped. Lana didn't know how everyone didn't slide into a pile. She stepped next to the King's dull-witted date. No doubt had she been sober, Theresta would have fled into the 'protection' of the crowd, but now she had only Lana's heated hands.

"You don't think Lady Theresta will be a valuable hostage, do you? I won't negotiate with terrorists," King Paul said, shrugging.

"That's one thing we can agree on. There will be no negotiations." Lana glared down at the woman. "Nice ring. Give it to me," she demanded.

Theresta's hands shook and she wobbled as people rushed around them. Her trembling fingers clutched the ring, offering it up to her. Lana snatched it away. Deep inside of her, in a place dark and hidden, she knew her humanity was fading, fast.

Stinging hands barely controlled the heat that danced, desperate to break free. Even after all of her training, the only way Lana could ensure control was to focus on single bursts of compressed air, which lit into small explosions. But now, with the thought of the last of her family gone, Lana was closer to unloading everything and letting loose a geyser of fire and fury upon the bloated leeches. Her struggle was never in starting the fire — it was in controlling it.

I could stop now and maybe save myself. The errant thought invaded, trying to coax her into submission. Floating through the air, a pretty lavender bow burned swiftly at her feet. Instead of releasing the spark and letting it wreck the room as it played, Lana swallowed it.

Lana watched the Preosian woman from before, her eyes wide with terror. She scanned the room but registered nothing. For a brief, frozen moment, Lana thought she looked like a painting; something named 'Portrait of a Desperate Woman'. The pause lasted only as long as it took for a younger man to strike out his leg, kicking an older woman into her husband. The elderly pair fell, and no one stopped.

There was a quiet roar as ladies' dresses rustled, and more high-pitched screams added to the noisy bouquet of pandemonium. The bedlam echoed in the once pristine hall as those dressed in silk and gold choked on smoke and the smell of burning flesh. The scent triggered a long-hated memory — Lana pushed that down too.

She had wanted to remember to make sure the bounty hunter's death wasn't in vain. At the time, Lana hadn't wanted to become a monster. Now she didn't see any other way.

"Get out of here. Run, Lady Theresta." Lana grabbed the woman by the hair and shoved her towards the King. She bounced off the wall of soldiers, scrambling, frantically pleading with them to let her in as they bumped and pushed her away. Lana kept her eyes locked on Paul. From the corner of her eye she could see the woman stumbling away, fading into the madness of the crowd.

Dimitri gained control of the bodies as they dropped, whether from the poison or the fire. He raised them to serve, and the well-dressed puppets fought the guards that were starting to spread into the hall, taking the brunt of the armed force's attention.

It's up to me now.

The guards rushed to stand shoulder to shoulder, blocking her path to the King. Their ruby and gray tunics still crisp and clean as they raised their swords, waiting for her to attack. Lana lifted her attention from the swords towards the blue-eyed King, who stepped forward, blocked by the armored shoulders, and stared into her soul.

She felt energy flex between them. It was a whisper of intrinsic knowledge — he knew her, and in return, she knew him. They were different sides of the same coin.

"Die now, witch, because later won't be a slow death. I promise I'll make sure you suffer," the red-cloaked guard spat. He held his sword in the only hand he had left with a wild glint in his eye.

"I said, don't kill her!" Paul shouted. Lana didn't think the command registered with the guard. His eyes targeted her every movement, focused on revenge.

Lana lifted her left hand and swiped up, using the air around the first guard to knock him into the first row of men. They collided like lighting and slammed down into a heap on the marble floor. Their swords crashed onto the floor, sliding a few feet away.

Some knights looked around nervously. Others shifted, uncertain on their feet. *Not too sure of yourself now, are you?*

Guards from the back rushed forward, pushing the King back. A smaller group formed a tight shield wall around him. Lana lifted her hand, ready to build the metis into something bigger, something more dangerous and impossible for her to control, when a distant disturbance dimmed her focus.

A rhythmic crunching noise echoed. Dimitri's warning cry came a bit too late, but it allowed Lana to pinpoint what was charging at her: a massive mechanical man.

The figure rushed through the smoke. It was eight, if not nine, lengths high with shoulders made of multiple alloys as wide as a horse is long. Metal gears squeaked as the hiss of a suspension system wafted the scent of icy iron and grease towards her. Angled steel and glass launched at her, its arms outstretched in a tackle.

Lana's head cracked against the stone, bouncing back up and into the metal chest plate. The armor's weight was probably closer to a horse than man, and it slammed her down just as determinedly as she had just done to the guards. Uncompromising metal edges dug into her body, pushing her into the unyielding marble floor. Something would have to give, and she'd put money on it being her ribs.

"Don't kill her. I want her alive!" King Paul yelled, reaching over the armored guards shepherding him away.

"No!"

With her hands pinned, Lana used her mind's eye and channeled her rage. Heat built, cooking the man in metal with her devastating fury. Lana didn't have much time left; her lungs hurt and her head swam. When her spirit finally fell spent, she looked into the eyes of the man inside the suit. He grinned, untouched by the heat, his armor burning red, but undamaged.

Two of Dimitri's men charged, their ashy skin burning from the prolonged contact with the red-hot metal. Lana mustered a forced gale of wind, and that, timed with the puppets bull rush, was enough to knock the mechanical man off her. She skittered to her feet, breathing deep into her now bruised lungs.

Through the wall of soldiers retreating, Lana caught sight of the King. He'd been attacked and nearly killed, but he was grinning. The people who served with and for him were scattered, injured, or dead and he was high off his victory.

The muffled sound of a hysterical scream broke from behind her, but her focus was now on the massive metal beast ahead. It struggled to climb back to its feet, lacking mobility. Lana slung shot after shot at the man, one after another. *Psst. Psst. Psst. Pap. Pap. Crack.* The explosions sizzled through the air, all connecting with the soldier, but his damned armor ate the hits. The man continued to struggle to his feet.

Frustration, fear, and a bit of bruised ego built a fever pitch inside of her. Before now, she had always held something back. Not this time. It was this metallic beast that stood between her and the monster who killed her family. *He will pay!*

A hand on her upper arm yanked. Lana, who was already off balance, spun around, her hand glowing with heat. Dimitri's soft and now soot-smeared face slowly came into focus. Lana's energy and control fluctuated, rebounding inside of her. It overwhelmed every nerve until it diminished down to a spark that struggled for a moment before it winked out.

Looking around the room blankly, sounds started to filter in disjointedly. The thunder in the background and the sharp sounds of metal on metal coming towards them barely registered. Dimitri pulled on her arm, but she still couldn't discern his words, only the frantic tenor of his voice.

Blood and grime pooled on the once pristine marble, spreading towards the center. Lana thought for a second that once it collected she would be able to step into the pool and would be transported to a place of wild magic, a place of madness. *Aren't I there already?*

The remaining puppets formed a wall, absorbing the hacking hits as the guards tried to get to them. Her stomach pitched and rolled, but she didn't have time to be sick; Dimitri would leave her behind like all his other puppets. She jogged outside towards the horses they kept stashed away. Dimitri climbed on his mount and took off without a backwards glance at her. *We failed. We actually failed.*

With her head pounding deep between her ears, she struggled to summon the metis once more. The best she could do was lift the air to form a low barrier that the guards following on horseback stumbled over. The terrified shrieks of horses cut through the air as they pitched forward, falling on top of one another before slowly climbing back up.

The two of them rode swiftly and frantically. Lana pressed her hand to her heated head, wishing she was wrapped in thick arms, roped with muscle and filled with strength. In the haze Lana was trapped in she could only guess whether the flashing eyes penetrating into hers were Ryker's, or just her wishful thoughts.

CHAPTER THIRTY-SEVEN

Lana

A black velvet and purple silk cape billowed behind Dimitri as he stormed through his castle and into the main dance hall that they had made their headquarters. Time charts and spell scrolls were spread out on the table, with little game pieces set upon the map. So much time and effort had gone into planning the perfect hit — in and out with the most destruction possible. They had been so close.

"What was that thing?"

"I can't believe you lost him!" Dimitri spun towards her, his blue eyes glowing with frustration. The puppets' heads lifted, eyes jumping from Dimitri to Lana.

"You were supposed to keep them off my back!" Lana's lip curled as she faced him. Was it finally going to happen? She had always had the feeling that they would end in a fight. Power demanded dominance, and that couldn't happen with peace.

If they fought now, Lana knew she would lose; the hit she took still left her dizzy and disoriented. But she would burn the rest of this infernal estate down to ashes with her. She would overload herself. She vowed it. And if there was anything left of her after that, she still had her vial.

"They wouldn't fall." Dimitri's anger evaporated as he puzzled the curiosity. "Those behemoth machines were impenetrable." He paced away, and the light dimmed out of the puppets until they were mere statues. "No doubt Preosian inventions."

"They may have been impenetrable, but they weren't perfect. They lack serious mobility. Once they're knocked down, they can't get back up." Lana rung her shaking hands in her skirt.

When Dimitri surprised her with the dress, she'd felt beautiful and deadly. She'd felt like a queen. Now it was burnt, ripped, soiled, and painted with her blood. *Thus ends the brief reign of Lana, Queen of Nothing and No one.*

"We failed, and now there will be no peace." Lana looked at the delicate ring that still rested in her palm. The stones were different, but the engraving was as she remembered: 'To tomorrow — together, always.' Lana's heart clenched and her body tightened around it. *They're all dead. That bastard killed them all!* Her eyes heated, but not in tears.

"It was definitely Preosian technology, but how? They've come a remarkably long way from what I remember."

"It ate up my fire as if I were slinging mud balls." Lana's heart pounded hard and steady in her chest, and she couldn't shake the feeling that there were only bad things ahead. They had grievously miscalculated their enemy. Tales of his madness and political turmoil seemed greatly exaggerated when compared to the intelligence in his eyes and his obvious secret alliance with Preos.

"Einharts and Preosians have held alliances for as long as I've been around. I shouldn't have been surprised they would loan their technology to the King."

"Preosians have advanced water filtration, mechanical lifts, and autonomous clocks. They make impressive ships, but there has never even been a rumor of something as advanced as that armor."

"It was a well-kept secret, Lana. They were better equipped than we had assumed, and that's it. Get over it," he snapped.

Get over it? That's your advice? Lana glared at him, but instead of saying anything she walked away, trying to release her pent-up adrenaline. There was no arguing with Dimitri, and at this point she didn't see it being worth the effort.

They had lost both the element of surprise and their anonymity. King Paul knew who she was, she saw it in his eyes. The recognition when their energy last brushed against one other was undeniable. She was somehow connected to the man who killed her parents. The hypocrite who condemned all others to death for what he lived freely.

"He's metisian."

"He's more than that. He's a Watcher."

That term itched in the back of her head — she'd seen that word somewhere around here. She rummaged through the sheets, books, and scrolls until she had the thick volume of Sir Jorson Edgall the third, a Preosian explorer, in her hands. The dried leather felt brittle in her hands and she opened the dusty tome cautiously.

"Don't bother searching for the term."

"I know I've read it."

"You've heard it, because it's a tale as old as time. Probably one myth that has endured until even this century. The Watcher and the Warrior, The Seer and the Scribe — they're all the same. In every hour of great need, the Fates provide the gift of True Sight. To maintain the balance of power, Fate provides a warrior to either work with the prophet or against them. If this legend is true, and he is who I think he is, then we're in big trouble."

"Who are the Watchers?"

"It's a curse bestowed upon no particular bloodline, but it was never meant to mix with nobility. The last time I lived, favor from the Watcher and the Warrior were closely guarded and highly sought. Why?"

"I've seen the future. It's saved my life."

"You should have told me sooner."

"I didn't think it was relevant," she hedged.

"Believe it or not, this is good news."

By the malicious grin stretching across his jaw, Dimitri saw hope. His pacing began soon after; in silence he turned, and with stiff posture he mapped the floor. It was a quick jaunt — only three and a half laps around the expansive ballroom before he beelined back to her.

"There is only one Watcher, but in my time he had a harem of seers who scried the future for him. Together they were the Watcher's eyes and ears; they shared a special connection. He would send them as messengers, spies, and gifts," he said.

"Is that the reason I've had such vivid dreams?"

"What do you mean by vivid dreams?"

Lana hesitated. "Sometimes it seems like I'm sharing a dream with Ryker."

"Are you sure it's not an actual dream?" Dimitri said.

"No. I mean…" Lana sighed. "I wasn't until the last time."

"What happened last time?"

"He said some funny things, and then he left first." Lana shifted uncomfortably.

"Why didn't you tell me this?"

Lana froze mid itch. *He has no idea what kind of dreams those were!* "Why didn't I confide in you about my erotic dreams?" Lana restated his question for him.

"Yes! Exactly."

"That's uncalled for." Lana drew up, her chin lowered, taking his measure.

"Oh! Here comes the Einhart prudery. Sound the bells, something titillating is about to occur! Kindle the fire, we'll burn her in the back." Dimitri rolled his eyes and huffed.

"I'm not a prude!"

"Did you really think that I couldn't have helped you?"

"I didn't want to admit it was more than a dream."

"It is, Lana. It's much more than me living vicariously through your sex dreams. Why did you not tell me?"

"You can't have a life in the present if you're living in the past, right?" Lana extended her arm to the surrounding puppets. One puppet hauling rubble was so old he had a sapling growing out of him.

"Spare me the lecture."

"I'm just saying. I've noticed you've created more servants."

"I need them to rebuild my castle," Dimitri quickly responded.

"Why? You can't stay here forever. We need to move on."

"I cannot let go of what happened to me. I will not let what that family did to mine go unpunished! I will have my revenge."

"Can't you take your revenge elsewhere? They'll be coming for us."

"Let them try."

"This castle has already lost one battle, why put it through another?"

"I'm not ready! Can't you see that? Leaving for the attack was terrible. Worse than I thought it would be. I felt so exposed and vulnerable."

Dimitri moved once more with purpose, his stride long and smooth.

"Now, if the King is the Watcher and he has no one to help maintain the burden of his sight, that is undoubtedly what turned the man mad."

Was that what Paul had meant when he said he wanted to pour into her? That he wanted to purge himself of his visions? Is that the real reason he keeps those women so close and so drugged up? So that he can ensure clarity?

"As a Watcher, he is a guardian of truth. It actually makes sense that your world has been so thoroughly laid low. The sentry meant to protect our people is the cause of its destruction. He's used his gifts to stomp us out. This new world, this time — it's so filled with perversion it's almost too much to stomach."

Twisting her mother's ring on her finger, Lana tried to quiet her thoughts and steady her control. One truth stood out above all the rest — they needed to leave, and Dimitri wasn't ready to abandon this estate.

CHAPTER THIRTY-EIGHT

Lana

"I am alone, as I've always been," Dimitri said to himself, looking down at the map now in pieces.

"You know Dimitri, when you say things like that I don't really feel appreciated." Lana looked at him sideways, trying to bully a smile from him as he often did to her.

Fragments of crystal, glass, and porcelain launched

through the air, causing the light to flash rainbow. The beautiful moment lasted for a long, breathless pause, suspended in time. Then the spell broke, and the sharp remnants pelted down around her, settling in her hair, dusting her shoulders, and leaving the faint residue of minerals on the back of her tongue. Lana shook out her short, loose hair, ridding herself of a few of the smaller pieces.

Turning back around, Lana saw Dimitri with his fist still raised, his palm now cut and bleeding. His normally fair face was red and blotchy with rage. Lana tried to judge his mood on a scale from a typical temper tantrum to one of his less frequent full-on rages.

For a moment, satisfaction lit his eyes and his body lifted with pride. Then, as usual with his temper tantrums, regret soon followed. His chest deflated, his eyes narrowing as he realized the damage he had created with his lack of control.

Tilting her head to inspect the damage, Lana picked up a large chunk of blue and white porcelain she had once admired. It had been a bowl that once reminded her of a happy, uncomplicated time in her childhood. Now the fragment would be quietly swept up and thrown away, just like all the other victims of Dimitri's turbulent anger.

"This is why we can't go out in public," Lana sassed with a smirk. She knew the danger she invited as she taunted him, but she did so at her own risk, all but daring another burst of anger. She had a still-tender cheek from a disagreement they'd had last night over dinner.

"Damn you, Lana," he sighed, waving a dismissive

hand. Even the lift of his arm and flip of his wrist was lazy and distracted. "How am I supposed to react? The King has sent his army. My protections won't save us from that."

She stood next to him, looking over his shoulder as he often, and annoyingly, did to her. He was staring at the map that she had studied furiously before their failed attack. The map was just a reminder of their epic failure.

"They'll bring their cannons again," he muttered.

Lana burned the map with a flick of her hand, ignoring Dimitri as he cursed and sulked away. She had really thought that they could sneak into the party and, in the chaos, the King would be cut off from reinforcements. What a fool she was.

Lana stared blankly as the fire burnt itself out. She didn't have to turn to know that one of Dimitri's puppets was pulling his mattress into the streak of sunlight. The slack look on his face was almost exactly what she imagined he looked like after he had dug himself up from nearly twelve feet of dirt and roots. Failure had caused him to regress, somehow.

It was only a matter of time before the King's men found them. How could they not with the Watcher leading them. This estate was hardly defensible, as the cannon holes could attest. They needed to gather their information on metis and hide it. With how little knowledge was left in the world, it couldn't be left behind to be destroyed. It had to survive.

They would have to move. But, even on his best of days, Dimitri was a hermit. He was already starting to curl up into a ball; soon he would cry, and by the end of the night he would most likely be in a rage. This time, she wouldn't be around for it.

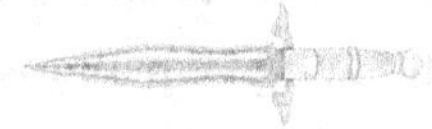

If she pushed her horse, they'd reach the nearest Shining Knights camp before midnight. The air just in front of her was dense and fuzzy, like charged velvet. The loose metis in the air beckoned her. It was a refreshing stroke that cleared her lungs and freed her mind. *I need this.*

Danger invigorated her. While Dimitri moped in his hovel surrounded by mindless servants she broke past his barriers and sought out her own justice. King Paul had sent troops, bounty hunters, and foreign agents after them. They were coming for her and they wouldn't hold back.

They were getting closer, converging now that they knew where to send their troops. According to Dimitri's spies, a small cell of infantry was making their way up from the southwest. Several smaller bands of Knights were spotted from Preosian outposts in the North heading right towards them.

She would go southwest. Like a swarm of locusts, the Knights surrounded a town with their aggression mounting, no doubt on the orders of the King. Small groups of Knights shook up sleepy villages, and they always left after sharing the name of who was to blame. Lana's name was smeared with blood and hate, but she'd be damned if she led a silent campaign.

Pushing forward, Lana used her abilities to subtly propel her. Whispers of sound drew her concentration. As she listened for the distant sounds of male comradery, memories of Orla and her group almost made her falter.

What ever happened to them? Did they ever make it out of that town alive? Nostalgia faded quickly when movement about fifty paces to her right rustled leaves.

She sank down, and though she still scanned around her, Lana was seeing her environment deeper than her eyes could ever penetrate. One straggler about twenty paces from his group — deep in his cups, judging by his fluctuating energy and staggered step — made his way towards a cluster of low, leaning trees.

Lana couldn't have asked for a better entrance than that. Changing her direction in the tall grass to cut him off, Lana kept low, trying to compress her own energy field in case any of them were sensitive. Any shift could alert them to an attack.

Creeping forward, Lana stepped up behind him as he shook his leg. He should have heard her approach; the thorns that clung to her cloak pulled and noisily shifted leaves along the forest floor. How had she been so naive as to think the noises of moving foliage were merely the wind?

Lana tried to control her field through her racing heart and spiking adrenaline, but as she approached the man, he tensed. She knew she had to attack now, as quickly and quietly as she could so he wouldn't alert his group. Her first step was a powerful lunge that broke the man's stillness. He spun, starting to pull out his long sword.

Shockingly cold hands squeezed his thick, chubby face, quickly heating to an inferno. Lana controlled the burn, letting the man drop after his face started to swell. Lana left the man alive, but he was as good as dead — as was his group. She smiled, turning towards the dense yellow and orange bobbing energy.

Then she felt their energy shift to high alert. Songs turned to shouting orders, and their energy turned from joyful comradery to that of a disturbed hive. The smile dropped off her face — in her excitement, she hadn't been compressing. *Should I turn back?*

The men spread out looking for her. They moved silently, probably trying to catch her unaware. After all, it was dark out, they knew the terrain, and they had the high ground with the advantage of numbers.

Lana made her move, sending a streak of air between two searching Knights headed towards her. They both gave chase, closely followed by the rest of the group.

While the men charged heedlessly towards her, Lana, with her traps set long before dusk, laid in wait. When they came upon her they found that their long swords couldn't penetrate her shield wall, and the more they tried, the faster their armor melted against them.

A man gasped, eyes wide in bewilderment, locked with Lana's. The showy but cheap metal boiled into his chest, and Lana knelt down and provided him a kindness in the dark. When she set herself forward, her feet never brushed the gold dew-dipped leaves. She continued, unaware of the dark roots firmly taking hold.

CHAPTER THIRTY-NINE

Lana

It was getting worse. Temper tantrums, full-body heaving, and desperate pleas, all gaining in frequency and momentum. She felt as if she were dealing with a toddler. Lana didn't think she could stand any more of Dimitri's antics.

She understood why he was having such a hard time acclimating to this new time, but when he had asked her to shoot upon a crowd of people she had to darken a part of herself. It was that quiet, cold part that just couldn't connect to his pain; she no longer empathized with his trauma. She didn't see anything relatable anymore.

Dealing with him was starting to consume too much time. They would soon have an entire army looking for them. Would the troops actually enter this accursed land? Lana bit her bloodied lip. Damned Dimitri! She needed him to pull himself out of his hysteria so she could talk this out.

How deeply entrenched is Einhart with Preos? Would there be more of that damned power armor? Were they such close allies that the Control Panel would allow King Paul, the Mad King, to lead an army through Preosian waters?

Preos had always been regarded as the golden standard. They were academics who ran their government like a business, affording an evenly-burdened working class with a say in their rights and treatment. Though they didn't allow many to see the mechanisms behind their power structure and command, the entire country was thought of as nonaggressive and diplomatic — not a threat.

Apparently the Preosian Control Panel had been playing everyone, and Lana's surprise attack had forced them to show their hand. Dimitri's' cultist spies whispered about the rapid spread of Einhart's spin. According to reports, King Paul was attacked by a band of fire insurgents, only to be saved by an advanced Preosian elite force.

She was surprised that news of a Deathless Master

hadn't surfaced. The official word was that the attacker was killed, but the Crown was still looking for those suspected of aiding the terrorists. Everyone was to be on high alert.

Shaking her head, Lana paced the halls. She pulled her shawl tight to protect against the wind that blew in through the gaping holes. If the home was a mirror to a family's health, Dimitri had much neglect to work on.

Like her father used to say, "Work always needs to be done, because it's never finished." Dimitri's work was just beginning. He had to work from the inside out, and it was something he needed to do alone.

That seemed to be the decision she needed to make. A worn and dirty green hallway runner led her forward, where both of their separate paths began. As she followed the sounds of ear-piercing screams and cries brimming with fear and self-loathing, Lana rolled her eyes. She inhaled slowly and exhaled a long, suffering sigh. As she made her way towards the great hall, she heard the deep pounding.

Lana started to jog, worried he was hurting himself in his grief. Shouldering into the side doors, she came to a stop when she saw him. He'd pulled his mattress to the middle of the marble floor, into the biggest patch of sunlight.

It was there in the center of the huge, empty room that Dimitri, clothed only in his leather pants from three nights ago, lay curled in a tight ball, sobbing into his sheets. Lana looked at him, lost in his own pain, then at his puppets, which stood around the room banging their heads against the walls mindlessly.

"I'm leaving, Dimitri. It's time."

Her words, which could have easily been consumed by his wails, seemed to jolt him out of his hysterics. His puppets stopped and, in an eerie move, all turned to look at her. He was in a fit one minute and fully aware the next. It made her wonder if he was just being overdramatic and trying to manipulate her.

"No! You can't go. I can't do this without you. You owe me!" he sputtered. His pale chest was pinkened by his fit, slim and smooth, completely bare of hair and free of either fat or muscle.

"Dee. I'm not giving up, but you can't move forward until you deal with it."

"Deal with what?"

"Your past."

"I said no. I just need some help."

"This is help. At least, it's the best I've got."

His largest puppet walked towards her, stiff legs making his march choppy and slow. After Lana's glare at Dimitri, three other puppets in the room started to move in on her. His tricks didn't scare her, and his power didn't impress her; she knew how fragile his situation was.

"Don't try to stop me Dimitri," she warned.

"You can't leave."

"It's only a matter of time before they find us. We need to go."

"Absolutely not. This is the site where thousands of people died, I'm strongest here."

"You're living on a pile of rotted bones. That's not going to do much against the Preosian soldiers."

"Enough, enough, enough!" His shout echoed loudly for a long moment in the empty room. When the sound cleared he held up his hand, silencing her next words. "I don't want to think about that," he burst. Then with shivering control, he took a deep breath and turned to her, quietly this time. In almost a whisper, Dimitri said, "I can't take this right now. Stay, we'll talk later."

"No, Dimitri." Lana was surprised with how easy it was to deny him. She must be running out of fear, or naivety, or perhaps she was just finally ready. There was no more hesitation in her; no concern of sparing feelings or sparing lives. She was being pursued by a great force, but that didn't mean she had to run away. There was no more wait left in her. A lifetime of passive resistance had done nothing for her.

"News has come that the King has mobilized his eastern contingency and they will pass the Devil's Split in three days' time. It's time."

"Yes Lana, we failed. Rub it in."

"We did fail, miserably. Why we thought we could plan an attack when neither one of us had any knowledge of battle strategy, I don't know. It was a mistake. We both wanted revenge and we jumped at the first opportunity. It was a bad idea, but I'm not done. Are you?"

"I'm not done. I won't be done until that bastard is dead."

It was then that she understood Ryker's words. When he had told her that her parents had been killed, he asked her not to make any vows in haste. 'The vows we make to ourselves can be the most destructive.'

Lana saw the damage revenge could create. Her ballroom lord could go from teasing smiles to a feral animal, injured and backed into a corner, at the smallest of sounds or changes. Lana refused to become like that.

"You survived out of reflex, Dimitri. Now you need to learn how to live. Work through this, and when you're right and ready, you'll know where to find me."

"No!" Narrow shoulders rolled forward and lean back muscles stretched as Dimitri shouted as loud as he could. Pallid puppets ran towards her, no signs of stiff joints as the closest and biggest puppet rushed her.

Everything about this room, from the cannon hole so big sunlight filled the room to the stinking corpses that fought for their hopeless master, made her blood boil with injustice. It wasn't in her nature to abandon a friend, but there was nothing left for either of them here, and she was the only one who could see it.

"I need you. You're all I have. I'm all you have!" His hand slapped at her arm in a desperate flash of panic.

"Maybe you're right, but I won't be enough to help anybody, including myself, if I stay here. There's nothing here but dust and bones. This isn't life, and you're not living. Not really."

"But I can't do this without you."

"You couldn't do it with me either, so let's face it, we failed. *Miserably.*"

"So, you're just going to leave? Just like that?" Dimitri's lips curled as his eyes raked over her. That was all the expression she could read on his face, but his tell was, as always, the puppets that surrounded him. They started to sway and shuffle. Restless ambulation fell over them so that he could maintain control.

"I won't let you."

"Like you wouldn't let me leave any of the other times?"

"This is different. I thought we were friends. I should have known."

The steel in her spine softened at the vulnerability in his voice, but Lana's resolve remained.

"I am your friend, Dimitri. But you have to realize this lifestyle you have is not healthy. It's not sustainable."

"Don't do this. Not yet." His lined hand reached up to stroke the scar on his neck, but the guilt was no longer hers to bear. She hadn't been the one to cut him into pieces, but she had been the one to put him together again.

"You siphoned plenty off of me, your body has healed enough. I won't stay here any longer."

"You bitch! I hate you!" His screech split the air as he fisted his hair and spun away.

"Ryker's close, I feel it," Lana continued, undeterred. "He won't understand. He will try to kill you."

"So you just go running to him? Tell me, are you worried for him, or scared of me?"

"Can't a girl worry for both of you?" Lana wanted to keep her tone lighthearted, but she didn't have an ounce of playful left in her. A bone-deep apathy had attached itself to her, and only the last threads of pity kept her from snapping at the man.

"You'll never have a happily ever after with him. You'll never have a family; your body has suffered too much trauma for that."

There was a long stretch where neither of them spoke. Lana's head spun, and she needed desperately to stay focused. Only the shambling puppets kept the silence at bay. As always, with their movements came the yeasty funk of shallow burial grounds — sugar and sweaty cheese mixed with dirt and stale blood.

Lana's nose no longer crinkled at the offensive smell. She didn't want there to come a time when her stomach didn't turn at the scent, or worse, she didn't notice the sweet stink of rotting meat. Every day here she got closer to accepting that rancid malodor.

"I don't want to be alone." His whisper was more for himself than for her, but Lana responded anyway.

"Then come with me." Lana knew his answer before she made the suggestion. What she didn't expect was his reaction. Dimitri's pale cheeks swallowed any remaining color, highlighting the dark, grayish scars lining his neck and body in thick but shallow grooves.

"You know I can't leave this land. It's the only place I'm truly safe. Do you want me dead for good? You do, don't you!"

Abruptly, his puppets turned towards her, knees bent, about to charge.

"Don't, Dimitri."

"If you want to kill me, why don't you just try it already?"

"I don't want you dead. I want you to live."

"I don't need you or your pity. I'm better off with my puppets anyway. They won't betray me." They attacked in tandem and with an aggression never displayed before in training.

"You're a fool, Dimitri. Do you know that?"

"Yes, I'm foolish for thinking a formless rat could ever be trusted! You're just like the rest of them."

Power swamped her veins and combined with a flood of adrenaline, an instinctual reaction he'd ingrained in her through hours and days of torturous training. With no circle of protection there was nothing to shield either one of them. Indecision held the burst of metis inside her, swelling uncomfortably underneath her skin.

Her hesitation lasted only a moment, just long enough for his puppets to snap their teeth and take a couple of steps, cutting the distance between them in half. Heat built quickly inside her, sweat beading on the back of her neck, but she didn't shy away from it. Not anymore. That was another of Dimitri's lessons.

Lifting her hands, Lana prayed she hadn't built up too much metis since her last battle. Despite what Dimitri wanted to believe, she didn't want to hurt him. With what little control she had, she focused on the attacking puppets.

They came at her with the ferocity of an injured animal. The lumpy yellow and red mottled skinned creatures were spared no restraint. Lana wanted to burn the endless stain of rot off the face of Thrae. Without a doubt, she hated these corpses.

At first she attacked to defend herself, but as soon

as their flesh peeled, euphoria followed the flames. Lana pushed her flames further, letting them dance from one puppet to the next. Her hellish heat surrounded the room, taking even the puppets he'd held back.

The flames would have consumed the room if the hall hadn't been devoid of burnable objects. As it was, Dimitri's shouts were swallowed by the crackling rush of fire. The orange flames darkened until they turned blue, and she tingled with warmth for the first time in a long time.

Slowly, Lana turned towards Dimitri, heat sizzling her hands. She had to move slowly, always careful to keep the fire — already hard to handle — under control. Her mentor rocked on his knees, holding himself as his favorite, most complete puppets turned an ashy white, then crumbled.

Dead bodies burned well, especially against her blue flame. He should have known.

"Do you want to continue?" Lana didn't feel anger, or fear — not even irritation. She was as deadened as the piles of ash surrounding her.

"No, no more."

"I can burn through your army of corpses and really leave you with nothing," she warned, lifting her hand once more. It was an empty threat; Lana didn't have it in her.

"No. No, just go." Holding himself tightly, he shook his head, turning away from her. It didn't keep her from seeing the tears glistening on his cheeks. Lana wanted to want to feel sorry for him; she wanted to be the kind of woman who sank to her knees and gave him comfort. But those days were gone.

And so, with a new line of puppets following her out, Lana left. She stepped out of a place of fear and pain and into something much worse — into the terrifying unknown. And this time, she was truly alone.

CHAPTER FORTY

Terra

J ust another day, and one more bounty. No big deal. No matter how much Terra tried to talk herself up, fear still coated her palms and weighed down her feet. If not for the steady, oblivious march of Mour, the seven-fingered thief, she would have stopped to hyperventilate by now. As it was, her bounty's constant movement kept them moving past the ancient sea stacks crowning the distant shoreline.

Mour, the friendly rogue, continued, unaware of her dread. Was it dread? Or, was it a fear remembered? Fleshy palms and foreheads, slick and shiny with sweat and disease. Terra shivered at the memory, covering it up with an exaggerated roll of her shoulders.

Still, the memory of the last bounty she had tried to collect played as nightmares in her sleep. The Shining Knights had not only denied her bounty, but had tried to keep her at their base. Their greasy smiles and nasty insinuations had sent every internal alarm screaming. If it hadn't been for Josef, if they hadn't been able to work together, neither one of them would have left that place.

But Lord Wyvier's down payment was long gone, and Terra needed the money. So she had found Mour, her first real bounty, in a small and well-hidden cabin about ten spans to the east of the town of Charmain. She and the thief had walked against the river for nearly half a day, her anxiety increasing with each step.

They were a quarter-span away from the smarmy lechers who had pulled, pressed, and pushed at her. She likely wouldn't encounter the same group; rationally, Terra knew that. After all, she was in another country. Still, hesitation weighed her down.

Their jovial faces and empty eyes had imprinted on her mind. *No. No, no, no.* Terra pleaded with herself to think of anything else, anything that wouldn't lead her back there. That memory and the emotions attached to it needed to stay locked away and swallowed down.

And then there it was — the sweet image of Josef.

Wild, curling hair caught and lifted in the air — motionless. He'd been there and they had saved each other. He helped her save herself. Josef wouldn't be there this time.

This time, it would be different. She'd changed. Now she knew who and what she was dealing with. Terra now had a jaded eye and a tried-and-true determination that replaced the naivety and desperation of before. She would need no help. Not this time. Straightening her spine, Terra looked forward. A glare made her squint and her jaw clicked with tension, but her feet pounded the trail.

If they made a move, she would be ready. And while making an enemy out of the Shining Knights was most people's last mistake, Terra was nobody's victim. Even as her heart twisted in her throat, Terra's knees lifted in a solid march. She might not be ready, but she was as prepared as she'd ever been.

When they neared, Terra walked through the walls made of staggered shields that made up the bulk of their outer defense. Mour had slowed his pace as soon as the camp was in sight. Now that they were near, his struggles were gaining in intensity.

"Don't do this. Please let me go. Do you know what they'll do to me? Please!" Mour pleaded while he dug his heels in the ground and shoved back. Gripping the rope tying his hands together, Terra leaned back with him. He outsized her, but she used his backward momentum and his immobile arms to lift him off his feet. All she could do was throw him on his side. He landed and rolled into a stack of crates that lined the wall. The shields were spread out wider than at the last camp. They seemed precisely placed to disperse a large group.

"Don't do that again," Terra warned as she pulled him back to his feet.

Nearby drag marks looked fresh. The voices and clanging from inside the camp told her they were active — preparing. All the bases she'd encountered so far had been on high ground and were well-fortified. Defensible. This one seemed to be hastily built, with the sole boon of having the waterway at their backs.

Standing taller and walking in long strides, Terra stepped into a false confidence. It was her own kind of armor, as comfortable as her own skin. Her spirit swam free, endorphins swamping her system in preparation.

Mour felt it. He stumbled into a slower step, turning to look at her over his shoulder. His long, pocketed cheeks flapped loosely with his open-mouthed gape. Terra didn't spare him a thought. The extra strength surging through her picked up his slack. If she were going to do this, there would be no hesitation.

Walking past the slanted quarter-walls on the eastern edge of the camp, Terra turned the corner and had nearly half a minute to assess before she was spotted. A few unarmored men were warming up in the belly of the base, while others unpacked and stacked crates. A group of fully-armored knights stood around a table to her left. There sat a short stack of papers, and the officers, plotting over a map. With her sensitive hearing she heard a man mention pulling off a 'sweep' before the 'shipment' arrives. That was all she could catch before a man turned towards her.

"Moursig Batuk, the seven-fingered thief, responsible for the Eulipian grain shortage, the Clypsan golden urn theft, and the pearl scam of '42. Here are his papers." Terra tossed down the tri-folded bounty on the table they were all standing over.

"Hey man, that pearl thing wasn't my idea. I swear! I got nothing from that."

One man straightened, and at the nod of an older man, turned and walked away, disappearing into a building across from the table. It was the only finished unit in the camp.

She watched him leave out of the corner of her eye. Terra had no intention of giving the group of men the benefit of her distraction. As four well-armored soldiers stood around her, one came forward. He was a young man with soft blue eyes and a newly bald head. No greasy slime on him, just open enthusiasm. She could almost trust those eyes. Terra shoved Mour ahead a step, but didn't release him until the first man returned with a jingling sack.

"What is that, twenty-five gold?"

"Try thirty," Terra corrected.

"The price has dropped," said another man. "The bounty's been open for nearly half a year already." He turned and faced her fully. He was a middle-aged man with a thick bulbous nose and sandpaper disposition. The way he looked Terra and the thief over was as if they were the same. Even his tone was grating; it was of condescending privilege, and an octave higher than she would have expected.

Terra pulled Mour closer, debating. At twenty-five, she would be nearly breaking even. And she still had to replace her rope and fix her grappling hook.

The last man's attitude and all this bother made her itch for a fight, but she had nothing to prove. Not to them. She knew better than to pick a fight with a pack. They might not be wyld, but she knew that when they hunted they marched together. For a difference of five gold, it just wasn't worth it. It took only a moment of Terra's silence for the group's tension to spike, and by then she'd already made up her mind. Terra shoved the bounty forward into the camp, towards the blue-eyed boy eager to receive him.

Scanning the base, her gaze caught a pair of eyes nearly hidden in the shadows of a cage. She damned those blasted devices. Her heart lurched hard enough to tug her almost off-balance.

Could it be? Impossible. Were those sad eyes Josef's?

It took roughly a quarter of a second for the eyes to register as too young, too sad. A child, crying silently in a cage. Bastards.

"Is she going to go, or what?"

"If only they all stood transfixed like that, our job would be too easy."

"Talk about easy target practice." The second-oldest man smiled over at his middle-aged companion with a strange kind of satisfaction, almost like a benevolent parent guiding their child along a long-determined path.

Reaching forward, she held herself back from snatching the bag. Instead, she opened her palm and motioned for it to be brought to her. It was a relatively simple power play, and the stoic runner obeyed her silent command to hurry it along.

When she stepped back, most of the group's eyes were already back to the map. It was a map of Charmain. From what she saw, it looked as if they were about to finish a *lo-roun*. By the sound of it, they wouldn't be driving their captured targets back to their base.

Terra left without incident, but her eyes stayed glued on her shadow moving steadily back and forth. She paid no mind to the stares that followed her out, but the muttering — the loose lips that whispered about an 'open season' — could not be ignored.

It seemed like this cleansing was about to get messy.

CHAPTER FORTY-ONE

Lana

So, *I have another bounty hunter tailing me. I should just kill her now.* Lana watched from a distance as the younger woman ripped her bounty sheet down from the board and added it to her bag. *Don't even try it, bitch. I'm way out of your league.* There was something different about this one —

a reservation in her eyes that was contrary to Lana's experience with most bounty hunters.

Not for the first time, Lana wondered what motive a person could have in hunting down their own kind. Fifty thousand gold, she reminded herself. And that was just last week's bounty sheet. The price on her head had spiked after she attempted to kill the King. All it had done was ensure that Paul knew she was coming for him. That revealed a darker truth that Lana wasn't yet able to face.

I wonder if The Shining Knight forces had enough time to increase their bounty after my latest attack on The Shining Knight's base?

With a dark smile, Lana stalked the hunter. *Does she know? Can she feel me watching her? Does she have any clue that the hunter just became the hunted?*

Lana hadn't expected to catch a bounty hunter in town. She had no trap set or circle scouted; in short, she was unprepared. Lana would have to think fast and improvise unless she wanted to start an explosion that could burn down the quaint town of Charmain.

Lana scanned the area just outside of town, on the dirt trails that ran a perimeter around Charmain. All she needed was a circle of protection. It was the one universal truth to metis.

It was also the only thing that could contain her uncontrollable rush of metis. Once she opened herself to her spirit, it would swell. It would happen hard and fast, and Lana knew from experience that there was no control without a circle.

She could only control the massive surge with a

protection ring. Despite all of Dimitri's lessons and training, Lana still couldn't command the torrent of energy inside her. *Maybe I'll never be able to.*

If I wanted to kill her, it wouldn't be an issue. However, I think it's time I elevate my attack on the Shining Knights. I need an insider, and if my instincts are correct, she'll do nicely. Which meant Lana couldn't just blast the problem bounty hunter away.

Lana found what she needed in a wild patch of violets. Hundreds of short-stemmed blue-violet flowers grew in tight circles along with another common weed, the firebell. A thick patch of dark green leaves filled the space around the flowers, and Lana's dark smile lightened.

You're always there when I need you. Lana walked the perimeter three times before stepping over the floral circle. This knowledge, Dimitri had nothing to do with.

This trick she learned from her grandmother. In an age that beat down metisians and locked them away, her grandmother had been the first noblewoman tried with Aumet-mur, but not the last. Six years later, Lana had been found guilty of the same charge: unlawful manip-ulation.

Some unlawful manipulation was now precisely what she planned to do. Stepping into the center of the circle, Lana took a deep breath and focused her mind's eye. The young bounty hunter strolled through the side alleys, taking her time. Sightseeing.

All right, girl, time to shake up your day. Let's see what you're made of. Lana exhaled. With the movement of her breath, she lowered the flood wall just a little.

With her eyes closed, Lana directed her focus. She pulled the air around the hunter's noisy steps with a steady hand.

Thump. "Mmph!" Lana squeezed her hand and pulled the air like an imaginary rope. She dragged the squirming hunter down two blocks.

"You are too easy, bounty hunter." *But she stayed calm — points for that.*

"Formless coward! Save your tricks and fight me like a man!" The girl's brown leather jacket squeaked as the hunter punched the air; her wild swings were a laughable attempt at battling her hold.

Lana dragged the woman until she lay sprawled before her circle. As soon as she stepped out of the ring, her control evaporated. The invisible hold on the girl was gone, along with most of her access to metis.

As the girl tried to sit up, Lana force-pushed the air before her, slapping her back down. Single-second bursts of fire of air were all she could control outside of the circle. *The girl should be grateful I chose air.*

"Stay down," Lana ordered.

"Like hell."

"Suit yourself." She'd be getting her answers one way or another.

Stepping back into the circle, Lana controlled the air around the woman's head and squeezed. The girl fought uselessly, like she had before, but the hunter could not strike at what was not there. The more she tried, the faster she faded until she slumped, her hand still clenched in a fist.

Sighing, Lana crouched before the girl's prone body

and lifted her over her shoulder. The girl was heavier than she looked, and Lana wobbled briefly. She still had a long way to go before her camp. Like with everything else, Lana focused on her first step, seeing only the end goal. This girl, this bounty hunter, would give her what she wanted, or she would die like all the rest.

CHAPTER FORTY-TWO

Terra

A light grumble woke her. Someone behind her tightened a strap across her chest. *Damn, the formless. I'm really starting to hate their trickery.*

But I can be a tricky bitch, too.

A gentle hand rested on her shoulder. Shortly after, another stronger grip against her other shoulder. The small touches gave Terra something to fight against, but she stayed still, pretending to still be unconscious.

When her attacker drew closer, Terra twisted her head to the side, and bit. Her sharp teeth sank into the gentle hand that rested on her shoulder. She bit down with the full force of her wyld bite and knew she broke skin and pierced bone.

The wail was for her alone as the form behind her pushed with one hand, trying to pull her wounded hand away. Like a taunted beast, Terra held on, grinding as she continued to twist, stretching against her binds and upsetting her attacker's balance.

Terra rolled with her momentum, sending the chair backwards. *Come on baby, break for me!* But the chair remained solid, leaving her with enough time to debate whether to attack again or flee. Either would be difficult with the ropes still securing her to the chair.

Before she could decide, that ghostly touch forced her down once more. It took all of Terra's strength, but she fought against the hold. She fought until darkness overwhelmed her, and she fought that too.

Not that it mattered; the harder she fought, the weaker she became. The invisible weight on top of her grew, pressing her from all sides. Time stretched as Terra's eyes watered and her lungs burned until it was the only thing she could feel. Until she felt nothing at all.

When she woke again, Terra understood the gravity

of what could have happened. *How long was I out? Where am I? Who is the formless asshole ready to die for kidnapping me?*

While she was glad to be alive, she awoke to find herself still tied to a chair in the middle of a dilapidated barn. *Who was it that had took me down, and why haven't they killed me already?*

"Time to wake up, bounty hunter," a calm voice cooed with good cheer.

"Release me," Terra demanded.

"I don't think so. You'll just run off and tell the Shining Knights where I'm at, and I can't have that, not yet. So, until I'm ready, here you'll sit."

"I don't work for the Shining Knights."

"Tell that to the bounties in your bag and their coin in your purse."

The one time I get paid for a bounty!

"I'm really getting tired of people going through my stuff."

"Then you should try defending it better."

Terra's attacker had never shown her face, but she could tell by the shadow she cast that she was tall, and by her stride that she was confident. Which made sense, since she not only took Terra by surprise, but knocked her out and transported her across town without being seen, no less. Yes, this woman was good.

"I do odd jobs for them every once in a while, when it suits me. Look, if you think that I am a blind servant to the Shining Knights, you should have just killed me when you had the chance. Because once I get free, you'll never get the jump on me again."

"I hear your confidence, girl, but I don't see your skill."

"Gah! Fuck you. I will kill you!"

"Temper, temper. There's no need to get so defensive."

The woman paced behind her. Terra could only see the lengthy shadow the stranger cast, topped with short, choppy hair. She heard no sounds of squeaking leather or scraping metal. *Like a well-oiled machine.*

"Perhaps you're right." The shadow stopped directly behind Terra, a dangerous place for her to be. "Maybe I should have killed you when I first had the chance. But I was always a sucker for losing a good opportunity."

"Who are you and what do you want?"

"That's better. My name is Lana Colton, and I'm the largest bounty you have in that thick stack of papers. I'm a bit harder to handle than you had expected, am I right?"

"Bullyshit! Come around here, let me see you."

There was a long pause, but the shadow shifted. Standing in front of Terra was a tall, rather leggy woman a few years older than her, somewhere in her mid to late twenties. Her cheekbones were sharp and her eyes hard, but behind that was a gentlewoman's grace. The woman may have been trying to hide it under layers of studded leather, but the smooth rotation of her hip and the mild set of her chin spoke volumes.

Shaking her head, Terra had to force herself to remember what Lana had done to become the highest female bounty across three countries, and enemy number one to the Einhart people.

"Well, Lana, I've spent a lot of time looking for you."

"I can tell. You have every bounty since the first. It seems I have quite the admirer."

"It's not what you think."

"How could it be anything else?"

"I travel by the secret order of Lord Wyvier, the Third Citizen of Taraq. I travel at his command. Here, check the pocket inside my coat." It was a partial truth, since she'd given up on finding Charlie. But she still had Lord Wyvier's seal of approval.

"He sent you to find me?"

"He's been desperately trying to find you," Terra said, instead of answering directly.

"Of course he is," Lana muttered, reaching into Terra's breast pocket and pulling out the letter. She glanced at it for a short second, then tossed it on top of the pile of belongings laying scattered near her bag.

"Let me go, and I can send for him. You can be reunited!"

"No, thanks. I'm good."

"No?" Terra's response fell short, escaping as a single croaked note. "Well then, what is it you want?"

"From you? Hm." Lady Lana tilted her head and pretended to think about it.

"Come on. You grabbed me for a reason. You kept me alive for a reason. You could have easily killed me back there, but you didn't. Why?"

"Well, I need an insider. Someone who can come and go within a Shining Knights base camp."

"Why?"

"The Shining Knights have already begun their lo-roun in Charmain, and I plan on stopping it."

Terra shook her head not once but three times, not sure she heard Lana right. Defeat the Shining Knights? Terra already toed the line by avoiding the Shining Knights' bounties, but to actively go against them was insanity.

"You're crazy! Why would you think you could do that?"

"Someone has to."

What kind of a person would try to go up against the Mad King's army? Not to mention the shame and havoc it would bring to her pack. *If I got caught.* Her people relied heavily on the Shining Knights' patronage. *They would be ruined.*

"They already did their first lo-roun sweep, which means they have a foothold in Charmain. They'll be back soon to pick up their claims, probably around noon when the sun is high and the sky is clear. I plan to stop that. They will not finish their culling."

"Isn't that kind of like trying to stop the tide? You could no more affect the Shining Knights' movement than stop the moon from rising."

"Careful, you're only as small as your thoughts."

Did she just call me stupid?

"The Shining Knights are a powerful force, far greater than any one person."

"The Shining Knights are weak. They're vulnerable because they expect submission. They come into town, high-polished and well-oiled so that they gleam as if touched by the heavens. Then, while pretending they have moral superiority, they stir up petty old drama. The citizens do most of the work for them, and then they fall into docile lines off to the gallows. They haven't encountered a real struggle or scrape since they were playing with wooden sticks in their mother's front yard."

"And you know this how?"

"This isn't the first band of Knights I've come up against."

Terra paused. "You're the one attacking the Shining Knights base camps."

"Now you're getting it," Lana said with a smirk.

"Look, I do what I can to work around the Shining Knights, but I can't directly challenge them. It's suicide."

"And yet, here I am."

I just need to get her to release me. She'll only do that if she trusts me, which means I have to play along.

"What would you even want me to do?"

"Well, it's simple enough; all I need is for you to tell them a metisian is hiding out in the old, abandoned barn, and then lead them here."

Terra was starting to understand. Lana wanted Terra to lure the Shining Knights into a trap. She could see now how the structure formed the organic line of a circle within the landscape. Josef had done something similar on a smaller scale, back when they were together.

"No, I can't. It's too much like cold-blooded murder. Sorry, that's not my kind of thing. I might hate working for the bastards and actively avoid them when I can, but I am not trying to take a stand, or make a statement, or whatever it is you're trying to do."

Whatever she said seemed to light a fire behind the woman's eyes. Mercurial lavender orbs flashed as the woman looked down at her in disappointment. Terra lifted her chin to face the woman's glare straight on.

"I'm trying to save innocent people's lives."

"Are you sure this isn't about revenge?"

"You know nothing! Pretty soon your kind won't be the pampered pets that get preferential treatment. Then, you will be the last guardians of an era highlighting their weakness. You and your kind will be the final trophy to hang on their walls."

Lana's stern eyes were filled with disapproval. She stared at Terra as if she pitied her — like she sympathized with the ignorant fool in front of her.

A small but curt shift in her stomach spoke to an uncomfortable feeling of truth resonating within her. It reminded her of the conversation she'd overheard. All of the things that she and Josef talked about, the worst-case scenarios they volleyed back and forth, were starting to pale compared to reality.

"How do I know you're not the unhinged radical that they claim you are? After all, a bounty as large as yours comes with a history of violence. How do I know I can trust you?"

"I don't need to prove anything to you," Lana said evenly. "The fact that I kept you alive should be good enough."

"If you let me go, I can prove to you I'm not a Shining Knights lackey."

"How?"

"In my bag there were a stack of papers—"

"You mean my bounty sheets?" Lana taunted as she thumbed through the pile.

"You'll find a slip of paper regarding a little boy named Teddy."

Lana looked it over before inspecting Terra once more. "What of it?"

"I know where he is."

"Where?"

"He's in the Shining Knights base camp."

"You know this for a fact?"

"I know they have a boy locked in one of their cages who matches that description. If I can set him free, that should prove to you that I don't work for the Knights. Right?" Terra shifted with what little room her binding allowed, watching Lady Lana's eyes carefully.

Lana held the paper, a look of indecision bunching her nose. In her hands she held Terra's life. She didn't think she would actually have to make the decision to remain true to Lord Wyvier's contract. Now she had to choose between honor or the massive sum of gold attached to the Shining Knights' bounty. Did she have it in her? Could she set Lana up? Did she dare risk betraying the people who had funded her family for as long as she could remember?

"They'll make their move right before noon, when the sun is high without much cloud cover. I bet they're already preparing."

"They were looking over their plans this morning," Terra confirmed.

"So, it is as I expected. You don't have much time;

get the boy, bring him home, and prove to me there's more to you than your Shining Knights alliance."

"You'll let me go?"

"Yes. Maybe I'll even keep the unit occupied while you get the boy out of the Shining Knights camp. But, I warn you — if you betray me, you won't find peace in death."

Terra swallowed hard as Lady Lana approached. A brutal gust of wind clawed at both their skin and clothes. The planks of the weathered roof rattled and a single ray of light lit the woman's dark hair, highlighting her short, sleek cut and her dastardly grin.

Terra tried to tell herself that she was making the right decision. But as Lana stepped through that beam of light with a knife in her hands, Terra could have sworn she saw an unnatural darkness shadow the woman's gentle face.

CHAPTER FORTY-THREE

Terra

It didn't take long to pen a letter and order a falcon, however it cost nearly half her wage, not leaving her much after her dagger. Hopefully Ryker would bring more gold, as he promised. However, if the articles she'd read were to be believed, her generous benefactor had lost it all.

For some reason, seeing the town of Charmain swarmed with Knights filled her with champagne-like bubbles. It was exciting, imagining the long-dreaded Knights meeting resistance. They'd run unchecked for so long that they had grown cocky in their culling.

Those giddy bubbles soured when confronted with the questions swirling around in her head. The fear of failure and indecision weighed her down, forcing her to reconcile the weight of her choices. Would she save Lana, or save herself?

Why would Lana free me? What motivated her to help save this boy she'd never met? What is she getting out of it?

Terra could only imagine what would happen to the boy when the Shining Knights returned. Reaching into her pocket, she pulled out the formal plea — a mere scrap of paper, where parents begged for any word of their child, Teddy.

A brief description and a rough sketch were barely enough for Terra to consider the boy in the cage, but the proximity could not be denied. He was the only child on the list missing.

Her steps were heavy as she hurried through the rolling hills. The tall, paper-thin grass reached her knees and provided little cover. Terra's naturally fast pace made quick work of the spans, and even though she was walking over sandy hills, loose soil, and upturned rocks, she did so with determined ease.

The shrill sound of metal on metal sounded to her left. It was a vulgar display of militant extravagance, screeching between the long lines of marching troops.

The abrasive noise cut through the thin line of trees and shrubs with the sharpness of a scimitar.

Ducking, Terra crouched behind a swaying tree, praying the branches' braided bark and fluttering leaves would conceal her. Whether it was her abrupt movements or the marching unit's loose control, something made the flutterbys nesting in the tree take flight. They hovered in the air, dusting her with puffs of pollen, only to settle once accustomed to the boisterous crowd. Terra tucked closer to the tree, nestling into the root system until the last of the clattering faded.

It took Terra not even a half hour after spotting them to run a perimeter around the Shining Knights' base. From what she gathered, two or three Knights had stayed to guard the grounds. One was the aged man from before. He stood staring down at the table, much as he had the first time she had seen him. There was another younger, chubby soldier who sat watch.

There was a shuffling deeper inside the base. Terra thought there might be another worker unloading crates. While the timing wasn't perfect, it couldn't get any better.

She had to give it to Lana. She was right — the Shining Knights had moved right before noon. Lana must have picked up on it from her other interactions with the Knights. A noticeable pattern, perhaps?

Crouching forward, Terra sank low on the balls of her feet and snuck back inside the base camp. She crept forward and opened the little boy's unlocked cage without a noise. The guards remained oblivious.

As it was, Terra had helped more people out of the

Shining Knights' cages than she had put in. *Some bounty hunter I turned out to be.* Terra had thought she wanted to be an enforcer; she needed to reevaluate. Did she really want to take after her father? Could she spend her time putting people into cages? Especially when breaking them out and returning their freedom felt so good.

When she and the boy made it back to town, ear-piercing screams warned her that she might be too late. Shouting surrounded the Charmain civic hall. The Shining Knights held a group of citizens back, keeping them from the high doors.

The young Knight she'd seen earlier paced before the crowd. He addressed them with grand gestures and bold bullying. He pressed himself into their faces, stretching to be as tall and wide as he could, pointing his blunt fingertip to accentuate his points. Terra had grown up around wolves and had never seen someone as wild and savage as the Knights. *I never thought that would stop being a compliment.*

Pressing her back into a stone wall, Terra looked at the young boy and asked him if he knew where his house was. He nodded. When Terra tried to disentangle him from her grip, he panicked, his fear sounding in tiny squeals. Hunching lower, nearly on top of him, she shushed him.

Tense as the people were down below, Terra had to lose the kid before she made her move. Picking him up with one arm, she carried him on her back, heading towards the town's edge. The blacksmith's forge was outside the downtown center, but all the commotion was further towards the front entrance. They could make it if the kid kept quiet.

CHAPTER FORTY-FOUR

Terra

Terra watched from behind the mob, slowly approaching the blacksmith. The Shining Knights focused on the group while Lana weaved through the crowd. Little did they know they were within spitting distance of a bounty large enough to buy an island.

This rescue might be the only way I can pull this

bounty. But I have to be careful. If Lana gets caught by the Shining Knights during their lo-roun, there's no way I'll get a payout. But I can use this to establish trust.

Now all she had to do was inform Teddy's parents that he was safe and sound. Then Terra could get her dagger paid for as a reward, and get close to the gold mine currently walking through the agitated crowd.

And if it goes south and she doesn't believe me, then what? Am I willing to confront Lady Lana, Mistress of Air and Snow? Terra's stomach dropped at the thought.

Finally, Terra and the child made it to the black-smith's shop. In front, a strong, well-muscled woman with a square jaw and an expression that reflected all bullshit stood facing the Shining Knights. The woman crossed her defined arms high on her chest. Her face and posture were that of an irritated heifer, ready to kick.

"And what do you want?"

"I found your son." Terra smiled, all too pleased with herself as she moved the child from the back of her leg, pushing him into his mother.

"What?" Terra noted the mother's tone: no thankful Blessings, only shock and disappointment. Not the teary-eyed gratitude she'd been expecting. Instead of happiness, the woman's mouth pressed into a thin line.

"You put a reward out for him," Terra reminded. A heavy cloud darkened her confidence.

"For information, and so our neighbors would still bring us work. I never thought anyone would be stupid enough to cross the Shining Knights."

Well, that changes things.

"You don't want him?"

"Stupid girl, what do you think I sold him for?"

Oh no, what did I just do?

"Don't look at me like that," the blacksmith snarled, her shoulders turned to Terra with her fists clenched at her sides. "Don't you dare judge me."

Teddy huddled into Terra, looking up at his mother like he was looking deep into the mouth of a monster. Now she understood his fear.

"There are worse places to send the boy," she argued. Then, after a pause, added, "we did right by him for as long as we could."

"Tell me, what makes a mother wash her hands of her child?"

"He's sickly and weak; I figured the Shining Light academy would handle both failings."

Terra felt only rage. She stepped forward, ready to raise fists at the bigger woman, but something inside her stilled. *She's not my mother, and that's not why she gave me up. It's not the same.* And it wasn't — it was worse. This woman sold her child to strangers.

Guilt hit her like a shield's bash. She was so sure she was doing the right thing that she didn't stop to assess all that didn't add up. With her eye on the prize, she nearly missed the real goal — not the reward, but the act of saving a child.

What the hell do I do now? She obviously couldn't give the child back to his parents. Who knew what they'd do? They didn't want him. What was worse, Teddy had to hear the appraisal directly from his mother.

Teddy's hesitant grip started to loosen from her hand, but she tightened her fingers, not letting go. Terra turned and walked away from the crowd, the mother, and the building violence. She had no idea what to do now, but she knew she couldn't make him return.

"Deceivers!" A barrel-chested, big-bellied man shouted at the crowd. He was an old Knight squeezing into his shiny armor. Turning to the citizens surrounding the hall, he punched the air with his fingers and hollered with all his might.

While Terra had never seen a lo-roun before, she was positive that this wasn't this man's first round-up. He was a less-than-impressive sight, but still, he commanded everyone's attention. *I have a bad feeling about this.*

She hadn't finished tucking Teddy into a hiding spot when the blacksmith's husband emerged from the shop. He scanned the crowd, then started his charge towards Terra. She had a minute at most before he worked his way through the crowd.

Untangling the child's arms from around her, Terra sank to his level. "You have to run, now. You have to hide. I'll find you when this is all over. Go. Now."

"What are you going to do? What's going to become of me?"

How am I supposed to know? Terra shook her head, uncertain. Teddy's eyes radiated fear, as if seeing all of the possible horrendous paths his future could take. She needed to say or do something to soothe him.

"Whatever you want. We'll figure it out later, ok?"

A part of her wished she'd gotten a chance to choose. Terra had been about Teddy's age when her mother had dropped her off. Luckily for Terra, her dad and his wife,

Jiema, had taken her in. But she wondered how her life would have turned out if she'd had a say in her future. *I certainly wouldn't have chosen to join the Shining Knights.*

Terra stood when she felt an intense pressure against her spine. The feeling was without temperature, but it weighed heavily against her flesh. Turning around, Terra found nothing at her back, and no one nearby. But, when her eyes scanned the crowd, they connected with Lana. A shiver rippled across her shoulders at the stare.

Terra shook her head. It was the only way she could communicate her failure. Now it was only a matter of time before her world fell apart.

CHAPTER FORTY-FIVE

Ryker

3742.08.08

The city was bustling with forty thousand people trying to get where they needed to be. In most urban settlements, the higher the population density, the more disparaging the people. Not in T'roack, also known as Rock City.

Ryker had nearly forgotten the unity that spread between individuals, like electricity shooting between lightning rods. There was a shared sense of purpose that Ryker had been cut off from for some time. As they pushed through the city streets — double stacks of kiln-baked brick layered in jagged lines — Ryker's horse, Chet, shifted from side to side, uncomfortable.

The mount could brave bandits and beasts but had no temperament for the busy city life. Genie slid out of the saddle without word or direction, taking the horse by his harness, a gentle hand on his cheek. Whatever the young woman said helped calm the horse, and strangely, it also comforted him.

"I've never been to T'roack before. It's just as I had imagined. Isn't it great?"

Ryker sighed and rolled his eyes, her enthusiasm taxing his nerves.

"Bellmore Square is up ahead. Once we get on the main road, it will lead us to Rock City's chamber hall."

"For our audience with the First Prime."

"No, for *my* audience for the First Prime. You'll be restocking."

The chances of a confrontation with Zuul going well and in his favor were high, as public opinion still held him in high regard. However, there were political mechanisms of unknown intentions that Ryker needed to keep in mind. He would be walking in ignorant and unprepared.

"If Ravetta's little visit told me anything, it's that the political climate has changed dramatically."

"You think you'll be thrown to the wolves?"

"Don't be so dramatic," his voice barked, but his stomach shifted — *too many unknowns.*

"It's not like you were actually banished, right? We're not breaking any laws by being here, right Lord Wyvier?"

The two men to their right twisted sharply to look them both over.

"Keep your voice down, girl! Do you want to get waylaid before we even make our move?"

"Have you been formally banished?" Genie persisted.

"No." *Not technically.* However, the First Prime had made it clear Ryker was not welcome back in the city, or in any city in the Northern realms. It was an unfortunate mix of mistrust and greedy ambition that kept him from the heart of his people for too long. *And here I am, not only risking war, but actively looking for it.*

Through all of Ryker's hard-learned lessons, he knew when war built there was no stopping its release. All you can do is get out of the way and prepare. Which is why they'd separated from Josef and sent the young man and his cart ahead; to prepare, just in case.

"Feed the mount, let him rest. Get the supplies and meet me at the inn next to The Raised Fisticuff."

"The gambling den?" Her eyes lit as she looked up at him.

"I thought you'd never been to Rock City before?"

"Everyone's heard the stories of Lord Wyvier's early fighting days. How you earned your reputation in the arena at night, all while going to the academy during the day. They were some of my favorite stories," she smiled sheepishly. *We'll see if reality holds up to her imag-ination.*

"Don't get your hopes up too high, kid. It's a shit-hole." His warning didn't diminish the stars in her eyes or the renewed energy in her step.

The capital city's chamber hall was a ten-minute walk away, which was fine by Ryker; his legs and back could use the stretch, and his mind could use the time to prepare. If all went well, he'd be heading the Tarquin army to push back the Einhart Shining Knights. Though he doubted things would go that well.

Time was against them all, Lana especially. He couldn't fail her again. Ryker had lost contact with her. Rubbing the brand almost impulsively, Ryker searched for the spark of light that was Lana. Nothing.

Where is she? He had only her bone-deep dread to comfort him; the last remaining knowledge that let him know she still lived. It was a pitiful reminder that he clung to like a child with their favorite blankie.

How he had lost himself so thoroughly to that damn woman, he'd never know. But he was laid bare without her. Her dreams haunted his nights; her voice teased him throughout the day.

With the beckoning image of her firm in his mind, Ryker lifted his hood to cover his face and took a seat in the back of the hall, biding his time. When the time for open questions came, as it did at the end of every meet-ing, Ryker stood.

"And what of the Shining Knights' invasion? Why are our troops immobile?"

"Who stands before me asking such questions?"

"I, the Third Citizen of Taraq, Lord Ryker Wyvier stand before you, First Prime. I also stand against this lax course of inaction." A murmur of surprise broke the crowd. Quiet questions spread like a rolling wave, starting from the seats nearest Ryker. His name was hissed throughout the assembled masses.

"Lord Wyvier, how unexpected." First Prime Zuul raised a dark brow and curled his lip in a flash of uncontrolled reaction. Contrary to the spark of emotion on his face, Zuul leaned back, relaxing in his stone throne. He lifted his leg over the armrest and rested his heel on the metal bolts that fastened the strip of engraved gold plate. It was a carefully casual move that showed how comfortable he was in his position of power, and how unconcerned he was of Ryker's surprise attendance.

"Well, what say you on the matter?" Ryker persisted.

"Rumors and speculation, that is all."

"I have heard multiple trustworthy, firsthand accounts of The Shining Knights' current invasion."

"Can I assume you've brought proof of these considerable accusations?"

"No," Ryker lied. "I have only my warrior's intuition to know we are on the brink of war."

"Then it is as I have feared: you are a warmonger."

"I refuse to relieve myself of my good senses or shield my people from an uncomfortable truth. The Shining Knights are here. Wishing it weren't so will not save us."

"The only truth here is your willingness to set us all to war to fulfill a promise of protection to a foreigner, and one of suspicious ancestry, at that. I have already disproven these false claims of Einhart invasions. If you want to fight phantoms for a stranger and a witch, you'll do it alone."

"She may have started as a stranger, but we're bonded in a way no law or sovereignty shall dismiss or transgress upon." Ryker pulled aside his shirt, revealing hopefully irrefutable proof.

"It's an Owein, the mark of a mate and protector. The Fates have marked Lord Wyvier," a woman to his left explained.

"How can we trust any of this?" Haggerdy Portellum, the beggar and swindler, asked. His chin jutted as he stood up from his seat. *So they released everyone from The Peak.*

"The integrity of my word has never been called into question. Can we say the same for you?"

Before anyone could get too close, he let go of the fabric and snapped his collar back into place. Ryker turned back to the only one that really mattered: First Prime Zuul. Both men surveyed the crowd and then reevaluated each other. Ryker saw a man flush-faced and jealous, but of what, he couldn't be sure.

"I understand, Lord Wyvier, I do. If I were in your position, I would try to move Heaven and Earth to protect the one Fate had sent me. But Fate has granted me this post at this time, putting me in a position to stop you. Perhaps because jumping into another war so soon would be a mistake for everyone."

"I am not—"

A loud crack echoed through the closed room.

Matron Sha-Zule, the First Prime's matriarch, stood

with authority. In her hand, the engraved white oak staff, the symbol of Tarquin council, snapped sharply against the stone platform she and her grandson sat upon. The noise brought immediate silence. Everyone — the crowd, Ryker, and First Prime Zuul included — waited patiently for her to deliver her assessment. With the bearing of a short and mild-tempered battle-ax, her silver hair was cut to graze her shoulders as she drew to her hunched height.

Her hazel eyes cut through the crowd and settled on Ryker, tightening in what most would assume was a squint of old eyes. He knew better. When the matriarch looked at Ryker, she saw not the Third Citizen but the biggest threat to her and her grandson's reign. Zuul might be the First Prime, but everyone knew he took his direction from Sha-Zule, his namesake.

"As Fate is such a fickle creature, let us not make assumptions about her intentions. We will keep this debate based purely in the here and now, in the realm of man, where it belongs." Her demand echoed throughout the chamber.

Unfazed, Ryker bowed as deeply as he could bear. Without the backing of the people, he couldn't make a move against the First Prime. There was too much at stake to throw his people into political chaos. They had a war to fight, but it couldn't be internal. Until he had enough proof to convince even the most conservative of skeptics, Ryker knew he had to walk the fine line of treason.

"King Paul called for war as soon as the Einhart troops turned hostile against our people." Turning to the crowd, Ryker scanned their faces. "The best time for them to attack is now, while we're unprepared and still rebuilding after the Chargers. There is no doubt. This is not just a coincidence. Just because it is inconvenient for us at this time does not change the enemy knocking on our door," Ryker said evenly.

"What kind of leader allows his people to be bullied and locked up by a foreign nation on our own soil?" Ryker tilted his head to the side to speak directly to the First Prime. "Who are you protecting if not them?" Then Ryker turned back to the citizens surrounding him.

"It's time we show our strength. Our greatest asset is our connection and the unflinching ability to aid one another in times of need. Well, that time is now. Our kin are crying out for us. They might as well be on the Seas as we speak. Will we let that stand? Should we start bowing in fear at the sight of gleaming armor? Maybe next, the First Prime will order our children not to play too close to the Knights lest they annoy one of them. Tell me, First Prime Zuul, who has the right of law here anymore? Is it us, or is it them?"

The crowd, which had been nodding in approval, went silent. Sometimes it was silence such as this that burned the most. This silence, however, rang like a bell through his soul. For him, they listened. It was all he could ask of his audience. As his argument sank in and the First Prime gathered his subsequent counterpoint, the people waited with bated breath.

The pressure of expectation in the air pressed heavily against his chest. Ryker wanted to charge forward while the crowd held him in favor, but a pearl of inner wisdom reminded him to stop while he was ahead. Still, his finger started to tremble. Uncertainty choked him harder than any battle he'd faced.

In the silence, shuffling feet scurried towards the entrance. A young page boy raced through the open doors. His blond head bobbed, nodding in quick shows of respect to the sitting lords and ladies and other high-ranking officers on his way to the side of the First Prime. He whispered something with great fervor into Zuul's waiting ear.

Whatever information passed between them quirked the First Prime's mouth in amusement before his face settled into a grim frown. From the entrance, more messengers spilled into the chamber. Genie's face was panicked as she jogged down the center aisle towards Ryker.

"My lord, my lord! News just reached the city. There was a failed attack on the Mad King Paul. It's Lady Lana, my lord. They're saying he's declared war on all metisians. Lady Lana has just become their number one bounty. They're calling her—"

"It sounds like your Lady Love has made quite a name for herself! Lana the Unlikely, Lana the Scampering Skag."

Ryker charged forward just one heavy step, and the room tensed.

"Watch your tone," Ryker warned.

"No Lord Ryker, you watch yours. This is precisely what I was talking about. Taraq never backs down from a fight, but we also know when to wait." First Prime Zuul turned to address the room.

"Third Citizen Wyvier seems to think every solution should end in violence. I hoped to help him overcome this shortfall by sending him somewhere quiet where he could reflect, because he is a hero, and I take care of the warriors under my command. They are always considered family.

"But still, he thirsts to raise arms against the Shining Knights and the rest of the Einhart army. He'd have us imprison the Shining Knights as he did the bounty hunters who entered his lands legally. I have tried being understanding." Finally, he turned from the crowd and faced Ryker, victory stamped in his eyes and conviction on his tongue. "But I will not drag still-weary Tarquin soldiers into yet another battle because you and your woman seem to be intent on starting a war.

"As for any warrior under the arms of your family name — once you and your beloved are legally married by Tarquin standards, you can do with them as you will. But you will not be drawing all of Taraq into a war."

"I don't need your army. All I ask is that you stay out of my way."

"Agreed, once you abdicate your title."

"Agreed."

"And revoke your active rank."

Ryker's heart clenched, but he thought he covered the tell by grabbing his wrist in a military preparatory posture. It was instinctual, and the First Prime wanted to take that away from him.

"Do what you will; there can be no dissuading me."

Another ripple went through the crowd, fading quickly into a silence that saturated his bitter heart. And with that, Ryker turned and left, his chin raised, his shoulders square and even. He left without looking back.

"You can't just take away a warrior's rank like that. That's his reputation, his credit. That's his everything." Genie looked from the First Prime to the confused crowd.

"Not so, child," Sha-Zule wagged her finger. "He has a Fated mate. That's more than most of us ever get. This matter is closed."

Genievet gathered herself high, and with a bullish glare, stormed off after Ryker. He was the Winter Lord and the General no longer.

CHAPTER FORTY-SIX

Ryker

The Raised Fisticuff was exactly how he remembered. The yellowed walls, tarnished by decades of yeezba smoke and highlighted with splatters of blood. Even the sour smell of spilled kublaas, an alcoholic milk made from the brewer's gut of the billy goat mixed with hay, stamped the air. Only the hollering crowd seemed to have changed; instead of a cacophony of excitement and cheer, Ryker now heard the deep groaning loss that filled the place.

"Hey, look who it is. I'm going to sign you up for a match, man." A heavily beaten stranger slurred.

"No." Ryker didn't bother with the man as he passed through the room. He had neither the time nor the inclination for drunken fools.

"Just one match. Easy money."

"I'm not interested," Ryker said with a glare.

"Come on man, for old time's sake."

"I said no. Now back the fuck up and get out of my face."

"Come on man, lighten up."

"This is me light. Now fuck off." Ryker slammed the door to his room in the rubbernecked slob's face, and it felt good. He almost wished he had taken him up on his offer. After the day he had, he wouldn't mind getting a bit bloody.

"Oh, I've caught you in a mood. Well, I may have something to help with that," a woman's sultry voice cooed from the corner.

"And what's that?" Ryker's lips twitched.

"I have something for you, something you want. But it'll cost you." Her sultry voice cooed from the corner.

"Who's to say this information is even worth my time?" Ryker smiled, keeping his back towards the heavy shadows of his room as he locked the door.

"Oh, it is."

"Prove it." Finally, Ryker turned. Ravetta sat in the

darkest corner of his room in the plush fireplace lounger, sitting with one leg crossed over the other, damn near demure. With a lift of her striking brow, Rav pulled out a small, folded paper.

"A letter from one Terra Hallowbit of the Wrenshaw Clan."

"And how did you get that? I know it wasn't addressed to you."

"If you want to talk specifics, let's talk numbers."

"Ok, what will it cost me?"

She winced, the smile never leaving her eyes. "You're really not going to like that." That's when she lifted her leg, and the slit in her wide-legged trousers exposed a long line of her smooth, lean thigh. She had picked her spot perfectly, the firelight prancing against her radiant skin.

With their long history, she knew his tastes well. Rav always played with cunning and deviousness. It was an invigorating challenge when they first met, but now a greasiness sat like sludge in his stomach.

"What is it?"

"I ask that you remove your name from Stella's blood right."

Everything in Ryker paused. Even his mind stilled in shock. *Surely I misheard her.*

"You expect me to abdicate my rights to shield and protect our daughter?"

"Your name will do more harm than good now. You've made sure of that."

"A father's name doesn't only serve to open doors. It gives me the right to protect and demand retribution."

"I know."

"How can you ask this of me?"

"Stella's nearing graduation. Soon she'll be scouting for apprenticeships. How can you expect her to get anywhere with your scandalous name so closely attached?"

"Damn you. You're a heartless bitch," Ryker said in a flat voice, still stunned. Of course, he'd already known that, but this took it to a new level.

"That's always been one of the things you like best about me."

Funny, he didn't appreciate it much at the moment.

"This missive has information concerning your Fated lady, and about the Shining Knights' movements. Choose quickly. I'm getting chilly, and might need to add fuel to the fire." Her arm dipped back, turning the letter as if to flick it into the fire beside her. It was a pressure tactic that set him off.

"Why would you have me choose? And how long have you known of this?"

"Long enough."

"And you sat there in the council chamber and said nothing."

"It means nothing! Ryker, don't you see? Yes, the King's men are here — that's not up for debate. Zuul has been kept fully apprised of their movements. But there is no invasion!"

"Just a cross-country witch hunt? Sending an army for one girl? That's not suspicious to you? And I noticed you and the First Prime are now on a first-name basis."

"That's just how things are," she shrugged.

"Am I to assume he is who you've filled my role with?"

"And why is that so surprising? As a General, and then the Third Citizen, you were a powerful force, to be sure. A terrifying protector. But as a stripped man…" In a most uncharacteristic style, she floundered for words. "You're nothing but scandal."

Rav continued, her face pinched delicately, trying to soften the massive blow she had just dealt him. But all Ryker could hear was *you're nothing* on repeat. Over and over again, it rotated in his head. *Nothing, nobody, a stripped man.* For a moment, his world tipped, and he was lost.

Tightening control, Ryker acquiesced with a tight jaw.

"If you and the First Prime are together, I congratulate you. He is undoubtedly a worthy catch."

On his tongue laid three insults he knew would hurt her as she'd hurt him, but he held them inside. Hurting her wouldn't get him near that letter, especially since he was damn sure he wouldn't give her what she wanted. He had to play this right. The two women that held his heart were on the line.

"I'm sure that was painful for you to say." Rav glared, suspicious.

"You're a hardworking, intelligent, and beautiful woman. First Prime Zuul would be lucky to have you at his side. However, I am not a fair-weather father. We have raised Stella not to depend on us, but to become something of herself. The name doesn't change her bloodline, and you know all too well that our bloodlines do not define us. Our actions do.”

“In most cases, that’s true. But the First Prime has a personal stake in this feud between the both of you, and I know you, both of you. Neither of you will let this go. I don’t want Stella to get caught in the crossfire.”

“I can only do what I think is best. Same as Stella. We will let her decide. Until I get word from her, nothing changes.”

“You would let our daughter be thrown under the wagon wheel to save your beloved?”

“No, Ravetta, I’m letting her make a choice that determines her future. That’s something you never seem to get.”

“Rationalize it however you must, but you’re still a selfish bastard, Ryker. I hope you know how much you’ll hurt her with this.”

“When she hurts, I hurt ten times as much, which is how I know if anything were to happen to her there’s no one better invested in bringing her home. No one would scour the land and seas to find her as I would. There’s no one as relentless as I. No one can replace my love for her, and damn you for saying that’s not good enough.”

“That’s not—”

“Get out,” Ryker rumbled deeply. When she hesitated, as if thinking of ways to continue her argument, Ryker stepped forward. He’d grab her by the arm and toss her out if that’s what it took.

The threat must have shown on his face because she shifted abruptly, stepping around him in a sharp snap with cold sidelong stare. If things weren't personal now, they were about to be. As always, Rav came with information, but she'd decided to keep it to herself this time. It was only a matter of time before Ryker had that damned letter.

CHAPTER FORTY-SEVEN

Ryker

Later that evening, Ryker sat at one of the Fisticuff's scarred tables. He sat in the back corner — the darkest corner — hoping to stay out of sight. Genie stood next to him, bobbing to the small band playing loud and off-key music.

"I'm having such a good time!" Genie's uncontrolled yell into Ryker's ear caused him to jerk away and give her an inquisitive look, but she turned back to him with a smile.

Her constant enthusiasm grated Ryker's nerves. *What does she have to be so happy about? Lana is gone, in more danger than ever. The First Prime just ripped away most of my power and authority, and our only clue is in the hands of my scheming, manipulative ex.*

"This place is exactly as I'd pictured it."

Yes, it's all fun and games until your face and body are bet on. A dark thought floated through his head. *I shouldn't. She could get hurt. If she gets hurt, that might keep her from smiling so much. Then again, if she gets hurt, she'll slow me down. But she won't leave me alone long enough to make plans.*

"Why don't you join a match?" Ryker asked.

"What, join the fights?" Genie looked through the open double doors where the four small arenas were set up outside the tavern. The fight rings teemed with people throwing their money away to bet. It would be the perfect opportunity for him to get some privacy without her lurking around.

"Why not? Try out your fists."

"Well, I couldn't. I don't have a sponsor or the coin to enter."

"Here, kid, go for it." Ryker handed her the entrance fee and his clan emblem, nearly ripping it off his cloak in his haste. *This will be worth twice the gold if her injuries keep that dopey smile off her face for a little while.* "Don't get so hurt you'll slow us down."

It was some of the worst advice he could give a freshie. Anything that splits your focus before a fight could prove detrimental. Genie's eyes lit with enthusiasm as she ran with her typical springing steps towards the ringmaster.

"A word." A deep bass rumble came from behind Ryker's right shoulder. A voice from his past he had wished to never hear again. Meaverik.

"Sit." Ryker offered the empty chair across the table. This meeting was why Ryker was here, out in the open, when all he wanted to do was sleep. Or, more accurately, dream.

"You did as I asked?" Ryker asked quietly.

"The recon reveals two possible entrances, neither of them easy to maneuver." "Recommendations?"

"A three-person team. We'll cause a distraction at the front gate, nothing too fancy. Then we sneak in through the back. The guards rotate every half-hour, so we'll have a narrow breach window."

"She'll keep it close, most likely in her room. She loves secret hiding spots, so we'll have to look for false walls and unnecessary hardware."

"Understood—,"

"Hello, Papa." Like a breath of fresh air, the soft and warm greeting immediately set his mood right. Stella.

Ryker blinked for a moment, thinking his eyes and ears deceived him.

"Leave us," she demanded of Maeverik, sounding more like her mother than ever.

"What are you doing here, Petey?" Ryker looked on in confusion. Stella only turned to look at the hulking man who remained.

"Leave us, but stay close." His old partner nodded his head and silently retreated.

"I came to surprise you."

"Well, you've succeeded. But you should have sent word, I could have met you somewhere safer."

"What, and miss my father in all his glory? I don't think so. I missed you, Father." Stella smiled radiantly up at him with all the trust and love a father could ask for. Ryker drew his daughter's full form into his arms and squeezed. Their foreheads touched, and for a moment, he wished he didn't have to let go.

When he pulled back and looked down at Stella, he saw a double image. Both the woman she had become, but also of the child he watched grow up. She would always be his baby girl, no matter how old she was; he just wished she hadn't had to grow up so fast.

"What are you really doing here, Stella?"

"When I came home today, I heard some troubling news. Some troubling news about you, Papa."

"Don't you worry about that."

"I have to worry because I also found Mother forging a letter from me to you."

Ryker's heart dropped. He should have expected the underhanded tactic. After all, it was what Ravetta did best. He just hadn't wanted Stella to witness it firsthand.

"I hope you know I would never ask to drop your name. I would never ask you to give up your rights as my father. You know that, right?"

"Your mother makes good points, Petey. I don't want my ruined reputation harming you and your future."

"How many people receive the mark of Owein,

Father? Fate has plans for you. But even if she didn't, I would still be proud to have you as my father. No matter what."

"Even if my name hurts your reputation?"

"Oh Papa, you give yourself too much credit. Scientists don't care about the war. They won't care about your name, and if they care more about you than what I can provide, then I wouldn't want them anyway."

"How did you get so smart?"

"Grandmos," Stella said with a grin.

Ryker rolled his eyes, but he had to agree. He came from a long line of powerhouse women, steadily growing accustomed to power and control. The intelligence he'd seen in his matriarch's hawkish eyes was mirrored in his daughter's. He knew that even if he left her nothing, she'd learned to thrive on her own. There was nothing that could have made him prouder.

"Which is why I come bearing gifts." Stella pulled from her pocket a familiar folded letter.

"Stella! How did you get that?"

"Come on, Papa. You think I've learned nothing by having a spy as a mother?"

"She'll be furious, you know."

"Not as furious as I am with her."

"You're getting older now, Petey; I'm sure you understand the complexities of walking the line of authority."

"That's not what this has ever been about. Mom's only goal is her ambition. Now she has what she wanted most with only one thing in her way. But you, you've always been on my side. You've always encouraged me to pursue my passion. Everybody else has tried to push me into a life of their choosing, but not you. You have no idea what that means to me. I love you, Papa."

"I love you too, Petey, and I know you're upset with your mother, but that's—" Ryker shook his head, unable to come up with the words that would help the rift between mother and daughter.

"I did it!" Genie grinned, breaking the intimate moment. Her toothy smile beamed despite the pink stain of blood.

"You won?" Ryker asked, aghast.

"Well, no, but he didn't get away clean."

"And who's this?" Stella asked, her voice a little louder, a little deeper. Before his eyes, his daughter changed, blossoming from a cherry-faced cherub into a mischievous imp looking for trouble.

"Stella, this is my riding companion, Genivet."

"Genie," she corrected, extending her swollen hand to his daughter, who took it with a blush and a discreet smile.

What is happening here? Not my baby girl, not with Genie. She's the worst. Ryker shook his head with a pained grin and ignored the two pairs of curious eyes on him. "Genie, get us some drinks."

"Yes, sir."

Ryker's fingers tapped on the table when Genie's eyes dropped to Stella's ample cleavage, then slowly swept back up to her eyes. *Yeah, that's right, watch where you're looking.*

"And you?" Genie asked, a small smile pulling at her busted lip. "How do you like it?"

"Hard and sweet."

"I can do that."

"We'll see." Stella batted her eyelashes before turning back to him. She had a twinkle in her eyes, but she focused on him with a stern look as Genie walked away. "Don't even start."

"All I'm going to say is that she comes from a family of liars and betrayers, and after having traveled with her, I like her less than I did before." *Which says something.*

"Papa, if there was ever a person I wouldn't take romantic advice from, it's you."

"Ouch, Petey. I'm not that bad, am I?"

"Even before your exploits with Lady Lana, a romance that might still start a civil war, if not a world war? Yes."

"Stella, your mother and I—"

"Oh, no. Papa, I don't have to remember you being together to know how wrong you are for each other. Which is why I wish you only the best of luck with Lady Lana. I can't wait to meet her once you bring her home safely. Now, I'm not having this conversation with you. I'm going to enjoy myself for a little bit before Ravetta realizes I'm gone."

"Stella, don't be too hard on your mother. She's only doing what she thinks is best."

"And that's where you're wrong, Papa. She's doing what *he* thinks is best. He wants me to stop reading, quit the science academy and join Asa Ve! He starts talking about physical requirements and now she's suggesting that I lose some weight. I won't do it anymore. I don't care if he is our First Prime. I refuse to be anyone's pawn."

A fury grew inside him at the pain in her eyes and the frustration in her tone.

"You don't have to do anything you don't want to. Not ever." Ryker's voice dropped. A vacuous feeling overwhelmed him at the thought of Zuul having any interaction with his daughter.

Giving me this letter was so much more than the simple act of rebellion I'd originally thought. Stella is fighting for her freedom, and I won't be there to help. Then, as if she didn't just tip his world on its side, his little girl leaned forward, kissing his cheek before spinning out of her chair and following Genie to the bar.

Glaring into space momentarily, Ryker motioned for Meaverik to join him again. "There's been a change of plans."

CHAPTER FORTY-EIGHT

Terra

Three Shining Knights built a fever in the mass of citizens. The first Knight, a thickly-built man with a forehead so tall it showed below his visor, mocked the crowd with vicious insults, pointing straight in their faces.

A younger man stood at the heckler's side, agreeing with everything his partner said. He added emphasis and layered shame on the crowd. Not even a block away, the Shining Knights, protectors of the good faith, beat a thick-bearded man into the fetal position. The crowd reacted as if already beaten.

Their commanding officer stood behind them, overlooking the crowd with a long face and stony eyes. He watched the group with a disconcerting stare. He was a warrior who'd stood the trials of battle and won. Terra knew though he had an almost minuscule stature, he was the biggest threat.

Her position in the back of the crowd gave her the ability to watch the full circus. As the heckler instigated the crowd and his companion built the tension, their commanding officer scanned the people. They were looking for whatever secrets may lay hidden.

The commanding officer was an experienced observer. With only a single nod, another soldier moved like a shadow. From there, the pleading and crying person was bound, sometimes gagged. The processing was finished when the Knights shoved them into a mobile cage with others found guilty.

The enforcer — the man that stood at the Commander's back — took orders only from the older, more experienced soldier, but he did so with contempt. He looked at the crowd as if they were squirming maggots, and when he grabbed an individual, his actions were ruthlessly aggressive. He made sure to cause as much pain and fear as possible.

The sight of one of their people being dragged away further antagonized the crowd. Their movements became progressively more chaotic, fear clouding their judgment, making them all the easier to threaten and control. Terra now saw it for what it was: theater. Each soldier played their part, riling the crowd, shaming them into cowardice, stirring up trouble, and then spotting the weakest link.

The citizens were pushing against each other, accusing each other of anything from the most horrific of taboos to the most petty of grievances — anything to get the attention off of them and their families. Curiously, a few families didn't reap the benefits of the Shining Knights' attention. And the blacksmith was one of them.

Terra didn't overthink it at first, not with all the other commotion. But as people fought for volume, the commanding officer didn't even bat an eyelash at the less-than-grieving mother. They had already sold their allegiance to the Knights before the commotion.

It was smart. By doing so, not only did the family rid themselves of a burden, but they also gained an ally in the Shining Knights. A partner that would turn a blind eye to whatever insinuations the mob threw at them. They got ahead of it without isolating themselves from their neighbors.

At least when Terra's mother dropped her off she had ensured she was with a family who would love and protect her. What protections did they give to their son? The more Terra thought about it, the deeper the tremble inside her became.

"Look what I found." Another Knight came around the corner. How many of them were there?

"Look at what we have here."

To Terra's dread, it was Teddy they hauled out from behind the general store. His chubby little arm struggled and fought against the Knight's grip. The little boy tried digging his feet into the ground and even reached up, throwing tiny fists into any small unarmored gap, but to no avail. The soldier dragged his twisting body, spinning him and throwing him towards his Commander. Teddy flipped and rolled into a pile. Tear tracks smudged the dirt on his cheeks.

Teddy didn't cry out. He just stood slowly, getting to his feet with fists at his sides. And his mother called him weak. Grown adults fell into a blubbering heap at the sight of a Knight coming for them, but Teddy stood steadily.

"Haven't I seen him before?" the Commander asked sternly.

"That's our new boy. How the hell did he get loose?"

"She did it!" The blacksmith's husband accused with wild eyes and a shaking voice, pointing his finger directly at Terra. *Well.* The dusty air dried her tongue.

It felt as if the entire town shifted to stare at her. Terra immediately became the source of shock and horror. Who knew saving a child would cause so much trouble? Terra felt her cheeks flush, but not in shame.

I could get out of this easily enough if I turn in Lady Lana. All it would take was reminding them of the massive reward attached to that graceful little neck. But then I wouldn't get the payout or the credit, only my life.

Moving forward, Terra set her sights on the back of the group nearest her. The two men in gleaming armor showcased their treasure victoriously, all too proud of themselves for catching a terrified little boy. Let's see them handle her.

"Yes, I did it. I saved the boy after his parents sold him to the Shining Knights. Now, let him go!" Terra felt a shifting inside of her. It was nothing an ordinary eye would discern, but she felt the wyld strength steady her arms and tighten her legs into a waiting spring.

Terra counted eight Knights, but couldn't keep her eyes on them all. Instead, Terra hooked her thumb near the fastener of her dagger sheath and stepped forward, prepared. She thought she would be shaking with fear, but she wasn't.

She was afraid down to her bones — terrified. But her nerves were as smooth as glass as the two closest soldiers marched towards her. One of the men left his guard on Teddy and stepped forward with the group, his armored feet pounding into the dusty soil.

They sheathed their weapons and approached her like they'd approached all the others — with bloated confidence. They would try to handle her like the others. Their mistake. *Bring it on, boys. I'll die before I let you throw me in one of your cages.*

The commanding officer realized the error, but it was too late for the three soldiers. Rolling her thumb and wrist, Terra unsheathed her blade and struck between the helmet and the gorget. The first man went down with a wet, choking cough and ended up on his knees, gurgling blood.

At first, nothing happened. All the attention was on the downed Knight and the thick red stains coating the shining chrome. It took until he fell to his side, dead, before anyone moved. The commanding officer was the first to curse. He barked out orders, sounding like foreign shorthand.

The crowd split, taking the opportunity to scatter while the Knights hustled into formation. Terra had seen tighter grouping from children. In two-by-two pairs they lined up, going for a flank. A scream was cut short behind the group coming at her. It took only half a breath, but Terra felt the sizzle of energy raising the hair on her arm and cringed. *Lana.*

"It's a trap!" the Commander hollered.

The first two men remained charged. They moved without communication, both coming at her directly. Crossing an arm over her body, Terra pulled one of the men into his partner and watched them tangle themselves onto the ground.

She would be at a significant disadvantage against them in their full suits of armor, which meant she had to capitalize on their lack of mobility. Though Terra might have added strength and speed, it was nowhere near what she would need to survive so many.

And yet, as adrenaline hit her, Terra felt clumsy in her wyld transition. *If I could access my wyld spirit consistently, I might be better at it. I could shift faster and smoother. If only I could coax her out without it being a life-or-death situation.*

A whooping wail came from the group Lana was attacking. The high note broke the staring contest between Terra and the incoming Knight; he followed the sound while Terra's attention fastened to the man's exposed throat. Terra had prepared for the jump, and it felt good and clean.

She went from woman to predator in that jump. It felt like rolling sunburned skin into a calm lake; from a place of anxiety to one of focus.

Terra pulled her body into the soldier by the straps of his chest plate. When they fell, Terra's knees rode his chest and crumpled a quarter of his armor. He squealed as the metal punctured his arm, the armor doing more damage than her attack.

Holy Unitas, I'm strong.

The third Knight looked from his downed partners to Terra. Terra smiled. He dropped to his knees, hands empty and spread wide. His soft brown eyes framed with dark lashes and chubby cheeks were both pretty and pitiful as he begged for his life. Terra held up her finger in warning before turning to the dust pile in the center of town.

From behind her, a rustling of the grass grabbed her attention. Crouching down by the sandstone rocks, Terra watched shadows pass through the drapery of the *basilar* trees. The deep cursing couldn't cover the scraping of their unsheathed weapons.

Two men sped forward with tense shoulders, hands gripping their sheathed swords. Their gleaming helmets darted back and forth, trying to assess the situation. Their focus left their flank open.

Terra crouched low as she crept behind them. Her body contracted and tightened, preparing for stealth. But the muffled sounds of a struggling child warned like a bell over all other noise.

Terra spun on her haunches towards the muffled shouts and sounds of scuffing boots in the dirt. Teddy's parents fought off to the side. Each pulled Teddy towards them. The boy swayed like a basilar tree caught in the wind.

"If my husband can't do what needs to be done, then I will. Come here, boy." His mother grabbed his wrist, pulling him towards the cage on wheels.

"No, mama, please! I'll be good." Teddy pushed at her grip with his other hand, digging his feet into the dirt.

"It's too late for that. I warned you that this would happen, didn't I?" She yanked hard, flinging him forward a step.

"He can stay, Hellaris," the husband decreed, grabbing Teddy's other hand.

"No. He needs to go back." Hellaris dismissed him quickly with her hammering tone.

Teddy wiggled, trying to escape the pull of his parents' strong arms. The boy twisted, kicked, and pulled, but it did little good. *This will get ugly quickly if it ends up being an all-out tug-of-war between the two.*

"I won't stand idly by any longer. Give him to me," the father demanded with another hard tug. Hellaris accepted the challenge with spite.

In a sprint she burst towards them, dry grass and

shifting sand crunching with each step. It felt like freedom, but it tasted like fear. *Protect the boy.*

Teddy cried out, and Terra could have attacked both parents. *Couldn't they see they were hurting him? Didn't they care?*

"Let him go, you're hurting him!" Terra shouted.

She didn't know if his father let go because he was concerned about Teddy's welfare or about the people watching the fight as they fled the Knights. But as soon as his hand dropped, Teddy was dragged into his mother's arms, struggling away from the direction of the prison cart she pulled him towards.

"Now I know where his weakness comes from. You're pathetic. You're both pathetic. He's going back."

The early evening sun warmed her. And, ancestors help her, she understood the temptation of the spirit now. A wyld instinct urged her to attack, and her body reacted in preparation for a fight. Reaching deeper, Terra tore after the couple.

Her focus narrowed, and her body lightened to torpedo her across the center of town. She raced forward to them, but not in time to stop Teddy's mother from twisting Teddy's arm cruelly as he resisted.

"I said no." The blacksmith's husband stood behind his wife. Slowly she turned towards him with staggering steps, a look of shock shared between them. She fell to her knees, then face-first into the dirt, a well-crafted dagger plunged into her back.

The unmistakable expression of satisfaction on the father's face as he clutched the boy to his chest left no room for misinterpretation. Teddy's mother lay on her stomach, legs sprawled, arms swimming in the air. She was unable to lift herself and unwilling to process why. Terra sank to her knees beside the woman, still feeling feral.

The woman must have seen the struggle in Terra because she immediately recoiled and tried to crawl away.

"Don't worry, I'm not going to kill you. If there is anyone who cares for you, they will get you help. But, I suspect no one will come for you. This is my gift to you." Terra cupped the woman's jaw and squeezed. After a long moment of satisfaction, Terra released her and walked away. She didn't want to linger in a puddle of blood.

The boy's father held Teddy as he cried, cradling him to his chest. With both arms wrapped around the boy and the unfettered focus shared between father and son, Terra doubted either one heard Hellaris' repeated pleas or the muted cries for help. Turning away, Terra's attention returned to the pair of Knights closing on Lana's flank.

"Watch out!" Terra yelled.

Now she had two pairs of hardened eyes taking her measure. Straightening out, Terra paused, looking between the two grinning men. Unnerved, she shifted and palmed her empty sheath, then swallowed loudly.

"What are you waiting for? Get her!" their Commander shouted. His stiff hand struck the air sharply.

Startled into movement, the younger man swung his body-length spear into a sharp slash. The deceptively long blade caught her side under her arm. The cold edge chilled her from the inside as it grazed a rib bone, and she had the hypersensitivity to feel it warm as blood bubbled to the surface.

Pulling herself out of her shocked paralysis, she snapped back to attention just in time. The spear was on its second jab at her. This time, it meant to impale. Twisting away against her wound stole her breath, so she fueled her muscles with stubborn resolve. Hopping to her side, Terra wrapped herself around the spear's shaft. Holding tight as he yanked the wooden stick, Terra dropped and rolled abruptly. The spear popped out of his grip, and he lurched, but kept his balance.

Stumbling to her feet, Terra swung the spear towards a pile of boulders and enjoyed the sound of it splintering. Terra had lost her blade at some point, and all she had now were the natural weapons of her thick, curved claws.

The remaining man took one look at her and ran. Terra sneered as she wiped the blood on her hands on the dead Knight's cloak. She vowed to herself to only hunt actual predators — no more scapegoats.

In the distance, another shriek rent the air. This time it was a woman's. *Damn. There goes my backup.*

And that's when the town exploded.

CHAPTER FORTY-NINE

Terra

Shaking hands pressed against a sloppy mixture of blood, sweat, and dirt. Terra stumbled a step, then struggled for another inch until her trembling knees collapsed under her. The strength that had once rushed through her muscles now rung them dry.

"Ah, you survived. Good." Lana strolled past her with a silky sway to her hips. Covered in dark smears and clumps of flesh, Lana tipped to the side and shook her head. Her short hair let loose captured ash and bone.

"You left witnesses. Smart." Lana said something else about reputation building, but Terra couldn't hear anything over the swelling of her ears. The downside to fighting against outsiders was that they were so loud. The screeching, scraping, and banging abused her sensitive hearing.

A sudden movement brought her back into the moment, and it startled her. Lifting her hands, Terra blocked the small, pudgy hands of Teddy. His round eyes looked deep, and Terra's eyes were struggling to remain focused. Teddy's grip on her shirt was the only warm and soft thing she had.

She wanted to scoop him up and cling onto that little bit of comfort, but she was so filthy, any contact with her would soil him. Leaning forward, she leaned her head against his. He smelled like forest and ocean. He felt like innocence.

Using the broken spear as a walking stick, Terra stood and surveyed the damage. There were a few Knights who still lived. Not for long, though — their wounds were too great, for this town at least. Terra knelt at the Commander's side, his sharp, frantic breaths a desperate attempt to control death.

She could see no wounds other than his burned palms. His hand lifted, and his slim finger waved in the space between them. His blackened lips opened, and an airy moan caught them both by surprise. He tried again as Terra sank lower to hear his last words. Though what could he say that would matter anyway?

"Onstr." He nodded and pointed his head behind her, where Lana chatted with Teddy.

"I don't—"

"Mon—, "His last syllable may have been his attempt to finish his sentence, or a death moan. Sinking back on her heels, Terra watched Lana smile at the young boy. The sorceress had gotten down to the young boy's level and played a magic trick with him. It would have been a beautiful moment if not for the wreckage and his mother dead in the background.

But, they both seemed to be enjoying themselves, even with the darkness that clung to the other woman. Terra didn't like her around the boy. She didn't know her, only that she was glad to have the help taking these Knights out.

"Please, help me." One of the Knights to the west started crawling away from the women, trying to make his way to the horse and cart that waited a stone's throw away. The blacksmith's husband got to his feet and, with shifting eyes and shaky legs, searched the carnage for his son.

Snatching him away from Lana, he continued to stumble, leading him towards the cart the Knight was crawling towards in desperation. Terra watched as Teddy shook his head and slipped out of his father's grip.

"Come, boy. We haven't got the time."

Teddy looked away from his father and the Shining Knight and looked to Terra. His face was a squished expression, as if he was contemplating the paradox of life. Whatever he saw, it ended with an all-knowing smile, and swooped down to help the injured Knight up to his knees.

Terra half expected Lana to strike the Knight down, regardless of his close proximity to the child. She had been preparing to do something should the other woman make a move.

It didn't come to that because Teddy's father, with a heaving sigh, took over for his son. Together they made their way to the cart, wondering why the women were letting them escape. Only Teddy truly understood the balance of compassion and duty.

"Well, come on. Let's finish this."

"Excuse me?"

Lana nodded to their right. Off in the distance, another Knight was trying to sneak out into the cover of night. His heavy limp and hissing breath gave him away, and they stalked their wounded prey. When they did, another sense of extra awareness overcame Terra — a feeling of oneness between the two women. Almost like an open mind and shared thought, which resonated within her on a soul-deep level.

It was a beautiful feeling until Terra dipped into the well. Pretty on the outside, but thoughts of death swirled like a cursed cauldron underneath the illusion. The truth was a thick fog of pain, fear, and aggression. The connection ended abruptly when Lana shielded herself, and Terra jerked away.

The two women avoided eye contact as they closed the distance between them and the limping man. Terra folded over carefully, scooping up a smooth chunk of wood. With a quick flick of her wrist she flung it at the man. It hit him behind the knee and he collapsed, falling back.

"What do you think, hunter? Do we kill this one?" Lana asked as she walked around him. She looked at him strangely — blankly. Like she was focused on another layer of the man that Terra couldn't see.

"Please don't. You don't have to kill me. I've got a family." He flipped onto his back and scooted away from them as they approached.

"I say let him live. Maybe next time, the Knights will think twice."

"Oh, how precious. Knight's thinking. And on their own, how funny."

"What? What do you want? I'll do anything," the knight sobbed.

"Did they warn you of me? Did your superiors tell you to be on alert?" Lana interrogated.

"No, they had no idea," the soldier swore, lifting his hand over his chest.

"That's what I suspected. We might as well just kill him."

"No! Please, no." He grabbed Terra's pant leg, pleading desperately.

"I don't understand. You want them to know?" Terra asked.

"They already do. This is the fourth band of Knights I've stopped. At each camp I've let people go. Their leaders know I'm targeting them, but they're keeping it quiet. They don't want to risk spreading the hope of rebellion. Their power relies on compliance."

"If you let me live, I'll spread the word to every village I encounter of your resistance."

"Deal," Terra agreed quickly. The thought of any more killing was making her sick. Nodding towards the deserted town's empty hall, Terra and Lana watched as Teddy's cart raced out of town. The injured Shining Knight lay in the cart surrounded by a pile of looted inventory from the city. *Live well, kid.*

Later, before the night had filled the sky, Terra sat across from a poised Lana with a full drink on the table. It was warm from sitting out, but Terra topped it off from a bottle behind the bar.

"I think it's a great building. The town did a good job." The young woman nodded slowly. "I'm glad the Knights never got around to burning it down."

Terra took a shot of some amber liquid that burned all the way down her throat, not doing a damn thing to rid her of her dry mouth. There were a few people in the bar, but everyone avoided eye contact. *Not much of a thank you.*

Terra knew it was a difficult situation. A few civilians had been killed in the attack, and most were still in shock. None of them knew what to expect. *Did I do all this just for the Knights to come back to this town?*

Terra tried to take another shot but choked as soon as the smell hit her nose. She coughed, spit splattering on the counter between her and Lana. She'd never gotten to meet a noble before, and while she didn't know genealogy, she could smell old money. Slowly, Terra wiped the spit with her sleeve, cheeks hot and red.

"You did well out there today. I didn't think you were going to show."

"Well, I couldn't leave the kid in a cage. That's just brutal. And then…Well, to be honest, I never made the conscious decision to fight alongside you."

Terra watched the woman to see how she reacted. Would she grow suspicious? Instead of what Terra feared, Lana laughed.

"I can accept an unintentional partnership if it's as fruitful as ours."

"You call that fruitful?"

"We saved people today, Terra. That's no small feat. Standing up to the King's army pales in comparison to this." She spread her hand towards the mournful crowd. "We've spit in the face of his propaganda campaign. Each victory spreads hope, and that's his greatest weakness."

"Right, well, like I said before, I'm not taking on a cause or trying to make a stand. I just want to make money and create a name for myself, and this isn't doing me any favors."

Terra was finally able to appease her thirst, and the sharp cut of alcohol washed away the layer of grit from her mouth. Finishing her drink in one big swallow, Terra nodded with ballooned cheeks, sliding to get up.

"Going so soon? We've just started our talk."

Terra eyed the exit, but the woman's power couldn't be denied. After all, Terra didn't need to remind herself she'd taken out multiple bands of Shining Knights. Though, it probably wasn't too tricky if all their armor was as faulty as these men's.

Still, Lana and her rebellion wasn't the direction Terra had imagined for her future.

"What's there to talk about?" Terra demanded.

"How about taking control of our lives?"

"I told you. I'm in it for the money, not to change the world."

"And I just happen to know how you can get both."

Terra hesitated. "You know, up until I met you, I had fully planned on turning you into the Shining Knights."

"And yet you didn't. I wonder why that is."

"I'm wondering the same thing."

"I guess that's something we'll both have to think about."

CHAPTER FIFTY

Terra

Far in the distance, Terra heard a horse scream in warning. Whipping her head towards the sound, she crouched, shoving a pile of gooseberry branches under her arm as she cursed her fate. *Bandits. Damn, I'll have to go around.*

Another greasy, leather-faced crony walked not even five paces in front of Terra. *Damn, they're close.* Terra shifted behind a tree, taking her time not to step on sticks or rustle bushes and give away her position. It was a good thing Lana had agreed to rest in Mour's secret cabin; if not, this might've ended in a blood bath.

There's got to be a way to get Lana's bounty. I can't strong-arm her — not with her level of abilities — but maybe I can convince her it's the right thing to do. But is it?

A heavy palm settled on Terra's shoulder, a root shoved into her mouth. Gasping around the root the big, calloused hand covered her mouth and pinched her nose closed. His other hand pushing Terra down to her knees. Bitter, milky sap coated Terra's tongue, and it took only seconds before her vision started to swim.

With the last of her focus, Terra pulled back sharply. The back of her head slammed into something soft. The crunch of cartilage popped in her ear, then a string of short, choppy curses.

"Get your hands off of her," a familiar voice warned with a deep ominous growl.

Terra sank to her knees after the thick body supporting her from behind moved. As her head swam, the world around her tipped until she felt like her stomach was now located at the back of her throat. As hard as she fought to focus on the sounds of a screeching sword fight happening near her, everything in the distance dimmed until even her hands in front of her face blurred.

Just before whatever root they'd poisoned her with pulled her into its deepest clutches, Terra saw a familiar face. She couldn't determine who it was — her head and eyes were too cloudy for that. But as the head dipped closer and the man's deep, soothing bass washed over her, Terra thought she heard a question followed by a devious chuckle.

Terra vaguely registered a patchwork rug and being tossed onto a cushioned bed mat before succumbing to darkness once more. Then, between one blink and the next, two or three men stood talking around her. When she was finally able to keep her eyes open, a dusty tan canvas stretched overhead. *What the hell?*

Where am I? What is this place? Blue and yellow tapestry divided the tent. Standing up on wobbly legs, Terra was pulled up short by a tie around her ankle. The soft but strong leather lead connected to a stake in the ground gave her enough room to get around the tent, but no further.

Terra took stock of her body, shaking her head to clear the remainder of the sap. No pain, no bruises, and no gear. She'd been stripped out of her armor and down to her leather pants and cotton tunic top.

Taking inventory of the tent, Terra saw a cup of water and cheese with crackers. Dumping the probably poisoned drink on the ground, Terra pocketed the dull cheese knife and tossed the food into the small fire. Looking up through the small smoke hole, she guessed the time to be about half way to dusk. *Not good. Lana was expecting me before nightfall. I must have been out for a few hours.*

Terra tried to untie the leash around her ankle, but the knots were too tight and the rope too thick for her dull cheese knife. Returning to the stake, she tried to pull it out of the ground, but to no avail. She walked as close as she could to the entrance and heard the faint sound of men laughing about thirty paces away. She couldn't tell if anyone was closer to her.

When Terra was comfortable enough with their distance, she began trying to dig the stake up, loosening the ground with the cheese knife. She nearly cursed out loud when she realized how long the stake was. Abandoning the task momentarily, she walked again towards the canvas opening, trying to get a look outside.

She watched shadows move until the sound of conversation grew close. Frantically looking around, Terra tried kicking and stomping the dirt back into place around the stake. She tucked the cheese knife in her side pocket quickly as the flap to the tent opened, and three large warriors walked in.

The first man scanned the room, his eyes following where Terra's movement had stirred the ground. He had a giant battle ax on his back, a long, nasty-looking scar running down his arm, and tattoos covering his bare head. His eyes were sadistically bright and ominous, and blue veins popped over his muscles.

The next man had a shaved head, with a long strip of hair running down the center. This warrior had different tattooed symbols running down the side of his face, bare back, and chest. He wore brown leather pants with boots to his knees. He had no weapon — only black gloves with spikes for knuckles.

The last warrior filled her with dread. *Allister.* He didn't look at her, not at first. The wyld hunter she'd met earlier — the one she left in a hard way — turned slowly towards her.

"Why do you have me tied up like this?"

His eyes traced up her body like he remembered the feeling. As he turned, Terra caught sight of her dagger strapped to his hip. It looked like a dinner knife compared to the bulky hunter.

"How else could I ensure you didn't sneak off again?"

"I don't sneak."

"Yeah, we could tell. How do you think those bandits caught you?" The bald warrior snorted a laugh.

"You must let me go. I have to leave, now. My friend needs me."

"Right. I'm surprised you didn't go with the sick mom excuse."

"I'm not lying."

"That's right, you don't lie. You prefer omissions."

"Fuck you. Let me go."

"No, but allow me to make some introductions. This is Ulmer," Allister said, pointing to the warrior without a weapon. "And this is Malin of the ax." Something about Malin's name had the other two men grinning while Malin scowled; obviously an inside joke. "Boys, what we have here is an undisputable she-wolf." Allister's voice lowered as his tone cooled.

"Just let me go, Allister. You know me. There's no need for this." Terra lifted the strap that bound her.

"I don't know anything about you. I asked around and no one had heard of you. Did you even give me your real name?" Allister accused.

Terra shifted, feeling heat flush her face and neck. "Yes, I gave you my real name." Terra glared. "Perhaps you should have asked around more. You clearly weren't asking the right people," she bluffed. Drawing in a deep, calming breath Terra tried not to show her embarrassment. Instead, she lifted her chin and looked him dead in his eyes.

After all the things I've done to make a name for myself, no one has talked about me? Not even Josef? No one! I've fought bascileons, travelled halfway across the world, survived some of the most brutal wyld shifter packs, and he spread none of it? Was it all for nothing?

"From where do you hail?" Ulmer stepped one foot closer.

"Who do you work for?" Malin demanded at the same time.

"Why carry this?" In Allister's hand was the stack of Lana's bounties.

"Which am I supposed to answer first?" Terra shrugged towards Allister.

"Do you work for the Shining Knights?" Malin asked plainly, with a heavy step. Each step they took shrank the room.

They wanted to know the answer to a question she'd been asking herself for the last three months. "Release me and I'll answer all your questions."

"No," the three men said at once.

Well, at least they're all on the same page.

"Well then, would you believe me if I said I just like reading the articles?" At their flat looks of disbelief, Terra tried again. "What, can't a girl watch the news boards?" Terra glared, lifting her chin as she planted her feet and crossed her arms.

Her answer seemed to disappoint Malin. Terra turned, trying to nonchalantly make her way to the other end of the tent. She refused to continue her retreat; not just for her pride, but because she would be cornering herself all too soon. Already her leash had little slack left to give.

"We should just sell her," Malin sighed.

"She's not the blue blood everyone's looking for, but with the right buyer we could still make some profit," Ulmer said, ignoring her disbelieving gasp.

Terra's breath caught in her throat, and she strode back in front of Ulmer and Malin. As she passed, she watched Allister shake his head. Terra silently prayed he had the common sense to disagree with selling her off. *They're joking, right? They're trying to scare me.*

"Less than fifty," Malin added.

"You wouldn't really sell me because I left you hanging, would you?" Terra stared up at Allister. She wanted to glare. She wanted to fight and rage and tell them how small and pathetic they were. Instead, Terra remained quiet and still, waiting for him to respond.

"Leave us," Allister growled. His eyes pierced hers and for a second she saw a desperation she'd never seen in him before. "Now, you're going to tell me everything you know about the Shining Knights and their lo-rouns, or I will sell you to the biggest piece of shit I can find. It won't be the highest bidder, it'll be the meanest mother fucker at the auction house."

While the two others left, Terra tried to contain the swell of unwanted emotion. She made it halfway across the tent before her leash stopped her short. Terra turned back, glaring at Malin's foot solidly on her leash. He laughed at her with a glare of his own while she regained her balance.

"You know what they say about a man with a big weapon, right?" Terra lifted a brow in defiance. She looked him square in the eyes and flipped him off. As he left with a sneer and an eye roll, Terra bent down and mimicked his earlier chuckle. She picked up her leash, throwing it over her arm, and waited until the ax man was out of sight.

"You know, there was one thing I did find out when I asked around about you. I heard about your father. I heard he's the top bitch for the Knights. That your pack are some kind of ultimate lap dogs for the Shining Knights. Is that true?"

Terra didn't respond. What could she say? His hostility towards the Knights was obvious.

"Tell me, Terra." Allister stepped forward again, closing in on her.

"You're not going to get me to gossip about my family. I don't care what you threaten to do to me." As strong as the desire to strike out and leave her pack had been, she still had love for them. She never wanted to do anything that jeopardized their safety or success.

"Unfortunately, that's not the answer I was looking for."

Terra's heart beat furiously as she stepped back and leaned against the table the food had lain on. Her head was fuzzy with confusion and emotion. *He couldn't be that cruel. That's not the man I knew in The Peak.*

Allister stopped in front of her. His finger crooked under her chin, and he tipped her head back. Terra's eyes dipped to his lips, and she waited. Panic and fear stilled as she waited for him to make his move. Something had happened to him, something that involved the Shining Knights', and now, somehow, she was stuck in the middle of it.

CHAPTER FIFTY-ONE

Terra

Wind lifted the tent flaps enough for Terra to catch Malin as he swung his full-length ax in front of a fire. Ulmer was kicked back, relaxed, staring up at the moon. Terra pressed her lips into a line, folded her arms, and gave Allister her full attention.

I'm so tired of being tied to this stake. Watch yourself

Allister, I'll do whatever it takes to free myself. Either keep up or get out of my way.

"Alright, if you don't want to talk about your family then tell me what you know about where the Shining Knights take their captives."

Is this why he went through all the hassle to grab her?

"Do you really think I'm going to tell you anything while I'm tied up?"

"I think eventually you're going to tell me everything."

"That's bold considering you drugged and kidnapped me, tied me up, and berated my family's allies. Who do you think you are?"

"Technically, I tied you down. Tying you up would be something entirely different. And I didn't drug you, the bandits did. You interrupted them while they were burgling us. After you passed out, I saved you. Again."

"It sounds like I saved you initially, so we're even. You may release me." Terra lifted her ankle between them, expectantly.

A smile pulled his lips as his eyes swept over her. His gaze rolled up the legs he'd kissed his way up, the hips that he'd palmed so thoroughly, and the breasts that he'd played with until she spasmed underneath him. When they finally made eye contact, Terra trembled.

Stamped clearly on his face were all the things he wanted to do to her, and she didn't think it mattered if she were tied up, tied down, or let loose. He had plans. And he wasn't going to let Terra's defiance stop him from getting his answers.

"No."

"Don't be petty. You're still upset with how we parted?"

"You mean because you played a teasing bedmate, or because you worked for Wyvier? Or perhaps, it's because while I was trapped on top of that mountain, you were in league with the same people who culled my family like sheep."

This time it was her turn to stay silent.

"Why did Wyvier let you out?" he asked.

"I was only sentenced for two nights." Terra eased up on him. *Maybe I'll get more by playing nice.*

"I assumed it was because you weren't a bounty hunter. So why have these?" He pointed to the stack of bounties.

"I'm not your average bounty hunter."

"And you knew the entire time." It wasn't a question. He turned and walked away, still out of her reach. When he leaned against the table, his face was unreadable. "And you said nothing."

"Why would I? It would only put me and my exit in jeopardy."

What would he have done knowing he had a limited time? Would it have changed how he possessed me? Would Allister have given in to the desires he hadn't tried to hide? Or would he have abstained from them all together? She had too many uncertainties to contend with, so she let them go.

"I told you when we got out—" he started, but Terra didn't need the reminder.

"I know what you said. And I believed you."

He'd planned on claiming her, taking her. Allister had kept track of everything he'd wanted to do but couldn't without drawing the attention of the others and risking another fight. Did he still want to make good on his promise? One thought kept spinning in her head. *What does he plan on doing about it?*

"And that's why you ran?"

"I didn't run. I left. Afterwards, Lord Wyvier offered me a job."

"And what job has your attention now?" Finally, Allister stepped closer. As soon as they were within arm's reach, her skin tingled.

"I've only come into the area to help a friend."

"I just don't trust you." He stared her down.

"When I needed a protector, you were there. You didn't hesitate, and you didn't ask for compensation. I learned everything that I needed to know about you that day."

"Maybe I'm looking for compensation now."

"I don't believe it."

"I'm not asking. You want me to make you? Is that it?" He glared, his hand grabbing her by the hair, pulling her close and forcing her head back.

"Anytime you feel big enough," Terra sneered as her eyes rolled up his seemingly never-ending chest.

"Soon, Terra. Soon. Believe me when I say, there is nothing I wouldn't do for my people." Allister released her abruptly, sending her stumbling back as he stormed out of the tent. Terra stared at the canvas door flapping behind him.

"It's a shame you didn't just let me loose, we might

have been able to help each other!" Terra shouted after him, kicking up sandy dirt in his direction. *He can't release me until I give him the information, and I can't trust him until he lets me free. Looks like I'll just have to help myself.*

CHAPTER FIFTY-TWO

Terra

Through the tent flaps Terra spied a small fire and stools. She could see that the land was cleared, and supplies were stacked. That sent relief coursing through her.

Well, at least they're not ready to move. That means I have time to either convince him or escape. Terra knew a few ways to convince a man, but Allister would be ready. She'd teased and left him wanting too many times for him not to remember her bite.

As soon as the flap settled, Terra immediately went back to digging. Her mind returned to the image of Ulmer's sharp, steel-studded gloves, and she prayed she didn't have to come up against him.

The cheese knife was so bent it acted more like a scraper, but she worked furiously. *Dig around the stake, wiggle, push, and pull more. I can do this, come on!* When the knife finally broke, Terra could move the stake to the edge of the dirt hole. The ground had turned progressively harder, but she clawed at the clay, ignoring how the compacted mud painfully separated her nails.

Finally, with a quiet heave, she pulled the heavy spike out of the ground. She couldn't untie the knot on her ankle, so she slung the rope over her shoulder and flipped the metal stake in her hand. It was big and dense, and while not the sharpest, she could beat the men over the head if she had half a chance.

Terra hunched over and tried to stick to the deepest shadows. She'd traveled to all three continents and fought monsters. She'd dived in after a bascileon and traveled through a howling portal that nearly turned her inside out. So why was her heart pounding loud enough to make her jump?

A small part of Terra wanted Allister to find her gone. She wanted him to come searching for her. It was the same instinct that wanted Allister to fight for her back at The Peak.

Outside the tent, the camp was small but solid. High ground, defensive terrain. Fortunately, it was surrounded by densely packed trees. They'd built a fire at the rear. Terra could barely see the horses, but they were close enough to hear. She moved as fast as she dared towards the fire while staying in the tree line. She tried to not make any noise; it was no easy feat.

It was times like this she wished Josef were here to mask the sounds of their steps. Terra focused so much on trying to hear footsteps that she walked straight into Malin, relieving himself. Jerking her head up, her rope fell back, and they stared at each other, wide-eyed.

Terra was the first to attack, lifting her foot and kicking his exposed and vulnerable area. Raising the stake in both hands, she smashed it over the back of his skull. As he fell, she ran.

He must have debated with his hand on his ax for a long moment, only to use it to climb to his feet. He charged at Terra. Both his arms swung to catch her. Ducking and spinning, she pulled his ax from his sheath, nearly dropping it; it was so heavy.

"Don't do it. You're not strong enough to—"

Holding it by the end of the handle, Terra spun herself around and around. Quickly she picked up momentum. It was enough to keep the giant warrior back. Finally, she let loose. The smooth wooden handle slid out of her hands, flying into Malin's chest, knocking him down again.

Terra jumped on the opportunity. Dizzy, Terra wobbled until she crawled to get behind him. Her legs wrapped under his ribs as her hands fisted the stake under his chin. Terra pulled the stake back into his throat, holding his head with all her might. It took longer than she'd liked, but he eventually slumped unconscious.

Gasping, Terra covered her dry-throated cough in her arm. Hungry, thirsty, exhausted, and probably still feeling the effects of whatever sap they poisoned her with, she didn't have much more energy to burn. *I should have eaten the cheese. When was the last time I ate anything?*

Quickly picking his pockets for anything useful, she grabbed his large pouch of gold and a small lockpick set. Terra chugged his canteen of water and tossed the empty container to the side. She had been hoping for a proper weapon, but the ax was not an option for her. Movement at the other edge of the camp caught her eye. Terra crouched lower, but no one turned towards her.

She could only hope they kept their distance. Terra lifted her hood once again, her hand shaking in fatigue. Standing, she crept around the back of the camp.

If she were going to leave here, she would have to be careful not to draw anyone's attention. Lana was already suspicious enough. If Terra made it back to camp too late, who knew what the woman would do.

CHAPTER FIFTY-THREE

Terra

The foliage underfoot was dry, making it impossible to move in complete silence. She followed the song of the strong river, letting it guide her across unfamiliar terrain. She'd taken Lana to Mour's cabin, and it had proved surprisingly sturdy. It was a one room shack with a solid roof and an escape hatch. Not even Lana could complain.

But as Terra stepped closer to the cabin, a bad feeling churned in her gut. Under the short overhang, the exposed sun-split steps lifted and curled like a grinning, buck-toothed smile. Behind the closed door, the room inside was eerily quiet and unusually dark. As Terra approached, each step she took creaked.

"Lana?" Nothing but an echo answered her.

Empty. Not good.

"Lana? Please tell me you've gone to pick berries." *And haven't done something stupid like take on the rest of the Shining Knights.*

"Imagine that. The she-wolf sneaks off, again." Allister leaned casually against the entryway, his body taking up most of the doorframe. With his arms crossed over his chest and an amused grin, Terra's stomach flipped from unease to a clutch of attraction.

"What are you doing here?" Terra forced herself to glare at him.

"I followed you."

"Clearly. Why?" Temptation lured her closer. Would she give into the desire to touch him, or knock him over the head? Both had equal appeal.

Allister stepped forward, but not closer to her. Instead, he walked around the hollow cabin. His hand swiped a thick layer of dust off the small fireplace mantle. His eyebrow shot up and he slowly turned to look at her, disapproving.

"Maybe your friend left to find better accommo-dations."

"We don't plan on staying here long."

"I guess not."

"Why did you follow me? I'm sure it wasn't to check on my domestic skills."

"No, I wanted to see if you were telling the truth."

"I was. And now my friend is gone and it's all your fault!"

"How was it my fault? I wasn't the one who drugged you."

"You might as well have by keeping me locked up the way you did."

"I wouldn't have to tie you down if you didn't tend to sneak off and run away." Finally, he turned to her. Terra felt the weight of his stare immediately. His intensity charged her skin, sinking deeper until it stirred her wyld spirit. *Careful. Stay calm.*

"Did you ever consider that if you have to tie a woman down for her not to run away, perhaps she's not interested?" Terra jerked her chin up and spun away, facing an empty wall.

"Now we both know that's not true."

She felt him move behind her. The heat of his body buffered her from the chilly night air. Would he reach out and touch her? Would he— *Stop. Stop. Stop. Focus on the job and not on your hormones.*

"It really is," Terra responded through clenched teeth.

"Well then, fine. I'll leave. And here I was going to offer to help you find her. After all, four wyld eyes are better than two. But fine, as you like." Allister turned and walked away, his heat quickly fading.

"No, wait!" Terra turned towards the door he had already passed through.

"Yes?"

"Since you are partially responsible for her running off, you should feel honor bound to help. And I accept." Terra graced him with her most magnanimous nod. It was something she'd seen Lana do when she didn't want to answer any more of Terra's questions.

"Well, that's an odd way of asking for my help."

"I wasn't asking." *I'll never ask for help again. The one asking for help is always the one who gets ripped.*

"I'll tell you what. I'll help you find your missing friend, then you'll help me find my missing family. Do we have a deal?" His massive hand stretched in the space between them, a gentle and open offering of peace.

"No," Terra snorted with an exaggerated eye roll.

"No?"

"I know where they most likely have your people. It won't be as easy as searching the forest. That's not a fair trade. No, if I help you, in return you and your friends will help get me and my friend to safety."

"So she *is* a job?"

"When I said I wasn't your average bounty hunter, I meant it. I try to take jobs that reunite families."

"Sounds like you're just the hunter I need." Allister looked down at her with a pensive inspection she found odd. "Do we have a deal?" Allister tried again.

Terra grasped his outstretched hand, sealing the agreement. "Was there really any doubt?" She cocked her head to the side, looking up at him through her lashes. *Is it weird that I want him to kiss me?* The thought and the desire surprised her. She would have thought she'd have learned her lesson with Josef — don't mix business with pleasure.

"Actually, no." Allister stared down at her like he was seeing a ghost, and pivoted away abruptly. "Uh, I think I found your friend."

Terra spun towards the door — nothing. Then, she followed Allister's gaze. *The escape hatch.*

"You're late. And you brought a guest," Lana said. Slowly she looked between Terra and Allister without stepping out of the hole in the floor.

"I went out for food and found reinforcements." Terra crossed then uncrossed her arms as she stepped from side to side. "Surprise!"

CHAPTER FIFTY-FOUR

Ryker

3742.08.14

"Oh. That is *not* good," Genie moaned.

The sentiment resonated within Ryker wholly. Though the trio had found Lana, it didn't look like it had been in time. In the center of the valley, Lana and a small group squared off against two full Einhart units.

"Damn her!" Josef hissed through his teeth. "See! She's led Lana into a trap."

"Wait." Genie shook her head, her hair bouncing as she leaned forward, resting a hand on Josef's shoulder. "They're back-to-back. They're fighting together. But who are the other three with them? They're huge!" Genie gasped and leaned forward, as if to get a better look.

"It doesn't matter how big they are. It won't be much of a fight if we don't get down there to help." Ryker pulled the young woman back from her gawking.

"It's a hundred to five. We don't have the odds even with the three of us." Genie frowned as she stated the obvious.

"I have an idea, but neither you nor the horses will like it." Ryker pointed to the southeast ridge of the hill they topped, where there was a little clearing.

"We'll break through there. That's where their forces are the weakest."

"Sounds like a good plan," Genie said puzzled. "Why wouldn't I like it?"

"Because you're going to be the driver."

"No, you know I'm no good. I'm not an experienced enough driver!"

"You can do it."

"But Lord Wyiver, these are extremely steep hills."

"You'll have to go fast, too. We can't risk being spotted before we close in." Josef added. His face showed no emotion, but his eyes told the truth of his mischief.

"No, I can't. Lord Wyvier, if I tip the cart we're all trapped."

"So, you'd better avoid doing that. Let's go." There was no more time for debate. Ryker had decided, and Genie had enough training to know his decision was final. Ryker watched Josef climb to the back of the cart, holding the top railing overhead. Genie eyed him with watery eyes.

"What I wouldn't give to have ears down there," Ryker muttered.

"I can do that. That's easy." Josef looked at the small army that surrounded both of their women and glared with an enhanced focus.

Ryker stepped on the back of the cart, tapping the side in two hard knocks. Begrudgingly, Genie cracked the reins and started the horses forward. Ryker watched Josef curiously as the man narrowed his eyes. His green orbs flashed quickly with heartache before focusing on the girls.

The cart lurched quickly, and Josef spilled forward. If it hadn't been for Ryker's quick snatch, Josef would have tumbled out of the cart. He stayed true to his focus, holding on to the cart with a white-knuckled grip, his eyes never leaving Terra.

Soon a whirlwind of air tunneled down towards the small group. Ryker watched dirt rise and grass part as it darted like a field mouse. Out of the vortex created in the palm of Josef's hand, feminine voices started to form.

"I never meant for any of this to happen."

"Of course, you didn't," Lana agreed. Like a tunneled gust of wind, both Terra and Lana's voices sputtered into the cabin of the cart. Ryker could hear with crystalline clarity the inflection of Terra's guilt and the dismissiveness of Lana's acceptance.

"We're going to have to do something. They'll be upon us soon," one of the men advised.

"We can try claiming you're my bounty, but without any rope that will be a hard sell."

"We agreed to help you get away, not fight an entire military flank," another deep masculine voice grumbled.

"It's fine, everyone. Relax," Lana soothed.

"Seriously? Are you really telling me to relax right now?" Terra hissed.

"Just wait."

"Wait? We need to get ahead of this. We can't wait for them to close in on us."

"Can they hear us?" Ryker asked softly. Without a word, Josef shook his head. *He must have to maintain constant focus to keep the spell working.*

"Let them come," said Lana.

"You want to get caught or something? Do you have a death wish?" Terra hammered.

"No, and no. I have something better. A plan."

"A plan. Okay, good. What do I do?"

"When my circle ignites, duck."

"Duck?"

"Just a little bit closer." Lana's whisper was especially breathy through the vortex.

"You knew the army was near, didn't you? Is that what you were doing when I left?"

"Oh, I knew we should have chosen the gold. This is a terrible idea," another man griped.

Lana chuckled. "It's not too late to run."

They never heard Terra's response; Josef waved his hands, and the spell faded.

"Good Josef, now to the Lieutenant."

"Which one is the Lieutenant?"

"We just passed him. He's the one in the back." Ryker pointed to the rigid armored man and horse flanked by two riders, each holding a flag. One flag man to the right held the emblem of The Shining Knights. The other, on the Lieutenant's left, proudly held the heraldry of the Einhart King.

"If only I could capture this moment. This image would be enough to send the Tarquin troops to the battle-fields. It's definitive proof of the Shining Knights' invasion."

"I can't help you with that, but we can listen now that I know where to look."

It was impossible to know who said what, but Ryker leaned closer to the soft blasts of air. Almost immediately he caught the scent of infected skin and sweaty horseflesh pushing through the wind tunnel — a powerful explosion of stink.

"We've been following this harlot for nearly a week now. I'm ready for this to be over. Wearing the suit for so long is starting to rub me wrong."

Ryker gripped the wooden edge of the cart, staring the tiny man down. At this distance, he was the size of an insect. *And if he keeps insulting Lana, I'll crush him like the bug he is.*

"Lieutenant, something doesn't feel right." The warning had to have come from one of his flag bearers.

"Damn it, man. I told you not to mention your feelings again. Do you want to be sent to the Preosian work camps?"

"No, sir."

"Then keep your feelings to yourself!"

"But there's something in the air. Something's wrong."

"Jessup. Not. Another. Word," the third man warned darkly.

"No, get him out of my sight. Send them to the front lines of the second unit."

"Yes, sir. Right away, sir."

That's when two conversations merged. One of the older men giving the younger soldier shit for his disobedience, and the other the Lieutenant griping about no good help and the general lack of moral character in today's youth.

"I've heard enough." Ryker sat back, looking over the valley.

Both men inhaled sharply, enjoying the new burst of fresh air that cleansed the wagon of its previous funk. The troops were closing in, and he felt a brief panic for Lana and the men surrounding her. Ryker had read the report about the first man Lana had killed — the bounty hunter they'd sent after her. If the Lieutenant had done his homework, he would know just what kind of trap he and his men were about to enter.

They were quickly closing the distance between them and Lana. He could feel it. A flood of adrenaline rushed through his system. His muscles flexed, warmed, and readied for one hell of a fight.

"Hold on!" Genie yelled.

Both men grabbed the cart's frame and braced themselves against the walls. The coach crested over another sharp hill. All four wheels lifted into the air and slammed hard when they touched ground again. If it weren't for the Preosian springs Ryker had insisted Josef install, surely an axle would have broken and their daring rescue would have been ruined before it began.

"Genievet!"

"Don't yell at me! I told you I wasn't any good at this."

"And I said don't tip the cart!"

"Well, then you're really not going to like this one. Hang on!" Genie pulled the reins, and the horses screeched in terror. Ryker couldn't see what was happening, but the rear cabin's framework twisted. *Holy Unitas!*

"Jump!" Genie shouted over her shoulder.

Gripping his weapon, Ryker closed his eyes before being launched out of the back of the cabin. He had a vague notion of Josef behind him, but his eyes were glued to the four armored Knights already drawing their weapons at the commotion behind them. That meant the men didn't see the wall of fire burst through the ground, but Ryker did. Ryker kept his blade holstered so he could raise his arms over his head and took a deep breath before the fire crashed over him.

CHAPTER FIFTY-FIVE

Ryker

Josef's guttural shout became quickly overwhelmed by the rushing inferno, exploding against a wall of wind in one wave after another. The sliver of a defensive wall only seemed to enrage the flames. Sweat beaded across Ryker's chest, the metal of his weapon turning slowly hotter.

His hair drooped and stuck to the sides of his temples. Ryker rolled his shoulder and wiped the large beads of sweat from his cheek. The neckline of his shirt became almost immediately saturated with sweat, which was the only thing protecting him from the heating chainmail strapped to his chest.

Already, the little armor he had was starting to get uncomfortably warm. Turning his head away to spare his eyes, he watched Josef hold both hands in front of his chest, another fierce look of concentration on his brow and stamped along his tight jawline.

By the time the fire faded, Josef had fallen to his knees. The man gasped, and even from a distance Ryker could tell he shook from exhaustion. *Great.* He didn't have time to worry about the other man; Ryker needed to keep moving.

Screams filled the area, and an armored man stumbled between Lana and Ryker, eyes open and empty with shock. That was a problem easy to rectify. Unsheathing his weapon, Ryker cut the knees from under the man, barely sparing him a glance as he fell. Ryker's eyes focused on more important things.

Directly in front of him, Lana and her group huddled in a pile. *Something's wrong.* Then the three men who accompanied Lana drew their various weapons and spun in a perimeter around the women.

Ryker's thighs swelled just before a new burst of speed shot through him. As if feeling his eyes on her, Lana's head lifted, eyes sparkling with irritation. Once she spotted him the power fizzled, consumed by confusion.

Twenty paces and half a dozen soldiers separated

him and Lana. His only saving grace was the Knights' split focus. At first Ryker didn't understand it, but as he passed by a fallen man, Ryker realized the extent of Lana's damage. Around him Knights gasped, shocked to find their protective gear still bubbled from the blast.

Whether from the cheap metal or the extreme heat, their chest plates had softened and seared to the flesh underneath. The men continued to burn long after the fire stopped. Those who avoided the direct flames seemed desperate to escape. Only a valiant few remained to help their comrades try to pull the pieces off.

The scent of burned flesh mixed with a pungent sizzle of melted metal. As frantic and disconcerting as they were, no one was brave enough to even look in their direction, let alone try to stop him from approaching. This was Lana's true power: fear. Not fire, and not death. Still, Ryker knew well how quickly their attention could shift. While they were distracted, he cut them down.

"You've been shot!" one of the men sputtered as Ryker neared.

"I'm fine. Hand me my weapon," Terra grumbled.

"You need to stay down," the bald man urged.

"I can do it," Terra snapped.

"Don't even think about it. Ulmer." A familiar-looking man snapped. Immediately Terra stilled, her eyes locked on the man as he flicked his sword and turned back to the charging army. Another man lowered his upper body to scoop a compliant Terra into his arms.

"What's this?" The first man took Ryker in with a quick roll of his eyes.

"I'm here for Lana. Who are you?"

"I'm impaled with an arrow, and there's an incoming army. Can we make introductions another time?" The young woman's howl of pain mingled an octave higher than the orchestra of cries around them.

"Come on, Lana. Let's go while our exit is still clear," Ryker said over the wails.

"Not yet." Lana glared at him, turning back towards the crowd.

"Now's not the time to get distracted," Ryker demanded.

"I'm not getting distracted. I'm getting revenge."

Ryker cast Lana a sideways look. Her voice, her expression — it was all off. He'd always been able to read her, even in her dream world; in a place where she had control of everything, she couldn't control her body's reaction or the reflection of her thoughts and feelings.

But now, there was nothing. There wasn't enough time to search for all she concealed, not that she seemed willing to look at him long enough to do so. Ryker wanted to take Lana into his arms and ensure she was all right. He nearly reached out and did so until another man stumbled closer to the group, and instinctively Ryker slashed with his sword.

As the Knight fell, Ryker saw his charred lips. The breath that came out of his mouth turned to smoke. Even the soft tissue surrounding his eyes was dry and ashy. The man was dead before Ryker struck — he just hadn't realized it yet.

All around him, Knights that had dropped to their knees cried in agony as they tried to rip the molten chest plates off their bodies. Their armor pulled and dripped chrome along the battlefield. Ryker watched in horror as men dropped, consumed by the lasting effects of Lana's inferno.

CHAPTER FIFTY-SIX

Terra

A second reserve pushed forward, marching with squeamish steps through the grisly remains of their ground troops. The rear cavalry drove the ground troop's hesitant momentum onward with lambasting curses. Terra pressed her fingers around the arrow shaft embedded in her side. Blood welled over her fingers and pooled on her stomach.

"Don't worry. We'll get you out." Ulmer looked down at her, unable to hide his grimace. *Great, so it actually looks worse than it feels.* He held her in his arms as Allister and Malin spun around them in a slow, tight circle. The two men cut down all who dared get too close.

"We won't be able to hold them off forever," Allister stated.

"The second wave is nearly here!" Malin shouted over his shoulder, unnecessarily loud.

"He gets like that in battle," Ulmer explained, oddly calm. His light green eyes scanned the battlefield.

"The cart's coming back. That crazy bastard is coming back around!" Malin shouted, looking between the group. His eyes were wide with a stupid smile on his face. That look was enough for Terra to believe they might actually survive this.

"Come, Lana. We have to get closer to the cart," Allister called. But Lana was already working her way towards the incoming siege. The woman used both hands to pull an invisible force in her hands, building the energy with one hand as she directed an incendiary blast with the other in a decisive push.

The men that stood against her didn't stand a chance; she mowed them down like a machine.

"The girl's a never-ending canon. A canon with unlimited munitions," said Ulmer. He looked at Lana with part awe, part fear, and with dark understanding. *Now we know why the King wants her alive so much.*

"She gets like that in battle," Terra explained, her eyes sparkling. She laughed, then she convulsed in a full-body wince.

"She's out of it!" Malin yelled.

"We've got to get her out of here." Allister shared a look with Terra and Ulmer.

"She's mine. Get to the cart!" Lord Wyvier ordered.

Allister and Ulmer stared after the man as he charged past, hacking into the spine of a Knight who crept up in Lana's blind spot.

"Well, you heard him!" Terra shouted. "Go!" Terra caught the look Lana gave Ryker. Surprise opened her expression until a wave of bitter anger darkened her eyes. *I'm not looking forward to explaining my involvement in this happy reunion.*

"Terra, are you okay?" Josef's wide eyes jumped between her face and wound, not waiting for her answer. Allister turned, saw the stranger startlingly near, and raised his arm to swing.

"No! Don't!" Terra jumped, attempting to launch herself out of Ulmer's arms.

"Hey! Don't do that either," Ulmer scolded. "Help me get her into the cart," Ulmer ordered Josef.

A young blonde woman steered the cart to a stop, impatiently angling the horses away from the incoming archers.

"Come on! What's taking them so long?" The driver worried her lower lip as she stared behind them. Josef pulled her into the back of the cart, but Terra was focused on Lana and Ryker as they fought back-to-back. The swarm of infantry was not even two paces behind them. It wasn't enough, even with Ryker dragging Lana, who continued to blast the hacking swordsmen.

"Get this thing moving," Terra yelled.

"But they're not even close!" The driver protested.

"We have to give them a chance. We can't just leave them, Terra," Josef scolded as he looked down at her.

"If we're stationary, they'll flip us over. Get moving! Go!" Terra squeezed her eyes closed and told herself the heat flaming her face was from Lana's fire or the pain of her wound, not the disgust on Josef's face. She didn't know what happened to him while they'd been apart, but it hadn't improved his opinion of her.

CHAPTER FIFTY-SEVEN

Ryker

Blood and melted metal pooled on the porous rocks underneath their feet. The dead would feed the land, eventually staining the dusty terrain red. Body after body dropped before Lana, and she just kept firing.

"Enough, Lana. We have to go!"

"They'll just keep coming!"

"Exactly, that's why we need to get out of here," Ryker insisted.

"There will always be more."

"Then fight them tomorrow. Because today, we run! Damn it, Lana, don't make me throw you over my shoulder," Ryker threatened.

That got her attention. Lavender eyes measured his sincerity. Whatever she saw had her turning away from the swarming mass and finally keeping pace with him. Ryker had reached a hand behind him as he extended his other hand towards the moving cart.

"Faster, Genie. Faster!" Ryker shouted. *We have to go a lot faster than this to escape the army.* He knew somebody would grab him and pull them in. They didn't have long before the second unit caught up with them. One of the men from the cart grabbed his hand and pulled. Ryker reached back, but Lana's shoulder had already launched herself into another man's arms.

"Josef, I need you to topple one of those piles of rock and block our exit. It's the only way," Ryker ordered as he pulled himself to a seat against the jarring jolts.

"You want me to tip a mountain?"

"Part of a mountain. Can you do it?"

Smiling with a silent laugh, Josef stood in the back of the cart, circling and spinning his arms. When he tossed them towards the vertical jetting rocks, his arm stopped abruptly. He pulled. A fierce look of concentration contorted his face until his knees gave out. "I can't, it's too much."

"Maybe I can help." Lana walked up to Josef, jostling with the bouncing wheels underneath them, and put a hand on his shoulder. Shock and wonder passed between them. She helped Josef to his feet, and they hugged heartily.

"We'll have better luck on the roof," Josef said, chilling Ryker's heart.

"No way! You'll be too exposed. It's too bumpy. Anything could happen."

"It's fine, Ryker. He's right. Come on, let's go."

But I just got you back! "No!" Ryker reacted immediately, reaching for Lana, who rolled her shoulder away from him.

"I'm not asking your permission. Now give me a leg up or get out of my way." Lana tried pushing him aside, but he refused to budge. Eventually, after a long, heavy second where they stared each other down, Ryker leaned forward and helped her follow Josef out of the top hatch.

Ryker couldn't help himself from leaning out of the back of the car. He watched Lana and Josef sway on top of the rough ride. It didn't take long before an ominous crack and groan filled the pass. Rocks toppled from their stacked position on either side of their racing wagon.

Cart-sized boulders tumbled and kicked up a gritty orange haze as a thick layer of particles caught the sunset light. A hoarse shout from a distance, a determined "No!" shot through the cloud. Ryker watched as the newly demoted flag bearer issued his desperate command with a raised hand, just before being crushed by a bouncing boulder.

The force tunneled through the dust into a whirlwind straight at Lana.

"Get down from there!" But it was too late. The force blasted Lana and Josef off the top of the cart.

"Stop! Stop the cart!" Terra shouted, crawling towards the door.

At the risk of being crushed by a rolling boulder, Ryker leapt over Terra's form to dive out of the moving cart. He couldn't wait for it to stop or even slow down. Instead, Ryker rolled when he landed, tucking enough to get his feet underneath him.

As soon as he had his balance, Ryker was sprinting towards a prone Lana. Josef sat up, shaking his head and cracking his neck as Ryker raced past him.

"Lana!"

Did we do all of this, risk all of this, only for me to lose Lana just as we've been reunited? Could Fate truly be so cruel?

"Oh man, she hit the ground hard," Josef said with a cough.

Ryker scrambled to cradle Lana's head. When he pulled back his hands, they were painted with blood. Ryker, Josef, and the other two men carried Lana back to the cart.

"Wait a minute. Where's Malin?" Allister demanded. Ryker looked up from the motionless Lana in time to see their third man, still swinging his massive ax into the throng of soldiers. Slowly, he disappeared behind the dusty rockslide.

"I'm sorry about your friend," Genie said softly into the silent void. "But where do I go from here?"

"I'll show you, Genie. I know a spot." Josef wobbled to his feet and Genie wrapped her arm around his waist to help him back up to the wagon. Terra craned her neck to watch the close-knit display pass by.

"Yes, I'm sorry about your friend. Thank you for helping," Ryker said, still cradling Lana to his chest. Blocking the exit bought them a little bit of time; at least a day, maybe more if the Knights decided to go around the pass instead of digging their way through. It wouldn't be enough. There was still too much land to cover. Their progress would be slow with the men's extra weight and two bedridden females.

"He was our brother," one of the men answered, bringing Ryker's attention back to the group.

"I'll compensate you in whatever way I can." Ryker laid Lana down next to a scowling Terra.

Before either man could spit a snarling response, Lana stirred. Dropping to his knees beside her, Ryker picked up her delicate hand, kissing each knuckle until she blinked at him.

"Wasn't a dream?" she asked, her eyes barely open.

"No, Vahejara. This is real." Ryker felt a ghost of a smile lift his cheeks.

"Damn," she muttered, turning away from him.

His smile wilted as he stared at the woman he'd spent so long trying to save. *That's not the welcome I've been hoping for. Damn, indeed.*

EPILOGUE

They spent the rest of the trip in fragile silence before they made it to camp. Genie and Josef sat up front, whispering back and forth. Ryker assumed Josef pulled the air around them to keep their words private.

Terra dozed in painful fits with Allister tending to her. Finally back on unsteady feet, Lana seemed determined to ignore Ryker's existence. All the while, the new warriors mourned the loss of their fallen brother.

Ryker watched as the evening lightened the air and darkened the sky. The crisp bite helped to relieve some of the dreary emotions within the cart. He knew those around him suffered from guilt and exhaustion.

Still, Ryker couldn't help but feel alleviated. All the turmoil and building desperation had led him to this. *She's back. After months of waiting and not knowing, she's here.* His enthusiasm was squashed under reality. *She wants nothing to do with me.*

Lana actively avoided even looking at Ryker. Instead, she helped Allister nurse Terra and checked in on everyone but him. He only wanted to pull her into his lap and wish everyone else out of existence.

Damn them for getting all the attention and affection I deserve. She's my wife! Not that she knows that yet, the dark voice reminded, whispering about how perilous their situation would be should she find out from someone other than him.

"Lana." Ryker didn't recognize his own voice. It dropped deep as he addressed her.

"Not now, Lord Wyvier."

So we're back to formalities, are we? "We need to talk."

"I said, not now." Her eyes shot around the cramped space before glaring at him. *Why is she so angry? She doesn't yet know all the reasons she has to be sore with me.*

"Fine, Lana. I'll give you time, but we have much to talk about when we make it to camp."

"Agreed," she relented stiffly.

For him, each minute dragged. All he could do was spend the time trying to rehearse how he would break the news to her. The life they'd both fought so hard to provide for was destroyed. There would be no peace, freedom, or justice until the high-ranking corruption had been laid bare. Lana had jump-started a war.

"Married? What the hell do you mean we're married?" Lana's voice grew. She paced around the small clearing he'd taken her to. Ryker looked over his shoulder and wondered if he should have gone deeper into the forest. "I know that's impossible because both parties must attend the ceremony. I know this marriage isn't valid because I was not there." Lana's voice became mechanical, as if she couldn't process the possibility of their marriage.

"I've got fifty people willing to say otherwise. Tell me, Lana, who do you have to corroborate your story?"

"You know I have no one," Lana whispered.

"Well then, wife. We have much to discuss."

"Wife?" Lana spat. "I don't accept that."

"You already did; it was a condition of your escort."

"I recall only agreeing to your proposal. I never—"

"Let's not get into semantics now. I proposed to keep you safe, and you agreed to marriage because you needed me. Nothing has changed."

"Everything has changed, and you know that. You knew why I had to leave."

"At first I didn't understand why. That is, until you pulled me into your dreams."

"I don't want to talk about that." Lana turned away sharply.

"I'm not surprised."

"Besides, you've lost everything. What makes you think I still want or 'need' you?" Lana looked him up and down in the moon's dim light. At first she scowled, but her gaze slowed, her eyes softening. The blush that followed was all the truth he needed to see.

"I don't know who told you I lost everything, but we'll get to that later. You. You told me every time you pulled me into your dreams. You invited — no, demanded I enter your subconscious mind's dark reaches. You drew me there and kept me with you, always close. Anytime you needed. Do you remember how often you needed me? You pulled me every night for weeks," Ryker whispered in her ear and watched as shivers rippled down her neck and chest. His hands slid down her shoulders, and her arms tingled in response. "Do you remember what you begged me to do?"

"Agh! I wish we were back in that dream world. At least I could make you shut your mouth."

"From what I recall, you preferred me to keep my mouth open." Ryker pulled Lana into his body. His grip had an angry bite, but as his hands roamed boldly, Lana fell into a paralysis of indecision.

"Watch your ego. If you recall, I didn't think you were real."

"I haven't forgotten, wife. I also haven't forgotten that you agreed to my terms without the intention of following through. You would have left me holding the bag, all alone." Once again, his touch turned hard.

"Stop calling me that. And don't be so dramatic,"

Lana scoffed as she broke free. "If you would have listened to me none of this would have happened."

"No, Lana." Ryker grabbed her by her shoulders and spun her to face him. "If you would have listened to *me*, none of this would have happened."

He didn't like the way she looked up at him in both shock and fear. The anger inside of him was colored with a hurt he couldn't acknowledge. It was a pain and insecurity that he didn't think he could ever explain.

"I will not allow you to bully me, damn it! So don't raise your voice to me!" Lana stepped closer to him, hands tingling with unspent metis, lighting her skin with a soft lavender radiance.

"That would be a threat if I thought you could do it." Ryker stepped closer until he could feel the pressure of her static against his body.

"I can do more than hurt you, Ryker," Lana warned.

She let loose the tight shield she kept around herself for a moment. The release knocked Ryker back a step. She looked at him with such a blank stare he believed her. Lana had seen death and had been in battles she had both won and lost.

"Vahejara, I have no doubt you can take a life. I've always known you were powerful. But still, no, I don't think you can hurt me."

Ryker grabbed her wrist, and all the hairs on his body immediately stood on end. Warmth lit his veins like sunshine from the inside out. That radiance swelled within him, but it didn't hurt. It felt fantastic.

"You don't have to fear hurting me."

"I don't fear hurting you, Ryker. I fear I'll like it." Lana shrugged off his grip and walked away. "And what about you, Ryker? Would you hurt me?"

"I might." Ryker dipped his head in remorse.

"And you wouldn't lie to me again, would you?" She closed all the space she had just put between them as she stalked forward.

"I might," he yielded.

"You might. Well, at least there's that." Her *tsk* of disappointment cut the air and filled Ryker with irritation.

He felt the swell of emotion itching for a fight, but he knew that was what she wanted. For whatever reason, Lana was trying to hate him.

"I can't promise I'll be perfect, Lana. I was never nice and gentle to begin with, but you are mine as I am yours."

"I reject this sham of a marriage."

"Only a fool would forsake Fate."

"How do I know you didn't brand yourself? How am I supposed to believe this isn't another lie? Another attempt to have a weapon at your side. Yet another manipulation by the great Lord Wyvier?"

"I would if I thought it would save you." Ryker shook his head at her attitude. He knew she would be pissed, but it felt like she held onto something else. "Why are you fighting this so much? This was the plan."

"Fuck your plan. I want nothing to do with it."

"You're just..." Ryker heaved a frustrated sigh before starting again. "There's no logical reason—"

"Just stop. Why don't you admit what you really want?"

"And what's that?" Ryker asked.

"You mean to use me as a weapon to get back at your Prime."

"I never planned for that."

"Tell me it wasn't always in the back of your head. Come on, Ryker. Lie to me," Lana dared.

"All right! If worse came to worse, why wouldn't you fight? I would never have forced you onto the battlefield, but when you have an army approaching, anyone who can help should."

"I'm not going to be your pretty little side piece."

"Are we still discussing warfare, or are we finally getting to what you're actually afraid of?"

"I don't know what you're talking about." Lana turned away stiffly.

"Yes, there it is. You're not afraid of battle — you've been chasing danger. Hunting it down, if the word on the boards is to be believed. No, you're still sore. Stop running away from this. Come here."

"Fuck you, Ryker."

She must have heard his suffering groan as his long legs closed the distance between them, but she didn't move. "We're married in a way that goes deeper, and binds more thoroughly than most could ever imagine. And when it happened, I wasn't scared. Not for a second, I knew what I had to do. It was my duty."

"I don't want to be a duty or a chore. I don't want to be your Fate-bound burden. You couldn't love me when

I had nothing. Why should I make this any easier on you now?"

"Let me show you Tarquin courtship."

"The last time you said that, you took my virginity and I didn't see you for two days. No, I'm good on your courtship."

"Why do you always make things so difficult?"

"If you want easy, go get your betnoir!" Lana spun away with a shrug.

"I didn't want her, I just wanted to keep the life I had. The life I knew." Ryker grabbed her shoulder, a small part of him tempted to shake some sense into her. "I just want you. As soon as you left, I knew it, I felt the mistake deep in my bones. I risked it all, sacrificed everything. I did that before I received the mark of Owein. I'm not doing it because of that, or out of some sense of duty.

"I'm here because there's no place I'd rather be than at your side, and if I have to spend every day proving it to you, I will. If I have to coax that charge back into our touch, if I have to risk your fire or your fury, I will.

"I'll face armies, monsters, or a deathless hoard. I will. Whether you like it or not, we are connected. Whether you like it or not, you are my wife. I am your protector. And I am not letting you go again."

"Maybe I don't want your protection."

"Well, you have it. Like it or not, it's yours."

"I can't believe this. This is crazy. There's no way."

"Unless you want this whole plan to go sideways, you won't dispute it publicly."

"Who do you think you are?"

"Haven't you heard? I'm no one. Except the only thing standing between you and an army."

"I didn't ask you to do any of that."

"Damn it, woman! Yes, you did. You came to me and asked for my protection. When I agreed to keep you safe, I meant it. When I make a promise, I keep it." Ryker stared her down, emphasizing his point with a glare. "But I need you to at least work with me so I can keep the illusion of my honor. You'll need it if we ever need an army."

Lana's eyes softened, and she stroked his cheek gently. He held himself still, trying not to give in to the need to lean into her touch. *Don't scare her off now.*

"I never wanted this for you. You knew that. I can't bear the thought of you suffering like my father did."

"No offense, Lana, but I am not your father. I do not run from a fight. And if the Einhart King wants to start a war on Tarquin soil, then he's sealed his own coffin."

"I don't see the point in killing thousands when we can target the real problem."

"Is that you talking, or Dimitri?"

"I'm not sure how much of me is left." Tears welled in Lana's eyes as she tried to brush past him. Ryker's hand slipped down her arm, his rough fingers sliding against her delicate inner wrist. He stopped her and guided her back to him.

"I understand, Lana. I thought I'd lost myself a few times in and after a battle. But you're there — I see it. I see you, and you don't have to be alone anymore. I'm not going anywhere."

For a moment, it felt like they were back in the

dream world. When Ryker pulled Lana into his arms, she melted for him. Until the background noise of Terra and Josef arguing brought the real world crashing back down like a slap. Once again, Lana looked past him, a hesitant withdrawal back in her eyes. *On my life, I will win back her trust even if it takes everything I have.*

GLOSSARY

Vocabulary

Aumet-mur - (trial of metisians) The law that makes it illegal for metisains to use their 'advantages'.

Bascileon - (animal) A large sea serpent.

Basilar tree - (plant)

Betnoir - (insult) Someone, male or female, who uses seduction for their advantage.

Blessings - (and also praying)

Bully goat - (farm animal) A mountainous goat known to be highly aggressive. Slightly domesticated as a farm animal due to the brewers gut each bully goat has that process sugars into fermented alcoholic milk.

Che-tro - (insult) Useless woman.

Epoch tree - (root is a painkiller)

The Fifth - (political position) Of twenty-five high ranking political positions within Taraq. Each with equal jurisdictional powers that have the executive functions and legislative review within their territory's.

Firebell - (plant) A climbing vine common inland, counterpart to fireburst.

Fireburst - (plant) A bushy coastal counterpart to the climbing vine, firebell.

Flutterbys - (insect) A fluttering insect with two pairs of bright and boldly colored wings.

Formless - (metisian) Widely considered to be one of the most destructive advantages a person can have. Most people can only connect to and harness one element.

Kataem - A non-blood-related adult who took an active role in guiding a child.

Kublaas - (beverage) An alcoholic drink made from the brewers gut of the bully goat.

Light Bearer - (prayer)

Lo-roun - (a raid/ inquisition)

Metis - (base form) An empowering energy.

Metisian - A person who wields metis.

Metitonne - The currents of metis that move throughout the universe.

Murdosh flower - (plant)

Myit - (metis) One's personal energy field or aura.

Owein - (fated brand) The mark of a mate and protector provided by fate.

Parlopean whale - (sea creature)

Sabic - (animal) A wild beast, a large feline.

Srikers -(animal) Rust chested birds with sharp pointed razor-like beaks. Piranhas with wings.

Unitas; the Divine Collective; the Great Equalizer (Religious pillar) - Understood as balance.

Vahejara - (term of endearment) meaning 'my hearts' vulnerability'.

Wild fbardi - (food that can be foraged) an edible starchy grass and grain.

Wyld - (metis) Spirit, a connection to the Instinct.

Wyldons - (metisian) The people with wyld spirit.

Yeezba - (plant) Sticky leaves are dried and rolled into a cigarette.

The Watcher and the Warrior, The Seer and the Scribe – (legend) In every hour of great need, the Fates provide the gift of True Sight. To maintain the balance of power, Fate provides a warrior to either work with the prophet or against them.

OTHER WORKS BY H.L. HINES

Seasons of Treason

Winter's Kiss

Vernal Tempest

Summer Reign

Savage Shadows

Will of the Wild

YOU CAN FOLLOW H.L. HINES AT THE FOLLOWING PLACES

Facebook- H.L. Hines
Instagram- h.l.hines
TikTok- hlhines
Website- hlhinesauthor.com

Where you can find H.L. Hines-
Amazon, Barnes and Noble, Google Play, Apple books,
available for wholesale order through the Ingram
Content Network, as well as on her website
hlhinesauthor.com

H.L. Hines is not the New York Times or USA Today's best-selling author. Her special interests range from collecting nature to saving old forgotten books. She enjoys learning anything and has a penchant for the deep, dark, and unexplored. She'd like to remind you to please, reduce, reuse, and recycle.